The Patriotic Assassins

by

Eric Stannard

Published by Pazapadap Press
P.O. Box 1409
Greenwood Lake, New York 10925 U.S.A.
pazapadappress.com

First published in 2013 by Pazapadap Press

LIBRARY OF CONGRESS CATALOGING IN PUBLICATION DATA

Stannard, Eric

The Patriotic Assassins

1. Kennedy assassination—fiction. 2. Lee Harvey Oswald—fiction. 3. Jack Ruby—fiction. 4. Office of Naval Intelligence—fiction.

I. Title.

PS3619.D47649F59 2013

ISBN: 978-0-9884597-3-1

Set in Garamond

Designed by Roger Tuttle

AUTHOR'S NOTE: This is a work of fiction. While drawing from historical records, I have attempted to fill some of the blank spaces and clarify some black outs and redactions in the known record. To do this I've started with real people in historically known events and invented characters, dialogues, but only a few plausible incidents. This book makes no claim to truth, although readers may find resemblance of truth here—a way of thinking about the assassination without being constrained by half-facts, or overwhelmed by statements made by officials of various sort and sundry in sheep's clothing.

PART I

1)

The gift

Sparky smiled nervously as he stood in Mr. Capone's office, a big room with a huge round table in the middle with a bright shiny chandelier over it, and Mr. C pointed a short, thick finger at him. "You can go a long way with a smile."

Mr. C had dark Sicilian features with thick lips, a big nose, and slicked-back jet-black hair. He looked at Sparky oddly as if he were considering what to do with him: he had lost the delivery bag. Sparky beat-up one guy and tried to chase down another who picked up the bag and ran during the scuffle but the second thief was too fast.

Mr. C said he was incredibly upset but he spoke in an even tone, which made him feel as if something violent was about to happen. Sparky, who had just turned 16, had run errands for Mr. C for quite some time but eventually advanced to running the numbers on the entire West Side. He got to know other people in the organization, like Mr. Sam Giancana, who seemed to take a special interest in him and show him the ropes. It was Mr. Giancana who, after he had been arrested for some petty stuff, showed him which gymnasium to exercise in and how to pay off the right police officers in the neighborhood. Later, because he had shown that he could be trusted and was tough, Sparky was handpicked to be a bagman and carry the cash from union kickbacks straight to the boss: Mr. Capone. Sparky wasn't sure if Mr. Giancana had arranged this or if Mr. Capone had actually smiled on his fortune, but he was grateful for the opportunity. But being a bagman was more difficult than it sounded because everyone knew the bags were filled with cash and everyone knew that it was, basically, stolen money. Some people thought that if they could steal the bag of stolen money it would be theirs—if they could get away with it. So, Sparky had to protect it, as Mr. Capone said, "like fresh meat in shark-infested waters."

Sparky had tried to take care of it, and he had done a pretty good job, he thought, getting into a few fights, and he had always delivered the bag before this last incident. He thought he was able to do this because of his reputation and his attitude, which was if anyone he didn't know came near him: BAM! he'd hammer them but good.

Mr. C looked at his fingernails as if he had just noticed something, then pinched Sparky's cheek roughly and slapped his face firmly. He had been daydreaming but Mr. C had his attention now. Mr. C finished his thought, "You can go a long way with a smile, but you can go a lot further with a smile and a gun."

Sparky raised his eyebrows and looked at Mr. C, who pulled out a short-barreled pistol. It was a .32 caliber and its dull gray finish had a few nicks in it. Mr. C turned his wrist as he plopped the gun down in Sparky's hand. It was heavier than he thought it would be and, for some reason, he pulled back the hammer with his thumb as he had seen James Cagney do in the movies.

Mr. C grabbed his ear and jerked his head sideways. "Watch out, it's loaded."

It was his first gun and Sparky felt proud, as if he had made some achievement, and who better to give him this gift than Mr. Capone? His goal was that some day he would impress Mr. C enough to work directly with him but he didn't know how that would happen. He knew he would have to work his way up, showing he could be trusted and be a moneymaker, and hopefully somehow he would be "a good earner" and Mr. C would want to take him on as one of his many, many business partners. But how could he be a good earner? Right now, he thought, he simply had to do whatever Mr. C said. That was easy. Sure, he got into a few fistfights but on the street that could pay a little money. He also had a few minor brushes with the law but nothing ever came of that, thanks to Mr. Capone's lawyers. Mr. C had heard about the fistfights and done nothing before, but now that Sparky had actually *lost* the bag, Mr. C was concerned. It was his money.

Sparky uncocked the hammer and gazed at the pistol in his hand. He wanted to say something important, a word of thanks, but all he could think of was how this would help his reputation on the street. He heard himself babble, "Yeah, I, um… I'm already known as a hothead. Some say I got a quick temper. But I roughed up them rats."

"That kind of reputation is okay," Mr. C said, turning from his pacing to smile at him. That smile, with a killer's stare in his eyes, scared the shit out of him. It was too quiet and he thought of Mr. C's words. It was true. He didn't mind a tough-guy reputation. He kind of liked it. "Now go use your reputation. Make some money."

Sparky widened his eyes. He had expected more but he got up quickly and left the office thinking about what Mr. C had said. He thought of that vicious smile and a shiver raced over his spine again. It was a challenge. No, it was an unspoken promise. Produce—or else.

Over the next few days Sparky noticed how people on the streets looked at him with even more fear and more respect. He was big for his age and he took care of himself by working out at the gymnasium with a little boxing, lifting weights, and throwing the medicine ball around. For as long as he could remember, Sparky knew that because he was Jewish he had to try harder. He was born Jacob Rubenstein in Chicago and his mother, his real mother, had told him that his heritage was very important. His parents had emigrated from Poland and his seven brothers and sisters, his whole family, had always said their Jewish heritage was very important. Once, when Jacob was seven, Gianni Marconi was telling a joke to a group of neighborhood boys. It was Saturday morning and Jacob was edgy from not eating dinner from the night before—he was too upset from being placed in his latest foster home—and Gianni Marconi, a bit of a clown in his baggy knickers and clean white tee-shirt, had five of the neighborhood boys listening to him. Gianni grinned, "How many Jews does it take to milk a cow?"

BAM! Jacob punched Gianni so hard it knocked out an eye tooth and bloodied his upper lip. But Gianni shut-up with the jokes. After that, no one teased him about being Jewish, or Polish, or about his mother, who some kids said was "a little bit crazy in the head."

One thing that his father, his real father, had said was, "In dees country… dees country great. A person raise himself, change himself into new person. Someone better." That appealed to Jacob. The streets of Chicago's West Side were a tough place but if you rumbled first, then you got a reputation for sparking a fight. So what? he thought. That's the way it is. And if that's the way it's got to be, call me "Sparky." Maybe he didn't have book smarts, but he knew one thing: he wanted to change everything about himself—his name, Jacob Rubenstein, his rough, pudgy face, and where he lived.

He also wanted to drop out of school and he wondered, Why should I go to school? Mr. C was the most successful man he knew, he was famous in Chicago, and Mr. C never finished school. He was the most important man in the city and he didn't need no school. So, why should he?

"Why should I go to school?" he asked his mother, his foster mother, his second one.

She couldn't make a good answer. She looked at him with her beady, screwed-up eyes, the tiny hairs on her chin twitching sideways as she grinded her teeth. He wondered if she would take a swing at him now. He was bigger now and ready. But she didn't answer. "That's it, then," he said, "I'm quittin' and you can't make me!"

Later, when they sat down to eat a dinner of boiled sausage and baked beans, she brought it up with his foster father, the second one, another weak, wimpy pencil pusher. "You can't make me go to school no more," he said, shoveling the brown beans into his mouth.

Neither of them answered. He looked up at his foster father and he looked away, staring at the dinghy peeling wallpaper. "Let's face it," he said, "this place is shitty."

"Hush that language!" his foster mother said then turned to stare angrily at his foster father, who shrugged in his three-piece navy blue suit. He continued eating and that was that.

It was because of his reputation that one nightclub owner hired him as a bouncer. The club was a dark, seedy place called "The Palace," with a revolving door of drugged-up or boozy sluts dancing for drunken men. Sparky saw a lot of money being made and that gave him the idea that this was how he could make his own dream come true. Sure, he would have to rough up some guys as the bouncer but that always came with drinking and loose women, plus some idiots were plain crazy and wanted to be punched out as a top-off to their miserable week, but this was how he could be a good earner. This could be the start of his great success. He made a vow to himself and he told everyone, including his best friend Leon Cooke, "Some day I will own my own club."

But then Mr. C got a raw deal and was sent up the river on some tax thing. Sparky thought, Who gets in trouble with the tax people so much that they get busted for it? It was unbelievable. Who even knew they could lock you up for that? But that was how Mr. Frank Nitti took over.

One of the first things Mr. Nitti did, through Mr. G, was to give him a job as a "union organizer." That was a hell of a lot better than being a bagman. He felt bad that Mr. C was in the joint, but Mr. G was looking out for him, and he liked this union job. Mr. G also arranged a job for his friend Leon.

Leon was short but he was strong, he could box, and they worked out at the same gymnasium. Leon had a way of looking at people from just under his drooping eyelids that frightened them. They laughed about that and also about Sparky's official title: "Secretary" for the Scrap Iron and Junk Handlers Union. But he was embarrassed to say that he didn't know what that meant. He couldn't type or do any office work, so he never said nothin'. But what he and Leon did tell people was they were "making money by the bucket-load."

After a few years of working for the union, just when he felt he was moving up in the organization, just his luck, he got into an "incident" that ticked off someone. Maybe word spread to Mr. Nitti, or Mr. G, but this one thing made all hell break loose.

It was a regular meeting for a scrap-paper plant that took place in an old Chicago beer hall. Mr. Paul Dorfman, who Mr. Capone had arranged to be the union big boss, was making his usual speech to the guys. It was going good. But then Sparky saw some asshole mouthing off with snide comments to his buddies to show he was a smart aleck. An asshole who knows everything. The guy wore a neatly pressed white-collared shirt and gray pants and a shit-eating grin. Then the asshole got a little bit louder so everyone could hear his big mouth. Normally this wasn't a problem because the people around a jerk would ignore the smart aleck, but this time the guys were turning toward him and away from Mr. Dorfman. He had to do something.

Then Leon bull-rushed the guy from the front of the room, swinging his black jack. He pulled out his weapon, the .32 from Mr. C, and pushed his way through the crowd. He was ready to double-team this asshole with Leon, clock this joker a good one, when the jerk made another wisecrack. People in the crowd laughed.

Mr. Dorfman kept up his speech but Sparky could tell it was affecting him. This gave the asshole more courage and he dodged away from Leon and moved up through the crowd toward the front and nearer the podium. Leon grabbed hold of the guy from behind but it quickly turned into a fistfight with the crowd of men surging away and then mixing it up around them. It looked like Leon smacked the asshole but a couple other guys near them also started fighting. It was getting out of hand and he felt bad because he should have popped the guy the very second he opened his mouth two minutes ago.

Sparky tightened his grip on his pistol, his old friend and reputation maker, and thought that maybe he could hit the asshole from here, deep in the crowd, and take him down. But he couldn't get a clear shot with the crowd surging around him. Then he thought maybe if he shot over them it would stop the fighting. Some of the other union organizers must have had the same idea because several gunshots rang out. Lots of people were pushing and shoving and BAM! Sparky's gun fired!

The crowd moved away like a wave receding and the guy was laying in a pool of blood, holding his side, curling up like a baby going to sleep for good. But then Sparky saw that it was Leon, not the asshole, who was hit! Leon bled from his side on the cement floor.

Sparky screamed, "Lee!" and rushed into the opening and knelt down beside him.

Leon's drooping eyelids hung heavy and then his eyes went glassy and fixed at nothing in particular on the ceiling. Sparky looked for a bullet wound to stop the bleeding, blood was pooling onto the floor, but Leon's eyes were pale, milky-white, and he was dead. "Aw, no!"

Sparky tucked his head down in agony. A lot of people were talking but he cried. He wondered, in the moment before his death what was Leon gazing at? He looked up at the ceiling to see a reddish-brown water stain and two pipes ran over to the side wall.

The gun felt hot in his hand as a thin wisp of smoke leaked out of the barrel. Suddenly the police burst into the back of the room. They were more angry than usual and yelled at the organizers and asked a lot of questions. It was only a matter of time until they worked their way up to him and Sparky could feel a sense of panic in the room. Lots of guys were looking about wildly. He felt hot, sweat was seeping from every pore, and the cops were closing in. They would question him next and he still had the warm gun in his hand. He put it in his pants pocket, wiped his eyes, and tried to act like he had done nothing wrong.

Two policemen confronted Sparky and the shorter one said, "Whatdya doing?"

"Nothin'. That asshole over there was mouthin' off." He pointed to the asshole, his white shirt torn by the collar, and a trickle of blood ran from his nose.

"Thanks!" the second policeman said, and immediately went over to the guy. A moment later they had him in handcuffs. Before they could leave, the police wrote down everyone's name and address.

Afterward Sparky went straight to McHale's bar for a beer and a shot of whisky. As he drank beer he worried about the .32. He had all sorts of ideas but finally he went outside into the alley and hid the pistol underneath a beer keg. He went back inside and, after a few more beers, he changed his mind again. He went out into the alley and grabbed the gun. Gift or no gift from Mr. C he had to make sure no one ever found this. He made his way over to the Chicago River, shuffled quickly onto the bridge, stepped under a streetlamp, and tossed the gun over the side. It seemed to fall slowly, down through the night, hit the river with a tiny splash, and was soon out of sight.

The next day Sparky had to answer a few questions at the precinct station, but not much happened. But then, later on, more cops snooped around the union hall, so the local politicians felt that something *had* to be done. It was those damn snooping cops that were screwing up everything. They took him into the station a second time for questioning about Leon's death. He didn't tell them anything. Not about the shooting, or how it worked with kickbacks, or how his boss should become President. But the "incident" taught him a valuable lesson: some cops were fine but some were "do-gooders" and if you shut up, even the best cops couldn't figure it out. When in trouble, just keep your mouth shut.

But the local politicians felt obligated to do *something* so they forced Mr. Dorfman's boss, John Martin, out of office. But even that turned out okay because Mr. Dorfman took over. Sparky continued to work as a "union man" during the day and as a bouncer at night with a little bit of hustling on the side.

It was a brisk autumn afternoon and Sparky was selling Chicago Bears souvenirs made out of tin, outside the stadium, when Mr. Giancana spotted him and came over to talk. He was embarrassed to be selling such crap, but he was making a few bucks, and maybe Mr. G wouldn't notice how cheap they were. Mr. G was wearing a long trench coat and fedora, and he put his arm around Sparky.

"You doin' okay?" Mr. Giancana said, looking around the parking lot.

"Yeah," Sparky said, trying to slip the handful of Bears trinkets into his pocket without Mr. G noticing them.

" 'Cause the cops are sweating people again." Mr. Giancana's cleaved chin was square and, apparently satisfied that no one important was around, he leveled his eyes to stare at Sparky. "But you's okay?"

Sparky shrugged and smiled. "Yeah. Okay."

Mr. G chuckled and patted his shoulder, then squeezed him high on his back near his neck. "You know where we went wrong, don't you?"

Sparky's mind raced over the mistakes: of how he should have popped that asshole right at the start, of several people firing their guns, of the .32 at the bottom of the river, and of Leon's milky-white eyes under his heavy eyelids that stared up at nothing. "No, what?"

Mr. G smirked and squeezed his neck. "It's a lot easier to get things done if you got *all* the police on your side. Go to the police *first* and make them your friends because some day you're going to need *all of them.* Whatever it takes to make the cops your friends, some day it will all be worth it."

"Yeah," Sparky said, taking his cue from Mr. G, who looked around again, so he scanned the crowd, too. Then Mr. G noticed someone, another man also wearing a dark gray trench coat and fedora, and he took out two football tickets from his inside coat pocket. Mr. G raised them in the air, announcing that he had their 50-yard line tickets, but the other man nodded upward and kept his distance. Mr. G lit a cigarette with a fancy lighter, closed it, and shoved the lighter into Sparky's palm as they shook hands goodbye.

Mr. Giancana said, "You keep your mouth shut!"

Sparky almost replied, but said nothing. He looked at the lighter, made of silver with an etched scroll on the side, and pinched it like a good-luck rabbit's foot. It made him feel very good. Mr. G walked away but turned to tip his fedora to him before shaking hands with the other businessman, who looked over at him.

What a great guy, Sparky thought. And the fedora gives him so much class. He decided right then and there that he wanted a fedora, too.

But then Mr. Giancana walked back to him, blew some cigarette smoke to the side, and spoke in a threatening, harsh tone, "You're going to Dallas to open a nightclub."

It was an order, not an offer. Mr. G punched his shoulder, slapped his face, and pinched his cheek before he walked briskly to the other man, who waited at the turnstile gate.

Sparky felt betrayed. He thought, Twelve years of picking up bags and beating up hustlers and pansies, of being loyal to Mr. G and Mr. C, and this was what he got? This was his reward? To go to Dallas and open up a nightclub? Dallas for Christ's sake? If he was being exiled like the Jews, why wasn't it to some place nice like Florida? Or California? Or at least Las Vegas, where a lot of the other guys had gone? Why Dallas? And didn't another guy, Paul Jones, already go to Dallas and fail?

Then Sparky had second thoughts. Someone must have told Mr. G about his wish to open a club of his own. And now they were giving him a chance in Dallas.

Okay, it's a shot, Sparky thought. Go down there and start up a club. Get to know the cops and make them friends. Give them plenty of booze and favors, and they'll all be eating out of your hand. Make Dallas yours. That will impress them. And if a Jewish man like Meyer Lansky can make it to the top, then he could at least be successful with his own nightclub. That would be the next step in being a good earner.

Sparky thought, Okay, maybe I can do this. The Jews got their own state of Israel and I got my own club in Dallas. His mother, his real mother, had always taught him to obey. Everyone from Mr. Capone to Mr. Giancana and all the way through to Mr. Dorfman, had also taught him to obey.

Okay, he would do this. For them. He would go to Dallas. It was their code: *Picciotto:* Mama says and child obeys.

2)

The secret

Dear Robbie,

It has been a difficult week for me. Kids at school make fun of me and most of it is pretty stupid stuff. I know there just funning but it makes me mad. I got in two fights—maybe Mason won't bother me now ha-ha-ha! I wish you were here. Write back.

Lee

P.s. How is the marines? Do you march a lot and do lots of drills? Do you shoot your gun? Pleas write.

Lee wasn't sure if he liked New Orleans or not, but he didn't think so. The people weren't as friendly as in Dallas. When his brother Robbie enlisted in the Marines, Lee and his mother moved into a very small apartment next door to his Aunt Lillian and Uncle Charlie Murret, who arranged it. The kids at school were not as nice or as smart as the kids in Dallas. These kids were assholes, for the most part, and he often got into fistfights.

New Orleans was a jambalaya of spicy Cajun food that upset his stomach, shifty people in his face, tourists gawking at shiny trinkets, and hustlers that Lee became adept at outsmarting. The block of Exchange Alley where they lived was full of bars and stripper clubs with a pool hall below them that was the haven of the slickest and meanest gamblers. Plus even though his Uncle Charlie had "found" this apartment for them, he wasn't sure if he liked his uncle.

Uncle Charlie never hurt him but he sometimes swore at other people or raised his voice in a very intimidating way, and that scared him. He wasn't scared in the moment, because the people Uncle Charlie yelled at never did anything back, they just kind of stared motionless at him, but it was afterward when he thought about it that he became afraid. If his uncle could be that mean to strangers, what would he do to his Aunt Lillian, or his mother, or him?

Lee's mother usually worked on Saturdays for District Attorney Raoul Sere, who schoolmates said was a "racketeer," but he wasn't clear what that meant. But his mother had this Saturday off and they sat in his uncle's living room and watched television with his aunt. His mother repeatedly patted her dark hair nervously and her light blue eyes were fixed on the television screen. She had pale skin, dark pointed glasses with tiny rhinestones on the points, and she was overweight.

Lee wasn't particularly interested in this show but television was fun to watch. None of the other kids at school had a television. Nobody else in their apartment building had a television.

Uncle Charlie stood out on the balcony with his big strong hands holding the iron grille work and looked out over the street below where a continuous maze of people flowed through the French Quarter. Uncle Charlie's booming voice yelled, "Where's Sammy?"

"How should I know?" Aunt Lillian answered. She had a pale but pleasant face like his mother. She was knitting something with brown yarn but it didn't look like anything, except maybe a long brown shawl, which it certainly could *not* be in this damp New Orleans heat. That she was knitting at all seemed odd and he sometimes thought for a long time on why she did it.

Aunt Lillian said, "He's probably hung up in traffic."

"He's a limo driver. He's supposed to get around dat!" Uncle Charlie came back into the living room and his face was flushed red. "Besides, what traffic?"

"There's traffic. There's always traffic!" She shrugged but did not look up from her knitting. "Especially if he went to da airport or somethin'."

"He went to da airport?" The veins on Uncle Charlie's temples stood out and he squeezed his rolled-up *Racing Form* newspaper. "I'm gonna miss da first race because he went to da airport?"

Aunt Lillian paused her brown knitting in her lap and looked up at Uncle Charlie. "He'll be here. He always is. So what if you're a few minutes late?"

He tried not to move as he sat facing the television. Sometimes the picture tube flickered but even then he could still make out Lassie, or Lucille Ball through the static, if he was patient and stared real hard. But he wasn't really watching it.

"I'm gonna miss da first race and da daily double! I can't bet da daily double if I miss da first race! Goddammit I knew I shoulda driven myself!"

"Baby, honey, relax." Aunt Lillian moved the knitting onto a doily covering the table next to her, stood up from her beige easy chair, and went to him. She rubbed his back with one hand while squeezing his right shoulder with her other hand. "It's gonna be okay. He'll be here."

"He's late already! For all I know he's sittin' at da airport waitin' on a flight from Havana dat ain't comin' because of some storm or somet'in'."

"Okay, so what if he is? You don't want to go to da track without Mister Trafficante."

Uncle Charlie's eyes widened as if this were heresy. "No. Dat's right. No. Alls I'm sayin' is I'll miss da first fuckin' race because of dat asshole."

His mother looked harshly at Aunt Lillian, who then looked down at him sitting cross-legged in front of the television on a round multi-colored throw rug. "Dutz, honey, don't forget da boy."

"Please and thank you very kindly," he said. He stared at the television but watched Uncle Charlie out of the corner of his eye. He couldn't believe he had said anything! It just came out.

"Yeah, you's a smart little kid," Uncle Charlie said. "Polite, too. Hunh."

He glanced at Uncle Dutz. That's what Aunt Lillian and their friends called him, Uncle Dutz, but he wasn't allowed to call him that. That name was reserved for his gang of friends, who everyone said were in organized crime. He and his mother had to say Uncle Charlie or just plain Uncle. He didn't even know what kind of a name Dutz was or what it meant. He once asked his mother and she said it was from when Charlie was a heavyweight boxing prizefighter and traveled through the South. But she also said that it may be some kind of card game or something. Lee wondered if maybe Uncle Charlie was called that because they were teasing him for his New York accent as in "Dutz what I said, or dutz right." Whatever the explanation, he didn't like saying it anyway. He thought it sounded stupid. Also, he wasn't even sure if he liked Uncle Charlie even though he let them watch his television.

A car horn tooted twice and Lee ran out onto the balcony as Uncle Charlie hurried out of the apartment. From the iron grille railing, he saw a black Cadillac slowly making its way through the crowded street below and pull up in front of their apartment building. He looked down at the shiny black car as people flocked around it, hoping to see the celebrity inside. He was also curious and knew it was someone rich and powerful.

Sam Termine, their neighbor across the hall, was the chauffer and he opened the Cadillac's driver's door and got out. Sammy wore his chauffer black suit and hat. He worked for Mr. Carlos Marcello and, although he was not quite six feet tall, Sammy looked very big because he was so muscular. People on the street quickly backed out of his way.

Lee liked Sammy because he sometimes gave him candy or gum, so as soon as he knew it was Sammy, with his tanned face and bright white smile, he shouted down, "Hey, Sammy!"

"Yo-hey! Lee!" Sammy smiled broadly, reached into his pocket, and flipped a fat silver coin high up into the air.

He reached over the railing and caught it. He immediately thought of a baseball player catching a fly ball in his mitt. He was a star and could hear the crowd roaring. Then Sammy cheered too, "Hey, nice catch!"

"Thanks, Sammy!"

Lee could feel his mother's washed-out blue eyes staring at him from inside the apartment. He knew his mother didn't like Mr. Termine or Mr. Marcello either. But he tried to ignore her and continued watching from the balcony railing. Then Uncle Charlie walked out of the building below and into the street, and Sammy opened the limo's back door for him to get inside. Sammy then closed the door behind Uncle Charlie, looked up at him with his quick dark eyes, tapped a salute of two fingers to the bill of his black cap, and got in behind the wheel. The limo pulled away slowly, making its way through the crowd of people on the street, occasionally honking its horn, then picked up speed and was moving away pretty fast. For as long as he could, he followed the big black Cadillac with his eyes, smiling softly to himself.

When it was out of sight, Lee stepped back inside and his mother examined him harshly through her thick, pointed glasses. Her stare made him feel as if the silver dollar had blood on it but he squeezed it in his fist. He could feel the image of "Lady Liberty" with her shining rays. The thought of "Liberty" inspired him to ignore his mother. This was a gift from Sammy and she should keep out of it.

That afternoon Lee slipped out of the apartment and walked to Pixie's Drug Store alone. He thought of his mother's scolding look and felt bad that she didn't approve of him. But he wasn't hurting anybody. She didn't know Sammy could be nice, so he decided he would simply ignore her about this. It was time for him to start becoming his own man, he decided, and he began thinking about what he would buy with the dollar.

At Pixie's Drug Store, he took his time picking out an assortment of candy. He knew he wanted a paperback book, a dime novel called "Diamonds Are Forever," but slowly dropped into a white paper bag a Clark bar, a Hershey's chocolate bar, and a whole lot of penny candy. On his walk back to the apartment, he ate the chocolate bars and most of the candies, making his way through the swarm of wandering-eyed tourists, and hustlers who stood still and stared like vultures. He protected the bag like a treasure and kept the book snug under his arm. He did not want to share any of the candy with his friend Eddie, or his mother, or anyone. The more he thought about it, the more it confirmed this was his decision, not to tell his mother about the candy or the book. Why did she need to know?

When he got back to the apartment, his aunt and mother were not there. He went into his room and lay down on the bunk bed, ate what was left of the candy, and relished reading this latest novel. It was a terrific spy story and he imagined himself as the hero. It was a delicious fantasy.

Later that afternoon he heard his mother and aunt enter the apartment front door. His aunt said something about "swimming at the *public* pool" and he shoved the paperback under the mattress just barely before his mother came into his room. She wore a plain brown dress and her dark hair was still wet and she occasionally tussled it with a simple white towel. She stood over him and said, "Where was you? We went swimming but you wasn't around so we just went."

"That's fine," he said.

"Where was you?" She stopped fussing with her hair and turned her head disapprovingly. "What you been doin' here?"

"Me? Nothin'." He could feel the lump of the book under the mattress. He smiled. "Just thinkin'."

His mother pursed her lips and shook her head disapprovingly. She looked around the room with a white glove mentality and he was glad his room was very clean. He didn't want to get smacked around by her again and felt the muscles around his eyes tensing for a blow. But his room was clean and there was nothing she could say about that. She shook her head disapprovingly again, shrugged, and walked out of the room.

He enjoyed having a secret that no one, not even his mother, knew. The best spies, James Bond and all the others, kept secrets. He smiled to himself. Yes, he could keep a secret. He enjoyed this very, very much.

3)

Three can keep a secret if two are dead

Sparky didn't like New Orleans. He didn't like Dallas either, but this wasn't even Dallas. It was god-damn New Orleans. It wasn't what he was first told—he was told to go to Dallas—and this wasn't Dallas. This was New Orleans. But he had to pay his respects. Okay. He'd say hello, tell Mr. Marcello what he was doing if *he* asked, and that was it—he didn't owe him nothin'. He wouldn't pay him nothin'. This was his deal in Dallas. Not his.

Sparky drove his beat-up blue Oldsmobile outside New Orleans, past the chemical plants where gas flared yellow and bright orange, and into a vast swampland with gray, moss-hung cypresses and bright green palmettos. He was looking for Mr. Marcello's estate and drove past oysterman's shacks set high on stilts above the marsh grass and then he saw its sign: Churchill Farms. He pulled off the blacktop and onto a dirt-and-gravel road, drove past a "No Trespassing" sign, and marveled at how big the estate was. There must be thousands of acres here. A white wooden fence ran alongside the access road for quite some time, he drove past a "Dead End" sign, and he thought more about this meeting.

Mr. Marcello's knick-name was "Little Man"—but no one dared say that to his face—and he wondered just how short he was. If he was very short, how'd he come to be the guy to get all this? He had heard that he and Nofio Pecora had been street thugs and made their money on drug trafficking a long time ago. It was rumored that Carlos Marcello now made over a billion dollars a year from his many businesses such as casinos in Havana, running drugs through Cuba, prostitution, motels, hotels, banks, a shrimp fleet, shipbuilding, and oil prospecting and drilling. Government officials from the Mayor of New Orleans to the Governor of Louisiana cozied up to him in his private box at the racetrack to drink bourbon and to collect a little something for looking the other way, or at least that's what Mr. G had said.

Of course Mr. Marcello's power didn't happen overnight, but Sparky figured he must be pretty tough, probably could handle himself in a tight spot, and was glad he had been keeping up with his boxing and workouts. Should he take off his hat to meet him?

Then the trees cleared and there it was: a huge, Italianate mansion with a very large porch, pillars, and two large wings on each side. He felt very intimidated by the size of this place and he was in awe. This was a hell of a lot more impressive than a fedora on Mr. Giancana's head.

Two big bodyguards with dark Sicilian features and wearing dark suits and ties stood near the door. Another muscle man was dressed like a chauffeur in black clothes and applied paste wax to a large black Cadillac off to the side, but he was watching too.

"You Jack?" one of the guards called out.

"Yeah," he said, taking off his fedora and leaving it on the front seat of his dinged-up Oldsmobile. He took out a cigarette and lit it with his lucky silver lighter, the gift from Mr. Giancana. He didn't smoke often but he found that it helped to calm his nerves sometimes. It gave his hands something to do besides flexing into fists. "Mister Marcello here?"

"Yeah, he's expectin' yous," the first guard said. The other guard, the quiet one, had a scar across his upper lip to his ear. It was red and looked fairly recent as it was still healing.

The guy who was waxing the Cadillac tossed aside the buffing pad and came over, eying him up and down as he approached. He was about five feet ten but muscular with very short dark hair and he wiped his hands on his black pants, making a chalky white smear. "I'm Sammy. Pleased to meet ya."

Sammy had a strong handshake and smiled. He was clean-shaven, his short black hair was slicked down, and his dark eyes were quick and seemed to catch everything. Sparky didn't know what to say, so he simply nodded, and walked for the front door. The two guards converged on him, quickly patting him down. The first guard found his snub-nosed, Colt Cobra .38 in his pants pocket, took it, and dropped it into his jacket.

"Anyt'ing else?" he said with a noticeable accent. His hands were scarred across the knuckles but he moved quickly in his searching.

"No," Sparky said.

Then the quiet guard found his knife in his coat pocket, a six-inch switchblade with a pearl handle, and he snapped angrily. "What's dis?"

"Oh yeah," Sparky said. "I forgot."

"You forgot?" Sammy the chauffer said, his eyes scanning his other pockets.

"Well, I thought you meant guns. That's the only gun I got. I don't think so much about my knife, you know?"

Sammy smiled, showing very white teeth under his tanned skin. "Yeah, I know. Go ahead."

Sparky smiled back to him and chuckled. The guy with the scar said, "What's so funny?"

"I ain't laughin'," the first guard said, but he was chuckling, too, and wiped his mouth.

"I wasn't talkin' to you!" the angry guard said and stared hard at Sparky. "What's so fuckin' funny?"

"Lighten-up, Tommy," the first guard said. "It's a knife. You's gettin' all touchy lately. Whatsa matta wit you?"

"Nuttin'," Tommy said, turning away slightly because of his scarred face, but quickly turning back with a vicious stare.

The first guard smacked Tommy across the shoulder with the back of his hand. "Whatsa matta wit you?"

Tommy shoved him back. "Nuttin'. Shut-up already!"

Sammy nodded to go inside. He looked tough just nodding as the two guards continued to argue and scuffle with each other.

Sparky headed into the mansion and was impressed by the huge entryway. Large paintings hung on the walls and two full-sized statues of naked women were on each side of the staircase. They seemed to be welcoming him and pointing the way up the stairs as a deep red carpet ran the entire length of a very long hallway. A short, bullish man wearing a suit with a thick, muscular neck, black glasses, and dark hair with silver on the temples and peak, came out of a side room off the hallway. It was Carlos "Little Man" Marcello, the man who ran the entire South and, as he came closer, Sparky admired his sharp gray suit with a red tie the color of dark wine. He was about five feet two inches with the rugged build of a Sicilian peasant, but he walked with an overpowering confidence. Another burly guy, dressed in black pants, a white-collared shirt without a tie, and a gray jacket, followed behind him.

Sparky shook his hand vigorously, "Mister Marcello, pleasure to meet you."

"Thanks for coming by," Marcello smiled warmly. "Can I get you something? A drink? Bourbon?"

"No, thanks," he said. He wanted to add that he had to drive back to Dallas but he didn't want to sound soft, like he didn't drink, or to make it seem like he was in a hurry. He was in a bit of a daze that this little man had become so powerful and he bowed slightly. "No, thanks."

Just then he saw a large ring on Mr. Marcello's hand and realized he should have kissed it. He reached out to take his hand but Marcello turned away from him, toward the big guard, and said, "Lou, I'll have a rum and cola."

Sparky withdrew his extended hand, then nervously fumbled with his cigarette. He stumbled to say something. "Yeah, so, yeah, I'm down here, in Dallas actually, to open a club."

"I know. Dat good, dat good. Joe Civello told me." Marcello spoke with a mixture of a New Orleans drawl and Sicilian accent. "Needle-nose Labriola and Jimmy Weinberg both said you all right. Then Santo and I talk it over. We happy for you, Jack."

The big shots called him Jack, which was better than Jacob, but he didn't dare ask Mr. Marcello to call him Sparky.

Marcello smiled kindly, "You ever need anyt'ing, booze, girls, steaks, whatever, you let me know." Then Marcello tapped his chest in a friendly gesture. "I get deals straight from de port. I can get you anyt'ing."

Sparky smiled, "Thanks. Thanks a bunch. That's real nice of you Mister Marcello."

"Call me Carlos. You got your license and everyt'ing?"

"Yeah," he took a quick drag on the cigarette and turned his head to blow out the smoke.

"What I mean," Marcello opened his hands and motioned them back and forth, "the police, they ain't no problem?"

Sparky laughed and said, "They're police! Of course they're dicks! But I keep 'em happy!"

Marcello laughed and patted him on the back. Sparky liked that he was such a friendly guy and he felt that he was getting in good with him.

Lou returned with a cut-glass crystal tumbler with the dark liquor on ice. He handed it to Marcello with a napkin and rolled his shoulders as if he were expecting a fight, and then held his fists in front of him with his legs apart like a military "at-ease" stance.

"Salute!" Marcello raised the glass to him and sipped the drink. "I hate drinking alone."

Sparky felt bad. He had made another mistake. First he didn't kiss the ring. Now he didn't take his offer of a drink. Shit. Maybe this wasn't going so good.

Marcello laughed, "It's alright, I'm bustin' your balls. You sure you don't want somet'ing? I was just about to eat. I'm having filet mignon wit potatoes au gratin, or somet'ing. You want some?"

"Yeah, I'll have one of dem," he said, pointing to the drink. Lou looked at him with annoyance but Sparky added, "And I could eat."

"Hurry up, Lou. We goin' over to de office," Marcello said as Lou nodded and stalked away with a snarl on his face.

Marcello motioned for him to walk with him and then put his arm on his back, about three-quarters of the way up his back, "I wanna show you de property. I got a lot of plans for it, an' we can talk good over dere."

He had heard stories of people "disappearing" here. Mob guys and average Joes went to meet Little Man Marcello and their bodies disappeared in the 6,400-acre swamp around his mansion. One time the Sheriff found skeletal fragments decomposing in lye, but he couldn't do nothing because the body was unidentifiable.

Mr. Marcello led them outside and bottle-green flies buzzed in the warm, humid air as darting swallows swooped down and made a meal of them without a sound. The shiny black Cadillac had been pulled up by the front door and Tommy, the annoyed bodyguard with a scar across his face, held open the back door. The other, talkative guard was in the front seat. Sammy, the chauffer, had put on a black hat and was behind the wheel but he turned to watch every move.

Marcello got in with his drink and then Lou caught up with them and handed Sparky his drink as he tossed away his cigarette. He scooted in next to Mr. Marcello. Lou followed him and sat down, and Tommy, after giving him another glaring stare, closed the door. It sounded final, like the slamming of a prison door and he immediately felt very, very nervous. The black Cadillac pulled away smoothly. Where in the hell were they taking him? Had he been set up?

They left the white mansion behind as the Cadillac bounced along a pitted, dirt road that cut through the dense swampland. It was very quiet as no one spoke but small stones dinged around the wheel wells or undercarriage and occasionally a white egret would take flight from the marshes.

"Dem herons," Marcello said. "Dat somet'ing like a crane. You find 'em on garbage dumps but they ain't no good to eat."

Sparky nodded, using a handkerchief to wipe a trickle of sweat from his forehead, and replaced his kerchief in his suit pocket. Then the car slowed down to a stop near a small shrimp-packing plant made of cinder blocks and a black worker came out of the plant. Marcello rolled down the window and the worker handed the boss a small crate of shrimp on ice, which Marcello passed to him and he juggled his drink. "Ain't no better shrimp dan I got."

They drove on and it was very quiet. The briny smell of the fresh shrimp filled the air. The box was cool on his lap.

Marcello gestured to the thick, dense swamp and laughed. "Dere's where we get rid of de bodies." Then he turned to him with a dead-eyed killer's stare, "Hey, Jack, you a Jew?"

Sparky didn't respond. He hadn't been this scared since he was 14 and alone and carried a brown paper bag of cash for Al Capone through the rough streets of Chicago's South Side for the first time.

"You look like a Jew. You know what we do wit Jews, don't you, Jack?" Marcello plucked a pink shrimp out of the box, flicking the ice onto the floor, and popped it in his mouth whole, chewing it and pulling out the tail that he flipped out the window. "We just roll 'em outa de car an' into de swamp. They plenty a snakes in dere."

He mustered a nervous chuckle and turned to look at Marcello, but his face was stone hard. It was his classic Mafia stare, a no-nonsense look that meant he would do what he said. A chill raced over him and he suddenly felt like peeing. He looked away briefly at the tangled swamp, felt hot around his collar, saw Sammy, the driver, eying him in the rear-view mirror, his dark Sicilian features intimidating, and looked back into Marcello's cold, gray eyes.

"How you like dat?" Marcello said.

Sparky swallowed hard. He didn't know what to say. Should he say he wasn't Jewish? Should he be defiant?

Marcello stared at him evenly. "De shrimp. How you like dat?"

Sparky chuckled nervously with relief. "Oh, good. Delicious!"

The Cadillac pulled smoothly around a bend and eased to a stop in front of an old lodge in the swampy bottoms. The building was weathered past the point of rustic charm with swallows' nests mud-stuck to the eves. A rusty pump was off to the side.

Sparky set the box of shrimp on the car floor, took his drink, and they shuffled through the sticky heat and into the lodge. Inside was a room that looked like a large den with a light oak floor and a ceiling fan spun at a lazy pace. A large wooden table, similar to a conference room, was in the middle with a big burgundy leather chair at one end and ten wooden chairs around it. Lou walked swiftly through the main room and went into a back area while Sammy, the white chalky smear mysteriously gone from his pants, went toward the porch but shut the front door on them. Inset bookshelves lined the walls but there were no books on them. Instead odd knick-knacks of fishing gear, hooks and ropes, and small paintings of Sicilian villages and fishing boats decorated the shelves.

"Nice place you got here," Sparky said, simply to break the silence.

A wooden plaque on the table read

Three Can Keep a Secret

If Two Are Dead

Marcello smiled and nodded. "It comfortable. Please, sit down."

Sparky walked around, not sure where he should sit, so he pulled out a chair from the middle, sat down, and felt lost. He adjusted his coat and repositioned himself on the small, armless chair.

Marcello followed in next to him, kicked aside a chair, and leaned his backside against the table and sipped his drink.

Suddenly a beautiful red-haired woman in a bikini came from behind a wooden panel at the far end of the room. He could see now that behind the panel of shelves was a hidden entryway that opened to the other side of the lodge. The redhead was gorgeous with green eyes, high cheekbones, and a very pretty smile. She was wearing a yellow polka-dot bikini under a very sheer camisole and her curvy body was stunningly beautiful.

"Dis here Ginger," Marcello said. "You want her to dance for you?"

Sparky felt warm and confused, but he stared at her voluptuous body. "No, it's alright. No thanks."

Marcello laughed again. "Not now, Jack, I mean she would, but I meant at your club. Whatdya say?"

"Yeah?" Sparky looked at Marcello then eyed Ginger. "I mean that would be great."

"Yeah, sure. I got a couple more gonna go over, too. Right, Ginger?"

"That's right," she cooed. "We'd love to see Dallas. Carlos told us all about it. There's Vicki and Jada, and Joyce may go, too. But don't you worry, we'll talk her into it. It'll be a great big party! Our own li'l Mardi Gras in Dallas!"

Ginger leaned over to shake his hand and her large breasts pushed against the small bikini top strings. He blinked hard as she sat down on his lap and she put her arm around him. "We want to give you a *big, Sou-thern* welcome!"

"Okay," Marcello said. "A little later. Go on out to the pool."

"I just came from there. It's getting hot."

"It's hot in here," Sparky said, and Marcello and Ginger both laughed.

"He's funny," she squeezed his left bicep, "Ooh, and strong, too. I like him!"

"Alright, go outside now. We got business to talk."

Ginger stood up immediately and walked toward the panel entrance that she came in and he watched her strutting away with a seductive walk. She turned to look at him over her shoulder, winked, shook her ass, and then sashayed out.

"Hoo! She's something," Sparky said.

"Yeah, she a good girl," Marcello answered. "And a real good liar!"

Sparky chuckled and said, "Thank you! Really, thanks a bunch Mister Marcello."

"Don't worry about it. My brother Peter fix all the dancers in New Orleans. We got five strip joints here. We set you up, make sure your club's running a-okay. It important dat you do good, you know?"

"Thank you Mister Marcello."

Lou walked in from the back with two sterling silver trays of filet mignon with green beans and mashed potatoes in the half-shell covered with melted cheese, all on fine china with silverware and a steak knife on a white linen napkin. He placed one tray on the table in front of the burgundy leather chair and slid the other tray in front of Sparky, and then went to the far bookcase and stood at ease like a classy waiter.

"Listen, I'm happy to help you," Marcello said. "Maybe you could do me a favor someday, so forget about it."

"Yeah, of course," he said, but he thought, shit, shit, shit. There it is. Do him a favor. Shit. He smiled and said, "Man, this looks great."

Sparky used a steak knife to cut into the thick beef. It was tender and practically melted in his mouth with a succulent peppery flavor.

Marcello moved around the table with quick, short steps, and plopped down into the tufted chair. He raised his glass. "Salute!"

Sparky felt he was making mistakes left and right. He quickly picked up the rum and cola and toasted him. "Salute! To your health!"

"Thank you, dat very kind of you."

Sparky chewed the delicious meal quietly. He thought that this was one of the best steaks he'd ever had. He could hear women's voices, laughter, and water splashing.

Carlos Marcello was also apparently enjoying the meal as he smiled to him. Then Marcello set down his steak knife and tapped the corners of his mouth with the fine linen napkin. He spoke slowly, "I'm glad you feel a willingness to help me."

"Yeah," Sparky said, knowing something was coming. What could it be? He was being so nice to him already. It couldn't be that bad. Could it?

"Dere a guy I want you to meet."

Mr. Marcello was staring at him out of the corner of his eyes, waiting for a response, so he spoke right away with his mouth full of food, "Yeah, okay."

"Good. Good. He FBI but he sound like he gonna help us."

"What?" he blurted out with shock and part of his steak fell onto the tray. Marcello was sending him to see an FBI guy? What kind of set-up was this? He'd be arrested and out of business within a week!

"Okay," Marcello sipped his drink. "I can tell you upset. He *ex*-FBI. His name Banister. You don't need to do nuttin'. Just go to his office, it here in New Orleans on Camp Street, tell him you new to de area and want to find out what kind of services he do. You don't gotta say nuttin' and you don't gotta do nuttin'. Let Banister do all de talking. But you let him know dat you know me. Tell him dat straight away and see what he offer? Understand?"

"Yeah," he said, looking down at the steak oozing blood.

"I can't just do t'ings bam-bam and fuck it up. I gotta know what I'm doin'. I gotta have confidence. If I don't have confidence, I'd rather not do business. I gotta know I'm dealin' wit somebody dat ain't gonna do me no shit. I don't wanna get in no damn fuckin' trouble or nuttin' like dat."

"Yeah," he looked over at Lou, who was watching his every move, and, just for kicks, Sparky raised his upper lip in a snarl. Lou tightened his fists and looked at Marcello briefly, then returned to staring at him.

"Look, we want you do good in Dallas. It good for all us, especially after what happened to Pauley. It good for business. Capeche?"

"Capeche." Sparky knew what that really meant. He doused the meat into a thick red steak sauce and ate. It was his first day in New Orleans and Carlos Marcello had him going to meet an FBI guy. Holy crap. *Picciotto.*

"You can do dat," Marcello said, sipping and setting down his drink.

It wasn't a question but Sparky responded, "Yeah." You don't refuse an order from a boss.

"You're just talkin'," Marcello said strongly.

"Yeah, I know. So what? FBI, *ex*-FBI." He rolled over his knotted fists, clutching the fork and steak knife. "We're just talkin'."

"Dat right," Marcello held out his hands and shrugged like it was no big deal. "Dat right,"

Sparky cut another large bite of steak, chewed it, and thought, No big deal, my ass. But he knew he must be respectful to Mr. Marcello. "Yeah, I can do that."

Sparky's mouth was overly full with the delicious steak and he swallowed hard but couldn't get it all down. "Yeah," he said, still chewing the meat. "Yeah, okay."

4)

I Led Three Lives

After Lee turned 15 he and his new best friend, Eddie Voebel, snuck into a movie theater without buying a ticket to see *On the Waterfront.* Lee was particular thrilled with the movie because the hero, Terry Malloy, who was played by Marlon Brando, was a lot like Uncle Charlie. They were both ex-boxers who knew some guys in organized crime, but that didn't mean they were *in* organized crime but sometimes they did some jobs for them. They were still good guys with strong moral values. The movie influenced him to consider his uncle in a new light even if Uncle Charlie did work for some guys who were criminals.

After their neighbor Sammy, the Cadillac chauffer, had given him a silver dollar, he watched keenly for him. One night Uncle Charlie came out of the kitchen, having fixed himself a drink, and saw Lee looking out the window in the middle of a television program, even before the commercials. Uncle Charlie spoke harshly, "Whatdya waitin' for someone?"

"No."

"You ain't got no Santy Claus on da way?" Uncle Charlie set down his tall glass of iced tea spiked with rum on top of the television cabinet and stood in front of the picture.

"No."

Aunt Lillian looked at him then his mother on the couch, who looked away. She stared up at Uncle Charlie and said, "Leave him alone. He ain't hurtin' nobody."

"You, shut da fuck up. I ain't talkin' to you. Was I talkin' to you?"

"No."

"Then shut da fuck up." Uncle Charlie turned his attention back to him and he dared not look anywhere except at Uncle Charlie. "Now. Some people say you ain't hurtin' nobody. T'ing is, I decided to take an interest in you. I t'ink you're hurtin' yourself, sittin' here watchin' T-V all hours of the day. What is you, sixteen?"

"Fifteen, sir."

"Call me Uncle Charlie, okay?"

"Okay."

"Now. What are you waitin' for," he pointed a thick finger directly at him, "and don't you fuckin' lie to me!"

He glanced at Aunt Lillian, but quickly realized Uncle Charlie's swearing was going unchecked. He also felt his uncle would know if he was lying. But *how* would he know? Maybe he should try to lie. No, he would definitely know and it would be worse. "I'm waitin' for Sammy. He gave me a silver dollar one time."

"Okay." Uncle Charlie took out his wallet. "You know Sammy lives next door?"

"Yeah, but I like it when he drives the Cadillac. Once he gave me a Liberty dollar!"

Uncle Charlie handed over two dollars and he gazed at the money in awe. He dreamed of buying another spy novel, maybe two!, candy bars, hard candies, gum, and started salivating. Uncle Charlie's wallet was fat with more bills but he quickly put it back in his baggy black slacks. He tussled his hair and said, "Come on wit' me."

His mother and Aunt Lillian stared as he and Uncle Charlie walked out of the living room. They hustled down the stairs and out onto the street where it was noisy with brassy jazz music and people calling out. The street lamp made a weird halo in the misty night air.

"Wanna walk?" Uncle Charlie said, but it didn't sound like a question.

He glimpsed at the balcony overhead and saw his mother looking down with worry and tears in her cool blue eyes, but when she recognized that he had seen her, she stepped backwards away from the railing but not completely back into the living room.

"Hey!" Uncle Charlie said, flexing his large right hand into a fist, then relaxing it and pointing two fingers at him. "Look at me when I'm talkin' to you."

"Yeah, sure."

"Alright." Without looking up, Uncle Charlie called out to Aunt Lillian and his mother, "We're goin' walkin'!"

It was warm and humid but a chill of gooseflesh raced over his arms. Men were playing pool in the billiards hall and they walked past it down the street. He saw a woman of the evening leaning against a brick wall and she smiled at him as they went by. A tough-looking hood glared at him with a lit cigarette dangling from his lips but the hood quickly looked away when Uncle Charlie stared at him. A drunken man stumbled out of a bar across the street and seemed to have trouble focusing his eyes as his legs wobbled beneath him. From the corner bar a wailful coronet moaned, a bass thumped a beat, and a tinny piano tinkled through the night air.

"Tell me, wha's your favorite T-V show? 'Lassie'?"

"I dunno."

"Some stupid kid waitin' for a dog to save da day?"

"I dunno."

"Whatdya watch for if you don't even know what one you like?'

"I like that spy show. 'I Led Three Lives'."

"Okay. Why?"

"I dunno." He knew that wouldn't fly and quickly added, "It's neat. This guy is a regular guy, that's one life, and he's also a Communist but he's just pretending, okay that's two."

"Two what?"

"Two lives. See he's got three. One is normal. Two is a pretend-Communist. And number three is that he's a counterspy for the FBI. But no one knows it because he's a normal citizen."

"An' you like dat shit?"

He looked up at him. "Yeah. I think it's kinda cool."

Uncle Charlie patted his back and let his heavy hand lay on his shoulder. "Yeah, I guess I can see how dat would be kinda cool," then he said under his breath, " 'cept for da fuckin' FBI."

A sickle-shaped moon sliced through the misty air between the buildings. They were walking away from town toward the warehouse district, over the train tracks, and, in particular, toward a slaughterhouse. As they came closer, the smell of blood was overpowering. A cow was screaming somewhere inside the main building and other cows were being herded through the gates into the receiving area.

They walked by the high fence, a guard waved hello to Uncle Charlie, and he thought the guard must know him, or have some power, or something, because he would never be allowed to come in here during the day. There was another scream but this one sounded more human-like and Lee felt a chill slide up his spine to his neck and all the way to his recently trimmed crew-cut. Tiny beads of sweat formed on his scalp and neck, and rolled down his armpits.

"Where are we goin' Uncle Charlie?"

"I wanna show you somet'in'." They entered the slaughterhouse from an open loading dock. A single fluorescent bulb flickered but a few more deeper inside were lit and cast an eerie bluish-white light. A worker with a white apron covered in blood and wearing blue rubber gloves and black boots, all doused in blood, waved at them cheerfully. Another man held a hose and washed down the cement floor that ran red with blood. Slaughtered cows, stripped of their hides and split in sections, hung on meat hooks.

"I'm not sure I wanna see this," he said.

"See what?"

"Whatever it is you're showing me!"

"What?" Uncle Charlie stopped and looked down at him.

Lee thought, What should he say? He was scared. But of what? Would Uncle Charlie hurt him? Would he show him some people who hurt other people? Kids at school said Uncle Charlie was in the mob and had friends who killed people. Was he going to show him some murdered people? He remembered a story from Jimmy Pamphilis, whose father was a policeman, who said they found an organized crime "rat" in a refrigerated truck hanging on a meat hook. Is that what he was taking him to see?

"What?" Uncle Charlie said again. "I gave you two dollars. Ain't you havin' fun?"

"No. Not really."

"Whatsa matter? I ain't said not'in'. How could I said somet'in' wrong? What?" He paused and waited. "What, for Christ's sakes?"

He missed his brother Robbie and wished the Marines were here. He blurted out, "I'm scared."

Uncle Charlie chuckled a little bit and patted his back again. "We're all scared. So what. Come on. You ain't even seen not'in' yet."

His legs trembled. They walked past several stations of the butchering line and the further they went into the plant, the more the cows regained their full body, their skin, became unchained, until they stood at the beginning of the line where a cow was led into a tight gate and its head stuck out through a narrow chute. It was shaking violently with wide eyes as it could see the cow in front of it had been killed and was being raised on a chain, then slaughtered into parts. A scream shrieked through the night air until a man with a hammer slammed it down squarely between the cow's eyes and brained it.

"Dat Elmer," Uncle Charlie said. "He a guy I know. Good guy. Did you see how he did dat?"

"Yeah." The brained cow was lifted with meat hooks on chains, Elmer released the gate, and its lifeless carcass was hoisted away, dangling and swaying with blood from the meat hooks dripping down to the cement floor.

"Watch. Anoda one's coming."

Elmer had closed the gate and was waiting for the next cow to be forced into the chute, it wailed, and the hammer came down precisely on its forehead.

"It's an art, really. A little dis way or dat, and da cow don't die. Dat'd be a real tragedy. Elmer don't miss dat often, couple of times a night maybe. Makes da cow goofy but he quick wit da second hit."

"You brought me here to see this?"

"Not especially." He looked at him hard. "What do you t'ink of Elmer?"

"I dunno."

"You suppose he got family? Do you t'ink he likes doing dis?"

"No. He probably hates it."

"Let's ask."

"No, I don't wanna."

"Come on. Hey Elmer, come 'ere." The man walked over. Under his white apron that was sprinkled with various shades of red and maroon dried blood, he wore dark blue overalls and underneath that a blue-and-red plaid shirt. His arms were muscular although he was thin, and the closer he came the older he looked. He was probably about fifty. "Dis's my nephew, Lee."

"Nice ta meetcha, Lee." Elmer had soft blue eyes. He turned to Uncle Charlie and said, "What are ya doin' out on a nice night like dis?"

"Catching a little fresh air. T'ought I'd show 'em da house. Say Elmer, do you like doin' dis?"

"Yeah, it okay." Elmer had wrinkles around his eyes and mouth, silvery stubble grew on his chin and cheeks, and he had a short crew-cut of white-and-silver hair. "I don't love it, but, you know… I mean I love the cows. It's a job, you know, I have to kill 'em but I'm glad it me. One guy misses a lot—he ain't as dedicated as he should be and he don't hit him quick. You know, makes 'em wait in the chute watchin' and screamin'. It awful. But, yeah, I like it okay. And it pay real good, too. Why, you need a job, Lee?"

"I'm fifteen, sir."

"So?" Elmer wiped his forehead with the back of his forearm, leaving his gloves on.

"No," Uncle Charlie said. "I just wanted 'im to see da ot'er side of his burger, if you know what I mean."

"Yeah, anytime, Dutz. I gotta get back to work. Quota, ya know."

"Yeah, sure."

Elmer looked at him. "You want a job, you let me know. I put in a good word for ya. 'Course Dutz can do more for ya than I can, but I help ya anyway I can." He smiled and waved, striding quickly back to the cow, waiting in the chute with wide whitened eyes.

They walked out the back of the slaughterhouse and the overwhelming smell of cow shit and blood hit him like a punch to the nose. He felt his insides well up and down and he grabbed a fence post and threw up. A cow backed away. When he finished, Uncle Charlie handed him a clean white handkerchief. Lee wiped his mouth and offered it back, but Uncle Charlie waved his hand, then pulled out a yellow butterscotch candy from his pants pocket. Lee unwrapped it quickly and it tasted very smooth and sweet.

Neither of them spoke as they walked back toward the city. It became louder and more raucous, and people were in various states of rowdy behavior. As they walked past the pool hall and reached their apartment door on the street, Uncle Charlie put his hand on his shoulder. "Now dat your brot'er's gone in da Marines, I feel specially responsible. You's a bright kid. Don't waste your time on T-V. And when you go for a job, go for somet'in' you love. Don't get stuck doin' somet'in like Elmer just 'cause it's a fuckin' job, you know. He does it 'cause he loves his family, and dat's honorable. But love whatever you do."

No one had shown any interest in him before, or said anything so kind to him. Lee didn't know what to say. He thought for a moment and realized he didn't know exactly what it was his uncle did for a living. He had walked with him through the neighborhood, seen him yell at people, and seen him stand at the door of a nightclub like a bouncer. But what was his "job"? He knew he couldn't ask that directly. "Do you love what you do?"

Uncle Charlie stared at him hard. He looked away and then looked back up at him. Uncle Charlie was still bearing down on him. Shit, Lee thought. Oh, Christ! Is he going to hit me?

Uncle Charlie moved very close so his face was almost touching his. He could smell his brand of cigar, his dinner of sausage and peppers, see his stubbly black beard. He spoke slowly, "No. No, I do *not* love what I do. I do it for my family. And for you, your mom."

Lee smiled nervously with tears in his eyes. He didn't know what to do and finally he hugged his belly and chest, but his arms couldn't reach around him. He hadn't realized how big his uncle was.

Uncle Charlie hugged him and lifted him off the ground, and then set him down and tussled his hair. Lee smiled and looked up at him but he never saw it coming WHACK! Uncle Charlie's slap stung his cheek. The force of the blow knocked him down and he caught himself on the first step.

"Dat da last time I smack you. Don't make me smack you again, because it won't be pretty. Next time it hurt a *hell* of a lot more if I gotta unload on you."

He looked up at him, trembling with fear and confusion, and he wanted to cry but he resisted that and his eyes watered. A strolling young couple slowed down to gawk until Uncle Charlie glared at the man, who quickly pulled away the girl by her upper arm.

"If I smack somebody, it to send a message. You understand?"

Uncle Charlie bent down with his hands on his knees and looked directly into his eyes. His cheek was stinging with pain and he thought, What have I done?

"But remember dis. Are you listenin'?"

"Yes!" A tear fell onto his cheek.

"Stop cryin', you ain't hurt. I didn't smack you dat hard."

He snuffled and swallowed, wiping the tears from his eyes. His legs were trembling uncontrollably.

"You listenin'?"

"Yes!"

"Remember dis. I love you and I will always take care of you. Anyt'ing I do will be because I love you."

Uncle Charlie turned and went up the stairs. He slowly stood up, dazed by everything. He stood on the doorstep for a long moment and let the sounds of the city at night wash over him. He could hear the television playing some soap commercial and he stepped back and looked up onto the balcony overhead and saw his mother, staring down at him. She lifted her glasses to wipe her eyes, turned, and went inside the apartment. He could hear his mother ask, "Is 'Lucy' on next?"

"She got a Cuban husband," Aunt Lillian said.

"But the show's funny," his mother said, "and he makes it funnier."

"No, in real life. She's got a fuckin' Cuban for a husband." Then he didn't hear them because of an outburst of cheering in the pool hall followed by two men cursing at each other loudly. Then Aunt Lillian said, "Lassie's on."

"Good, I like Lassie," his mother said.

Lee watched the people on the street, sometimes intoxicated and staggering, and thought for a very long time. He thought about his uncle, and about what he had seen in the slaughterhouse, and about what he had said. Uncle Charlie said he loved him.

After thinking for a long time, he noticed the brief stinging in his cheek was gone, but Uncle Charlie's words echoed in his memory: "I love you and I will always take care of you. Anyt'ing I do will be because I love you."

Lee resolved from now on he would only watch his favorite television show "I Led Three Lives" and read books. He smiled. He thought of his uncle for a long time and decided. Uncle Charlie is a great man. I love Uncle Charlie.

5)

Guy Banister Associates

Sparky wasn't sure if he wanted to meet this guy Banister. What good could come of it? He found the building but drove past it, continued around the corner, and parked two blocks away. He walked slowly down the streets of New Orleans, looking up at the buildings. Jeez, there's the FBI building. Ain't no exes punching the clock in there. What's that building? Holy crap, the Central Intelligence Agency? Talk about walking into a den of thieves. Alright, we're "just talking." Okay, maybe the best way to avoid the FBI is to pay this guy to watch them, as they watched us, and do it very closely. That's what Mr. Capone always said, "Hold your enemies close."

The words "Five Forty Four" were on the second floor of the building, so he went up the stairs where a glass door was stenciled with white letters:

Guy Banister Associates

Private Investigator

Okay, this is the place, Sparky thought. We're just going to talk. No, no, let *him* do all the talking.

Sparky rapped on the door and when no one answered he looked inside and saw a woman sitting at a desk typing. She had some small white electronic headphones in her ears so he opened the door. She looked up over her pointed black glasses, but continued typing.

"Excuse me, ma'am," Sparky said.

She was middle-aged and blonde, with her hair in a beehive hairdo, and she held up one finger, typed very fast, and then hit the black tape recording device on the desk. "May I help you?"

"Yeah, I need to talk to Mister Banister."

She took the wire from the machine out of her left ear. "And what is the nature of your business?"

"Nothin'. We're just talkin' here."

"No, sir," she looked at him over her pointed glasses. "I mean, why do you want to see him?"

"To talk," he said. He felt uncomfortable with this lady so he left his hat on.

"Mister Banister is very busy right now, do you have an appointment?"

He looked behind her at an open door and inside the office he could see a man had his shoes on the desk. That might be Banister, he thought, so he spoke loudly, "Mister Marcello asked me to talk to him, that's all."

The shoes came off the desk quickly and a husky man's voice called out from inside the office, "Hey, come on in here, you!"

Sparky walked past the snooty secretary, tipping his hat and then took it off. Banister was stocky and past his prime, but he looked like he could still throw a punch. He had a pug nose like he'd been in a few fights, steely gray eyes, and big, bony hands. He shook hands forcefully and spoke with a gravelly voice, "I'm Guy Banister."

"Hey."

"Have a seat, have a seat."

The office had a gray metal desk covered in papers, gray metal filing cabinets, some of which were open with folders sticking up. More file drawers were open with stacks of papers on top and a single wooden chair was opposite the desk. Banister gathered up a stack of folders off his desk and set them on top of the nearest filing cabinet and sat down again behind the desk. "What can I do for you?"

"Well, that's it," Sparky said.

"What's it?"

"What you said."

"What'd I say?"

"Hunh?"

"I'm sorry, I'm missing something. I'm Guy Banister."

"Yeah, I got that from the sign on the door."

"And you're an associate of Carlos Marcello." Banister stood up again, crossed the room to shut the dark wooden door, and as it was closing Sparky noticed the blonde-haired secretary looking in with her pointy glasses. Banister shut the door, then leaned his backside on the edge of his desk very near him.

Sparky sat motionless but looked up at him. "What?"

"What can I do for you?" Banister said, with a hint of a rough smile.

"That's it," he said.

"That's it. What's it?" Banister had a Chicago accent and it reminded him of the guys back home. "What *I* can do for *you?*"

"Yeah," he said. "Mister Marcello wants to know."

Banister laughed. "I don't talk about that."

"Well I ain't talkin' either, so I guess this conversation is over." He stood up and Banister slid off the desk with remarkable quickness to cut in front of him at the door like a boxer cutting off the ring. Sparky thought, Maybe this guy is tougher than I figured. He looked down at Banister's hands. The knuckles were roughed-up.

Banister smiled and put his hand on his shoulder. "I don't talk about any of my clients or their business. It's all confidential. Anything that goes on, stays with me. You have my word."

He nodded. There was something about Banister. . . something that reminded him of Mr. Capone, besides his Chicago accent, but he couldn't quite figure out what it was. Then he remembered some of the Chicago guys had said Banister was there when the Feds killed John Dillinger. He looked more closely at him. Banister's dark hair was white at the temples, cut short in a stiff crew-cut, and he had a look of experience etched on his hardened face.

"I'm going to make it easy for you," Banister said, "because I was expecting to hear from Mister Marcello. Let me show you something." He motioned for Sparky to follow him over to the windows that overlooked the side street. He pointed down to some men loading wooden crates into an Army surplus truck. "See those men down there?"

"Yeah."

"Those guys are working for me. I'm being paid very well by, um, a friend of Uncle Sam." Banister chuckled at his own joke and put his hand on his shoulder again and it made him very uncomfortable. He thought, Who is this guy?

"They pay me to make sure certain things get delivered." Banister smiled with a playful glint in his eyes.

"Yeah?" he said.

"Yes." Banister smiled more broadly but he didn't see anything funny. Sparky thought, This guy needs a good clock cleaning. That'd wipe the smile off his face. This whole thing just doesn't feel right. Banister had that same shifty, *smiling* attitude Mr. Capone had. That was it. Smiling while Mr. Capone grabbed Vito Agnello from behind and repeatedly jabbed an ice pick into his jugular. Maybe Banister smiled when John Dillinger was shot dead in front of the movie theater?

"Look closer." Banister picked up a pair of binoculars that were lying on top of the last filing cabinet and handed them to him.

Sparky looked at Banister oddly and thought, What kind of guy keeps binoculars in his office? He didn't trust Banister one bit and was going to keep a close eye on him. He set his fedora on the desk and raised the binoculars part way up to his eyes, stopped, and looked at Banister again, who wasn't making a move but stared down at the street.

"Go ahead," Banister said. "What do you see?"

He lifted the binoculars all the way up and gazed at the men. They looked dark-skinned like Mexicans or Latinos. There was one colored guy. Yeah, one colored guy and a bunch of Latinos loading a truck. So what. "Yeah. So what?"

"Can you read what's in the boxes?"

"Hunh?" He focused the lenses down onto a wooden box but the men loaded it into the back, so he moved over to the stack of boxes at the side of the building directly below them. It was stamped in black letters

U.S. Ammunition

Mortars

Another box read

M-16 Rifles

10

He lowered the glasses but he wasn't about to say anything. They stared at each other. They stared for a long time.

Finally Banister said, "It's guns and ammunition. Can you read?"

This guy was insulting now. One more word and that was it. He'd smash the fuck out of this guy whether he was a friend of Mr. Marcello or not.

Banister looked confused. "I'm sorry, you said Carlos Marcello."

"Yeah."

"I've been expecting a call. You see, that shipment is headed to Guatemala. Some friends arranged, with my help, to give Uncle Sam a hand down there. You follow me?"

"Yeah."

Banister was smiling again and Sparky thought, What is so fuckin' funny?

"And Mister Marcello may be interested in my services. I believe he has some friends in Cuba. . . " his rough voice trailed off.

"Yeah?"

"You can tell Mister Marcello that I could offer him the same type of shipment at the same price."

"He knows the price?"

"It's negotiable," Banister shrugged his shoulders like an Italian with his hands out. "If he wants to do business, we'll work it out."

Sparky looked at Banister closely again, noting the white hair on his temples and the deep creases around his steely eyes. He thought, Who in the hell is this guy? He's offering to send guns to Cuba? Why would Mr. Marcello need guns in Cuba?—That was Santo Trafficante's turf and there was no way in hell he was getting in the middle of a turf war. What in the hell is going on here? He simply stared at Banister in disbelief.

Banister picked up his fedora and handed it to him, put his arm on his shoulder again, and walked him toward the door. He tried to make his gravelly voice soothing, "I know what you're thinking. A tiger doesn't change its stripes. Well, I know how this world works. Believe me, I've seen plenty of things in my day and if Uncle Sam or *anyone* needs some help, I can give it at the right price. It happens, you know?"

"Yeah."

"So, you can tell Mr. Marcello that I'm not happy with the situation in Cuba any more than he is. And with the right business deal, we could work something out. Okay? Can you tell him that?"

Sparky cocked his head to the side. He couldn't wait to get out of this place. This guy was probably going straight to the feds. If this was a set-up, he needed to act cool and just walk away. He didn't *do* anything wrong. They had nothing on him. He didn't even say anything. He hated these smirking, smart aleck feds.

Banister opened the door and Sparky walked out. The blonde was filing her nails, chewing gum, and talking to a very strange-looking guy who had painted on eyebrows and a bad black-haired wig. Sparky wondered if the secretary and this weird guy were listening the whole time? Probably.

Banister called out, "You'll talk to him?"

He tipped his fedora to the secretary politely but thought, Who does this jack-off think I am? Of course he would report back to Mr. Marcello. He was going to wait a day or two though, in case he was followed. He didn't trust Banister one bit. And who was that kook-ball standing by the door? What a fucking zoo! "Yeah, I'll tell him."

He waited a week until he returned to Mr. Marcello's Italianate mansion. Once again they drove to the old lodge in the swampy bottoms where Sparky told him that Guy Banister was willing to ship guns to Cuba if the price was right. He didn't ask why Mr. Marcello would want guns shipped to Cuba, Mr. Trafficante's turf, because that was none of his business. He would let Mr. Marcello and Mr. Trafficante settle that. Yes, he would stay the hell out of that.

The following day Sparky drove his Oldsmobile back to Dallas on the Stemmons Freeway and along the way he thought about his bizarre meetings, first with Mr. Marcello and then with Guy Banister. Well, he had seen worse and done worse. The end result was that he had Mr. Marcello's approval on his club and he had done a favor for him, too. Now he would finally get to open his own business. As he entered the Dallas city limits he felt strangely happy to be back in this hellhole.

6)

To tell a different truth

Lee missed his brother Robbie and he felt it was *his* time to start out on his own. But at 15 he was too young for the Marines plus he wanted to do something Robbie would never do. Something that Robbie *couldn't* do. He tried to think of the coolest thing he knew. Playing sports and being the star was neat, but a lot of boys did that. Hmm. All the boys thought flying was tops. Yes, flying was cool. But he could never be a pilot. Or could he? Why not? Maybe he'd try to be a pilot. Yeah, that would be cool.

His best friend Eddie Voebel was in the Civil Air Patrol so he decided to ask him about it. On the way home from school, they stopped at a vacant lot where a construction crew was building a house. He and Eddie both wore dark blue jeans and striped shirts, but his shirt was brown and Eddie's was red. Eddie also wore new Converse sneakers. They sat on top of a large mound of dirt, tossing pebbles into the hole near the cement foundation, and watched the men hammering two-by-fours into a wall frame. "Hey, Eddie, what do you do in your Civil Air club?"

"It's not a club," Eddie said, pushing aside his schoolbooks and leaning back with both hands on the dirt. Eddie had dark brown hair and a few freckles high on his cheeks around his brown eyes. "It's a squadron and our C-A-P unit does lots of things. It's kind of like the military 'cept we work on aviation stuff. You should join. It's pretty neato." They talked for a long time about many things and watched the house wall take shape. But he had decided.

The following Monday Lee joined the Civil Air Patrol unit that met at Moisant Airport, just outside New Orleans, because it was much closer to his uncle's apartment. Eddie went to a different CAP unit but that's how it had to be. It was a small camp of fifteen boys, aged fourteen to eighteen, led by three instructors called commandants. One of the instructors was an odd but tough man named Mr. Ferrie but everyone called him Captain Dave. He was tall and lanky, with an odd appearance—he didn't have any hair or eyebrows because of his disease of alopecia, but he had dark eyebrows that he drew on with a woman's eye pencil. He also wore a dark wig. Captain Dave stood very close to the boys and sometimes, if a boy bent over to work on an engine, he stared at their backside.

"Check it again," Captain Dave said to Milton, who had a trim blonde crew cut and was slim but muscular for a sixteen year old. Lee noticed Captain Dave eying Milton closely instead of examining the engine.

On the first Friday night sleepover Captain Dave and the other commandants built a bonfire in a clearing in the woods not far from their cabins. Flames danced high in the darkness and Mr. Tom Baroni, another one of the commandants, asked Captain Dave, "Why don't you tell the boys a story about one of your *dangerous* flying missions?"

Captain Dave chuckled. "Yeah, after I left Eastern Airlines I got on the CIA payroll. They pay pretty good. This one time I was flying low over the jungle of Guatemala at night. It was dark and hard to see in the cockpit let alone find my target. I had a map and the target was a fort, well not really a fort but a fortified house. Turns out I dropped a bomb on Presidenté Arbenz's house!"

"Gosh!" Several of the boys said.

"That's right. I was responsible for overthrowing that dipshit communist dictator."

"Whoa," he said.

"That was me! Yes, sir. They give me the coordinates, the target, maybe a photograph. And I do my job. It's dangerous to fly a small airplane, loaded down with guns and military supplies, at low altitudes over the ocean, or over the jungle at night. But that's what I do. I fly mostly at night, deep into the jungle, over the mountains of Guatemala—"

Mr. Baroni, who had been staring at Milton, elbowed Captain Dave, apparently to get him to finish his story.

"It takes skill to land on an airstrip in the jungle at night. But there is nothing I enjoy better than blowing the hell out of every damn Russian, Communist, or Red. And right here boys, we're cooking up crews that will bomb them to hell. I want to train killers, however bad that sounds. It's what we need. I *love* this country."

"Alright, men, time to hit it!" Commandant Baroni said, clapping his hands. They all went back to their cabins.

Later that night in their cabin, after the lights had gone out, two boys began talking about comic books but another boy said he did not believe Captain Dave's story. Then another boy spoke from a top bunk across the room. "If he was really in the CIA, he wouldn't be telling us about it. You know, just talking about it like the CIA was nothing special."

Then Winston, a small boy with a lot of freckles, on the lower bunk beneath his, said, "The CIA gots people who look like Richard Carlson from that television show "I Led Three Lives."

Lee was curled up in his sleeping bag, on a top bunk, but that caught his interest because that was his favorite television show. He said, "That's the FBI."

The second boy continued "Okay, so Carlson's in the FBI. But they probably got someone like Cap'n Dave who's tough and smart."

Then Winston said, "The CIA don't hire tall ugly guys like Captain Dave."

But Lee thought that maybe they did have pilots just like Captain Dave, someone who would take-off at night from a remote air base, loaded with guns, and fly to Guatemala and land in a field to drop off small artillery or supplies, and return before dawn. And so what if he was tall? That wouldn't stop him from flying. Maybe the CIA didn't care what Captain Dave looked like or what he acted like, if he was patriotic, could fly an airplane, and was willing to risk the danger of doing it when and where they said to do it. Maybe Captain Dave *was* just like the counterspy in "I Led Three Lives." In that show, Richard Carlson was an advertising executive with a family life but he was also a secret, undercover FBI agent pretending to be a Communist. But with Captain Dave, if the night flights to Guatemala were one of his lives, and the Civil Air Patrol was part of his civilian life, then what was his third military life?

The next day, the boys learned to chart air routes but they also trained in military techniques like going through an obstacle course and firing rifles. After a dinner of canteen rations, they built another campfire and Commandant Tom told a story about flying from New York to Los Angeles and back—in one day! It turned out he made a lot of stops, so it was more of a marathon endurance and not that interesting. No one was killed and no one was fighting Communists. When the fire died down it was time to go back to the cabins, but Lee wanted to know more about Captain Dave and what his third life was. So he approached him as casually as he could and asked, "Are you in the military?"

"No, they kicked me out," Captain Dave said. "They were a bunch of prudes. Air Force dicks with their heads up their asses. But I'm twice the pilot of any of them jokers. You won't see any of those pansy-ass fuckers flying at night in a single-wing plane over the ocean at two hundred feet."

"Hey, David," Mr. Baroni said, "watch your language."

"It's true." He paused for a moment, pricking the fire with a stick. "I can't help it if they're dicks with their heads up their asses."

The boys around them laughed, but more boys were heading back to the cabins. He could see that Captain Dave was serious. It was in that moment he knew Captain Dave was telling the truth about his night flights for the CIA.

Captain Dave noticed Lee's gazing stare and tossed the stick in the fire. He motioned to him and said, "Come on, let's take a walk. I've got something to show you."

Lee wiped the ash from his hands on his shorts. "Yeah, sure."

There was light from a three-quarter moon rising over the pine trees around the lake and Captain Dave led him to the main path covered in wood chips, then took the path that went away from the lake, through the woods, to the firing range. He was about ten feet ahead of him and walking fast, but spoke as they walked. "I could tell you liked my story yesterday."

"Yes," he said. "It's true, isn't it?"

"You bet your ass it is. I don't lie, you little cocksucker. And don't you ever forget that. If I say something, you can bet your ass it's true. Now, part of it might be a whopper, like me saying I dropped a bomb on Arbenz's house. I ran plenty of night missions and I dropped plenty of bombs—so maybe one did hit Arbenz's house. But I was fighting the Commies 'cause I love my country."

Captain Dave stopped, looked at him, and put his hand on his shoulder. "You know what I'm talking about, don't you?"

"Yes, sir," he was suddenly nervous. The moonlight cast an odd white glow to the woods and heavy shadows veiled the deeper woods. Captain Dave had a large nose and the moonlight reflected off his shiny painted-on eyebrows. Something moved in the woods nearby and a soft squeal like a cat called out.

"Call me Davey," he said with a mischievous smile.

He thought, That's a little weird. Why should he be so special to be able to call him Davey? He was confused and felt that something wasn't right.

Dave put his hand on his cheek and then stuck a finger in his mouth. He felt warm and very uncomfortable, jerked his head away, and spoke quickly with irritation. "What was it you wanted to show me?"

"Just what goes on in the pilot's cabin," Dave said with a smile. He took him by the wrist and walked with long strides toward the firing range.

Now he was very confused. There were no planes or simulator modules in this part of the camp, so there would be no pilot's cabin back here. Then they reached the clearing where a series of three bulls-eye targets were attached to three bales of hay on tripods. Lee heard that soft squeal again, turned toward the noise and, vaguely through the bluish moonlight, saw one of the other instructors, was that Mr. Baroni?, leaning against a tree a few feet away. It was a large oak tree, so it wasn't clear at first, but now he saw the instructor had his hands on Milton's head and he was guiding his face up and down on his shaft. Milton squealed and Mr. Baroni moaned softly, "God damn, that's it."

"Ain't that a pretty sight," Captain Dave said, still holding his wrist.

He felt sick and shivered, and didn't know what to say. He looked over his shoulder, but no one was around. He didn't want to be here. He suddenly felt very mad and turned away violently, jerking his hand back. He walked away quickly, staggering to find the path again, and heard Captain Dave call out, "It's the benefit of being a pilot. All pilots get it."

What in the hell? he thought. He needed to be in another place. Now. So he ran. As quickly as he could go, he stumbled over the path and felt his legs pounding. He ran past the dying embers of the campfire and sprinted toward the cabins. He ran as fast as he could, thinking about what he would say to the Squadron Leader in the morning in order to leave the camp. When he got back to the cabin, the lights were already out and one of the boys asked, "Why were you running?"

He didn't answer. He breathed heavily and lay down and thought about what he should do. He finally decided he would start packing, now, and he got up, turned on his flashlight, and put his clothes and paperbacks into his duffle bag.

He didn't want to get Captain Dave in trouble but he didn't want to stay either. He didn't want anything like that happening to him again. But how could he leave? Maybe he'd tell them his mother had called and she was sick. No, his uncle had called and said his mother was sick in the hospital, and he had to go back home. Yes, his mother was sick. He had to go.

The next morning, shortly after dawn, he took his bag and went to the Camp Director's cabin and knocked. After a moment the Camp Director opened the door in his bathrobe and Lee said, "Um, my mother is sick and I need to go home."

The Director was overweight with wire rim glasses. He scratched his big belly, tied the robe belt tighter and scratched the back of his head. His dark hair was sticking up all over the place and he mumbled, "What's that you say?"

"My mother is sick and I need to go home." This time the director raised his eyebrows and nodded, but said nothing.

After a moment, Lee picked up his bag and left. He thought, That was an odd response. How could he ask to leave camp and the Squadron Leader didn't ask him about the telephone call, or ask about his mother, or say anything? Did he know what had happened last night? Or did he not want to know?

He hiked out to the main road, flagged down a bus, and took it back into New Orleans. During the long bus ride, he thought of what Captain Dave had done but he didn't know what he should do. He didn't want Captain Dave to be hurt, because he seemed like an okay guy, plus he probably was in the CIA and who knows, maybe someday Captain Dave could help him get into the CIA to be a spy. Also, if Captain Dave was in the CIA, maybe he could have him killed for talking about it. There was no way he would tell *anyone* about Captain Dave. But then again maybe Captain Dave shouldn't have been messing with boys. When he arrived back home he did not tell his mother, Uncle Charlie, his friend Eddie, or anyone what had happened. When people asked why he came back from camp so soon, he simply said that the Civil Air Patrol had taught him a lot but he also learned very quickly that he did not want to be a pilot. That worked for everyone. Everyone but Uncle Charlie, who looked at him sideways, sensing that something was wrong.

The next day, Uncle Charlie sat in an overstuffed chair by a circular fan that rotated and blew hot, humid air around. They were alone in the living room as his mother and Aunt Lillian had gone grocery shopping. Uncle Charlie looked up from the *Daily Racing Form*. "Why'd you come back early?"

Uncle Charlie had that scary look on his face—the one he used to fix problems on the street—the one that promised violence—and he recalled the time Uncle Charlie slapped him with the back of his hand and said if he ever had to "unload" on him it would hurt a hell of a lot more. He also figured Uncle Charlie would know immediately if he tried to lie. Finally he decided to tell a different truth just as his television hero Richard Carlson would do. "I still like aviation, but I don't want to be a pilot."

Uncle Charlie eyed him quietly for several moments, so he added, "They finished the training part with drills and shooting guns and I didn't want to stay any longer for the pilot lessons. It was sissy stuff."

Uncle Charlie smiled with his thick lips and nodded. He returned to his horseracing guide and used a pencil to circle something in the newspaper.

A large bead of sweat rolled past his ear. He remembered Captain Dave sticking his finger in his mouth and shivered.

Uncle Charlie looked over at him again and he quickly wiped away the sweat with the palm of his hand. His uncle looked at him hard, as if he suspected he was lying, and an ass whipping would be coming. He could feel himself sweating everywhere all at once but he slowly eased his breathing, slowed down his heart rate, and casually smiled. Then the moment passed. It had worked.

7)

A lifelong dream become reality

Bureaucratic red tape delayed the opening of Sparky's nightclub, but with a few introductions by Paul Jones, who was the mob's first man in Dallas, and Police Sergeant Dean, who had some pull in the Dallas Police Department, he was able to get through all the paperwork and licensing. Together, Paul Jones and Sergeant Dean knew all the right people, and with a fifty here and there, he officially filed as owner of a nightclub. He proudly called it "The Silver Spur." It was up one flight of stairs but had a nice main stage, two side platforms for more dancers, a small dressing room, a back office, an odd slanted wall in one corner that made a small triangular area that was just large enough for a band to sit, and a beautiful wooden bar that was forty feet long. The restrooms were wallpapered with a fancy red velvet pattern and he hired an attendant for each. He also had a nearby delicatessen deliver corned beef or turkey sandwiches and kept a pot of coffee brewing, all in a back room for the police or anyone important who stopped by. It was his lifelong dream come true.

For the Grand Opening he took out a help wanted advertisement in the Dallas *Morning News* for exotic dancers. He hired local dancers, a few girls he knew from clubs in Chicago came down, Carlos Marcello sent over a few girls to help him get started, but everything had to have Joe Civello's approval.

Mr. Civello was one of the top mobsters pinched in the crazy Appalachian raid in 1957 when they caught most of the Mafioso capos in a meeting in upstate New York. That raid made the FBI realize how large and how organized the mafia was. So Sparky got Mr. Civello's okay on everything to be respectful, even though he was dealing with Mr. Marcello, who ran New Orleans and most of the South.

After a successful Grand Opening, some people in the neighborhood complained about the noise but they were paid lip service or ignored by the police because a lot of cops came into the club, usually after work but sometimes during their shift, to be entertained. Within three weeks he had a full staff, plenty of food, a happy clientele, and the police were on his side.

Sparky stood at the bar on a slow Wednesday afternoon. Around four p.m. police officer William "Blackie" Harrison and his partner Julius Kimball stopped in on their usual round. He recognized Harrison from previous visits because he wore his trademark beige business suit and a white Stetson hat. His partner was new to him and he wore the standard Dallas blue police uniform with a white hat and his badge on the crown.

Sparky slapped Blackie Harrison on the back and welcomed him, shook his hand warmly, and offered him the best table in the house. Andy, the black bartender with short hair, watched them closely. Fortunately one of the girls, Magical Melissa and Her Mesmerizing Melons, had just started to dance on the side stage in a tiny spotlight to "Honey Bun" from the musical "South Pacific" on the jukebox.

"'Fraid I cain't sit," officer Harrison said. His beige suit was crisp and he tapped the bill of his white Stetson. His words sounded serious but he had a shit-eating grin on his face. "I'm here to close you down."

"What? Come on! Call me Sparky." He playfully boxed Blackie on the shoulder and smiled. "Want a sandwich?"

Harrison smiled and turned briefly to his partner, who smirked and gazed in the direction of Magical Melissa, who had pulled out her pet snake and was flicking her tongue while gyrating her hips.

"No. For what?" No one answered, so he cleared his throat and spoke a bit more forcefully. "Close me *for what?*"

"Okay, Sparky," officer Harrison smiled and winked at his partner, who chuckled but did not take his eyes away from Melissa. "Call me Blackie. That's my partner Julius. Seems you didn't pay the Liquor Board for your license and—"

"Now wait a minute, it's right there!" Sparky pointed to the framed license on the wall behind Andy, who was making two mixed drinks and had one of the beer taps pouring into a glass pitcher.

Officer Harrison leaned over. "Yup. Through *this year* only, plus—"

Sparky smacked the bar loudly with his open hand but the cop continued. Officer Kimball, not fazed by the theatrical slap, winked at Melissa and stroked his billy club crudely. He was of average height but thin with shifty quickness. His dark hair was greasy and he had cool blue eyes and a scar ran from his left juggler vein to his ear lobe as if a knife cut him as he wrestled away.

Blackie continued, "*Plus,* apparently you, your bouncer, *someone,* ruffed up a customer named Harlan."

"I have no idea who that is!" he said. "Guys get bounced all the time. Practically every night someone gets liquored up and needs to be, ah, excused from the bar."

"Well, this here Harlan..." Harrison smirked at his partner and this time officer Kimball turned sharply to him, smiled, and a deep dimple popped in his cheek over the scar on his neck, giving him a look of disarming friendliness. He stared into his eyes with intimidation and completed Blackie's set-up, "This *here* Harlan is Chief Curry's cousin."

"The Chief of Police? Oh come on, Blackie, you're killin' me here," he said. "How'm I suppose to know that?"

Harrison wound up and slapped down a citation on the bar, even louder than his smack down, and rested his hand on his holstered pistol as if he was challenging him. But he spoke sideways through this mouth. "It ain't me, Sparky. You know that."

"Yeah, alright, Blackie. Julius. You come back next week—I'll get this all straightened out."

"You betcha," Harrison smiled and then hollered, "*Sparky!*"

He smiled back even though Blackie had yelled it in a derogatory manner. Alright, he had lost this round, but he was getting to know them. He patted Blackie on the back and then shook the other officer's hand warmly. "Julius, nice to meet ya."

Officer Kimball was very strong and began to squeeze his hand hard. He grimaced through the pain and pressed harder but Kimball had him. He crushed his hand.

Then Blackie used the back of his hand to tap Julius on the back and he released. They turned and walked for the exit, a pair of old western-styled swinging gates, painted black, at the top of the stairs. Julius looked over his shoulder at him, winked, and his dimple popped as he whistled sexily at Melissa writhing on the stage.

"Alright," he said, massaging his hand. But he called out with a forced smile, "You officers take care now."

8)

Father Knows Best

When Robbie had joined the Marines, it seemed like forever ago, Lee felt lonelier than ever before. Why did he have to stick around here—just because he was sixteen and the legal enlistment age was seventeen? He wanted to enlist now and his friend Eddie Voebel and others said there were ways it could be done. He wanted to ask his Uncle Charlie to help but he hadn't seen him for a few days. Also, his mother seemed to know something was going on, she seemed suspicious of everything he did, and she would interrogate him with forty questions if he was too late coming home from school. He often stayed out after school, observing gangsters, pimps, and tourists on the street, simply to be away from her, but he also loved observing people. He felt he loved his mother in some odd way that had nothing to do with emotion but was more of duty, but he couldn't stand to have her watching his every move and smothering him.

Lee read *Time* magazine in his uncle's living room and his mother tried to get his attention during a commercial break of "Father Knows Best." She was sitting right next to him in a stuffed easy chair as he sat cross-legged on the round carpet but rather than tap his shoulder she cleared her throat, several times, until he looked up. She said, "I know you want to do something and you're itchin' to get on with it, but I don't think you're ready to leave just yet. You don't think I know best, so I've made an appointment for you to see a very smart man. He's a lawyer."

"A lawyer?" His mind flashed on last Saturday when Eddie lost a tooth roughing up a drunk to steal his wallet. Did Eddie get caught and talk to the police and now his mother knew? No, if he did the police would have arrested him, wouldn't they? Maybe the drunk had seen him and figured out who he was and told her?

"He's a very smart man," his mother said. She adjusted her pointed glasses on her nose. "My boss fixed it with him."

"Mister Sere? Oh brother! I don't want to go to a lawyer's office."

"We won't. We're going to his house. I have the address."

He looked at her with contempt and distrust. She fidgeted with her dark hair, twisting it around one finger and releasing it. He thought, Why was she always meddling in what he did?

The next Saturday morning his mother wore her green Sunday dress with a yellow floral print and she borrowed Sammy's Ford Fairlane. It was a terrific car, turquoise and white, but his mother drove with her hands glued to ten and two on the steering wheel and never went above twenty miles an hour. Even though he didn't have a driver's license, and had never driven before, he wanted to drive Sammy's car and floor it, open this baby up, and see if she honks! But his mother drove overcautiously and much too slow. Not even the city bus drivers went this slowly. It took them almost an hour to go across town, during which nothing was said. She pulled the Fairlane off a side street and they went down a ritzy lane with huge houses. She eased down even more slowly and inched the wheel into a gravel driveway. "Here it is."

A man who was as big as a refrigerator in a black suit with a thin black tie stood near the doorway. He sat in the car staring at the giant, ominous man until his mother grabbed her green purse and said, "Come on, honey, he won't bite."

His mother explained something under her breath to the man in the doorway, who smiled and nodded at him as they went inside. He wondered, Now what did she say?

Inside the house was a large living room with two sofas and immediately to the left was a rich-looking office with lots of law books and a large desk. He felt an odd sensation similar to entering the dentist's office and the room smelled of disinfectant. Further inside the room, in the far corner, a smallish man with glasses sat in a burgundy, tufted-leather chair under a tall brass lamp. He inserted a red silk-ribbon bookmark, closed the book, and stood up with his thin hand extended. "I'm Clem Sehrt. Thanks for coming."

"Thank you for seeing us," his mother said with a polite nod like a small curtsy. "Especially under such circumstances."

"That's quite all right. It happens quite frequently actually."

Lee was shocked by his mother's words "under such circumstances" but he tried to remain calm as he shook the lawyer's thin, soft hand. He recalled that horrible incident last Saturday night and felt his eyes welling up with tears. He had stood lookout as Eddie and Leo rolled a drunken tourist in an alley. The drunk had lost his balance when Eddie shoved him and the bottom of the whiskey bottle smacked Eddie's freckled right cheek and knocked out his eyetooth. He also felt bad about the way the guy fell, kind of ass backwards into a heap, but he wasn't about to say a word. What did they know? Did Eddie talk?

No. Maybe Leo had been caught and was trying to make a deal through this lawyer. That was possible, he thought.

Mr. Sehrt smiled and looked at him through circular wire-rimmed glasses. He motioned to a brown-and-white plaid sofa to the left and walked delicately behind the desk with an inset leather-writing pad. Did he have on slippers?

His mother sat down on the sofa and he looked at her, and then at the lawyer, and then sat down.

"Tell him, honey," his mother said.

Maybe she knows. He thought he got all the blood out of the bottom of his pant legs but maybe some had splashed up or something. Or maybe the guy got a look at him before Leo clocked him with a blackjack. Yeah, maybe the guy saw something—saw him—but it was Eddie's idea. What did Eddie tell them? Maybe Eddie had to explain to his mother how he lost his eyetooth? What should he say? Where should he start? "I'd rather not talk about it."

"That's okay," Mr. Sehrt said. "But if you don't say something, I have no idea how to help you."

Help me?, he thought. How serious is this? "I. . . don't know where to begin."

"Oh, Lee, honey! Mister Sehrt, he wants to join the Marines. But he's only sixteen. Is there some way you can help him?"

He looked oddly at his mother. She didn't know. So this was about joining the Marines? She was trying to help him?

"Yes, I can help," Mr. Sehrt said cautiously. "But tell me boy, why do you want to join up?"

"To serve—"

"And don't give me that serving your country crap. Who or what are you running from?"

He looked closely at Mr. Sehrt. He had a long curved nose and sharp, dark eyes that reminded him of a hawk. He realized his heart was racing and he felt himself sweating. He couldn't tell Mr. Sehrt about wanting to leave home to get away from his mother. And he didn't want to say anything bad in front of her, not with her sitting there and smiling at him. So he thought of the positive side of why he wanted to join. "Ever since I can remember, I've wanted to serve our country. My brother Robert joined the Marines and he's had a very good experience. It would be a very good thing for me as well."

Mr. Sehrt stared at him with the same attitude as the principal, or his mother, who knew when he was lying. But this wasn't a lie. He really felt that way.

Mr. Sehrt grunted with disbelief. "Okay. If that's what you say. I know a guy," he flipped through a black leather address book, "Let's see, here it is. On

Canal Street. He has a store at number two-twelve. He can get you an identification card. Don't mention my name. You don't know me."

"No, sir," he smiled. This guy was cool. Maybe he should tell him about that other thing? Maybe he could help cover it up? But how would he start to tell him about that? Should he mention some of the other work Mr. Sehrt was famous for, sort of tie that into the conversation, and then go from there? Or maybe mention his mother's boss—District Attorney Raoul Sere and his corruption charges? Or maybe mention his Uncle Charlie and his alleged involvement with organized crime? Or maybe go straight to the top with his uncle's boss, Mr. Marcello? He said, "I understand that you were able to help Carlos Marcello get off murder charges?"

"Who told you that?" Mr. Sehrt seemed disturbed and offended, but he also had a slight smile of pride.

"Oh, come on," he said, trying to act boldly. "Everybody know that."

"Who dat?" Mr. Sehrt spoke with a gut-reaction New Orleans' drawl in spite of all his book smarts and education.

He smiled knowingly and played along. "My uncle, dat who."

"Who yo' uncle?"

"Honey, shush now!" his mother said in a high-pitched whine. "He's done helped you already. Why do you have to bring that up? How much do we owe you, Mister Sehrt?"

"There's no charge, ma'am. I do what I can to help friends of friends. Especially friends of Mister Marcello."

It was suddenly quiet and a short grandfather clock on the wall tick-tocked. His mother stood up and opened her green pocketbook. Lee stood and the lawyer came from around his desk, motioning them to the front door.

His mother's eyes were watering with happiness as she gave Mr. Sehrt a whole five-dollar bill. "Thank you, sir."

He followed his mother out of the office and Mr. Sehrt's cool hand fell on his neck. "If you or your *Uncle Dutz* ever need any help, *Lee*, please come see me."

He was startled, turned, and slid out from under Sehrt's clammy grasp. The huge doorman opened the door, grabbed him by the forearm, and then vigorously shook his hand. "Okay, thanks for coming by."

On Monday Lee went to the drug store at 212 Canal Street and asked the man behind the counter for Ted Allen. The man returned with two postcards showing New Orleans during Mardi Gras with an identification card laid in-between. The name on the card was "Ted Allen."

Next Lee went to the downtown Marine Corps enlistment station. The Sergeant was a brusque muscular guy who seemed in a bad mood. He showed his new ID and said, "I'm here to join."

The Sergeant looked him over, grunted, and asked, "Do you have some additional identification?"

He didn't have any other identification in the name of Ted Allen, so he shrugged and said, "No, sir, I don't have any other I-D."

The Sergeant was sunburned but had a clean-cut look. "Come back with two pieces of I-D, some mail addressed to you at that address, and some more peach fuzz on your chin. In other words, try again next year, boy."

He thought, Shit, his first chance to do something covert and he blew it! Why didn't he take time to plan this? Of course the Sergeant would ask for more ID! He should have known better and planned more. Damn! He had to be smarter. He tried to be positive and asked, "What do you suggest I do in the mean time?"

The Sergeant opened the top drawer of his gray metal desk, took out the Marine Corps Manual, and handed it to him. "Study that like the Bible, son. Do that and it will save your life."

He wondered if his brother Robbie had received his Marine Corps Manual in the same manner? No, Robbie would never try to enlist underage, or get a fake ID. But how did his mother know to go to Mr. Sehrt?

Studying the manual sounded like terrific advice and he ran his hand over the book. He vowed he would know it by heart and next year it would take him away from his mother. Yes, he would study this, follow it, and memorize it as if his life depended on it. Because it did.

9)

If the Feds knew, they'd be here lending a hand

Sparky looked at the Cubans with disgust. They moved slowly. They were supposed to be loaded by now and the pilot, who was the strange-looking kook-ball from Guy Banister's office, David Ferrie, was supposed to be half way to Cuba by now. Ferrie should be flying over the ocean while he still had some daylight but these fucking, slow, moronic Cubans were screwing everything up. "Vinny! Pick up the pace!"

His buddy, Vinny Browder, lifted a crate of rifles by himself and shot him a smart-assed look. "How 'bout you help us, huh?"

"I'm watchin' out. Somebody's gotta watch out."

Vinny was a big guy with dark hair, in good shape, and he quick-stepped under the heavy load and slid it into the single-engine plane that was cleared of seats to allow more cargo space. Two Cuban men inside the plane grabbed the box, dripping sweat in the June heat, and hoisted it further into the plane. "Watchin' out for who?"

"Feds." He stared at Vinny's small brown eyes, then looked at the jagged wound over his left eye where somebody popped him a few days ago. Why was Vinny giving him lip? It wasn't like this was the first time they had done this. Plus Mr. Marcello had paid them cash up front. Vinny should have no beef.

"Jesus fucking Christ!" Ferrie called out. He wore olive green fatigues and an Army hat with an old, dark wig underneath. He was tall with a lanky frame and leaned on the wing with one boot propped up against the airplane's wheel strut. He chewed gum quickly as he gazed at the sun nearing the horizon with his large, Romanesque nose. "Would you dipshits get a move on so I can get the fuck out of here!"

"There ain't no feds," Vinny said. He paused to think, then added, "If the feds knew, they'd be here lending a hand."

"So?" he said strongly, rubbing his fingers over and over. He could feel himself breathing faster and his lip rose in a snarl of disgust.

"So, we ain't gotta look out for 'em," Vinny said with a smart-aleck grin on his face.

As Vinny bent over to pick up a small box of mortar shells, Sparky boxed him on the back of the head with a snapping right jab. It stung one knuckle but it was worth it. He had to keep these fuckers in line, even if Vinny was a friend.

"Hey, wha'dya do that for?"

"Shut up and get a move on!" Ferrie yelled. "Jesus!"

Ferrie was a good guy, Sparky thought. A weird fuckin' fruitcake, but a tough nut. Yep, he was very strange but a good guy. He could be counted on.

Ferrie noticed him looking at the small, unmarked plane. "You wanna come with me?"

"Fuck no."

"Then why don't you help load?" Ferrie said, spitting on the ground.

He turned and looked around the small airstrip, which wasn't much of a landing place for planes as it was simply a large open field in a clearing of woods outside New Orleans. The pine and ash trees were thick just beyond the clearing.

He raised up his shoulders, wagged his neck from side-to-side, and threw a couple of punches like he was loosening up for a fight. It was one of his old boxing moves that he picked up in the gym in Chicago. His jacket felt tight around him but his actions caught Ferrie's attention and he raised his fake eyebrows. "I'm the lookout. I don't do no loadin'."

"Alright," Ferrie said, then added sarcastically, "Good thing we got you!"

He walked back and forth like he was cutting off the ring, staring down Ferrie, who looked at his backside. Ferrie's eyes wandered down and stared at his crotch.

He cocked his fist and yelled, "You want your teeth bashed down your fuckin' throat?"

"Who's gonna do that?" Ferrie said. He stepped away from the plane with his bowed legs in black boots.

"I'll kick your fuckin' ass," he yelled. "You son-of-a-bitch!"

"You wanna dance?" Ferrie stood with his arms out, waving his hands inward for him to come forward. "Come on, tough guy."

He rushed the bastard, taking a glancing punch off his shoulder, but he grabbed him. Then Vinny wedged between them, pushing him on the chest and yelling, "Hey, hey! Take it easy, Sparky!"

A few more men gathered around and one Cuban jumped between them. He tried to throw a punch and yelled, "Let go! Motherfucker's a homo!"

"That's right," Ferrie said, his dark wig askew under his Army hat. "So what? What're you, bitch?"

"What?"

"You heard me." Ferrie pushed at the Cuban between them, wheeling his arms away from another, who grabbed at him.

"What the fuck did you say?" he yelled.

"You heard me."

He breathed heavily and Vinny swung around, locked his arms through his, and forced his arms behind him. He jumped and struggled but couldn't move. "Goddammit! Lemme go!"

"Settle down!" Vinny screamed. "Christ, we're all on the same side here."

"I ain't with this motherfucker!" he hollered.

He bent down, turned away, and violently pulled his arms free from Vinny. His jacket ripped by the armpit. "Jesus! Look what you fuckin' did!"

"Le's go," one of the Cubans yelled, "we're almos' finish!"

He stared at Ferrie, who winked at him. Bastard. Why did he have to eat all this shit for Carlos Marcello? He was sick of it. It was a damn good thing Mr. Marcello paid so well. Otherwise he'd be out of here. That was certain. Damn. Creepy motherfucker gives me the creeps. "Creepy motherfucker."

"You love me," Ferrie said. He straightened his Army hat and wig, winked again, and puckered a kiss.

Jesus, Sparky thought. He'd ask Mr. Marcello to find somebody else to do this. He needed the money, but not this much.

Ferrie climbed into the cockpit and started the engine. He slid open and leaned out the small window as the Cubans loaded the last few crates of rifles in the back. The two men in the plane jumped down, shutting the hatch behind them. One rapped on the body of the plane, Ferrie spit his gum out the window, and leaned back into the cockpit.

The plane's engine revved louder and it slowly began to roll away. It spun around and bounced over the grass, picking up speed slowly, lifting and dipping and rising again, straining under the heavy overload, and the engine whined louder. It rose slightly in the air then suddenly dropped, speeding closer to the trees at the end of the clearing, then lifted just high enough for its wheels to clear the pines.

Vinny slapped his shoulder and said, "Come on, let's get out of here."

"I hate that creepy bastard."

"Yeah, okay," Vinny said, spitting to the side.

He was still breathing deeply. He would tell Mr. Marcello he didn't feel comfortable working with that son-of-a-bitch. Well, that probably wouldn't work because Mr. Trafficante was involved, too, but at least he'd tell Mr. Marcello that Ferrie was a problem, in case he had to use his brass knuckles to beat the shit out of Ferrie one day. Creepy motherfucker.

"You know what," Vinny said, punching his shoulder, "We should use boats. Get Banister to get one of those big Army surplus boats and run it out of Galveston."

Sparky thought about it. It really was a great idea. That would eliminate Ferrie, it would be cheaper, and they could haul more guns. But he wondered if he could get Mr. Marcello to agree to it. If he liked the idea maybe Mr. Marcello would let him keep the extra money. Or maybe he should do it and not tell Mr. Marcello at first. No, Mr. Marcello had a whole fleet of shrimp boats running in the Gulf from New Orleans to Galveston. He would find out *immediately* so he sure as hell better tell Mr. Marcello up front.

"Yeah, I like that." He could hear the whining engine of the plane in the distance, but it was fading. He still wanted to beat the hell out of that creepy bastard. Then he thought again about using a military surplus boat to run an even larger load of guns. "Yeah, let me talk to the boss and we'll do that from now on."

PART II

10)

aka Alek Kovich

Lee sat cross-legged next to John and sited the target as John squeezed the trigger smoothly. John was his bunkmate, a bookish but tough kid from the streets of Philadelphia, with dark brown hair in a Marine buzz cut and soft brown eyes. John's last name was Heindel but everyone called him Hidell as a knick-name. His knick-name was Alek Kovich, which was a combination of two names: Alek, which was short for smart-aleck and Kovich because he loved everything Russian. Ever since he was a boy reading James Bond novels he wanted to be a secret agent and he had been intrigued with pseudonyms. Now his Marine buddies called him Alek Kovich but he wanted to find one of his own choosing.

John fired again and stood up swiftly with a salute to Sergeant Brisken. He took John's place, hitting the dirt and laying down into a field-firing position, ready, as the Sergeant stood above him squinting in the harsh California sunshine. They waited for a group of eight runners to dash out and take down the perforated targets, post a new black-and-white target that was in the shape of a man's head and shoulders with rings around it, and run the perforated target back to the Sergeant for an accurate reading. Their runner finally came back, breathing heavily from the 200-yard distance, and handed the target to the Sergeant, who tallied the bullet holes for the score.

"Forty-eight. Not bad Hidell." He looked up at his buddy and smiled to John. The Sergeant barked, "Alright, let's go Alek Kovich!"

"Da, da, Kommandant!" He felt the hard clay-dirt under his belly, smelled the fresh earth, as sweat rolled down his temples, down his forehead and around his eyes, and under his helmet. He pushed the helmet up and re-sited the target. He exhaled evenly, held his breath, and squeezed the trigger easily. A puff of dirt kicked up on the berm behind the target. He pulled the bolt back and reloaded. Eased the site down, leveled the crosshairs across the bulls-eye around the back of the head, and exhaled slowly, squeezing the trigger. Another puff volcanoed out of the dirt. "Shit!"

"Three more shots!" Sergeant Brisken hollered. "Go Kovich, you've got ten seconds!"

Lee thought, This is all a bunch of bullshit. What did this have to do with Intelligence? Who cares? He squeezed, jerked back the bolt, slammed in another round, and squeezed again, feeling the recoil punch his shoulder and pulled back the bolt, watching the spent shell cartwheel out of the magazine, and shoved another shell into the chamber. He yelled and fired, "BLAM!"

The result was the same. He stood and looked over at John, who lensed the target with his binoculars, brought them down, and stared hard at him. John cursed under his breath, "Maggie's drawers" —meaning he had missed not only the two rings around the bull's-eye but had missed the entire sheet of the target as well.

He glanced at John with a look of indifference to mask his seething anger. He knew it would be a few moments until the runner came back and the whole time he felt as if he were on trial and awaiting the executioner's axe in the form of the Sergeant's verbal abuse. He was furious with the whole system, including taking orders from this moron the Sergeant, when he wanted to learn the trade of a spy in Intelligence. Finally the clean, empty sheet was handed to the Sergeant, who barked the result loudly for all to hear. "Maggie's drawers!"

Another Marine laughed with ridicule, "Maggie's drawers!"

The Sergeant stood inches from his face and continued hollering at him. "You're disgusting! You slimy piece of shit, Kovich! You're better off with the Reds 'cause you sure as hell can't shoot like a Marine!"

When Bravo company had finished drilling on the firing range, Sergeant Brisken ordered their platoon to jog back to the barracks, shouting out the cadence with an obscene verse that he made up on the spot about Lee's mother's drawers and how she sucked-off Nazis. He was exhausted by the two-mile run with gear by the time they reached their hut. The other Marines cleaned their rifles and their area, and fell out for dinner, but the Sergeant made him do fifty push-ups and mop the floor.

As he mopped, Lee thought of the time he had to mow the lawn, and then trim its edges with a pair of scissors. He also recalled the time he had to sweep the walk, twice, because the Sergeant spilled peanut shells all over it as soon as he finished cleaning it. The first punishment was because he couldn't dismantle and assemble his rifle quickly enough and the second offense was because he talked back to the Sergeant, calling him "a loud-mouthed idiot," which he immediately regretted but fortunately the Sergeant had not quite heard his comment. But a few fellow Marines laughed, which alerted the Sergeant to him and he never repeated his comment despite of one hell of a tongue-lashing and a few stinging slaps on his cheeks that caused his eyes to tear.

When Lee finished mopping, he stood at attention near the Sergeant's office in their Quonset hut. He wondered if the Sergeant would spill something on the floor to make him mop it again, similar to the peanut shells. The Sergeant rose from his desk, walked up to him, and pressed his forehead into the top of his skull. He jabbed two fingers into his chest and hollered, "You're a slimy piece of shit that doesn't deserve to be in my unit! You think about that the next time you're on the range! Think about how you oughta drop out of my unit, soldier! Or, maybe, just maybe, you should shoot better!"

The Sergeant walked away and he exhaled heavily, feeling the bruised area of his sternum. He then noticed that John had hung around, pretending to polish his boots on the bottom bunk when all the others had left long ago for the mess hall. He thought that maybe the Sergeant was less mean because John was there, but then realized that wouldn't affect the Sergeant at all. Still he appreciated John's being there.

"Why'd you do that?" John asked, his dark eyebrows pressed together over his round brown eyes.

"I wasn't trying to miss. It just happened."

John neatly placed his gleaming boots into his locker then put his hand on his shoulder. He gazed at him with concern. "I'd hate to see you kicked out of the Corps."

"Don't worry, I won't."

John looked confused. He seemed to be thinking, how could he not be expelled with such horrible shooting? But John tried to cover his confusion and being upset with a joke, crooning a line from a popular Elvis Presley song with a horrible impersonation complete with a snarling upper lip, "Aw, you ain't nothin' but a hound dog—lying all the time!"

"Trust me, it'll be alright," he said. "I've got a plan and, from all indications, it's working fine."

Lee hadn't told anyone in his unit of his plan, which was to specialize in Aircraft Maintenance and Repair, but he also had a second, secretive part, which was to request special assignment with the Office of Naval Intelligence. He had heard they were highly selective and it was far from a sure thing, so he didn't want to say anything to anyone yet, not even Hidell. He looked at Hidell with a sphinx-like smile on his face. "It'll be fine."

"Okay. Come on, I could eat three Philly cheese-steaks."

"M-m-m, po' boys sounds great!" he laughed. "But instead how 'bout a big helping of that shit they slop in the mess hall?"

"Yeah, even that." Flecks of dried sweat-salt dotted John's temple and he smiled. "Let's grab some chow."

"Da, borscht. Yum-yum. And vodka for all my fun-loving comrades!"

John laughed, then tightened his arm into a headlock, and punched him playfully in the gut. "I'm gonna kick your ass, you Commie bastard!"

11)

The Carousel Club

Sparky sat in his office at his metal desk, piled high with overdue bills, another letter from the IRS, and dancer's headshots, and he gazed at the bare wall across the room. He was tired of spinning his wheels with Sam Giancana, Carlos Marcello, Joseph Civello, Santo Trafficante, and the other bosses. Guys were always taking advantage of him and he wasn't getting anywhere. He knew he would never become a made man because he wasn't Sicilian, but why wouldn't they show him more respect? Why couldn't he be in a little better position? He had been in Dallas for several years and he was still stuck here. He had done everything they asked of him and more. His new nightclub, the Carousel Club, was making a little money for them and the cops were okay with it because he had fixed that perfectly. He had a gift for working the police but the big shots acted like it was no big deal, or at least that was what they said, and he was tired of not getting their respect.

Sparky had made plenty of friends in the Dallas Police department. He often visited their headquarters just to say hello, bring them sandwiches, and invite them to his club with free passes. But some of the best connections he'd made on the police force were with officers who stopped by the club on their own. They said they appreciated the coffee and sandwiches he had for them, every night in the back room, but he knew the real reason they came in was for the girls. He knew that some guys would do almost anything for sex, even if they were a Bible thumper, and if they partied once, they would probably be back for more. And then they owed him a favor.

"You never cash in a favor unless you absolutely need it," Mr. Capone taught him. "No. You build them up, until you really, really need something."

The more favors he built up, the more leverage he would have with the Dallas police. But he used his favors wisely. In his time in Dallas, he had been arrested seven times, by naïve or rookie officers—twice for carrying a concealed gun, three times for licensing laws, once for assault, and once for a traffic violation. Each time the arresting officer quickly learned from senior officers that when the court date came it would be best for everyone if he took a day off, was a "failure to appear" in court, and the case would be dismissed. With all the favors owed, the only offense he had to deal with was the traffic violation.

Sparky had a lot of friends on the force and his dancers, the regular girls, liked him a lot, too. But none of them was the type of person he'd want to be with for the rest of his life. Sure, plenty of girls liked him—what wasn't to like? Some gals were runaways and some had been in trouble in other states, sometimes with the law, and none of that mattered to him. He wanted to help all these poor girls. But that didn't mean he wanted to be close with them. He'd fool around with them to make sure they knew what they were doing in the sack, to be cooperative about it, so they could be used properly with a local businessman, politician, or cop. But he wasn't about to marry one of them.

He got up from his desk and walked through the club to make sure everything was running smoothly. He opened the dancers' dressing room door and saw only two dancers.

"Hey, Sparky, can you lend me fifty dollars until the end of the month?" Daisy Porter, a pretty-faced platinum blonde asked. She sat at a narrow table crowded with makeup trays, hair sprays and brushes, paper coffee cups, perfume bottles, and tissue boxes. The other dancer, Wanda, a dark-haired beauty from Oklahoma but dumb as a fence post, sat across the room applying her pasties. "I gotta pay back rent or my landlord's gonna boot me."

"You can stay with me again," he said.

"Aw, Sparky, you're sweet," she cooed. Daisy had a nice smile even if her front teeth were misaligned. She jumped up, her perky tits bouncing against his belly, and adjusted the collar of his white shirt, under his dark suit coat, and stroked his chest. "I don't want to impose on you again. Just lend me the dough. I'm good for it."

"I know it, sugar," he said. Then he remembered a job that Mr. Marcello needed during the coming week. "You know, I got a friend who needs a package delivered from New Orleans. He needs it here by Friday. Whatdya think? You wanna go to New Orleans and make a few bucks?"

"Will it pay for my rent?" Daisy asked.

"If it don't, I'll make up the difference. Whatdya say?"

"I'd love to go to New Orleans," she said with excitement. "But how will I get there and back?"

"I can buy you a bus ticket there and I know a guy driving back, I think he's coming back Thursday? Yeah, that's right. That would be perfect, okay?"

"Yeah, okay!" Daisy kissed him and he could feel her bright red lipstick smear on his cheek. She ran her hand over his leg and it crept up to his crotch and she grabbed his dick through his pants. She moaned a bit and asked, "Mmm, you want a little head?"

He looked over at Wanda, she was wrapping some kind of swan costume around her torso, and he licked his lips. "Yeah, that'd be nice. Let's go to my office."

"Oh, you shy boy!" Daisy nodded in Wanda's direction. "Maybe she wants to help? Wanda, honey?"

Wanda had finished dressing with lots of feathers and practiced a shimmy in the mirror to the faint music that could be heard from the stage. She looked over at him and then down at the bulge in his pants. She asked, "Hunh?"

A scattering of applause could be heard and then a man called out, "Fuckin' bitch!" followed by a woman shouting, "Hey, don't touch me!"

He ran out of the dressing room and saw a small, nebbish man groping Betty Lou, who was trying to pick up dollar bills, pick up her sheer camisole, and get off the stage. The man was obviously drunk and held tightly onto Betty Lou's arm as she bent at the knees and pulled back but couldn't get away.

He dashed over and smashed a running haymaker into the man's face. Drool and a single tooth went flying. He then ripped two right upper cuts into his gut and the man held onto him to keep from falling to the floor. He shoved him down and stomped his shoe onto his head, feeling him squirm. Reaching down, he pulled up the sloppy drunk by his blue work shirt and dragged his small body across the room, letting his head and arms bump into tables and chairs along the way. Other men pushed them along, causing him to lose his balance and they hit the floor again. He kneed the asshole in the back but the drunk fought back, swinging his fists at him, so he pummeled the guy's head, feeling greasy hair cream and blood smearing onto his fists. The hair grease annoyed him and he pounded a little harder until the man whimpered with both hands covering his head and curling up his knees into the fetal position. He grabbed the jerk by the ear and yanked as hard as he could, the guy stood up and followed his lead to the door, where he tossed him out and watched him tumble down the steps to the landing, where he spilled out onto the dirt-and-gravel parking lot. The guy's clothes were dirty now and he rolled over, looking up at him. His face was a bloody mess.

Sparky yelled, "Get the fuck outta here before I have you arrested!"

He wiped the slimy hair grease and blood off the back of his hands onto his pants, and then looked back at the stage. Wanda was dancing as the band played a strumming grind and he smiled to know that they were professionals who carried on with their jobs in spite of a little difficulty. These were good people. He was proud of his club.

He walked to the bar where Andy, the bartender, had a rum and coke waiting for him. He asked no one in particular, "Any of you guys seen Daisy?"

"Yeah," Glen answered, a regular and also a cop, but a guy who was having some trouble at home with his wife. Glen glanced briefly at him before returning his stare to Wanda's writhing body as she danced. "She said to tell you she's waiting for you in your office."

He smiled and thought, If the big bosses could see his club tonight, they'd be proud of him.

12)

aka Alek Hidell

Lee flopped over the bunk with exhaustion. His feet hung over the metal frame and every muscle ached from running the obstacle course with a forty-pound pack, followed by a five-mile jog with gear, the obstacle course again, followed by an exercise called "chase the rabbit," a series of push-ups then kicking his legs, alternating back and forth, and finally bobbing in the ocean with his rifle over his helmet. On his bunk he folded his hands on his chest. "I'm dead."

"Me, too," John said. He laughed a little but let it grow into a howl. "Ha-ha-oooooh! Shit. I *am* dead!"

The lights were out and it was a very dark moonless night, but he stared at the ceiling. His head ached and he wondered if he was dehydrated. Sweat was caked all over his skin. His ears rang. He didn't want to move, not even to get up and shower.

John said, "If you're dead, what are you going to do?"

"Shut-up, Hidell!" another Marine yelled.

Lee floated in a state of half-sleep and half-remembering the torture he had endured: hours of rolling in the sand, climbing over logs, up rope bridges, and standing in the chilling Californian ocean in water up to his neck, bobbing up with the waves, holding his M-16 over his head. A large wave lifted him up and splashed saltwater into his mouth. He spit.

"You awake, Alek?"

"Huh? No."

"I'm droppin'. I cain't take it no more."

Sergeant Brisken stumbled out of his room, growling like an angry bear awakened before its hibernation was over. He hollered, "We got four hours! And if you don't shut up, *I'm* gonna kill you!"

"You can't kill me," he said. "I'm dead."

John laughed, as did a few other Marines. The ringing in his ears continued. After a moment he whispered, "Did you ever watch 'I Led Three Lives'?"

"You mean that tee-vee show?"

He was quiet. He didn't want to tell all these Marines what he had in mind, even if they were in his unit. He was proud of how far he had come and he didn't want to tell *everyone* his plans. He knew this process of indoctrination was also the Marine Corps method of weeding out the weak. His mind was strong enough to make up for his weaker-than-average body. He knew he could endure their forced marches, obstacle courses, middle-of-the-night inspections, physical abuse, and more.

Most of the Marines were snoring and John's foot punched up from under his mattress. "What about it?"

He whispered very softly, "That's what I want."

"How you gonna manage that in the Corps?"

He knew the answer and mustered the strength to raise his tired eyebrows and felt the seawater lifting his body again. He was floating between sleep and consciousness in a delicate, beautifully dazed reality.

"If anyone can do it, I reckon you can," John whispered hoarsely. "You're the most determined, smart, quiet, s-o-b I know. And you never talk about your folks, so I guess you don't care much for your family so you got nothin' to lose. If anyone can do it, you can… Alek Kovich."

It was very still and the sound of the snoring seemed to go up and down with the waves of the ocean. He was bobbing and floating in his beautiful dream.

Hidell whispered, "You know, I never told this to anyone before. I guess I never felt it before. But I consider you my soul mate. I'd do anything for you. I know that may sound queer, but I'd give my life for you. If there's anything you ever need from me, anything, just say the word."

He felt honored, smiled, and exhaled loudly. I'll need an alias, Lee thought. Hmm. If I took half of your name I'd be Alek Heindel. No, Hidell. Yeah, Alek Hidell. That would be a fine pseudonym.

"You awake?" Hidell said. Men were snoring, including the Sergeant's recognizable deep wheezing inhalation followed by a loud, staccato blubbering exhalation. "Alek?..."

He would need to put in extra target practice to improve his scores on the shooting range. He would also need to apply himself to studying a foreign language like Russian, but that would be a labor of love. Yes, his dream was so close he could almost visualize it. Alek Hidell: citizen, Marine, secret agent. It had a nice ring to it and he smiled again. He repeated it again. Alek Hidell: citizen, Marine, secret agent. He repeated it again and was soon asleep.

13)

What's he do if he don't like you?

It was a sunny, hot day but a fresh breeze blew off the ocean and everything seemed free and light, floating on an air of great potential. Sparky had prepped for a long time, in Dallas and now in Havana, and he was still nervous about this introduction. This could mean his career. Who you know can make a big difference. He knew that from the old days in Chicago. One little helping hand at the right time and suddenly you're *the* guy running things in Dallas, not Mr. Civello. No one could dispute Mr. Trafficante's word if he said so.

Sparky and Lewis Coviello, a friend he initially met in Dallas several years ago, entered the lobby of the Sans Souci Casino. Lewis had done well for himself and was now the manager of the Tropicana Casino in Havana. He dressed well for a big guy, wearing a dark blue pin-stripe suit, but his receding hairline made him look older than he was, which was his same age—48.

The Sans Souci Casino was a very fancy place with beautiful crystal chandeliers, gold leaf walls, and brocade drapes. The women wore diamonds and everyone was dressed to the nines. Even the dealers wore tuxedos.

"Remember Sparky," Lewis said, smoothing back a few hairs on the side of his head, "that if he holds out his hand, kiss his ring."

He barely heard what Lewis said because he was staring at a celebrity walking through the marble-floored lobby. The famous man was with a small entourage of assistants and bodyguards, and his gray suit was wet with sweat on the pits and around the collar, and beads of sweat formed on his upper lip.

"Hey, was that what's his name?" He couldn't think of the politician's name but the guy was all over the television from the McCarthy investigation and, oh yeah, he was the Vice President. "Nixon? Was that Nixon?"

"Maybe, yeah I think so." Lewis said. "He's been making speeches for us about getting the Commies out of Cuba."

"I think it was. Why's he sweating?"

Lewis shrugged. "Maybe he's hot."

They walked past a beefy Italian guy, who pulled back a red velvet rope for them, and they stepped into a special elevator where the operator, a thin black man in a maroon suit with a round hat with a black strap under his chin, shut a metal gate and started the car for the top floor of offices. But before they reached it, the operator stopped between floors, asked to search them, and patted them down. Lewis had told him not to carry any weapons and he didn't. The operator started the elevator again and when they reached the top floor he nodded with a smile, opened the metal gate, and kept the elevator stopped and open. The operator said "Okay" to a big, muscular guy in a black jacket with a black collared shirt underneath who stood by the elevator. Further down the hall was another guard in front of the last door at the end of the hallway. That guard also wore a black suit with a black shirt and a thin black tie.

As they walked down the corridor, Sparky realized that he was very nervous. He hadn't been this nervous in a long time, since the early days with Mr. C in Chicago, trying to impress the big shots. What would he say? Be casual, he thought. Hi, howya doin'? Yeah, call me Sparky. Or, Sure, Jack's okay but you can call me Sparky.

The guard in front of the door rapped it with the back of his fist, then opened it, and stepped out of the way, but he looked them over with an attitude as they entered. Sparky looked over to Lewis, but he didn't seem to notice as he flicked beads of sweat off his forehead, wiped his hands, and entered with a big grin.

"Hello, Mister Trafficante," Lewis said, but Mr. Trafficante did not look at them. He recognized Mr. Trafficante from his photograph being in the newspaper. He had very little hair on top of his head, large ears that stuck out at the side, and wore tinted glasses. He was sitting at a very large desk with no paper on it and a black telephone was off to the side. A sweet-smelling scent of expensive cologne hung in the air. Another man stood with his back to them, wearing a red silk shirt and black dress pants, and he had black hair slicked back. He glanced at them briefly, with menace in his dark eyes, and then gazed out a window at the endless blue-black ocean at night. A few sailboats' tiny lights rose and fell on the water far below.

It seemed that he and Lewis had entered in the middle of their conversation because the other guy, the slick, black-haired man at the window, said in a rough voice, "That's what I don't get. Why would he do that? Is he fucking stupid? No. He's doin' it to send a message."

"Either that or he's fucking stupid," Mr. Trafficante said. He wore a gold chain bracelet on each wrist. He tapped his fingertips together and—he saw it—there was a ring on his pinky. It was a gold band with a nice, big rock. Sparky thought, Whoa, that's impressive. I oughta get one of those.

"Mark my word," Trafficante continued, "this man. . . this man is in trouble and he will get what is coming to him. . . He is going to be hit."

Lewis said, "Mister Trafficante, this is a guy I know from Chicago—"

"Very pleased to meet your acquaintance," he said. "Please, call me Sparky."

"Sparky?" Mr. Trafficante looked at him oddly through his tinted glasses.

"Or Jack. You can call me Jack." Mr. Trafficante sat motionless behind the desk. He didn't offer his hand even though he had his hand out and was waiting. He thought, What is this?

"Look, we're in the middle of something here," Mr. Trafficante said, putting his hands out in a typical Italian gesture that meant, What are you interrupting me for?

"I'm sorry," he said, and then thought, What am I apologizing for? What a load of crap!

"Yeah, I figured," Lewis said. "But I wanted you to meet Jack. He's in Dallas for us."

"Yeah, actually," he said, trying to sound impressive, "I been there a few *years* now."

"Everything okay for you, Lewis?" Mr. Trafficante said, eyeing Lewis up and down closely as if some information could be gathered from how he was dressed. Lewis looked neat and professional, but he did not wear any jewelry. "How's the Trop?"

"Not that hot, but it's okay, you know? Could be better, you know?" Lewis said, waiting patiently, but there was no response. Mr. Trafficante seemed to be making an all-important judgment. Lewis spoke, he could tell, just to fill the quietness. "Alright, then."

"That's great." Mr. Trafficante made a motion as if they were a nuisance and should go away and he thought, Of all the nerve!

"Okay," Lewis said with a slight bow. "Good ta see ya again. Nofio, take care." The man in the red shirt waved with the back of his hand and shot him an evil look and he recognized him as one of Mr. Marcello's men, Nofio Pecora, but he stared at the sailboat lights bobbing on the ocean below.

That's it? Sparky thought, as they left the room. He intentionally nudged the bodyguard at the door to feel if he was carrying a piece in his jacket and he felt a pistol against his side.

When he and Lewis got to the elevator, the guard stood there stone-faced. The thin, black elevator operator was ready to close the gate as soon as they stepped on.

Lewis said, "Geez, that went really well. I think he liked you."

"That's good," he said as the elevator doors closed. It gave him some satisfaction that someone as important as Santo Trafficante liked him. First Al Capone and Sam Giancana, then Joe Civello and Carlos Marcello, and now Santo Trafficante. He felt he was making an impression on all the right guys.

When they reached the ground floor the elevator bounced roughly. The operator swiftly opened the gate and doors for them and he turned to Lewis, who looked like a classy businessman in his pinstripe suit. "What's he do if he don't like you?"

Lewis laughed and punched his shoulder as they crossed the marble floor. "You don't wanna know." Lewis chuckled again, "You don't even fuckin' wanta know."

14)

Do you know what ONI does?

"Close the door behind you," Lieutenant Charles Donovan said dryly. He had a golden Californian tan that belied his firm chin and he spoke through clenched teeth. His intense hazel eyes followed him as pushed the door close, reminding Lee of the killer tigers he had seen in the zoo as a boy, staring at him like prey as they paced. He sat down on the metal chair with a green padded seat opposite the Lieutenant's desk, which was clean of any paper or knick-knacks.

Lee had worked hard to specialize in Aircraft Maintenance and Repair, he had learned about radar and air traffic control, and had been officially assigned to that unit. He had taken aptitude and intelligence tests and was "above-average." He graduated seventh in his class of thirty and finished as an Aviation Electronic Operator. Still, in spite of all this, he had been waiting to hear about his request for special assignment and was now slightly nervous in Lieutenant Donovan's office.

"The Navy appreciates your interest in volunteering for special duty," Donovan said with a tone as crisp as his starched white uniform. He took out a file, scanned the paperwork briefly, and continued dryly, "We have found your commitment to our requirements exemplary and you seem particularly capable in world affairs. I understand that your study of Russian passed basic conversation and you were able to do this in less than two months."

He recalled meeting with Major Weber's aunt in Santa Ana and talking with her in Russian for about two hours. It had seemed a little weird at the time when Major Weber pulled him out of aircraft engine repair class, handed him an address, and said, "You'll please say hello to my aunt, as long as you're in town?" Now he knew its true purpose was a covert test of his Russian proficiency and perhaps to test his ease in an unusual situation.

The Lieutenant continued smoothly, "Your experience is well-suited for special consideration and the Admiral was particularly pleased with your background in the Civil Air Patrol, your keen interest in Russian politics and philosophy, and your quiet demeanor and professionalism. In short, you're very bright, aggressive, and can button it up, if needed."

He wondered if the Admiral had really said all that or if Lieutenant Donovan was buttering him up for a crappy assignment. So far, it sounded pretty good but he prepared himself for the worst. He bit his tongue instead of smiling.

"It is with distinct honor that we would like to place you in the Office of Naval Intelligence with eventual assignment at an air base related to activities in the sphere of the Soviet Union."

His life-long dream had come true: he was being assigned to ONI! He couldn't wait to tell his best buddies, Heindel, Carter, and Thornley, and also Eddie, Robbie, and even his mother! He smiled slightly and Lieutenant Donovan looked up from the folder. "What do you say soldier?"

"I am honored to serve my country and if the Office of Naval Intelligence feels this is the best use of my skills, which I concur, I would happily accept such an assignment."

"Do you know what ONI does?"

"I have some idea, yes sir."

"No, you don't." The Lieutenant stared into his eyes with an intimidating flat gaze that he had seen his uncle and some of his "associates" use. He was certain Lieutenant Donovan had killed. "If you knew what we did, we wouldn't be doing our job very well, would we private?"

"No, sir," he said.

"The fact is that everything ONI does is top secret and you have no fucking clue what we do, isn't that right?"

"Yes, sir."

"You're god-damned right. Now. Now that you have no idea what it is that we're asking you to do, are you still willing to accept assignment?"

"Yes, sir. I've heard that it's an honor to be in ONI and I would be privileged to do so."

Lieutenant Donovan's eyes took him in, studying him grimly. "Very good. You are to begin immediate duty as outlined here," he handed him a sheet of paper across the wide desk that he had to rise from his chair to accept, "and you'll report for assignment in three months."

"Thank you, sir."

"You will never speak one word of your relationship with ONI with anyone. Not Sergeant Brisken or any of your buddies in your unit. Not your mother, your girlfriend, or your Aunt Sally. No one. Ever. Is that clear?"

Damn, he thought. Of course. "Yes sir, never a word to anyone."

Outside a platoon of Marines jogged by, singing in cadence as they ran,

"It was way back in Seventeen Seventy Five/That's when the Marine Corps came alive."

"You will follow orders explicitly and never discuss any aspect of any assignment, including any person involved, any location, any event, time of day, and so on, unless you are reporting back to your commanding officer. That is the only person who will discuss *any* aspect of ONI with you. Is that clear?"

"Yes, sir." He was theirs wholly, implicitly, always. Not part of the time, not a negotiable part of the time. Always. Semper Fidelis.

It was his dream becoming reality and at the same time it meant his life as he knew it was ending. He recognized that but truly, what was he giving up? Midnight chats with Eddie Voebel or a Marine buddy like Carter, heart-to-heart discussions with Robbie, disjointed as they were with his brother so distant and removed from who he really was, closed door "talks" with Uncle Charlie on how the world worked, and childish confessions to his mother. Okay, not much.

"If anything goes wrong, we will *not* recognize you. We will deny you have any affiliation with us. If you make a mistake, you're on your own. Do you have any questions?"

He had lots of questions—where would he be stationed, how would he learn all the detailed aspects of spying, what would be his cover, who would be his CO, would he have special tools and gadgets that enabled him to get out of tight jams, would he be trained on resisting interrogation techniques if captured and tortured, would he have an expense account or a sports car like James Bond? In short, what would he do? But he simply tightened his lips and nodded. "No, sir. It's a great honor."

"Congratulations and good luck."

"Thank you, sir." He stood and saluted, wheeling and smiling in one motion, and headed for the door and celebration. The hallway smelled of polished wax and he began reading the typed sheet of paper. It was a long numbered list. Number one was to learn self-defense and weapons handling, including all types of firearms. Number two stated that he was to become fluent in the Russian language. He inferred that to mean that ONI must, somehow, want him to talk with Soviets. Maybe he would interrogate MiG pilots? He scanned down the list. Another item was to memorize the codes and cryptonyms of operations and their own special language. Nothing was overwhelmingly difficult. Nothing was out of the ordinary. It was a task list that he would throw himself into wholeheartedly, without reservation, and with pride.

He took an intensive-study course in Russian at the Monterrey School, which was an institute of the Defense Department specializing in language. He was one of only a handful of recruits who could speak Russian. To practice his Russian and to keep tabs on Soviet propaganda, he subscribed to a newsletter, two magazines—*The Worker* and *The Militant* despite their conflicting philosophical differences—and a newspaper, the *Moscow News*. He also kept his multiple band transmitter tuned to Radio Moscow, a station that broadcast news in Russian all day and all night. He turned up the volume when he had to do yard maintenance duty around the barracks in spite of complaints from his fellow Marines. They ridiculed him for being a stinking Communist, but he played along with their comments until they saw that he was not going to give in to their ribbing or humiliation. Some suspected he was ONI, but he denied everything or played along with them. When he noticed officers meeting, he called them a Soviet "party leaders conference" and once, when the Master Sergeant stood on top of a flatbed truck to give instructions, he said, "Ah! Another collectivist farm lecture!"

But when Sergeant Brisken officially filed a complaint report about his strange interest in Communist literature and his continual playing of Communist propaganda, in Russian over the loudspeaker, the top brass told Sergeant Brisken to mind his own business. It was then that his fellow Marines looked at him differently. They changed, literally overnight, from showing an amused but sometimes disgusted confusion to a look of respect. Most of them still kept their distance from him but he could see that they admired him. He did not mind that they kept their distance, because most of them had no interest in Russian literature, or politics, or philosophy, certainly not to the degree he did, so he never felt close to any of them. He still joked around with Heindel and Thornley, and occasionally played chess with Carter, but for the most part he felt separated from his unit.

It was an average Monday night and he was playing chess with Joe Carter, who had typically Irish features of fair skin, full lips, light blue-gray eyes and freckles, and jet-black hair. He was engrossed in the game when he felt distracted from the combination he was trying to set up. Carter was staring at him and not the pieces on the chessboard. "What is it?"

Carter asked, "Did you ever wonder if our unit was different? Special?"

"No, what do you mean?"

"It kind of hit me last week," he said under his breath. Carter looked around, but their hut was empty as most of the men were watching the film "The Bridge on the River Kwai" for the second time. He rubbed his nose and continued, "Well, I don't know a lot about the Marines, but from what I can tell, our unit's pretty unusual."

He looked at him seriously. He had to dissuade him from talking about ONI if he broached the subject. "Yeah?"

"Think about it. Gomez is fluent in Spanish and is also being trained in bomb detection and assembly. Torrey's a genius when it comes to anything related to math, numbers, and he's learning encryption techniques. Jackson's a whiz at damn near everything and I saw him going into the ONI building."

"Yeah?" He wondered if he had also been seen going in the ONI building to study their manuals of codes and other documentation, which did not leave the premises, but he deftly avoided the topic and countered with a completely different question, as trained. "But what about you?"

"What do you mean?"

He said evenly, "You lose to me in chess all the time and you're as dumb as a box of rocks."

Carter laughed, slowly at first, and then harder and harder. It gradually took him completely and he fell into a fit of uncontrollable laughter. After a moment he caught his breath and wiped the tears from his eyes.

"Ew, oh. That was a good one," he cleared his throat, then laughed a little more and caught himself. "Yes, I guess that must be it."

He moved his bishop to threaten Carter's rook and king. He kept his finger on the bishop while he surveyed the board and the move. "I'm going to say this once and I can't let you ask any questions about it, but. . . I'm simply following orders. I'm trying to indoctrinate myself in Russian theory in conformance with Marine Corps policy. Check."

He took his finger off the bishop. Carter looked down at the pieces, grazing both palms over his short, stiff Marine haircut, and then grabbed the back of his neck and exhaled loudly. He studied the board for another moment and then gently knocked over his king.

"It's true." Carter rubbed his nose again and gestured with his hands. "This has got to be the smartest unit in the entire corps. And even if only half of what I'm thinking is true, it makes this an elite unit."

"Right," he smirked. "We're going to think the Communists into submission."

"No, be serious for a minute."

He started setting up the pieces for another game and rotated the board so he would be black this time. "I don't think it's any of our business."

"And then last week Sergeant Brisken was basically told to leave you alone. Now, holy smackers, milk and crackers, that just doesn't happen in any regular unit. So, if *half* of this is true…"

"Yeah…"

"What do you suppose they have planned for me?" Carter stared with deep concern.

"Well, I wasn't suppose to say anything, but—" he looked over both shoulders. It was quiet.

"Yeah?"

"They're bringing in a special K-9 unit of bloodhounds."

"Bloodhounds?" Carter's eyebrows raised with surprise.

"Sh-h-h!" He looked at the door again and whispered. "That's right. A new special unit."

"Yeah? For bomb detection? Or sniffing out Russian spies?"

"Sort of. They need someone to clean-up after them!"

Carter laughed again and was doubled over, holding his ribs with glee.

"I volunteered you. You're the super-duper pooper-scooper!"

Carter rolled onto the floor, doubling up with heavy laughter. Another buddy, Kerry Thornley, came in holding a small dish of vanilla ice cream and a wooden spoon. Thornley was a smart, very fit Marine designated for the Communications unit, who had aspirations of writing a great novel. He walked by and gave Carter an odd look, who was still giggling and getting up off the floor. Thornley swung himself up onto his top bed a few bunks away, took out a paperback book, and began reading and eating his ice cream.

Carter composed himself and sat back in the metal folding chair. He tapped his knee and said, "Watch this," and then called to Thornley and asked, "Hey, Kerry. Whatcha readin'?"

"Nineteen eighty-four by George Orwell."

Carter's eyes blinked repeatedly. "See. What kind of Marine reads a book like that? From talking to the guys in the other units, what I heard is most Marines read Playboy. Hell, they don't even *read* that!"

He stood up, stretched, and patted Carter on the shoulder. "You've got a bright mind, Joe. It may be a little adventurous at times, but you've noticed things that most people may not. But you see, Gomez is from Texas, near the border, and probably learned Spanish when he was in diapers. Yeah, Torrey's a math whiz so what better place to put him than encryption? And I suggested that book to Thornley. I'm sure the Corps will find an appropriate spot for you."

He walked back to his bunk and sat down. Carter was still watching him, so he took out *Time* magazine, snapped it open to great effect, and winked at Thornley, who was also looking at him, and then began reading. He added, "If you want to play chess anytime, I'm game."

Carter had a point but he decided to stay away from him for a while, hoping this would blow over. Other than Carter, there were only a few of other buddies who he liked to be with, but he found himself more and more mentally separated from his unit. In many ways he felt as if he had already been transferred to a higher mission and he accepted it with pleasure and pride. His dream had become a reality. He led three lives: he had an ordinary life with his mother, brother, and uncle at home; he was in the Marine Corps; and he was a spy.

15)

This is what I've been aiming to do all my life

Dear Robert,

Things are really going my way. I'm going to be shipping out soon and I can only say that this is what I've been aiming to do all my life. It's a great thrill for me and I have found my pot of gold at the end of the rainbow. Let me know what is going on there—how are you, ect.

Lee

16)

Nothin' like a funeral

As they drove down the two-lane blacktop road in Cuba, Sparky figured it was a good thing to do, no matter what. The guy was in trouble and he needed a friend. Who wouldn't help out someone in that position? That was one thing his mother taught him, his real mother before she was put away, not one of the two foster mothers, both weak-minded and helpless. He recalled his mother, sitting at the dinner table like a queen before her court, and she said, "Be a stand-up man and help your friends in need. And go to your friend's and important people's funerals. That's when they need a friend the most. Anyone can go to a wedding. It shows you're a good friend if you go to the funeral. The family knows. They recognize your respect. There's almost nothing more important in life than going to funerals."

He turned to Lewis, driving his shiny blue Edsel down the asphalt road, and said, "This is as important as going to his funeral."

"This ain't nothin' like a funeral!" Lewis was instantly furious and the blood veins stood out on his temples up to his dark, receding hairline. "And don't you dare say nothin' like that to him. He'll cut your fuckin' tongue out."

"I didn't say it was *his* funeral. I said it was important. You know, like a funeral."

"It ain't his funeral! Jesus fuckin' Christ!" Lewis breathed heavily and gave him a vicious stare. He was a very big man and a professional gambler but this was no poker-faced bluff.

"I know that."

"Well, shut-up with that," Lewis said, and adjusted the short sleeves of his white, collared shirt around his muscular biceps. Perspiration wet his armpits.

"I'm sayin' it's important. *Like* a funeral."

Lewis had become a little bit heavy, but he was tall and imposing, and he swerved to the side of the road and slammed on the brakes. The tires squealed to a screaming stop. "You say that word one more fuckin' time, *I'm* gonna rip out your fuckin' tongue!"

It was quiet. A crane flew up from the marshy roadside. Lewis slowly pulled the car back onto the road and then stomped on the accelerator. Neither of them spoke.

He recalled his job for Mr. Trafficante, shipping guns from Mr. Marcello to Mr. Trafficante in Cuba, and obviously that didn't work out as planned when Fidel Castro took control of the country. There was no way he was going to say anything about *that* during their visit.

He remained quiet as Lewis pulled the Edsel into the dirt-and-gravel parking lot of Trescornia, a prison detention center that resembled a camp with a high fence running around the grounds. He got out and smoked a cigarette quickly, knowing that Lewis didn't like him smoking in his car. The prison had a guard tower near the main gate and a cement office building was off to the side that probably monitored all the visitors. He noticed that there weren't a lot of prison officials or cops around, but a guard with a rifle stood in a tower by the main gate and watched the parking lot. Barbed wire topped an inner wall that was about twenty feet high.

Lewis opened the car's back door and slipped on the gray jacket to his business suit, then reached down to the back seat and took out a large dish of lasagna and two loaves of Italian bread.

"Come on, take this," Lewis said, tucking the bread under his arm and handing him the glass tray of lasagna. It was still warm. He stepped on the cigarette stub, mashing it into the dirt parking lot.

At the guardhouse, a police officer sat behind a teller's window. He set down the tray of lasagna on the window ledge and Lewis put the bread on top of it as they signed in. He forgot to use an alias signing in, and watched as Lewis wrote the name "Harry Truman." He chuckled and thought Lewis was a pretty funny guy.

The guard at the window asked in a Cuban accent, "Do chew have some ideentifeecashun, Meester Truman?"

"Nah," Lewis said, "I don't got no fuckin' ID." He grabbed his crotch through his black dress pants and shook it. "But you can blow me if you don't think I look presidential."

He laughed.

"Did chew drive heer?" the guard continued.

"That's none of your fuckin' business. Are you gonna let me in, or do I tell Mr. Trafficante that you're bustin' my balls?"

The guard immediately turned to him. "How 'bout chew, Meester?"

He sharply flipped open and closed his wallet with attitude as he had seen the Dallas detectives do. He was impressive. One clean motion for them to understand: don't give me any shit. I'm the boss here.

The policeman squinted at him and then motioned them to go through. Another guard opened the gate for them. Still another guard was standing ready with a fork, and stopped them to poke through the lasagna and the bread in search of contraband.

"You bring files in a pie," Lewis said to the guard and laughed at his own joke with his big body shaking. He elbowed him in the side.

"Que?" the guard said, and after a moment of simply staring at each other, he waved them inside. Another guard swung open a wooden door and led them down a long corridor, where they had to sign in again and have the food inspected again. This guard seemed to take even longer and, when Lewis exhaled and looked at the ceiling, the guard said in perfect English, "Something wrong, Mister Truman?"

After a few more minutes of waiting they were frisked and then allowed to enter the main courtyard, a holding area where about twenty prisoners milled about or sat around the outside walls on dark wooden chairs. It looked like a dining hall in an old lodge with two long tables and Mr. Trafficante was seated at the far end, with his back to the wall, so everyone was in front of him. He wore his tinted glasses and his large ears stuck out. Even in the open air of this prison, Mr. Trafficante's expensive cologne was in the air.

Next to Trafficante sat Nofio Pecora, the guy he had seen in Trafficante's casino in Havana. He knew Pecora was Mr. Marcello's right-hand man, but here he was, sitting on the high back of a chair and watching the entire area. Maybe he happened to be with Trafficante when he got pinched. He was thin with dark hair, dark eyes that surveyed the yard, and he smoked the end of a cigarette in the European fashion with the hand-rolled stub neatly tucked between the tips of his first two fingers and thumb.

He set down the lasagna on the long table in front of Mr. Trafficante and, with some hesitation, offered to shake his hand. He thought, Would Mr. Trafficante insult him again by not shaking hands?

Mr. Trafficante did not stand up but remained seated, shook his hand vigorously, and Sparky lifted it and kissed his ring. "Thank you, sir."

"Thank you. This looks delicious."

Sparky turned to Lewis and smiled. It was going better this time.

Lewis said, "It's from Trocadero's. I know it ain't easy to get good food in here."

"Dat right," Pecora said in his deep voice, smiled, and nodded to him. He wore a black turtleneck sweater with a black dinner jacket and black pants.

"If there's anything else I can do," he said, "just let me know."

"It's okay. Truly, this means a lot to me," Mr. Trafficante said and nodded his head slowly. "It really let's you know who your friends are. You get pinched, it takes some nerve to stand up and visit them. I appreciate it."

"Okay," Lewis said, and gave an acknowledging grin to him.

He smiled back. He was appreciated. Maybe now they'd take notice of him in Dallas and give him something more important to do.

"How's everything with you?" Mr. Trafficante said.

"It's good. I mean, you know, it's Dallas but it's good. The cops *love* me." They all laughed. "So it's going good. You know."

"Carlos helped you out, right?" Trafficante continued, adjusting his tinted glasses higher onto his nose.

"Yes, yes! Mister Marcello was a big help in getting the club off the ground. It's going great now. We're earning some money, you know, and the cops are okay."

"Good," Mr. Trafficante smiled and nodded to Pecora, who cut out some lasagna with a white spatula and, almost magically, a fine china plate, silverware, and a linen napkin appeared by way of another inmate, who performed as perfectly as a classically trained waiter. He then just as quickly disappeared in the crowd that kept their distance on the periphery. Pecora placed the lasagna on the plate and used his small, muscular hands to tear off the head from the loaf of bread and set it next to the lasagna for Mr. Trafficante.

He thought again about his involvement in shipping guns to Mr. Trafficante, how he had already helped him previously, but he again decided not to mention it. That didn't work out and it wouldn't be good to rub it in his face. After all, that was part of why Mr. Trafficante was sitting in this jail. Obviously Presidenté Castro appreciated the gun shipments, but it was small peanuts against the huge amount of money that Mr. Trafficante had taken in running some of the biggest casinos in all of Cuba. Castro was on a self-serving, image-promoting, mission to rid the island of corruption and now that he had taken power, he couldn't turn a blind eye to the casinos and the mobsters who ran them. No, he definitely wasn't going to mention the gun running or Castro.

Mr. Trafficante looked around the prison grounds and spread out his arms. "You know, this just shows that we didn't take Mr. Castro seriously enough. It was really our mistake."

"Dat right," Pecora said. "Our mistake. But now we need to handle it."

"Yes," Trafficante continued, as a bottle of Chianti appeared in another, surprisingly well-dressed, prisoner's hands and he poured it into a glass in front of him. "Now, what you should do," he stared at Pecora, "is get word to Jimmy Hoffa. He's got some connections with the CIA. Have him talk to those people. I hear they've been trying to hit Castro but—"

"Very clumsy," Pecora said.

"That's right. Stupid. Amateurish."

"Dey don't have de right technique," Pecora explained, tugging at his black turtleneck. "Dey try to be too smart like it a big secret! One time dey try fungus seashells to poison him dat dey hope he pick up de poison seashells at de seashore. Shit! And, and, another time exploding cigars!"

Pecora laughed heartily and raised his hands high before bringing them down quickly. "I mean come on, *really!*"

They all laughed because Mr. Trafficante laughed. But he thought it was a very funny idea. Castro would light up his cigar and BOOM! he would be left standing there like a cartoon character with a shredded cigar, blackened smoke on his face, his hair standing out, and his eyeballs swirling. He laughed loudly.

"No," Mr. Trafficante continued seriously and they were all immediately attentive again. "They need our help. And now, we're in a position where it would benefit us as well."

"Our benefit," he chimed in, but Lewis shot him an intimidating stare. Everyone looked at him with disgust as if to say, Who in the fuck are you to talk?

"Yes," Mr. Trafficante raised his glass to everyone, then took a single swallow. "You get word to Jimmy that he is to call on those Washington people and let *us* handle this thing."

Pecora nodded. "It's done. Hoffa will handle it."

"Good," Mr. Trafficante smiled broadly at Pecora, and then smiled around the group to everyone watching, and began eating. "Mmm, good!"

He smiled back. It was nice to be appreciated. He was very happy he made the trip to Havana and he had helped himself, too. They *had* noticed him. He had a very strong feeling that sometime, and maybe it would be soon, sometime he would be given something more important to do. He just knew it.

17)

Atsugi Air Base

Lee was stationed at a top-secret air base that did not exist. Marine Air Control Squadron No. 1 (MACS-1) at Atsugi Air Base, a few miles southwest of Tokyo, was so secretive that very few people in the United States knew of its existence. No one in the media, the Congress, and certainly not the American public, had any idea that such a base existed. The Pentagon officially denied its existence.

As the bus drove across the base, he saw a group of about two dozen buildings with a signboard that read,

Joint Technical Advisory Group

As Lee unloaded off the bus with the other newbies, Captain Gajewski was waiting for them in their hut. They stood at attention, holding their unpacked olive drab duffel bags. The captain was of average build but was in good shape and had a tough-looking gaze with a long nose. He eyed them coldly for a long time, and then spoke slowly with authority. "If you want to get in trouble, walk over to the hangar where they keep the black airplane. You don't talk about the black airplane. That black airplane isn't there. Do I make myself clear?"

They all barked, "Yes, sir!" and the captain went on for fifteen more minutes about what they didn't see, what they didn't hear, and what they didn't know.

While most radar operators had a high-level clearance, he was given a specific exemption with an even higher clearance rating of "Secret." This was because most of the flights out of Atsugi Air Base were routine sorties by Navy jets on practice missions, but they also tracked the top-secret flights of the mysterious black jets. Those flights were rumored to be reconnaissance missions flying directly over the Soviet Union at altitudes that were undetectable by radar and beyond the range of any guided missiles. The jets did not have names and the pilots were sequestered in a separate barrack. Most of the base personnel did not know anything about the missions they flew, who exactly the pilots were, or why the jets were so secretive.

Lee had worked at Atsugi for ten weeks when he was promoted to shift supervisor. He felt very good about that and, additionally, he was given an even higher security clearance in order to access the file storage room where he would enter his shift reports. He now coordinated all the radar operators on his shift, still under the supervision of the captain, but he was proud of his achievement. Part of their job was to direct aircraft to their targets by radar but they also scouted for stray Chinese or Russian planes and, as shift supervisor, he had more access to what was happening on all the radar screens. Still, it was generally very boring, but occasionally they had a moment of excitement, which usually turned out to be an errant weather balloon and not an incoming Russian MiG.

It was an ordinary Tuesday when a pilot asked for the weather, which was not interesting by itself, but then the pilot called in for clearance for an emergency landing because he was running low on fuel. As the shift supervisor, he could authorize ground control approach to clear the jet for landing, but when he requested the specifics of the incoming flight—its current altitude and location—the pilot responded with "Charlie Vector Niner Nought Nought Nought Nought."

Ninety thousand feet? He was confused. Civilian airlines flew at about 35,000 feet and the Navy's best jets, even on secret missions, flew at 65,000 feet, which was right at the limit of where guided missiles could, with considerable skill, hit a target. What in the world was a Black Bird doing at 90,000 feet? Also, no one had weather information for 90,000 feet, so obviously this pilot was showing off. Or he was signaling that he was the pilot of a Black Bird.

He looked over at Captain Gajewski, who was the supervisor on duty, and then around the room at three banks of operators who stared at their radar screens but were obviously listening. He waved to get the captain's attention and Gajewski stared down at him from the raised platform. Gajewski twitched his long nose but did not move, so he nodded for the captain to come over, and placed his hand over the radio microphone. He whispered, "This pilot is calling for an emergency landing."

"For what reason?" the captain spoke in a calm, normal voice, which was one aspect of his fine, professional manner. The whole world could be on fire and Gajewski would serenely ask, what facts do you have?

"He's low on fuel," he continued to whisper.

"Affirmative." Captain Gajewski held a clipboard, checked his watch, and wrote down the time with a pencil. "Clear a lane and prepare emergency vehicles."

"Roger that," he whispered. "But he's asking for weather at ninety thousand feet."

Captain Gajewski's eyes widened. He spoke firmly under his breath, "No he is not! Repeat. There is no aircraft in that position."

"Yes, sir! I'll clear a lane."

He maneuvered other jets out of its flight path, guided the Black Bird onto the base, and after it softly touched down, surrounded by fire emergency vehicles, he continued on his shift without saying anything to anyone. He didn't say anything at dinner, or the next day, to anyone in the radar room or back in the barracks.

On Saturday Lee relaxed with some of his buddies on the tarmac and they playfully tossed a football back and forth, sometimes with force, while still sitting down. He asked Richard MacInnes, another radar operator, "Mac, how high do you think the Black Bird can fly?"

"Sixty-five. Same as any other. Why?" Mac took a swig of a beer and looked at Rick Daly, who took off his tee shirt to work on keeping his tan. It was early September but it was very warm and sunny.

"I cleared a pilot on Monday who was asking for weather at ninety."

"Bull crap," Mac said.

Then Rick got up with the football and Bob Halberstam, another radar operator, walked out a few steps across the tarmac while still holding his beer, and tossed the ball further.

"I know what you're thinking," Lee said, clearing his throat, "and you're right. No, he wasn't on our radar. But he appeared about a minute later at sixty-five. Cruised in on fumes."

Mac picked at the corner of the label of his Japanese beer. "Yeah? Maybe he read his altimeter wrong."

"Yeah. Maybe my ass."

Rick flung the football side-armed to Bob, who spilled some of his beer to catch it. He set the beer on the cement as Rick took off running and Bob threw a long, arcing, perfect spiral pass to him. Rick caught it and kept running, finally holding his arms up as if he had scored a touchdown.

"Did you tell Gaj?"

"He was there."

"What'd he say?"

He mimicked the captain with a flat voice, "There is no plane at that position. Repeat. There is no plane at that position."

"Well, there you have it." Mac rolled up the wet, peeled label and tossed it at his face but he swatted it down in mid-air. "It was a bogey."

"Yeah," he chuckled. "Until that long Black Bird landed about five minutes later."

Mac was quiet. He stared at his dark label-less bottle, and then looked around to see if anyone else could hear them.

Lee looked around, too. Across the tarmac, a ground grew worked on a fighter jet's wing struts in an open hangar. No one was near. He knew they could get in serious trouble for talking about it, but his curiosity was too much and he had been thinking about the event all week. He also knew that everyone else on the base was thinking about the mysterious, long black jets even if they were silent. "What do you suppose he was doing at ninety?"

"Probably not breathing. Can't fly at ninety and breathe, too."

"That's silly. They've got oxygen tanks. According to that theory, no one could go underwater either." He felt the warm sun on his face and he leaned back against a sandbag. He picked a blade of grass that had wedged its way between a crack on the tarmac, nibbled the stem, and put his hands behind his head. "Let's suppose they can fly at ninety. What could they do?"

"Get us in a hell of a lot of trouble for talking about it, that's what they could do!" Mac instantly changed the subject, "Hey, tell me about that hostess at the Queen Bee. She was too beautiful for someone like you. How'd you meet her? She's top-flight."

"Friend of a friend." They were both very quiet as a Navy fighter plane landed on runway 27 and taxied around toward the hangars. Rick and Bob threw the football back and forth, a fair distance apart, and were well out of earshot. Obviously he and Mac were both still thinking about it, but he figured he has said enough and avoided the subject. "How 'bout them Auburn Tigers? National title again?"

Mac didn't respond.

The warmth of the late afternoon sun felt wonderful. He closed his eyes and daydreamed about the beautiful hostess at a swank officer's club in the city. He had only met her once, through an introduction by another ONI officer, and he didn't know her name. But he found himself thinking of her often. She was remarkably beautiful with a refined style that was very graceful. But maybe Mac was right. She was too incredible for someone like himself. Still, it was nice to think about her.

"They've got cameras," Mac said.

"I know." He thought about spying cameras and recalled seeing a picture of a miniature camera and an article in the *New York Times* that described how the spies Julius and Ethel Rosenberg took extremely small photographs of objects, and then placed the film into a microdot that fit inside a hollow nickel. The article stated that a paperboy had dropped the nickel, it popped open, and the microdot came out. The boy reported it to the local authorities and that was how the government first heard about the Rosenbergs. That started the great paranoia over Communists and spying because if someone as plain-looking as the

Rosenbergs were living in Brooklyn and spying for the Communists on our nuclear weapons technology, then couldn't the Communists be anywhere? For Lee, it was one more reason why he wanted to join the service and defend his country. He thought if the Rosenbergs had a very special camera then the Black Bird probably has a special camera, too.

Mac finished his beer and offered one from the six-pack carton to him. He kept his eyes closed and shook his head negatively, he didn't drink. He heard Mac open another bottle and then heard him peeling the label after the first swig. Mac continued, "Those cameras have powerful lenses that can take photographs from extremely high altitudes. So, if I had to guess, but you didn't hear me say this, a jet flying at ninety would take spy photos. They could confirm Soviet air bases, missile defenses, hell they could probably see where Premier Khrushchev took a crap in the woods."

Lee chuckled and opened his eyes. Yes, a powerful camera was certainly possible. The thought of it gave him a rush of excitement. He was helping top-secret jets to fly spying missions over the Soviet Union! The more he thought about it, the better he felt. The warmth of the sun gave him an overall wonderful feeling and he sighed and closed his eyes again.

Lee thought again about the hostess at The Queen Bee, of how beautiful she was, and he wanted to be with her. He desperately wanted to lose this "innocence" that clung to him. Then he thought of a way that he could be with her: it would be an enormous risk, and a stiff price to pay, but he knew how it could be done. Yeah, maybe it was time for someone besides pilots to get some of the perks.

18)

The inmates are running the asylum

Dear Robert,

The base is a lot different than I imagined. I can't talk about it in detail but some might say the inmates are running the asylum. Beer cans all over the barracks. Nobody talks to the pilots—accept over the airwaves, of course (ha-ha-ha). But all in all I'm having the time of my life. Got a weekend pass and I'm going to see the sights in Tokyo. I will whoop it up with thoughts of you, brother.

Take care,

Lee

19)

Do you think I sound like a homo?

It was early evening and Sparky's roommate, Dick Senator, sat on the sofa eating a bowl of sugary cereal and watched "The Milton Berle Show" on his black-and-white television. Dick was a big bear of a guy with brown hair but soft and pudgy, with large pink hands that he often rubbed in lotion. He was angry that Dick was not using a t-v tray—what'd he buy them for if he wasn't going to use them?, and try to keep the place neat—but his anger was distracted because Milton Berle was doing a funny shtick: wearing a dress and smoking a cigar.

He had to hurry to get ready to go to the club, but the whole thing annoyed him. He asked, "Do you think I sound like a homo?"

"What?" Dick said, scooping another bite of cereal into his pink mouth and spilling milk on his chin, dribbling down to his lap and onto the brown, white, and orange floral-patterned sofa. He had bought the country-style sofa on sale last month and here Dick was ruining it already.

"Come on, use a tray!" he raised his voice and breathed heavily. "Why do I gotta tell you everything two, three times!"

"Sorry," Dick stood with the bowl, sloshing some of its contents out onto the green-carpeted floor, and grabbed a rickety tin tray, setting it up with one large hand. He sat back down on the sofa, keeping an eye on the television and laughing at Berle's double-take to the audience. Dick's brown wavy hair, greasy with hair cream, was messy and he shoveled the food into his mouth and stared at the television screen filled with static snow.

He was heavily into debt to Joe Civello with the loans to start his nightclub, and more loans to keep it running, and he was obligated to pay tribute money to Sam Giancana and Carlos Marcello. He worked hard, tried to promote his club as much as possible, and here Dick was barely working, barely paying his share of the rent, but eating his food and getting his new furniture dirty!

"Hey, look at me when I'm talkin' to you!" Sparky said.

"What? You ain't said nothin'."

"I asked you a question," he said with tensed eyebrows. "Do you think I sound like a homo?"

"What? No. Whatdya mean?"

He snapped, "Then why are you always tryin' to bugger me?"

Mabel came out of his bedroom, wearing one of his white dress shirts and black panties. The shirt was unbuttoned but she held it together and gave a drowsy glance at them as she made her way for the kitchen. She had been asleep since late afternoon and he must have awakened her when he got up to get dressed for work.

"Hey, come on! Put somethin' on!"

Mabel gave him a look that said, what's with you?, and then tied the ends of his shirt together in a knot. She had a great body, with incredible tits, and he stared at her. He looked down at Dick, who was also staring after her with his dark brown eyes, and smacked him with an open hand across the top of his head. "Stop it!"

"Hey, what the fuck!"

That angered him even more, Dick was mouthing back to him, so he boxed a short right cross into his ear that knocked him off the sofa, crashing the tray onto the floor and spilling cereal and milk everywhere.

Dick stared up at him, confused and dazed, and finally said, "What the hell has got into you?"

"Shut the fuck up! Why do I always gotta tell you somethin' three times before you do it?"

"I got the tray already! Now look at it!" Dick stood, his greasy hair in a tussled mess, and picked up the crumpled and bent tin legs of the tray. He pointed at the mangled tray legs. "Is this my fault, too, you simple fuck?"

"What the fuck did you say, you lazy, worthless piece of shit!" He breathed heavily and flexed his fists.

"Nothin'."

He lunged forward, grabbed Dick by his thick throat with his left hand, and rammed him against the wall, and drew back his right fist.

"Hey!" Mabel called out. "You're acting like a jerk."

"I'm a jerk? He's the one eyeballin' you!"

She raised her eyebrows and smiled, strutting into the kitchen. "Well, that shows he's a red-blooded American man, honey. He ain't done nothin' 'cept look!"

Mabel took down a bowl from the cabinet, poured some cereal from the box that Dick had left on the counter, and opened the refrigerator. She bent over, the white shirt rising seductively over her black panties, the black triangle of her love region exposed, a bulls-eye target, and she playfully hummed "The Yellow Rose of Texas," her signature song from the club, and twitched her ass.

He released Dick then shoved him back into the wall. He charged over to Mabel and grabbed her by the arm.

"Hey!" she said. "I'm getting something to eat."

"Later!"

He smacked her with his open hand and pulled her toward the bedroom. He couldn't decide if he should make her suck him or just put on more clothes, because he was so angry at her, prancing around and flirting with his roommate, who was a slob. "Come 'ere! He acts like a caveman. Don't encourage him!"

Mabel glanced over her shoulder at Dick and giggled in a sing-song voice. "Some-body's jeal-ous."

He closed the door behind them, ripping open the white shirt and exposing her amazing tits. They were nice and full, and the nipples were pink and round and had a slight rise to them. She dropped to her knees and quickly undid his belt, unhooked the pants, unzipped the fly, and pulled down his trousers and underwear in one swift motion. Her mouth was quickly working on him, slurping and moaning at once. He felt the hot sensation growing in his thick shaft. He grabbed her hair by the back of her skull and eased her head over him.

"That's it, make me do it," Mabel said excitedly. She stroked and caressed him with one hand, holding him stiff at the base in the other, and slid her sweet, wet, mouth up and down.

Sparky enjoyed the building sensation but couldn't hold it anymore and released himself, bucking into her tiny mouth, holding her head close, jamming it into her like the whore she was.

God that felt great, he thought. And a little more, you bitch, "Unh! Unh!"

"Yeah," Mabel smiled up at him. She wiped her mouth with the back of her hand. "Not mad at me anymore?"

He chuckled and pulled up his pants. He pinched her left cheek and caressed her face. "Put some clothes on if you're gonna go out there," he said, and then shoved her away.

20)

Call me Harvey

As a mission it seemed pretty easy. Lee as "Alek" would meet his contact, a Japanese aircraft mechanical engineer who also spoke English and Russian, have dinner and sake with him, and go to his place of business afterward. His source would let Alek into the company President's office and he would use a specially made, pocket-sized camera to photograph any documents of business orders, engineering blueprints, or jet specifications from the Soviets.

Alek recognized Hiroshi, that was the name he called himself, from the personality or p-file photograph. He shook his hand strongly outside of Kenjo's Restaurant. "I'm Alek."

"The maintenance man," Hiroshi smiled. Apparently that was Alek's code name from the Japanese contact. He was slightly uneasy with this, so on the spot he decided to change his code name from Alek to Harvey.

"Yes, but call me Harvey."

"Like the bunny!" Hiroshi said.

Alek recognized the reference to the theatrical play and smiled. "Yes."

Inside the restaurant, a very pretty woman with white make-up and a royal blue silk kimono seated them in a private room with bamboo-and-paper screen walls. Hiroshi politely declined the menu and immediately ordered dinner for them as Alek adjusted himself to sit on the pillows around the square, black-lacquered table. Another pretty woman came from behind a back screen and knelt next to him with a tray of hot tea. She ceremoniously poured it for both of them. After a gracious moment, she nodded and left, and Alek began calmly, "I work at Atsugi."

"I don't want to know," Hiroshi put up his hand to stop. His brown, Oriental eyes seemed pleasant but fearful, and then he looked around the empty room as if someone may be just beyond the thin walls. "There are many things that should be left unsaid."

"Of course." He smiled politely, "I was making conversation to ease our situation."

"Do you enjoy painting?"

"No, I'm a —" Alek was about to say radar operator but he could see intense hope in Hiroshi's eyes. "Oh, you mean like art?"

"Yes, artistic painting." Hiroshi's dark eyes darted back and forth under his wrinkled brow.

"No." Disappointment washed over Hiroshi's face so he smoothly added, "I mean I know some, but I don't claim to be an expert. I've always wanted to know more. Please do tell me about it."

Hiroshi smiled and nodded several times. "I enjoy it a great deal. I find it very relaxing. The gentle movements relax my hands and my mind after a long day. There is much to be said for a painting by Van Gogh, for example."

"Yes, I've seen pictures of 'Starry Night,' 'Café at Night.' Oh, and the 'Sunflowers'."

"Ah-h-h!" Hiroshi smiled broadly and sighed. He seemed very happy and at peace. "That is something magnificent. If I could master the patience and technique to relate such an expression of my soul, I think that I should die a happy man."

Alek nodded and raised his teacup in a toast, and then sipped the tea. The meal was an assortment of delicious sushi treats including freshwater eel, octopus, and several types of fish and sauces. He had prepared himself to discuss haiku, but throughout the meal Hiroshi talked at length about his favorite artists, many of whom had painted still-life flowers.

Hiroshi enthusiastically drank a cup of sake but Alek only let it touch his lips as he did not wish to lose any concentration of what documents he should photograph, or to compromise his physical capabilities in any way. After Hiroshi's fifth cup of sake, Alek became worried that he would not be able to function, but then he abruptly stopped drinking when they finished eating. A bill for the food and drinks never came and Hiroshi explained, "It was prearranged… like many things in life."

They stood and Alek watched him carefully to make sure he could walk without weaving and he seemed, remarkably, fine. Hiroshi led him a few blocks to a very large office building, where a night security guard smiled and nodded as he opened the glass doors with his keys. They took an elevator up to the penthouse that opened onto a beautifully decorated corridor of many leafy bamboo plants, a small bubbling waterfall surrounded by bonsai cedar trees, and a pool with several goldfish with enormous eyes. They were gold, and red-and-white, and black.

Hiroshi made a polite bow to draw Alek's attention to the main room, a very large office with an incredible view of Tokyo. The city's dazzling lights spilled into the room in washes of neon green, red, running white lights, and blue.

Hiroshi turned on a few simple brass lamps and, off to the side, a miniature mock design of an airport was on a large display table that was about fifteen feet long and six feet wide. Many design drawings and specification sheets were on a desk in the corner and he quickly took out the camera from his shirt pocket and began photographing everything in sight. He was so preoccupied that it took him a moment before he turned to look over his shoulder at Hiroshi. His eyes were closed and his hands were in a prayerful gesture in front of his lips. He continued taking photographs as quickly and accurately as he could, looked around the room and found a few more documents that he photographed and, after quite some time, finally felt he had captured everything in the room.

Alek whispered, "Hiroshi!" and he opened his eyes, extinguished the lights, and they left the room. They made their way downstairs, where the security guard stood up from behind his desk and bowed. He smiled politely and they left the building.

Out on the street, Hiroshi shook his hand firmly. He spoke with tears in his eyes and the pungent smell of sake on his breath. "It has been my pleasure to share with you my delight in painting, Harvey-son. It is my honor to serve. I wish you and your family well."

Alek shook his hand strongly, many times, and felt touched. He wanted to respond with something equally emotional but realized he knew nothing of Hiroshi's family, or he of his, or that he had shared any information about himself at all. Hiroshi turned and walked away but Alek could see him bobbing up and down as he walked, a bit taller and larger than the others, and he thought he heard the sound of crying. He watched Hiroshi for a long time, moving among the crowd of dark-haired Japanese, and as he drifted away he felt a little piece of his soul go out with him.

Later that night Alek reported back to his commanding officer, Lieutenant Zapata, a grizzled, craggy officer with a dull stare that implied he had seen plenty of action himself, and he turned in his camera and film. He felt dirty, as if the evening had tarnished him personally in some odd way, and the CO noticed the distant look in his gaze. Lieutenant Zapata stood up, very thin but muscles rippled under his uniform, and he reminded him in rapid-fire statements that he had shown he was willing to take risks, he followed orders, he was serving his country, and he was helping to defeat Communism. He slapped him on the back and gave him an envelope of Japanese currency and another two-day pass for Tokyo.

He did not return to the barracks but immediately went out, riding in a taxi-cab as the driver sped recklessly toward the glitzy lights of downtown Tokyo. He was uneasy with the whole night, felt nauseous staring at the swirling neon lights, and wanted to vomit.

Alek rubbed his forehead and closed his eyes. He had been holding another thought in the back of his mind and now he focused on it. He wanted very much to be with a particular woman at The Queen Bee, the elite club for officers and rich men. The taxi came to a sudden stop and there he was, in front of the very exclusive and restrictive Geisha parlor. He nodded okay, flipped over a few bills, and went slowly up to the building. He thought for a moment, but he was positive he wanted to do this. Even if it went badly, how much worse could he feel?

Alek had to pay handsomely to enter, but he now had some extra cash. He eyed all the pretty women and then motioned to the older but nice-looking and gentle madam, a kind of floor supervisor, to come over. He whispered into her ear, "I've got some money and. . . and some information about the Black Bird."

The madam nodded but it seemed that she did not understand. He again whispered into her ear, smelling her sickly-sweet floral perfume, "I know all about the Black Bird. Do you know where to present such information?"

She leaned back and stared at him for a very long time without blinking. She then nodded ever so slightly and bowed crisply several times.

Alek placed a very fat wad of cash into her hands. "I want the most beautiful and talented woman here. The one I saw before."

The madam demurely accepted it, slipped it into a hidden pocket in her kimono, and escorted him with tiny steps to a remote room that was up two flights of stairs and down a long hallway. It was clearly the only room on this wing of the building. The madam knocked briefly, paused, and opened the door for him, bowed again, and inside, kneeling on a silken red pillow in front of a large canopy bed, was another Geisha with white make-up and fine features. She was posed in a position of graceful reception and ultimate respect, and looked down to the side. He stood still to stare at her and, after a very long moment, she glanced up shyly and in that brief gaze he saw again how incredibly beautiful she was.

"Tell me," he asked the madam, "what is her name?"

"Midorii," she smiled and gave another deep, graceful bow. She closed the door behind her as she left.

Midorii, the Geisha, smiled shyly and looked away.

"It's okay. You can look at me," he said. "I'd like that."

Midorii smiled but kept her eyes down. She had silky black hair and she slowly moved to pull back a cover on the bed to reveal red silk sheets. She bowed to him to sit on the bed and she slowly unbuttoned his shirt.

"It's okay," he said. "Please look at me."

Midorii stopped, knelt down at his feet, smiled again and, keeping her head bowed, looked up at him with her dark eyes. She was stunning.

Alek wanted to confess to her, as if she could purify the recent transgressions he had taken from Hiroshi, but she looked so pure and innocent herself that he wondered if she would understand. Did she even speak English? Tears welled up in his eyes. He did not know where to begin. Finally, he flushed and said simply, "I feel unclean."

Midorii moved delicately to his face, taking a silken white cloth from some hidden fold in her kimono, and gently wiped his eyes. He cried more and it seemed not to faze her as she delicately continued dabbing his cheeks, taking away each tear patiently, until he pulled her close and hugged her tightly. Then his tears flowed easily into her silken dress and after a few moments he stopped. But she continued tending to him with graceful movements as if it were her utmost duty. When he had stopped crying completely, she stepped over to a door, opened it, and offered a hot bath but he shook his head no.

Midorii cocked her head to the side, moved her arms elegantly around the kimono wrap, and slipped it off effortlessly, spinning gracefully with each arcing gesture, and stepping out of her open-toed shoes. Her nude body was as beautiful as her face and he spent the night with her doing everything he could think of, and she did a few things he would never have imagined. He felt incredibly strong physical pleasures that he had never felt before and it made his entire body feel electric and powerful. The evening was an intense, erotic pleasure festival that exhausted him and when it was over he slept very deeply in her arms.

When Alek awakened, he did not care what time it was but took a hot bath with special oils to relax and invigorate his skin. Then he experienced more pleasures of Midorii's flesh in yet more creative and memorable ways. Through it all, she led him to feel no embarrassment, or shyness, and she seemed to anticipate every thought he had with a graceful reception. She moved in a subtle language of sighs and hints, artfully done to make him feel wise and powerful. It was completely satisfying on a physical level and when he had finished with her, the madam gently guided him down the corridor, back down the stairs, and to the front door of the club.

Outside, a day had passed and it was nighttime again. As Alek rode in a taxicab through Tokyo on his return to Atsugi Air Base, he gazed at the flashing neon lights and thought of Midorii, and then of his mission. As he went by noodle shops and bars, saw Japanese women hand-in-hand with U.S. servicemen, he realized that even though his time with Midorii was stimulating and very fulfilling physically, he had no desire to be with her again. He had fond thoughts of her, her body, and her graceful manner. But more importantly, he realized he could not wait for his next mission. He realized that the mission, in its entirety, was very, very exciting. He had served his country in a dangerous and covert way, and he felt incredibly proud that he had, in some way, made a difference in this world.

Alek could not wait for his next mission, whatever it may be.

21)

ZR/RIFLE

The base CO, the Colonel, had always been a distant, aloof son of a bitch, who always found something to rub Lee's nose in, and he felt uncomfortable sitting in his smug, little office. Lee's time in Japan on this tour had passed very quickly and he had come to like it very much for the refined Japanese culture that was so different from America. People respected one another as a given, there was a sense of duty among his contacts, and there was no racial disharmony.

The Colonel chomped on a small cigar and rifled through papers in a folder that was obviously his p-file. Lee saw the pink copy of the firearm discharge complaint, his pay stub receipts (but nothing of the cash received from his mission in Tokyo), and a transfer order off the base as well as a slew of other official papers.

"Son of a bitchin' file's a god-damn mess," the next part the Colonel growled distinctly, "Just like you."

"Sir?" Lee said.

"Can't find your assignment order. Should be right here on top. JENKINS!" The Colonel hollered for his aide, who came scrambling through the office door. "Where's the god-damn assignment order?"

"ONI doesn't send one, sir. That's part of their MO." Lieutenant Jenkins stood at attention in his Navy whites, crisp and neatly pressed. He appeared to be in his early thirties, in great shape, and was meticulously groomed with a fresh crew cut. Tiny nicks and bumps dotted his jaw line with razor burn where he had obviously scraped at any excess beard this morning.

"How's this son of a bitch going to know who to report to and so on?"

"Nothing's written down, sir. For deniability, of course, should something happen to the recruit," he glanced over at him, "that was, um, unforeseen."

"Right." The answer placated the Colonel momentarily, although he was still visibly upset. "So, do you know your assignment?"

"No, sir, no one has informed me of that. This is the first I've heard of any mention, that is, from anyone of a new assignment."

"God damn it, JENKINS! We look like a couple of monkeys trying to fuck a football! What in the god-damn glory of the U. S. A. is going on here?"

Jenkins leaned over the Colonel's desk, a tiny part of an anchor tattoo was barely visible under his short sleeve on his upper arm, and he whispered something into the Colonel's ear, who stared harshly at him.

"Yes. Oh? Yes." The Colonel leaned back in his chair, away from the Lieutenant, and eyed him suspiciously. He then wagged a stiff finger at Jenkins. "Alright, you brief him! You've got all the details. I guess I don't need to know! I'm only the god-damn base CO, for Christ's sakes!"

The Colonel continued flipping through his folder and was breathing heavily. "Here's a sick pay check request! You been sick, boy?"

"Not exactly, sir. I'm in excellent shape."

"But you got paid for, Jesus H. Key-rist… JENKINS! Since when does the Navy pay. . ."

The Lieutenant leaned over again and whispered more into his ear, probably explaining the extra pay for his mission and the sick pay check request. Lee figured that Jenkins probably knew nothing about the cash bonus he had received from his ONI CO and he wasn't about to mention it.

The Colonel had apparently had enough. He leaned back and waved his arm upward as if he were through with him, so Lee jumped up to attention and saluted. The Colonel stared at him with a level eye. "Frankly, son, I'm happy to get you off my base. You sneaky ONI sons-of-bitches creep me out. Dismissed."

Lee snapped a salute and thought, what on earth are you doing running a top-secret base if you can't handle ONI officers? But he said nothing. Or maybe that was precisely why the Colonel was perfect to run this base?

Lee wheeled and went into the outer office, where Lieutenant Jenkins informed him of his next mission. It was all off the record and a high-risk program, but he would be one of a few selected Marines to attempt what he was about to do.

Lee spent the next two weeks being trained by his direct CO, Lieutenant Zapata, who was a wiry, copper-faced man with a gritty no-nonsense personality. Lieutenant Zapata was thorough and detailed, and educated Lee in observation and recording techniques, photography and drawing, and how to use elaborate encryption and coding systems that would allow a very ordinary letter, to his brother, for example, to contain hidden intelligence information. Lee also studied a booklet of codes and one stunned him:

```
ZR/RIFLE - to use a professional assassin to kill a
           foreign leader
```

Lee's skin crawled with gooseflesh. To assassinate a world leader. It struck him solidly that he was doing very important, highly secretive work. But he doubted that they would ever ask him to kill someone. He read the line again and noticed it stated "professional assassin." Observing, taking photographs, and reporting back to his CO was probably all he'd do. Still, he would do whatever they asked of him and be ready if his country called on him.

When Lee completed his intense training, Lieutenant Zapata walked with him around the perimeter of the complex, over a fresh cement walkway that encircled the Quonset hut-style buildings. Lieutenant Zapata spoke with a tough snarl in his voice that was filled with confidence and expectation, "This is the mission of a lifetime. There aren't ten men in the entire Navy qualified to do it. We're counting on you, son, to do your patriotic duty and do your best."

"Thank you, sir."

Lieutenant Zapata stopped and shook his hand vigorously. "You're a good observer with a tough mind. Be patient. Be ready. Your service will come. When it does, do your duty."

"Yes, sir." The Lieutenant did not salute but walked briskly off the walkway, zigging between two buildings, and was gone.

Lee repeated the Lieutenant's advice over and over to himself. He was honored to take this assignment. He would, once again, do his best to serve his country and do his patriotic duty. He was incredibly proud and happy, and very anxious of what the future would bring.

22)

To work for an export firm

Dear Robert,

I am embarking on the biggest thing in my life. Pretty soon I'll be getting out of the Corps and I know what I want to be and how I'm going to be it. You'll know all about it soon enough, and obviously I can't talk about it until it's done, but I am going to New Orleans to work for an export firm. My life seems to have had a lot of funny twists and turns but that's what makes it interesting, huh? I do want to let you know how proud I am and what a fine thing it is to live in America. It is BIG, brother. Very BIG. Wish me luck cause I'm going to need it. Don't write back—I'll be gone by then. I'll let you know my address when I can.

Love,

Lee

PART III

23)

Tell them everything

Lee felt slightly nervous, but ready, as an actor in real life. It was a beautiful October day and the leaves on the trees lining the Moscow River were radiantly red, yellow-and-brown, with some still green, and their brilliance against the high blue sky gave the crisp morning air a brightness and hope that anything could be done.

Lee as "Alek" entered the United States Embassy in Moscow with a highly optimistic attitude and marched to a desk where a receptionist with pointed, horned-rimmed glasses similar to his mother's, seemed to be looking for something to do. Alek handed her his passport and spoke smoothly and clearly. "I affirm that my allegiance is to the Union of Soviet Socialist Republics."

"I don't understand, sir," the receptionist said flustered. She looked young and maybe she was new on the job.

"I have made up my mind," Alek said. "I'm through."

She stared at him blankly, then adjusted her pointed glasses with her long, manicured red nails.

"I'm defecting."

"Oh," she gasped with a squeaky high-pitched voice. "Oh my!"

Alek said, "You better get someone important down here and contact the Soviet Embassy, please."

"Um-m-m," she looked around feebly until she caught the gaze of a Marine guard in dress uniform. She raised her eyebrows and pointed one finger at him but she appeared lost rather than an official of the U.S. Embassy. Her high voice peeped, "Help!"

Later that day Alek was escorted to the Soviet Embassy by the Moscow police and a few men in dark trench coats, who were probably KGB agents, he thought. One guy was tall and thin, with a scar over his left eye, but the guy who was calling the shots was fairly quiet, of medium height and build, with short blonde hair and cool blue eyes. He carried a black satchel as they took him across the street and into a remarkably ornate building, up a palatial staircase, then down a long corridor with many closed doors, and then turned down another even longer corridor, and they traveled the whole length before entering the last room on the left. The room was empty except for a simple wooden table with two chairs behind it and one chair in front of it, and a large mirror on the wall to the left that was probably a two-way mirror.

Alek stood very politely with his hands clasped in front of him at ease. The head guy with blue eyes glared at him, perhaps he was upset at coming in on a Saturday, and he motioned to the tall, lean guy with dark hair, who pushed him to sit down in the single wooden chair. He looked up over his shoulder at the second man, who, because of his wiry thinness, seemed to be acting tough instead of being tough.

The lead investigator opened his very large black satchel and placed a reel-to-reel tape recorder on the desk. Next he took out a folder, filled with a number of papers, and opened it. His light blue eyes conveyed a smug boredom. "You see, we know something about you already."

Alek thought back to his training in California with Lieutenant Zapata and recalled his gritty, calm voice. "Be relaxed. If you look too nervous, it looks like you're hiding something and they won't trust you."

"You think you are the first," the investigator exhaled heavily, as if he had better things to do with his Saturday. "But you are not. You are not even the first Marine in this room… and you won't be the last."

Alek ran his hand over the back of his scalp and felt the sharp hairs of his Marine haircut. He wanted to make a statement to put this guy at ease, but his rehearsed speech seemed inappropriate. Finally he smiled and simply said, "I look forward to contributing to the Soviet system in the highest possible manner."

"My name is Aleksei Kirilenko."

Alek recognized the name of the lead investigator of the Moscow KGB from studying the files and he tried not to flinch or register any response. His real name was Sergei Broda and the fact that Alek was speaking with him was a good sign that he was being taken seriously.

"Would you like something to eat?" Kirilenko said flatly.

"No, thank you, Aleksei… Kirilenko?"

Kirilenko nodded with the hint of a smile. Alek wondered, Was he on to him?

The tall guy leaned over, "Perhaps Coca-Cola?"

Alek thought for an instant. "Yes, thank you, that'd be real nice."

The tall man thrust a swift karate-like jab to the side of his head while shouting a kiai. His left ear rang from the blow and he grasped it to see if it was bleeding.

"Tough titties, cowboy," the tall guy said. "We are not being here to make party."

Alek looked up at him, noticed a trace of Asian influence in his dark features, perhaps Mongolian, as he snarled down at him with the crack of a smile bending the corners of his lips. His dark beard showed about two days of growth so apparently hygiene was not his first concern on Saturday morning. The thug walked behind him and, as he turned to follow him, somehow the guy swung around with a wheelhouse kick that snapped into the back of his head and knocked him out of the chair.

"Jesus Christ, what's your problem?" Alek said harshly.

"We are being here for long time." The thug pointed for him to get back in the chair.

Alek picked himself up and felt his mouth. His fingers were wet with dark red blood. It was oozing down his nose and into his throat. He slid onto the chair nervously, keeping an eye on the tall goon.

Kirilenko settled into his chair opposite the desk and scratched the silvery stubble on his chin. He used a sharpened pencil to point to an official-looking form that was filled-in with information that Alek read, in Russian, upside down. "We know, for example, that you served in Japan. Tell us what you did there."

"Well, if you got it all on the form, why don't you tell me and I'll letcha know—" Alek saw it out of the corner of his eye, a wrecking ball of two fists clenched together, coming down squarely into his right eye. Pain shot through his skull.

"We are not to be leaving here," the goon breathed heavily. "Not tonight. Not tomorrow. I am, as you say, warming up." The cracks of his smile twisted into a full sadistic grin as if he were proud of his English.

Kirilenko pressed the red record button and the two tape reels starting spinning slowly. "Tell us what you know."

Alek could hear his CO's voice as clearly as if Lieutenant Zapata was standing next to him. "You should tell them everything, and quickly, because they're going to get it out of you anyway. We're changing all the codes, so don't worry about that. There's nothing you know that we aren't changing, so you may as well *tell them everything*. They'll like that a whole lot better… And you may save yourself a tooth or two."

"I have something of special interest for you. I was shift supervisor of radar operators at Atsugi Air Base near Tokyo. We flew Black Birds, U-2 spy planes, and I monitored all the flights."

"Yes?" Kirilenko seemed intrigued but not satisfied. He continued coolly, "And?"

"So, from what I hear, Aleksei, do you mind if I call you that?"

Kirilenko shook his head no. "I prefer Alek."

"Oh, me, too. . . "

Kirilenko was silent but kept his amused grin.

Alek locked eyes with him. "You've been having a hell of a time even knowing that these birds exist, let alone know how to find them, so here's a clue: they fly at ninety thousand feet. I know the authentication codes for any aircraft entering and exiting U.S. Air Defense Identification Zones and I can also give you all the radar codes and tactical call signs. Where do you want to begin?"

For the following four days Alek talked, under more civil conditions, and he told them everything he knew. He repeated the same details again, and again, and again. It was all true and easy to describe repeatedly because he had lived it. Finally on the fifth day of interrogation Kirilenko and the Soviets appeared pleased although still very suspicious. Unlike other Marine "defectors" before him, because of all the information Alek had given them, they decided they would let him stay. Alek had won the first battle.

Next Alek requested several times to live in Moscow so he could enjoy the cultural benefits of Soviet society—the radio stations, music, theatre, and opera—but Kirilenko stated that there were no positions available for him in Moscow, which he knew was obviously not true. That showed they weren't ready to trust him completely, to place him anywhere near anything of importance, and they shipped him out to Minsk. It was a place where, Alek figured, the KGB could watch him continuously and there was probably little of intelligence value.

The Monday following his defection, the U.S. Navy, Marines, and Air Force, issued a statement of their shock at this "surprising" news. They did not mention that they had changed all of their tactical codes and call signs the previous week.

In Minsk, the Soviets assigned Alek to a job as an "assembler" at the Byelorussian Radio and Television factory, placed him in an apartment that was beyond any ordinary worker's wildest dreams, and surely bugged by the KGB, and gave him an allowance every month that was more money than he could spend, although he tried.

Alek quickly formed a friendship with Pavel Golovachev, a co-worker. Pavel was apparently affluent but it was not clear if his money was from his family having once been aristocratic or from his father's service in the military. Pavel was of average build, athletic with a dancer's firm, fluid body, but unusually strong. It was one night, after drinking nearly a pint of Vodka, that Pavel "accidentally" let slip, in broken English, "My father general in Red Army and is knowing where all MiG aeroplanes station."

Alek was aware that the U-2 flights had most likely captured that information from their surveillance photographs. So he acted nonplussed even though he was extremely curious as to why Pavel had used English, which he had never done before. After a moment of extremely awkward silence, with Pavel staring at him with slightly wandering, boozy eyes, Lee changed the conversation back to Russian and the best local chess players.

For days Alek thought about Pavel's use of English and determined that either Pavel was considering defecting to the U.S., or the KGB was using Pavel to feel out whether or not he was a secret agent. It didn't take long for a more definitive answer.

The following Saturday night, he went to the opera with Rimma Shirokova, one of many lady friends he was dating. She was a tall, statuesque blonde with thick Slavic facial features of full lips, a prominent nose, and heavy blonde eyebrows. After the opera, they went to the Dancing Bear and, after two tall glasses of vodka, Natasha, a "friend" of Rimma's, leaned over and whispered in English, "I am having location of lab for making interior missiles."

"What?" Alek asked coolly, as if he couldn't hear in the noisy bar.

Natasha, thin with dark hair and middle-aged, gave a quick hiccup. She spoke a little louder. "Missiles. Continent ballistic-hic rockets and nuclear warhead is making design."

Alek again remembered his training and acted as if none of this mattered in the least. He chuckled and spoke condescendingly to her, in Russian, "That's nice!" and turned away from her to rejoin the group conversation about the opera.

Alek waited two weeks, as advised in his training, before acting on this tip. He sat with Rimma in a small café, sipping a chocolate liqueur and eating chocolate mousse. He casually asked her, in Russian, "Is Natasha a close friend?"

Rimma smiled slyly and spoke with a beautifully throaty, strong voice. "She's a friend. I have lots of friends and some are closer than others."

"Is she close?"

"Why?" She raised one eyebrow. "You like to sleep with her?"

He chuckled. "No, I wondered if perhaps she would like to attend the next opera with us?"

"No." Rimma's eyes blinked nervously. "She, ah, had to move back to Stalingrad."

"All the way to Stalingrad? Was it for a job?"

"Yes. The State moved her." She sipped her liqueur from a porcelain cup, looking around the café. "State moved her."

Alek nodded casually. He now knew that it had been a ploy to monitor his interest in information. He would no longer trust Rimma and he would never again show the slightest interest in any hints she or any of her "friends" dropped. But he did enjoy dating her for two more months until she became engaged to a shifty, handsome bureaucratic official, who was an upper level official of the State and, Alek thought, probably in the KGB.

Alek continued to go to parties with Pavel and occasionally Rimma, but he never drank. He enjoyed their friendship and easily made more friends, but he never pressed anyone for details, and certainly asked them nothing if they offered information.

After his affair with Rimma broke off, he began dating several different women. He spent every evening with a pretty woman on his arm at the movies, theatre, opera, cabaret, or jukebox bar. After a few months in Minsk, he decided to write a letter home to his brother Robbie in New Orleans. He knew the KGB would read the letter thoroughly, again and again, trying to figure out codes or ciphers. So he figured he should write something that would be simple without any codes, and something that he knew the KGB would want to read.

24)

Minsk is cold

Dear Robert,

Minsk is cold, much colder than New York, and all the time. They built up Minsk pretty good after the war. I have a job in a radio factory and have made a few friends—we have our fun! After the Russians assured themselves that I was really a naïve American, and believed in Communism, they arranged for me to receive a certain amount of money each month. I'm living big and love it here.

Your brother,

Alek

The KGB would spend the next two and one-half years wondering if any of it, other than the Minsk weather, was really true.

25)

Don't lie to me

Sparky stood outside the door of his sister Eva's house, holding a copper-colored mold of green gelatin, while Gail "Boom-Boom" Curtis, one of the girls from the club, checked her hot-pink lipstick and makeup with her pocketbook mirror. He could hear the other partiers inside, he knew it was supposed to be a surprise birthday party for him even though his birthday wasn't for another week, but he decided he'd play along with them. He rarely went over to Eva's house even though she was his closest relative and lived in Dallas, it just wasn't something he was interested in doing. So when she invited him over three weeks in advance for a "barbeque" party, Eva didn't own a barbeque grill, he knew something else was happening.

Boom-Boom used a white plastic comb to poof-up her dyed-blonde beehive hairdo and chewed her gum with a snapping noise. She glanced at him over the mirror, winked with her long, fake eyelashes, and said, "Put a smile on your mug! You look like you're going to the morgue."

"Take the jello," Sparky said, suddenly wanting a cigarette. "I feel weird holding it."

"Alright, keep your socks on. I gotta make sure my lipstick's even."

"It's even. Come on."

Boom-Boom looked in the mirror. "It ain't even! Don't lie to me!"

"It's fine," Sparky said. A dog yelped inside with a high-pitched voice. "Whatsa matter with you?"

Boom-Boom curled up her lips and wiped the lipstick off her teeth with a tissue. "Don't you fuckin' lie to me!"

Sparky yelled, "Shut up already!"

He pushed the plastic doorbell repeatedly and heard the two-tone chime ring inside several times, followed by a quieting of voices. He thought, wasn't anyone looking out the window to see them come up the walk?

The white curtain on the picture window drew back, a man's eyes peered out, they looked very familiar—was that his brother Sam?, and the curtain fell back. The dog's yelping howled into a continuous high scream with barks.

"There. All set," Boom-Boom said, and tucked away the tissue and mirror, and took the green gelatin mold.

Sparky reached into his shirt pocket and tapped out a cigarette, lighting it with his silver lighter in one motion. He exhaled smoke as his sister Eva opened the wooden door, wearing a fancy yellow-and-green party dress with a pattern of calico kittens and flowers on it. She had straightened her dark hair into a nice hairdo but she had on enough makeup for a circus clown. She had also let her weight balloon but Sparky decided long ago that he wasn't going to say anything to her about her appearance, especially after the last big blowout. He took another drag on the cigarette and opened the aluminum screen door, stepping over the threshold, and inside everyone yelled "Surprise!"

"Yeah, okay," he said, managing a smile.

Boom-Boom punched the back of his shoulder with her purse and spoke harshly, "Sur-*prise!*"

"Yeah, yeah," Sparky said. "This is nice."

Sparky looked around Eva's living room and saw about a dozen friends and there was his brother, Sam, tall like himself but not in good shape, he was a salesman and a bit of a slob, and another one of his sisters, Mary, with her hair in a simple pony tail but also wearing a fancy, poodle dress that made her look like a car hop girl with white socks and patent leather shoes. Some of the men were smoking and almost everyone had a drink in their hand. They raised their glasses in an impromptu toast and began singing, "For he's a jolly good fellow!" and they continued for two verses and laughed at the end with a hearty cheer.

"Yeah, yeah, okay," Sparky said.

"Here's a whiskey and cola," Eva said, handing him a tall glass with a lot of ice and liquor.

Sparky didn't like ice because he thought it watered down the drink and weakened it, but he took it anyway and raised it in a toast. He said, "Hey, thanks a lot. To the good life!"

Sam, his brother, called out in his deep, heavy voice, "Here! Here!"

Sparky downed the drink in a long gulp, to get rid of it, and then said, "Next time no ice, hunh?"

"Sure, Jackie," Eva said.

It upset Sparky that Eva called him "Jackie," like he was a boy again, and he snapped at her. "Call me Sparky!" and then, hearing how loud his voice was, he chuckled a little bit and added, "Or Jack."

"Why so angry?" Eva said, turning to Mary, who looked down nervously and went into the kitchen.

"Hey, come on," he said, "Let's have a party now!"

Sparky saw Andy, his bartender from the club, over by Eva's record-playing console and he nodded to him. Andy was the only black person at the party and he immediately placed the needle on an album by Frank Sinatra and everyone livened up. People started talking with each other, Boom-Boom wiggled her hips and Mary returned from the kitchen with another whiskey and cola, and he hugged her. He was glad that only his close friends were here and no one from the "organization." He didn't like explaining anything to anyone.

"Salute!" he called out to Dick, his roommate, across the living room. "L'achaim!"

Dick was in his best dark suit with his hair neatly combed, he looked polished and clean, and he smiled his full, great smile. His big pink hand raised his glass, and a few other people looked at Sparky and raised their glasses, but mostly people were talking and laughing.

Sparky hugged Eva and thanked her for throwing a party for him, then began shaking everyone's hand around the room. With each person he repeated a phrase he had heard one of the bosses say, and he liked it very much, which was "It is an honor and a privilege to have you as a friend. Thank you."

The dog continued yelping in the kitchen and Sparky turned to Eva. "Did you get a dog?"

"Yeah," Eva smiled. She went to the kitchen, her party dress made a swishing sound, and picked up a small dachshund. It was only a puppy. "It's for you! Happy Birthday!"

"What? For me?"

"Yeah," Eva said.

The small puppy fit easily in Sparky's hands. He held it up and looked at it closely. It was all brown with black near its paws and nose, and it licked him repeatedly. Sparky laughed and nuzzled with the puppy as it licked him more.

"We thought you'd like it," Mary said.

Sparky didn't know what to say. He never had a pet growing up, mostly because he was never in one house long enough to keep one, but he always liked the idea of owning a dog. But this was a little one. He'd have to buy it dog food and take care of it.

"You're always picking up strays and helping people," Sam said.

Boom-Boom shot Sam a dirty look and said, "Hey!"

The pup licked Sparky's face more and he laughed again. "He's cute! But he's so tiny!"

"So now you'll have a regular companion," Eva said, smiling and patting down her straightened dark hair.

Dick was on the other side of the room and not paying attention. He was talking with Andy, and had his soft pink hand on Andy's shoulder, which Sparky felt was being a little too friendly to a colored guy, whether it was Andy or not. He'd have to remember to have a talk with Dick at the apartment later and straighten him out.

"Do you like her?" Mary said.

"What, it's a girl?" Sparky asked. "Sheesh! Another cute stray bitch?"

Sparky laughed at his joke and Boom-Boom cuddled up to his arm, pressing her face against his and puckered her hot-pink lips for the puppy to kiss. The tiny dachshund licked her lips again and again, and then his face, and wagged its whole back end with its tail. The puppy then wet his hands and Sparky held it out at arm's length and watched the pee hit the brown carpet before he stepped onto the linoleum tiles in the kitchen.

Sparky tipped the dog up and said, "That's about right. Two minutes and the bitch pisses all over me!"

Sparky laughed again and his sisters and Sam laughed, too. Everyone was in a great mood and he was happy that he had gone along with Eva's "surprise" party. Then Sparky thought about his club, all the money he owed to so many people, and when Dick walked into the kitchen he handed over the puppy into his large, soft hands and said, "Here, clean-up this mess. Now I need to whiz."

Just then Boom-Boom handed him a folded-up note. She put her hands on his forearm as he opened the note. It read,

Don't be mad at me!

–Gail

P.S. I want to suck your dick *right now*.

Sparky pointed to the bathroom and said, "Gail and I got something to talk over."

He watched Gail sashay into the bathroom and followed her, shutting the door behind them. He ran the water in the sink and washed his hands, then unzipped his fly, but let the water continue running. Boom-Boom dropped to her knees quickly and reached into his pants, taking out his floppy member. She stroked him and took him into her mouth and he liked seeing the bright pink lipstick go around him.

"Don't you ever do that again!" Sparky shouted, and she stopped to look up at him. He lowered his voice to a whisper and thumbed in the direction of the door. "Keep going, I'm yelling for them."

Sparky yelled again, "God damn it, I said to *do it!*" and Boom-Boom smiled, winked, and took him into her mouth again, smearing her pink lipstick all over him and around her mouth. She was an expert at doing this, he was rock hard in a moment, and he enjoyed the way she slid her hand up and down his shaft in rhythm with her tongue curling around his head. He wanted to focus on the sensation but so many things had annoyed him that he wanted to explode and be done with it, get back to the party and have another drink, and he couldn't hold back any longer anyway, and he let loose a tremendous bucking load of his cream. When he finished, he tucked himself back into his pants, zipped up, completed washing his hands, and turned off the water. He didn't look at Boom-Boom as she got up off the floor, but he opened the door and smiled to Eva and Mary standing nearby.

"So, yeah, thanks for the dog. What should I call him?"

"How 'bout naming her after Eva?" Mary asked sweetly. "Like Evie?"

"Nah, he's a weenie-dog, right? How 'bout "Hot Dog"?" Sparky chuckled.

"It's a girl!" Eva said loudly.

"Yeah, so what?" he said. He turned to Boom-Boom coming out of the bathroom. "Girls like weenies, too, ain't that right?"

"Sure, Sparky," Boom-Boom said. Her lipstick was bright-pink and even again, and she winked at him with her long lashes. She turned to Eva, who was staring coldly at her. "It's true! You can't hate me because it's true. I'd just as soon eat a fuckin' hot dog as a hamburger."

"How 'bout Sheba? Like the show?" Sparky said, but everyone in the room was looking at Boom-Boom. Sparky knew that for most people this would be an awkward moment but she was used to being on stage. She raised her eyebrows, let her mouth drop open wide, and put on her "dumb blonde" look just like Marilyn Monroe. Then she said, "Hey! Wasn't this supposed to be a barbeque?"

Everyone laughed and Sparky picked up the dachshund pup. "Good thing for you it ain't a barbeque, Sheba! They'd be grilling you like a big hot dog!"

Eva and Mary laughed. Sparky nuzzled Sheba's nose and it licked him repeatedly.

26)

No secrets

It was a characteristic dance party in the Soviet style. Workers and medical students hung around the gymnasium floor as a disk jockey played all Soviet music that was supposed to sound hip but everyone knew that they were poor imitations of Chuck Berry or Jerry Lee Lewis with ill-fitting lyrics of propaganda. Soviet banners and red streamers hung from the rafters and ceiling beams. Young men wore black leather jackets or tee-shirts with rolled-up shirt sleeves, holding a pack of American brand cigarettes, for status only as they would never smoke them, and stood around the periphery of an open area for dancing as red and white lights flashed hypnotically.

Alek spoke with Pavel, in Russian, while watching the crowd. Pavel, as usual, had asked about America and it was somewhat tiring. His favorite subject was California and Pavel often asked if all the women there were blonde. But tonight he asked, "Have you seen a colored person?"

"You mean a Negro? Yeah."

"I have never met." Pavel took out a silver flask with an inscription on it, in Russian, that had been presented to his father for his bravery during World War II. Alek had never looked at it closely, but Pavel used it so often that he could make out the words "Berlin" and "1945."

"Do they dance?" Pavel asked.

"Yes," Alek chuckled, and then stopped. "Wait, what do you mean?"

"I saw film. They dance and eat watermelon."

"No, no," Alek replied sternly. "They're just like you and me, in every way."

"No," Pavel laughed easily and drank again.

"Yes, they are. Do you dance?"

"I am best dancer!" Pavel started a pirouette on his toes, stumbled out of the turn, and caught his balance. He shrugged a frown and took another drink. "I need to be inspired by California ballerina."

Alek chuckled again, then picked up the conversation. "Negroes are just the same as you and me. They're ordinary people."

"No. Not same. To say is propaganda lie because America has more colored peoples."

Alek thought that the only propaganda in it was that they were considered second-class citizens in America, which disgusted him, but he didn't know how to say this in Russian without sounding elitist, or to the opposite extreme, to the alleged even-playing field of all workers in all jobs. He could see Pavel's awareness of his frustration but he also had a look of disbelief, as if Alek were lying, which frustrated him more. Finally, Alek said, "No two people are alike or equal. Black people are good and bad, just like anybody. They are smart and stupid, talented dancers or not, great thinkers or. . ."

Pavel was not paying attention but staring at a group of women who had just entered the gymnasium. One was a gorgeous, blue-eyed, dark-haired woman and she had two friends. She strolled with another brunette who was heavy-set with thick features, and the last woman was a blonde who dressed in a reflection of a Western prostitute with a very short dress, black nylons with a seam in back, a jeans jacket, and too much eye make-up and lipstick.

Alek tapped Pavel on the shoulder to come along and he approached them. Pavel was quickly talking with dyed blonde and, after a few words, the heavy-set woman continued walking away, deeper into the party and toward the dance floor.

"My name's Alek," he said in Russian to the beautiful brunette. He felt fairly comfortable as he had been able to practice his Russian for a few months, plus the first few days of intense interrogation by the KGB had sharpened his skill. "How's it going?"

"Okay, not bad," the woman said, glancing at him with her bright blue eyes and looking out onto the dance floor. "My friend Vera is to meet us here, but I don't see her anywhere."

"Oh?" Alek asked. "What's she look like?"

"Dark hair, about my height."

"Okay, that eliminates about thirty people. Only one hundred to go."

She looked at him and laughed. "Who are you?"

"Alek. It's my pleasure to meet you." He shook her hand but she did not respond, looking past him, so he did not let go. She was too good-looking. Alek continued, "This music is the worst I've heard since the last time I was here."

She giggled. "Me, too."

"What's your name?"

"Marina. Would you let go of my hand?"

Alek smiled and kissed her hand softly and released her, but Marina backed away only slightly. "I think your friends will tell you when they've found Vera. Plus, she'll be looking for you, right?"

Marina flashed an intrigued, quick smile that held promise. "Are you always this forward?"

"Only with the most beautiful women," Alek grinned. "Tell me more about yourself."

Marina spoke about her recent graduation from pharmacy school and how she wanted to travel. She wasn't happy with her family, well, they weren't really her family after all, but she wanted to go to America and see the sights.

Then she stopped and looked at him directly. "Do you have anything to drink? Some vodka?"

Alek tapped Pavel on the jacket and Pavel pulled out his flask, handing it to him without much concern. Alek unscrewed the top, pretended to take a shot that burned his lips, and handed it to Marina. She turned away briefly to hide it, slammed back a chug, and spun around with an enthusiastic Russian folk dance move with her arms out. "HEY!"

They spoke for quite some time, then moved over to the wooden bleachers that were pulled out with three rows of seats. Alek sat close to Marina but leaned back on his elbows on the top row, keeping an eye on the entire gymnasium. He learned more about Marina's family, that her father was not who the government, or her mother had first said he was, but that he was a soldier in World War II who had actually been captured, or was a traitor, she wasn't truly certain, and was shot in Germany. After her mother died, she moved to Minsk and was raised by her aunt and uncle and—

Alek interrupted her and said he could relate to and appreciate that. "Sometimes your family, they know things about you, like what you're doing or where you've been, but mostly they don't understand you at all."

Marina turned and looked deeply into his eyes. Her bright blue eyes were searching his and Alek locked on to her with his eyes. He leaned over and whispered into her ear, "I understand you and I want to help you. Would you let me help you?"

Marina nodded, unblinking. They spoke more, without looking away from each other, and the evening melted away until they noticed that the bad music had stopped and the bright gym lights were turned on.

"We're off Dancing Bear," Pavel said. He wavered next to the bleachers on shaky legs.

"My uncle expects me back by midnight," Marina said.

"We wouldn't want to upset your uncle's expectations," Alek smiled mischievously. "Would we?"

Marina laughed and playfully punched his shoulder. Pavel drank from his flask with a grand gesture, raising and lowering it over his mouth to show it was empty. A young woman with dark hair, who might be Vera, came over and tugged on the sleeve of Marina's gray sweater to leave. Marina broke from her friend's grasp, took hold of his collar, and kissed him suddenly. It was warm and wet and wonderful and timeless and he wanted it to go on and on, but she backed away tenderly an inch from his face. "I'll go to the Dancing Bear tomorrow."

The dark-haired woman pulled her again, "Come on, leave the American alone."

Marina looked at her friend with confusion. "Alek? He's a worker in the radio factory."

"What?" Now the dark-haired woman looked confused, while still searching for another person in their small group, as the students and workers filed out of the gymnasium.

He nodded. The time at the Monterrey School near the Marine base in California had paid off. He did not have a noticeable accent. He continued in Russian, "Yeah, I'm American. I defected a few months ago."

Marina's confusion and tensed brow was replaced by a broad smile. "Your Russian is excellent."

"Thank you. So is yours." He laughed and stood up. He offered to shake hands with her friend. "You must be Vera."

"Yes, how did you know?"

He wanted to say playfully, "I'm a spy, I know everything," but he knew that was his emotional response to Marina, wanting to show-off, and he resisted. "Lucky guess."

Now Marina stood up and pulled Vera away. Pavel slapped him on the back and said, "Come on, we must go bear… to bar. . . To the Bear Bar! Oof! Somebody drank all the vodka!"

The next night Alek met Marina in front of the Dancing Bear. It was cold and he hopped from foot to foot to keep warm. A wooden sign overhead creaked back and forth in the wind. Finally, Vera approached with Marina, who pointed to him, still bouncing to keep warm, and said, "Look, the Dancing Bear is outside!"

He laughed at her good joke and opened the door for them. As Marina started to enter he stopped her, grasping her shoulder. "I wanted to see you."

"Yes. Here we are," Marina said with a big smile. "Come on, let's go inside. It's cold!"

"Not yet. I want you to tell me the truth. No secrets."

Marina looked at him oddly, but her bright blue eyes were beaming. "Yes, of course. What is it?"

"More than anything else today, what did you want to do?"

"To come here," she smiled and her teeth were beginning to chatter from the cold. "Come on, our friends are inside."

"Yes, and that's what I wanted, too. I thought of you all last night and today. And more than anyone else here, who did you want to see?"

Marina's mouth opened slightly and she looked down. He touched her chin tenderly to make her look into his eyes. She said softly, "To see you."

"And I you. Please, let's not waste our time with drinking."

"But all our friends are inside." She looked confused. "Russian boys always want to drink first."

"I'm not Russian." He took her by the hand and led her away, slowly at first but as she let herself go, he walked faster. His apartment wasn't far and the frigid night air had his cheeks burning. He was able to afford a one-bedroom flat to himself because with his salary at the factory plus his stipend from the Soviet government, he was making more money than the factory director. He could afford this lavish, arranged apartment. He smoothly opened the new, polished wooden door.

"It's so large," she said, admiring the living room.

He felt the warm air on his face and hands as he quietly closed the door. He watched her as she tip-toed around and it reminded him of an animated movie he had seen where a lowly commoner stares with astonishment at the grand ballroom before she becomes the princess. He took Marina's coat and hung it on a simple rack, then drew open the curtains to reveal floor-to-ceiling windows with a balcony. His apartment was on an upper floor overlooking the river with an incredible view of Minsk.

He stood closely by her at the window. His lips were inches from her ear and he whispered softly, "No secrets. Only truth."

Marina nodded, staring out into the beautiful expanse of the city lights below twinkling in the night.

"More than anything else. . ." he held her hand with tenderness, "have you wanted to be with me tonight?"

"Yes."

"More than anything else, have you wanted love in your life, a deep love that can transform you?"

Marina turned to look into his eyes. "Yes."

"Will you let me make you happy?"

She said in a breathy whisper so softly it barely escaped her lips, "Yes."

He took her gently by the back of the neck and kissed her deeply, feeling her warm mouth open to him. She dropped her purse and put her arms around him. He kissed her more and moved his head slightly sideways, feeling his passion rise. He clutched at her clothes, feeling for the clasps, then stopped and looked into her eyes. "Let me love you."

He kissed her again, beautifully, and her eyes closed. She kissed him more and placed her hands around his head and stroked his cheek. He eased her back and she danced smoothly backward to his steps and he broke his kiss, only for a moment to bend down quickly and scoop her up into his arms. He kissed her mouth again and carried her gently into the bedroom and lay her down softly on the made bed.

"I," Marina said. "I don't know you."

"You've known me—as the person you've been looking for, for so long."

"Yes, I've been saving myself," she said.

"Thank you," he said softly. "And I've been saving my love, my deepest feelings for you."

He unbuttoned her blouse and kissed her breasts tenderly, seeing the pinkish brown nipples rise slightly and harden. He touched her neck, kissed it, and smoothly slid his hand down to her chest, caressing her as she writhed with sensual delight. He kissed her mouth again, solidly, again and again, sliding his tongue into her, feeling her take it, and wanting to let it all go, now, but put his hands around her head, stroking her hair, and kissing her deeply again. He felt himself becoming thick and gently lay on top of her. He whispered, "Oh, Marina."

"Please," she said.

He unbuckled his pants and slipped them down, pushing up her skirt and feeling her wet panties. He kissed her neck and breasts, feeling their supple weight, and pulled off her panties. His hand reached down to her soft tenderness, wet with anticipation, and he slid himself in, softly, gently, wanting her to want him. He looked into her eyes and tears were streaming down her face.

"What is it?" he asked. "Am I too rough?"

"No," she smiled. "I'm so happy."

He smiled broadly. He felt the beautiful wave building inside him, gradually getting stronger with every loving stroke, and looked into her eyes. She was amazingly beautiful. He wanted this moment to last forever, kissed her strongly on the mouth, their passion growing hotter still, unable to breathe enough, and feeling stronger until he felt overcome with incredibly intense waves of ecstasy, pulsing through him, to the core of him, until he slowed down to a gentle rest with his head on her bosom. Time seemed to have stopped when he was with her and now the world was back—the honking of a car in the distance; a drunken man shouting about the people's revolution.

A moment later he was peacefully, blissfully asleep.

27)

I miss the Texas heat

Dear Bro',

Minsk is dog-gone cold. The city is filled with hard-boiled Communists and newer buildings. I'm not having as much fun as at the beginning—maybe I'm settling down at twenty-two ha-ha-ha! People here don't discuss politics and the system as they would have you believe, so that's a disappointment, but I guess all in all, there people just like home. I miss the Texas heat. My job is menial work and I don't like it. I would rather be studying and writing, but they seem to have their place for me. Their rules, their system. I put in an official request to study in Moscow. Wish me luck!

Your bro',

Alek

28)

Why is his name popping up across the South?

The Director of the Federal Bureau of Investigation, J. Edgar Hoover, sat at his desk looking over various reports of strange events happening in Louisiana. He bit hard on an unlit cigar and ran his palm over his neatly combed but thinning hair, then checked that his tie was snuggly knotted.

As Director of the FBI, Hoover felt he always had to put together the pieces of the puzzle. No organization ever came straight out and told him what they were doing. But this was quite an evidence trail and he couldn't ignore it any further. At the end of the trail, there was a spike in the fighting in Cuba by anti-government guerillas using U.S. Army munitions and weapons. One step back on the trail, surplus weapons and ammunition were being bought in large quantities, or stolen from U.S. military installations, around southern Florida and near New Orleans. Also, there were reports of gunshots and explosions at a makeshift training camp for anti-Castro rebels in a heavily wooded swamp just outside of Lacombe, Louisiana. The latest report was of a group of demonstrators fighting on the streets of both New Orleans and Miami. Sprinkled along the trail were common names of CIA agents he recognized like Hunt and Phillips, but then there was this new name popping up frequently: Oswald.

Hoover thought for a moment, Who in the hell would be fighting *for* Cuba? Commies. Reds! He ground his teeth on the cigar and thought, There will be no commie bastards demonstrating on the streets of America!

Hoover's aide, Wilbert Darrow, a meticulous, bright, middle-aged man, wore an identical dark suit and tie, and sat patiently, looking at the green linoleum flooring. He was ready for any action the Chief decided to make.

The Director of the FBI continued in deep concentration, oblivious to the humming of some song by his aide. Hoover thought, It was one thing to turn a blind eye, but he should be *informed* of what was going on. This is American soil and the FBI is in charge *here,* goddamnit! He would cooperate, for now, but he had to let *them* know that *he* knew what was happening, that he smelled a rotten fish, and *he* would be watching *them!* He took out the unlit cigar from his mouth and turned to his aide.

"Send a telegram. From my office. To the Office of Naval Intelligence and copy it to the Office of Security at the State Department." Hoover felt the light hair cream on his well-manicured quaff and pursed his lips.

"Yes, sir. Go ahead." Darrow wrote on a small steno pad with a pencil.

"Since there is a possibility that an imposter is using your man's birth certificate, no, strike that part about 'your man.' Put his fucking name in the telegram: Oswald. Let them know that *I know* what they're doing. Wait a minute. Didn't his military record state he was obligated to service until December sixty-two?"

"Yes, sir. Military or CIA, I saw that as well. Umm-m..." The aide reached over and sifted through the papers on Hoover's desk and found the typed form. "Here it is. Yes, he's committed through December eighth, nineteen sixty-two."

"Well, that's it, then. He's their man! But if he's in the Soviet Union for a two-year re-enlistment. . . What's all this god-damned activity? Why is his name popping up across the South?"

"It begs the question, sir."

"It's like a god-damn three-ring circus! And someone in a clown suit is going to get fucked. Maybe it's a trail of damning evidence for deniability. Still, I want them to know that *I know*. So, from the top."

Darrow read, "To ONI, copy to the State Department, Dear Sir, Since there is a possibility that an imposter is using Oswald's birth certificate..." he did not even look up, knowing that Hoover would finish this quickly.

"Yes. Any current information the Department of State may have concerning subject will be appreciated."

"Yes, sir. Is that all?"

"Rat bastards." Hoover chomped down on his cigar. "That'll show 'em."

"Yes, sir. It will go out today." Darrow set the memo on a stack of papers piled in Hoover's outbox, looked up, and smiled slightly to his boss. It was another productive day in the fight against communism.

29)

Be patient

Alek was thoughtful of his mission and patient. They had drilled that into him: Be ready. Be patient. So he asked himself if he was ready if an opportunity, no, *when* an opportunity arose? He decided he must take steps to become ready.

Alek's friend Pavel liked to hunt and they often went to the woods on a large farm that Pavel's uncle owned outside Minsk. He didn't shoot well but neither did Pavel so it didn't matter much. What did matter was that he allowed Pavel to drink just enough vodka to lose count of the number of shotgun shells they had fired at grouse, or pheasant, so when the day was done, Pavel wouldn't notice the two shells he had placed in his sock while retying his boots. After two months, he had about forty shells.

Next, at the factory Alek found a scrap of two-inch pipe about ten inches long with screwed threads on the end and a twist top that fit snugly on one end. But it was deformed on the other end and thus tossed into the garbage. He asked a co-worker to solder the other end shut, and he did it during a lunch break for three rubles and two tickets to the Gorky Theatre production of "The Seagull," which he had already seen four times. He took the finished pipe back to his apartment and the following night borrowed a drill from a neighbor and a bored a tiny hole in the middle. He carefully emptied the powder from the shotgun shells onto a piece of paper, then poured the explosive into the pipe. He screwed it shut, then took a monkey wrench and twisted it as tight as he could, having wedged the pipe into the crevice between the radiator and the floor. He bought some string, dipped it in wax, and tested how long it would take to burn as a fuse. When it wasn't fast enough, he bought thinner thread and soaked it in gasoline first, then added a bit of powder to the thread, and sealed it all in wax. It sputtered and jumped, but burned effectively. He bought an alarm clock and glued three match heads to the alarm striker with a flint board, then attached the fused. In all, the project had taken him four months from the time he had first gone hunting with Pavel in early October, but he had built a pipe bomb. Now he was ready.

And then he waited.

~ ~

It was one of those days at work where everything seemed to be out of synch and everyone blamed him. It was easy to blame him—he was the foreigner. He didn't understand some of their technical jargon in Russian, but it wasn't his fault that the line broke down. He was keeping up, for the most part, but when Ivan, the line supervisor, lay a tray of rejected transistor panels at his workstation, there was no way he could inspect and fix those, and keep up with the line. Also there was Boris, who was a short, squat Latvian who chatted constantly and made funny faces and noises, smirking off to the side and hoping the line would shut down so he could have another drink of vodka with Pavel and Sonya. But when the line stopped for the third time after lunch, everyone except Boris immediately glared at him because the loss in production would mean no bonus pay at the end of the month.

After a long day at work, Alek was ready to relax at home with Marina, who he had asked to live with him, and then, a month later, married in a quiet civil service. But when he arrived home, the luxurious apartment was a mess. Newspapers and magazines were littered across the sofa and floor, dirty plates, cups and saucers lay on the dining table and in the sink, and dinner was not ready. None of this was as it should be, as he had learned growing up with his mother, and he had spoken with Marina about it many times before. It immediately upset him.

Marina sat on a large stuffed chair, uncrossed her legs, and looked up at him as he walked through the living room. She asked how his day was, in Russian, and he ignored her. What had she been doing all day?

He opened a kitchen cabinet, which he had painted white when she moved in, and took down a glass, moved a plate dirty with spaghetti and sauce in the sink, and filled it with water. As he took a drink, he thought about how it was only the third week of the month but they had already spent his entire monthly allowance fixing up the apartment, and going out with Pavel and Vera, and he wondered how they were going to eat on the little money he had left.

Alek asked curtly, in Russian, "How much do you have in savings?"

"What?" Marina remained seated on the sofa, looking at him with some confusion and wanting attention with her big blue eyes. "Some but not much. I already told you that."

"How much is it again?"

"Not a lot."

He was growing madder. Why did he need to ask everything three times or more before he got an answer? "God damn it! Will you tell me *how much* it is?"

"About two hundred rubles."

He calculated meals and other expenses and breathed a bit easier, but he was still upset with her. Couldn't she see how they were living and *do* something about it? "We'll need to use it."

"Yes, I know." Marina approached him in the kitchen and hugged him, nestling her head on his chest and stretching up on her toes to kiss his neck and cheek. "Tell me about your day."

He looked down and saw piles of dust under the cabinets and a few drops of white paint here and there along the baseboard. Near the stove was a red splotch of sauce on the floor as well as around the stainless steel pot, which still held mixed spaghetti, sauce, and a wooden spoon. He was growing madder and turned away from her and saw yet another spot on the floor that was greenish-brown and apparently growing mold.

"God damn it! I asked you to clean the kitchen floor!"

"I will."

"When?" He could feel the veins on his neck pounding but he didn't care.

"I'll do it soon. It's not a big deal. Tell me about work."

"When?"

"Soon. It's not important, is it?"

"God damn it, answer me! *When* will you do it?"

"Tomorrow morning. What's wrong, sweetie?" She put her arms around him but he pushed her off. "Tell me about work."

"Work was shitty!" he yelled. "What in the hell have you been doing all day?"

She backed away from him and stood with her back to the stove. "I made lunch. Read the paper."

"When are you going to act like a proper wife?"

"Honey, I'm here for you. Tell me what you want."

"I want you to clean the fucking floor! Is that too difficult?" He took a swing in her direction and slapped the pot off the stove and it went flying across the room and crashed on the floor, spilling its contents into a lumpy, red mess.

She looked at it with fear and horror, and the expression on her face made him think that it could be *her* lying on the floor in a lumpy mess oozing blood. But he was so mad he didn't care.

Marina looked at him nervously and her voice trembled. "Alek. . . "

He was furious and thought that none of this was working out. He had learned nothing of value for ONI and was tired of writing letters with monthly production rates coded into the text. He worked at a menial job that bored the shit out of him. He was sick of his friends, who only wanted to know about California, and Marina's friends, who seemed to aspire to nothing more than drinking and fucking. He had married her because it was the right thing to do, and here she was sitting at home and doing nothing. He exploded, "I'll do whatever I god-damn well need to do! You can't keep this home in order! This isn't even a home—it's a pigsty! If you won't listen to me, maybe I'll have to beat the shit out of you!"

He grabbed her by her blue sweater near her neck and she cringed away, slinking down to the floor. He tightened his fist into a ball and flexed it back, cocked and ready.

She cried out, pleading through her tears, "Alek, don't hit me! You'll hurt the baby!"

He froze. My god, what was he doing? He breathed heavily and loosened his fist. He pulled her close and tried to kiss her, but she turned away, still fearing him, so he sat down next to her and kissed her cheek and petted her hair. "My darling, I'm so sorry. I'm sorry."

Marina cried hard and held onto him, heaving deep sobs into his chest. She mumbled something in Russian and it sounded like "The rooster rules the roost," but he couldn't quite understand her through her garbled and choking tears. He held her tenderly and continued to kiss and stroke her.

She was a beautiful person and he hated what he had done. This whole situation was not what he expected. What could he do? What could they do? Would he have his child grow up here and live under constant surveillance? To live in a city mired in the past with poor education and where the people had no dreams or ambition?

He had to do something. As a family they had to live in a better situation. He knew right then that they had to leave the Soviet Union. He also suddenly realized that he was incredibly homesick.

She looked at him and wiped her eyes. "I'll clean the floor now."

He kissed her on the lips and she let him. It was a sloppy, wet kiss of both their tears and happiness, in knowing that they were the most important thing here and not the floor, not this apartment, and not his crummy job. He kissed her more and more, and clutched her passionately, tearing off each other's clothes, and they made love on the dirty linoleum floor.

30)

If de dog head cut off, de dog will die, tail and all

During a standard "review of documentation," two federal agents handcuffed Carlos "Little Man" Marcello in his home. He wore only suit pants, but without the coat, and a white shirt buttoned-up but no tie. They did not have search warrants or arrest warrants, and they also did their job with a holier-than-thou attitude. The agents wore business suites but they threw him into a waiting black-and-white with two more policemen and drove him straight to the airport, where a small eight-seat jet was waiting with its engines running. Marcello had no idea where they were taking him and the whole operation made him furious. He had drunk a few glasses of Montepulciano wine the night before so over the course of the long flight, wherever it was he was being taken, he had to relieve himself in the plane's small, makeshift bathroom while still handcuffed.

By the time the jet arrived at the airport in Guatemala City, Carlos Marcello's veins pounded like thick chords in his bull-like neck and he breathed heavily. Two more federal agents were waiting at the top of the flight ladder and one un-cuffed him. Before deboarding, Marcello turned to one of the agents who had escorted him from New Orleans and bumped his chest directly into him, an officious, pasty-faced man who was apparently the chief of this squad. The agent, Captain Raymond Lewis of the New Orleans FBI, was about five inches taller than Marcello but chubby. He smirked.

Marcello ground his teeth and bit off his words viciously as he vowed a Sicilian oath, "*Livarsi 'na pietra di la scarpa!*"

He defiantly spat in Captain Lewis's face and flexed his fists, expecting a response, but none came. The agent wiped off the spittle from his still smirking face. Marcello then walked down the stairs where the Guatemalan policeman, wearing a light blue shirt with a short dark-blue tie, pointed him in the direction of the only terminal.

Marcello trotted with short steps, carrying his muscular weight easily as he jerked his head from side to side, looking for any challenger, and continued a string of Sicilian curses directed at the man responsible for this hasty deportation: the Attorney General of the United States. His parents were from Sicily and he was born in Tunisia, but he was taken to Guatemala because he had one of his attorneys file a "found" birth certificate from Guatemala. But he had not had any type of hearing or opportunity to defend himself, and the manner of deportation was an aloof, humiliating, and degrading event that set him plotting revenge. It was an unforgivable lack of respect. It would not be forgotten until the person responsible for it was thrown out of power. Marcello had the money, the connections, and, now, the motivation to do just that.

In Guatemala City, only six hours later, Carlos Marcello watched as Captain David Ferrie landed a single-engine plane at the airport. Marcello strutted out onto the tarmac, ignoring the police and officials, who yelled something at him in Spanish, all short and squat with dark complexions. He greeted Ferrie as he climbed down from the plane.

Ferrie was tall for a pilot with odd-looking features. He wore a faded red toupee with dark grease-paint eyebrows. He handed Marcello a briefcase that Nofio Pecora had personally packed.

Marcello rested the briefcase on his knee and opened it immediately, smiled broadly, took out a packet of twenty-dollar bills, and closed it. Marcello patted Ferrie on the shoulder, squeezing his black leather bomber jacket, and then opened it up and stuffed a wad of twenties into his white shirt pocket. He pinched and slapped his cheek playfully.

Ferrie chuckled and said, "Thanks!"

They walked away from the plane, hearing more shouts in Spanish that Marcello silenced with a few more twenties here and there. He also gave huge tips of American cash to a taxi driver, who had a vast knowledge of the city and escorted them everywhere they went; to a very short tailor who had the finest shop in town; to the chef and owner of a restaurant with a beautiful view overlooking the city; and to a lanky Cuban exile who ran a very clean cigar store. Within an hour, Carlos Marcello had bought a new suit, had a late brunch of eggs benedict and lobster bisque, and bought the best Cuban cigars in town. Later that same afternoon, Marcello, wearing an expensive navy-blue pinstripe suit and smoking a Cuban cigar, was flying back toward New Orleans with David Ferrie, who also smoked a cigar.

During the flight back, Marcello and Captain Ferrie talked for hours. Marcello found Ferrie to be very intelligent and they shared many of the same ideological beliefs, mainly that they both wanted the Cuban communist ruler Fidel Castro out of power. When they landed at Lacombe, a small airstrip just outside New Orleans, Marcello handsomely rewarded Ferrie for his prompt help with another huge wad of cash.

But Carlos Marcello always thought long-term and so he also gave Ferrie a job as his legal aide. Ferrie's new job would be to assist Marcello's squadron of lawyers in finding any loophole in the law to fight off such a rude deportation from ever occurring again. It did not matter that Ferrie was a pilot first and foremost. It was a desk job that paid well, gave Ferrie something to do, but mainly kept him available to fly a plane on a moment's notice.

A few days later, David Ferrie strolled through Little Man Marcello's conference room in the lodge at Churchill Farms. Nofio Pecora sat in a leather wing chair at one end of a long table, while the boss sat at the head in another leather chair. Ferrie gazed at a painting of a Sicilian fishing village market that had colorful fruits and vegetables, and bright white sails on the boats. A big bodyguard stood nearby and they all listened intently to a small wooden radio console, placed squarely in the middle of the conference table, which broadcast a speech by the President of the United States. "There will not, under any conditions, be an intervention in Cuba by United States armed forces, and this government will do everything it possibly can—and I think it can meet its responsibilities—to make sure that there are no Americans involved in any actions inside Cuba. The basic issue in Cuba is not one between the United States and Cuba; it is between the Cubans themselves. And I intend to see that we adhere to that principle."

Marcello motioned to his bodyguard, Lou, to shut it off. He had had enough.

Lou, very large and wearing a close-fitting black blazer and dress pants, strutted over to the radio, turned the knob, and then collected their drinks to refresh them. When Lou left the room, David Ferrie took long strides to the head of the conference table, leaned his lanky frame over, and whispered his idea into Carlos Marcello's ear. It was a bonus but not surprising to Marcello that Ferrie, very bright with an ability to think unconventionally, came up with an idea of how to relieve Marcello's more pressing need to fulfill his Sicilian oath, literally translated, "to take the stone out of my shoe!" Ferrie devised a plan that used the deposed anti-Castro guerillas he personally knew in a paramilitary maneuver to "eliminate" the deportation menace.

Marcello simply listened, nodded, and a gradual smile came over his face.

"Don't worry, man, 'bout dat Bobby," Pecora popped his fist into his hand. "We gonna take care a dat sonofabitch."

Captain Ferrie had a clownish appearance with droopy eyelids, a new, brick-red hairpiece, and reddened eyebrows. He looked confused and scratched the back of his scalp where the wig was pasted down. He said aloud, "What you mean you gonna take care of Bobby?"

"Little fucker constantly nippin' at your heels," Pecora said.

"He's like the tail of a dog. He's not the head man!" Ferrie said.

"He not de head," Pecora agreed. He rubbed his small, right fist into his left palm. "It easy to lose sight of dat."

"Dat right," Marcello said, becoming louder and more boastful as Ferrie's idea sank in. "Yeah, what good dat do? You hit dat man an' his brother come out wit de National Guard. No, you gotta hit de top man and what happen wit de next top man? He don't like de brother."

The fullness of the idea settled and the room was quiet.

"But it's taking a big chance to go to Washington," Ferrie said. "You're not even allowed out of the state."

"What's a matter wit you, man?" Marcello said angrily. "When did I ever have to lift a finger to hit a man? But I tell you as sure as I sit here, somet'ing awful gonna happen to dat man."

"Dat's all I'm sayin'," Pecora added.

"Don't worry about that little Bobby son-of-a-bitch," Marcello said, seething with fury and vengeance from his deportation ordeal and growing more confident in this plan. "*Livarsi 'na pietra di la scarpa!*"

"Dat right," Pecora confirmed the oath.

Marcello nodded again. His eyes squinted with the knowledge that this would work. He smiled ever so slightly at the corners of his mouth. "De dog keep biting you if you only cut off its tail. But if de dog head cut off, de dog will die, tail and all."

Carlos Marcello smiled knowingly.

31)

A local spa can provide complete and final rest

Alek knew Minsk forward and backward, all the bus lines, the side streets, alleys, and thoroughfares, and still it felt like there wasn't much to it. Certainly nothing to report. Before World War II, the city had over 300,000 people but it had been annihilated by the war and reduced to less than 60,000 citizens. The Soviets had built it up as a model city with faithful, loyal, boring communists.

In his days at the factory, Alek occupied himself by meandering down every hallway to every locked door. He made annotations on every little nuance of the plant, the workers, and Soviet life, things only a trained observer would detail, and wrote encrypted letters back home to report his findings on production, manpower, and the Soviet system. It seemed that all they did was build radios and televisions for elite party members. There wasn't even a research-and-design laboratory in the factory. They simply retooled the line and made new devices based on the specifications from an engineering team in Moscow. He felt there wasn't any significant information to pass along from his work, or so it seemed, and the rest of Minsk also seemed dry of information.

The winter was very cold, which he hated, and, although he was very taken with Marina at first, the parties they attended began to feel the same. Even Pavel's drunken jokes became routine and stale. The theatre recycled old Chekov plays, which were pretty good, but then what would he do until the next production three months later? The opera was entertaining, but he did not like it enough to attend more than twice a month. But most of all, he knew he had to leave because he was not being effective as a spy and this lifestyle was taking a toll on his psychological frame of mind.

His boredom and ennui were becoming so overwhelming that he considered telling the Soviets precisely what he was doing here. What would it hurt? He had already given them all the radar codes and signals, about a year ago when he had first "defected," so what else could they do but let him go? Then he recalled from his training that they may try to make him work as a double agent. What would his response be? No, he couldn't even entertain that thought.

Alek needed to persuade the Soviets that the reason he wanted to leave was for Marina and his family to have more opportunity in the United States. But how could he convince them of that? For the Soviets to do that would be to admit that the good old U. S. of A. was a better place to live than the Soviet Union and they would never do that in a million years. So what could he do?

Maybe he should simply go into the U.S. Embassy in Moscow and announce his wish to return to the United States and let the Embassy work out the diplomatic paperwork. Yes, that's it. Sounds simple enough. But what about Marina and his wonderful daughter June? He loved them both dearly and wanted very much for them to be a family. He enjoyed family life and tried to make their life everything that he did not have as a child growing up. He gave June stuffed animals, and made a mobile, and read books to her in Russian even though she was still a baby. But there was only so much one could provide in the Soviet Union, especially in Minsk.

In order to marry Alek, Marina had taken a vacation leave from her pharmacy position in Moscow. She was then reassigned, but continued on a leave of absence, when she "officially" moved to Minsk and into his apartment. As her pregnancy became more noticeable, she stayed in their apartment more and more and she never did report back to the pharmacy to work. That did not go over well with her comrades at the pharmacy, or with the Soviet party officials in Moscow. But Marina and Alek never really knew her Moscow coworkers, nor she them, so she did not care.

Marina liked to attend twice-weekly meetings of a sewing club. This troubled Alek because she showed very little interest in actually creating any sewn garments. Still, she attended the meetings religiously and it made him wonder if that was how Marina reported to the KGB. Another reason he was extremely jealous of the meetings was that one of the other sewing club members was a suave, good-looking blonde man named Sasha from the ritzy Lenin apartment complex and Marina often talked about him. But when he confronted Sasha after one meeting and found him to be flamboyantly homosexual, or an exceptionally good actor, or both, it seemed to confirm the true intent of her attending the meetings: she *was* a KGB informant.

Alek took Marina and June, all bundled up, for a long walk along the Karchina River. He quizzed her about the sewing group, at first tangentially, because it was not an organized event where one person routinely led the group to learn more about sewing but seemed more of a gossip circle. Was anyone in the group prying into their private lives? Was the sewing room bugged? But even as he discussed it he realized why would she need to go all the way across town to a meeting when their apartment was probably bugged? What could she tell them at a meeting that she couldn't simply speak into the hanging lamp over the dining table? Maybe someone stopped by their apartment at a regularly scheduled time when he was at work? Finally he couldn't stand the doubt any longer and decided he had to ask her, in his now-fluent Russian. "Does anyone visit you regularly during the day?"

"No."

"No one?" he demanded.

"My aunt sometimes comes over," she smiled, using her fingers to amuse baby June.

"No one else?" he pressed.

"No, darling." Her smile faded and her bright blue eyes were searching. "What's the matter?"

Alek said nothing. How could he tell her that he suspected she was a KGB informer? He couldn't, but what the hell did she do during the day? He stared at her with angry suspicion and she simply looked at him as if he were crazy. The more he stared, the more she fidgeted until she spoke out with a tone as if she needed to explain something. "I go to the sewing meetings to learn about sewing and to talk to people. I need to get out. It's fun. You should get out more, too. Look, if it bothers you that much, I won't go anymore."

"No, no. It's, ah, it's okay." He was conflicted about telling her to act more like a wife as well as wanting to find out more about this sewing group to determine if it was really a KGB cover. Part of it made him upset that his wife was across town on a regular basis but he definitely didn't want that to be the focus of their talk. After stewing for a while, he decided he should simply let it be. But it irked him so much that he couldn't let it go. "You don't talk about it that much other than Sasha."

Marina looked at him blankly. What was she thinking? He then realized that if it were a KGB group or a weekly reporting, they would be wary of his questioning her. He needed to quickly cover this and he smiled broadly. "But you enjoy it, so yes, you should go!"

The rest of their walk was uneventful but he was extremely quiet and brooding. How could he figure out a way to certifiably establish if she was in, or reporting to the KGB?

Late one night after a sewing meeting, he sat down with her in the dining room. They had a white Formica table with a silver star-pattern and there were four white vinyl chairs around it. A simple old metal green lamp hung above it, although he carefully noticed the black cord appeared new and shiny, and it probably had been spliced onto the lamp's receptacle with a tiny microphone in place.

"Sweetie, I've made a decision." He took her hands, still cold from the bitter March weather, and warmed them in his. June lay peacefully sleeping in her cradle in their bedroom, just a few feet away. "I love you and June very, very much."

"What's wrong?"

"Nothing's wrong. I want what's best for all of us." He squeezed her hands warmly. "And I decided that what we need is to get back to the States where my family can help us out."

"Yes? You mean it? You want to take us to America?" She was very excited and smiled brightly.

"Yes! You need the help, too," he said carefully. "I can tell Junie's wearing you out."

"You mean it? No fooling?"

"Yes," he smiled.

"Where would we go?"

"To America."

"No, *when* would we go?" She gazed at him eagerly.

"Just as soon as I can arrange it. I don't think they'll be happy about it in Moscow, but I'm still an American citizen. If I want to go back, I can. I could create quite a stink if they tried to stop it."

"I cannot believe this!" Marina turned away, and then turned back quickly with tears in her eyes. "This is my dream, yes?"

"Yes, I know."

"This is so beautiful, Alek! I can't wait to meet your family and your mother. She'll be very happy to see June!" She stood up, leaned over the table, and kissed him excitedly. She ran into the living room for a notepad and pencil and began making a list. "This is the best news!"

Marina's reaction was overwhelmingly positive and she seemed so sincerely happy to move, to have their family grow-up in the United States and to meet his family, that he felt ashamed to have even considered her to be a KGB source. He shook his head in amazement at his own doubting ignorance.

Then he thought about his mother. He had not written to her in a few months and, in fact, the last time he had communicated with her was when June was born. She responded to his carefully worded, indubitably censored, five-page letter with a cheap greeting card with a stork and a baby in swaddling in its beak that said "Congratulations!" Inside was a very brief note. "Good luck. Mom."

He knew what that meant. It meant that he had always been a burden to her and now he would have his own burden to carry and good luck with that! Well, let her think that. He loved his family, which was Marina and June now. He didn't need her luck—not that she ever had any. What did she know of luck? Her husband Robert died before he was born and she had a hard time keeping a job because she took everything personally and was highly emotional. They moved often in pursuit of her worthless jobs, or in search of a cheaper place to live. Good luck, indeed.

He didn't need anything from her to help them through difficult times. He had Marina, and a beautiful daughter, and he was serving his country to the highest degree. She couldn't touch any of that. Still, he dreaded the moment that would inevitably come, maybe not the first day, or the first week back, but soon after they returned. She had moved back to Dallas, after her job in New Orleans was lost, and it struck him that if they lived near his uncle in New Orleans, then she couldn't run his life from Dallas. Mother would need to adjust, in Dallas, and that was the end of it. She would have to learn that he was a man now, he had his family, and she had to butt out.

Marina returned to the dining table with a quickly drawn up list of things to do before they left and she hugged his neck and kissed him on the cheek repeatedly. "I'm so excited, I don't think I'll be able to sleep tonight. It will be so beautiful! America! Oh, this is so fabulous. America. *America!*"

As she read the list of tasks to do, she did a little dance around the dining table. Her dancing, singing, and rejoicing had awakened June, who cried at first but stopped as soon as Marina went to her in the bedroom and picked her up, danced with her, and sang softly into her ear. "We're going to America! We're going to America to see your grand mama!"

He smiled again. Yes, it seemed like a wonderful idea. Why hadn't he thought of it before? He looked up at the lamp above him and examined the shiny cord leading into the shiny new-looking receptacle area. He stood, screamed, "Yee-hah!" and whacked the new receptacle as hard as he could.

He had a plan. Now he simply had to wait for the Soviet bureaucracy to allow him to leave, hopefully with his wife and family. If not, well, he did not want to think about that.

The following morning, he officially requested, in writing, that he be allowed to return to the United States with his wife and family. Now he had to wait for the KGB, masked in Soviet bureaucracy, to blink.

~ ~

Two months later Alek's formal request to leave the Soviet Union was denied. He was very depressed for quite some time but continued observing people and the factory inventory. Then, for the third time in four months, he officially requested in writing that he be allowed to return to the United States with his wife and family. His request was promptly denied for the third time.

Then suddenly a traveler came to Minsk on an Intourist tour, became "separated" from her tour group, and found him in the only outdoor coffee shop on Saturday morning. It was part of his Saturday ritual as he had been briefed, before he defected, that this would be how he would be contacted. He struck up a conversation with this traveler but he was surprised because Mrs. Marie Hyde was an elderly woman. After only a few words of polite introduction, he quickly realized that Mrs. Hyde was a very sharp cookie. She may have been an elderly tourist but she knew the Moscow subway system by memory, casually mentioned the names of a few of the local politicians who were also confirmed KGB agents, and she did this with a calm and ease that seemed to be a part of any casual conversation. It was as if she was an old friend and this was their weekly meeting at the neighborhood coffee house. Then one item stuck out in their conversation: Mrs. Hyde said, "Premier Khrushchev Z-R rifle is planning a trip to a local spa."

Alek's eyes widened. "ZR/RIFLE" was the code to assassinate a foreign leader. He was shocked and dumbfounded on how to respond. He thought quickly. "Oh, how wonderful. Spa treatments can be so restful."

"Yes," Mrs. Hyde stirred her tea nonchalantly. "A local spa can provide complete and final rest."

Alek looked around, took another drink of his cappuccino, and wondered if he should ask her to repeat it, but Mrs. Hyde was already on to the topic of visiting the art museum later in the afternoon with her two companions. She was with two American women. One was a sweet-mannered, rich blonde from California and the other dark-haired, spastic, and outlandish New Yorker. Both of them were oblivious to their conversation and were clearly tourists.

After a few more minutes of small talk, Alek stood up from their table in the outdoor café and asked the blonde, an innocent young woman named Janice, to take a photograph of them, and then subtly arranged for the newly built radio tower to be in the background. Unfortunately, Janice stepped back and turned slightly away from him to put the Palace of Culture in the background instead of the radio tower. Alek could almost hear the cursing of ONI officers in Annapolis, and later at the CIA in Langley, when they would unload Janice's camera in their "routine" check of overseas travelers and find yet another photograph of the Palace of Culture.

He spoke easily with Mrs. Hyde and the two women for another forty-five minutes about his work, the local political rallies, and life in Minsk in general. When Mrs. Hyde pointed out two dark Mercedes Benz cars pulling up, she subtly wiggled her nose and upper lip, and he left their table swiftly. He was quickly down the street and fifty yards away when he turned back to see four men approaching the three "tourists." The women pulled out their passports and Mrs. Hyde flailed her arms in a huff, and he chuckled and continued down the street.

His mind was racing, knowing that he was ready, but wondering when Premier Khrushchev would visit. It was exciting. He had another mission but this one would be much more dangerous than anything else he had ever attempted. His mission was to assassinate Premier Khrushchev!

~ ~

Alek waited for two more months. He patiently tried to find out more precisely when and where Premier Khrushchev would visit, which local spa, but no one seemed to know or care. He continued methodically, expertly, to casually ask people about spas, about the Premier, and about the chances of Khrushchev's visiting their city. Finally, the following spring, it was announced in the newspaper that Premier Khrushchev was coming to Minsk for a speech and to enjoy the spa in Verbinsk. He scouted various locations: the airport gates, the hall where he would speak, the spa in Verbinsk, just outside the city limits, and finally decided that the only place with any certainty, with a definitive time, would be the hall where Khrushchev would speak.

Alek expected that on the day of Premier Khrushchev's speech that security would be very tight, so he went to the hall very late at night the day before the speech. He had paid a trustworthy prostitute very well to come with him, turned her loose on the only guard on duty at the back entrance, picked the lock, and went to work inside the darkened hall.

He hurried to the podium at the front and, from a large brown paper bag, he pulled out a small hammer and chisel. He wedged up the floorboards next to the microphone jack very slowly and very carefully so as not to damage the wood. He used the chisel to dig a hole in the plywood subflooring, then down a little deeper into the cement foundation. He had pre-set the alarm time, pulled out the striking switch, and gently lay the pipe bomb into the hole, covered some debris around it, and gently tapped the floorboards back into place. Next he took out a small bottle of wood glue from the paper bag, squirted some over the floorboards, and spread some dirt around. Then he pulled out an old work shirt to wipe up the excess dirt, wiped the entire area clean, and placed the tools back in the paper bag. He stood back and examined the area closely in the dark. He could see the loose floorboards if he looked closely but it would probably be okay. Who looks at the floorboards in a hall?

The next day, when Premier Khrushchev came to speak, Alek was careful to be noticed at work by creating an argument with the foreman that he was running the assembly line too fast. When the foreman, a tall Estonian named Carl with a casual, happy-go-lucky approach was willing to let the incident go, he had to press him into making an official report in the manager's office, during lunchtime, around 12:30, which was exactly the time of the Premier's speech. Carl was not happy to miss part of his lunch break in order to file the report. The manager was also more interested in eating his corned beef on rye sandwich, and so at exactly 12:37, Alek was satisfied that he had a definitive alibi.

He waited, but not long. The public address system at the factory squelched followed by an urgent, special announcement from the State-run *Radio Moscow*. The radio announcer spoke smoothly but his voice was filled with concern. "Premier Khrushchev was unharmed by an explosion at Lenin Hall. Premier Khrushchev arrived in Minsk yesterday and was to give a speech in Lenin Hall, but as he was still greeting officials a bomb went off. Premier Khrushchev was shaking hands and speaking with his many admirers outside the hall when they heard the explosion. No one was killed but many party officials were injured. We do not know exactly how many people, perhaps as many as seven, including some high-ranking State Party officials, but, we repeat, our party leader Premier Khrushchev was unharmed. His speech will be posted in the newspaper."

The address system screeched as the radio broadcast was turned off and then went silent. Alek scratched the back of his head and returned to his position on the assembly line, which Carl began running promptly after the news announcement was finished.

The next day, the KGB went into the factory plant manager's office and questioned several people. After about twenty minutes, they pulled Alek off the line, asked a few brief questions as to his whereabouts in the last three days, and then took him downtown to the main KGB building. They interrogated him for seven hours, but as they questioned him he determined they had arrested him simply because he was an American with a military background. They had absolutely no evidence and he felt relieved.

It was also clear from their questioning that the KGB had not trusted him all this time and they had, indeed, bugged his apartment. Some of their questions contained phrases or direct quotes from him or Marina.

Later that week, the KGB arrested all his friends and associates, including Pavel, Rimma, Sonya, and all the women he had ever dated. They also questioned Marina for nearly ten hours. After twelve days of intense, thorough questioning, they still had nothing. But the KGB was not taking any more risks with this American.

The following Monday, Alek's original written request to return to the United States was declared "found" after having been "misfiled." He had filled out many bureaucratic forms and waited nearly one year, but this time they replied with an official declaration from the State Department.

He read the crisp, new letter with chagrin because they had "officially" responded to him three times before, but this new document carried veracity in the Seal of the State Office of Emigration. Officially, Alek was being deported by the Soviet Union and, as a special courtesy of the Office of the Politburo, he may also take his family, Marina and June. They were not, of course, part of his original request, so someone had put those facts together. Alek smiled to himself.

Then he smiled broadly despite his failed mission. Lee was going home again.

PART IV

32)

It's not every day a defector returns

At the airport in New York, Lee, Marina, and June were processed through the typical customs routine until the agent, a middle-aged man with glasses, looked at his passport. He looked up from under his hairy eyebrows, picked up the telephone on his desk, and said, "I've got a situation here."

"There's no situation." Lee was aggressive because he didn't want this guy getting physical or calling in any goons. This was his wife and child, and there was no need for them to be searched.

"It's all routine, sir, as you can understand." The customs official held up his passport as if it were an exhibit on trial and he was a dramatic trial lawyer: "Entering from a Communist country!"

The agent was a tense man and cleared his throat often. He clutched their passports and eyed their five pieces of luggage. "We'll need to—"

"No, you won't. Call the FBI or State Department." He was surprised that his English was a bit rusty and he had to search his memory. "Someone was supposed to meet us here. They're probably just late."

The man raised his eyebrows as if to say, Who is this talking *to me* in this tone of voice? He said, "Oh? *Who* was supposed to meet you?"

Lee crossed his hands in front of his suit jacket. This was characteristic bureaucratic harassment. "My wife and daughter are legally entering the United States. I have never disavowed my citizenship and we have the legal right to enter. Would you please let us pass?"

"No, sir, I can't do that," the official turned to look for the security agents.

A short, heavy man walked quickly through the door marked "Supervisor's Office". He wore a dark blue suit with a mustard stain on his blue tie, still chewing something, swallowed, and spoke with food still in his mouth. "This the one, Evans?"

The customs agent handed over their passports to the short supervisor, Kurt Orloff, who took them back to his office, waving at their luggage as they passed by it on a cart, and mumbled, "forget about it."

Orloff's office was a mess with papers on his desk and a thick, partially eaten tuna sandwich in white paper spread out in the middle. Two filing cabinets stood against one wall and a dull mirror hung on the far wall that probably held an observation room and recording devices. Still standing, Orloff made a brief telephone call to the State Department and hung-up. "They said your party is on his way."

Marina rocked June in her arms, adjusting her pink sweater around her small body, but the baby wanted more attention. Orloff said, "cute girl," trying to make light conversation, but when Marina bounced on her toes and cooed a Russian lullaby he raised his eyebrows with alarm. Now Orloff was suddenly nervous and hurried to his desk, picked up a three by five notepad, flipped it open, and wrote down something with a pen. He sat down and continued his questioning, dropping any pretenses of formal niceties. "Why did you defect from America, only to come back now?"

When Lee didn't answer, Orloff spoke his mind: "Are you working for the Russian Union now?"

He chuckled because of Orloff's blunt delivery rather than his misinformed question.

Then Orloff looked at Marina. "How 'bout you?"

"What?" she asked, still staring into June's pretty blue eyes.

"You K-G-B?"

Marina laughed. "Yes, here with daughter. We want top secrets. Where you are hiding rockets?"

Lee laughed, but Orloff took it seriously. He made a note in his small pad with his thick fingers pushing the pen and occasionally smearing the ink.

As was his habit, Lee studied Orloff's behavior. Perhaps this agent thought this incident would provide a break for his career and gain him a promotion. He strolled past his desk, to the far end of the room as if pacing, but watched Orloff closely. Orloff looked back at him and curled his hand over his notepad. "Move over there!"

June began crying and Marina bounced the babe up and down on her bosom. She cried louder, she was probably hungry, so Marina turned her back and sat on the edge of the agent's desk. She then unbuttoned her blouse and offered June her breast.

"Do you have to do that here?" Lee asked in Russian.

Marina responded, in Russian, "Where else do you suggest I do it?"

"Jesus Christ."

"Alek," she continued, "she's hungry."

Orloff didn't know what to make of the exchange in Russian but finally turned away from Marina, which left him facing the wall. Orloff fidgeted and then quickly stood up and went to the door. He seemed lost away from his desk, but he was politely respectful not to look in Marina's direction.

Lee waited for another question, but Orloff never said anything. Perhaps Orloff gave in to the idea that this was a family that needed a private moment or, more officially, that he would leave the whole matter to the officer from the State Department. After a few quiet moments, the agent from the State Department arrived, entering with a quick knock and bumped into Orloff's big belly. Marina stood with June and turned toward the corner, shielding them both. Lee moved forward to shake hands with the official but was blocked as Orloff stepped in front of him.

"Orloff?" The agent wore a plain gray suit with a white shirt and gray tie, and a gray fedora, and looked over Orloff with a frown of disapproval.

"Yes, sir," Orloff said.

"Agent Raikin," he flipped open his wallet to show his ID. "State Department. I'll need to use your office for about thirty minutes." Raikin had a quick, efficient manner that matched his thin physique. He set his black briefcase on the cement floor and took off his fedora, placing it next to Orloff's tuna sandwich. His hair was thinning, dark black with gray at the temples.

"Oh?" Orloff held onto Raikin's wallet awkwardly to examine the State ID. "What's the Traveler's Aid Society?"

"It's a division of the State Department that I like to call none of your god-damn business!"

"Well! Where's the CIA? Someone from the Domestic Contacts Division?"

"Are you not hearing me?" Agent Raikin barked, immediately flushed with anger. "I'm handling this. You're done!"

Orloff again looked at Marina, still nursing, then spoke toward the mirror on the wall. "I thought I contacted the appropriate office. The CIA handles stuff like this, maybe military intelligence. It's not every day a defector returns to—"

"Get the hell out!" Raikin screamed.

Orloff faced down Agent Raikin. "I haven't finished my investigation into their activities here. They were talkin' Russian about—"

"You're done." Raikin now spoke with an even tone, perhaps aware that he should not have raised his voice. He nodded at the door where two men in trench coats flashed badges that read "FBI" and another officer in a policeman's uniform looked into and around the office. Orloff started to close his notepad to leave when Agent Raikin said, "—And I'll need your notes."

Orloff handed over the small notepad and pointed to their passports on his desk. He was obviously miffed and pushed his way between the FBI men at the door. "They're your problem now!"

The FBI men nodded and the police officer closed the door behind them, leaving them alone in the room with Agent Raikin.

Lee asked, "What took you so long?'

"Traffic's a bitch. Musta been—"

"Please watch your language in front of my wife."

"Sorry. —An accident on the bridge or something." He looked at

Marina, as if seeing her for the first time. "Ma'am let's find you a private room. Murph!"

The door opened again and one of the men wearing a trench coat, with thinning red hair, looked in. "Take her down to Aiello's office—it's empty. We'll come down when we're finished."

"Right. Do you want me to start the Form Sixty-two 'E' for her?"

Raikin looked at Lee and gave an almost imperceptible negative glance with his eyes. "No, that won't be necessary."

As Murph pulled Marina by her upper arm, she looked to Lee with alarm and screeched, "Hey!"

"Please don't touch her!" he said sternly and Murph backed away with his hands up in mock horror.

Lee caressed Marina's shoulder to comfort her, but he thought, this is her introduction to America: more bureaucrats? He wanted to calm her so he whispered, in Russian, "It's alright. They're taking you to a room so you can feed June. I'll answer their questions."

Marina stared at him with a fearful, concerned look. He immediately realized that she was worried about any State official, as she had often mentioned her experience with lascivious bureaucrats in the Soviet Union, and she had also told him stories of her friends who had been raped in back rooms.

"It's okay," he squeezed her shoulders as she buttoned up her dress. "They won't bother you. He said it will only be a few minutes."

He kissed her cheek as Murph held open the door for Marina and June. Murph exhaled sardonically and rolled his eyes, and Lee thought he'd like to pop him once between his eyes.

Agent Raikin spoke with Lee for a very long time, much more than "a few minutes." It seemed that the information he had provided through letters, post cards, and photographs via Intourist travelers during the past two and one-half years was of little use. Now the State Department had a chance to obtain many more details about Minsk but Lee had nothing substantial to add. After about forty-five minutes, Raikin was becoming annoyed and snapped, "You expect me to believe that?"

"It's Minsk, for Christ's sake! They watched me constantly. What do you want me to say, I know where the ballistic missiles are built? They gave me no opportunity whatsoever and from what I saw there's nothing of strategic value."

"Okay. So what did you do for two plus years?"

"Mostly I went to parties, then I got married," he said.

"Parties and got married. Geez, that's tough," Raikin chuckled. "Sounds like a typical *special* agent's life. We'll see if we can change it up for you and find a nice desk job away from all the pressure of parties. Okay, tell me about your wife. Marina?"

Now Lee was annoyed. They obviously had documents on his marriage and monitored his mail. "She's innocent. Just a woman I met."

"You're positive?"

"Absolutely. Not even Marina knows why I came home."

"Okay. There was no one of circumstance at those parties?"

"A General here and there. The son of a military leader. They teased me with fluff information. I've told you all that. Didn't you monitor my mail?"

"Okay, okay. I'm just following procedure and making sure. Of course we read your mail. I have one note here, ah, we deciphered everything you sent, which was minimal, but what does "I miss the Texas heat" mean?"

He looked up quizzically. "It means I missed the Texas heat. It's colder 'n a sumbitch in Minsk."

"Oh. Okay." Raikin scrawled a note and said, "no meaning." He looked up, "Um, just for future reference in your transmissions, if circumstances should arise, leave out any phrases about 'heat,' 'over a hundred degrees,' anything like that, okay?"

He knew the code phrases for extreme tension or political unrest, and nodded.

"And nothing about coming in from the cold."

"Yes, sir."

"Okay, let's go over the Khrushchev event again."

"I gave you all the details," he said.

"I know, I know. I need to make sure it wasn't something else."

He was puzzled. "You mean my loyalty? Because I just spent three years of my fuckin' life overseas, behind enemy lines!"

"No, no, hey relax!" Raikin held his hands out and pressed the air downward. "Nerves and—"

"No, sir!"

"—and that you had done everything as planned and that you didn't miss any detail due to nerves or . . ."

"No," he said. He exhaled heavily, rolled his shoulders, and immediately relaxed. He stepped closer to Raikin and stared at his cool, dark eyes. "Or what?"

"Or fold."

"No. No, sir."

"You were certain of every detail. You never doubted your technique after the event?"

"No, sir. I performed my duty by the book. Khrushchev was gabbing outside the hall and went well past the time of the speech."

Agent Raikin nodded. He seemed satisfied and paced away from Lee, and then stopped to scratch the back of his neck. He had avoided something and finally he came out with it, slowly, in his roundabout fashion. "We've reviewed your file, had a meeting over at ONI, and you've done acceptable, no, *fine* work. It's clear that—"

"What is it?" he asked, wanting Raikin to get to the point.

"We want you to go to Dallas."

"But I, *we* want to live in New Orleans."

"We want you to go to Dallas." Raikin's bloodshot, brown eyes were unblinking. "Doesn't your mother live there?"

"I'm closer to my uncle and my brother's there, in New Orleans. I know people there. I can do more work there."

"Dallas. But we've got an office in New Orleans and maybe sometime, later, you can work there, but it's already been decided to send you to Dallas. We've got a man there who's very good and he's worked in Minsk, too, so you'll have that in common."

He spoke firmly, hoping this would settle it. "I'd *prefer* New Orleans."

Agent Raikin raised his voice and pronounced it with finality. "Dallas!"

"Yes, sir." He knew there was no denying them, once they had an objective in mind, so he realized they must have something already lined up for him. Hmm. What could it be? "Okay, who's my contact?"

"George de Mohrenschildt. Here's his p-file." Raikin handed him a personality folder and he flipped through it, studying the contents carefully. This may be the only opportunity he had to view its entirety and there would be documents in here that were nowhere else. There were a few typewritten pages, a card with his physical description: 6'0", 180 pounds, brown hair, blue eyes, no known scars or tattoos; a document with an official Nazi stamp on the top of it with a photograph next to it; State Department notes; a biographical report from the OSS with another passport-sized photograph of the same man in a French beret; and what must be a current photograph of de Mohrenschildt, much older now, middle-aged with gray hair, and standing in an oil field with derricks in the background.

"He's one of ours?" Lee asked.

"He is now. He's been around but he's top notch." Raikin exhaled heavily. "Look, we want you to learn more. Get ready for another assignment."

"Shit. I just got back. I haven't even seen my family."

"Not now, not now. The assignment's down the road. Don't sweat it. Take your time. Learn."

Learn? Lee thought. He just spent three years undercover. Who's this s-o-b to tell me "learn"?

Raikin pulled a folder out of his briefcase and rifled through it. "We'll help you get set-up in Dallas," he handed him a check for $435.71, "and just sign here."

Raikin handed him another filled-in form with a signature line at the bottom.

"What's this?"

"It's a promissory note to the State Department."

Lee signed it, scratched his right eyebrow with his left hand, and turned his attention to the documents as he thumbed through de Mohrenschildt's p-file again.

Raikin took hold of Lee's arm and shook his hand vigorously, so much that a few of the papers spilled out of de Mohrenschildt's p-file and onto the floor. It seemed an odd ending because almost two hours had passed in his "interview." But then Raikin grinned. "Welcome home, Lee."

He smiled back, remembering the "acceptable, no, *fine* work" comment. So, people had noticed and he was moving on to another assignment, which was good. But more importantly, right now, he wanted to comfort Marina and get a good steak. He thought about all the wonderful things he could have again in the United States that he had missed so much: the foods, movies, sports, music, but then found himself thinking about what his mother would say about Marina. And about June. She would disapprove, of course. But Marina and June were his family now. His mother would have to butt out and for good. Of course, she wouldn't. She never would. Well, that was too bad. She'd just have to understand *they* were his family now and that was that.

Okay, Lee thought, he would need to move with Marina and June to Dallas. As a child he had grown up in Dallas, so living there again wouldn't be too difficult. But who was this de Mohrenschildt?

33)

The twist

Sparky had to do something about his money problems. The club was only bringing in a total of about six grand a week, before expenses, and at that rate, it would take him fifteen years to repay Joe Civello and Carlos Marcello, if he wasn't rubbed out before then, and now the IRS was hounding him for back taxes of almost $40,000. The thought of being busted like Mr. Capone or Mr. Nitti on some tax thing made him very nervous. When the government doesn't have any evidence and can't do anything, this is how they take you down, he thought.

Sparky had to do something to make more money and he was constantly looking for new ways to do it. He tried to win money gambling, mostly on sports, but he was always a streaky gambler. He'd win two grand and then lose three. Sometimes a winner, usually a loser, coming out about the same. He needed something that could make him some big money and he needed to make it *now.*

One afternoon Sparky chatted with Andy, the Carousel Club's bartender, as he tried to think of a way to make more money. It occurred to him that it was fun to exercise in the gym and everyone was doing this new dance called "the twist." Young, old, it didn't matter, everyone was doing the twist. Chubby Checker had more than one hit record with the twist and other performers were trying to work it into their act. It came to him as he watched one of the girls, Ruby Rockets, dancing onstage, doing the twist while stripping down to a bikini. She was limber and smooth, and made her moves with seductive ease.

Andy was deep in thought as he worked on a crossword puzzle from the newspaper with a pencil. He pulled on his short kinky hair and his lips moved silently, testing words.

Sparky said, "What if there was something that made it easy for everyone to do the twist? And, better than that, to exercise at the same time as dancing? What could be better than a twist board? You just stand on it and twist. You're dancing and you're getting a workout on your hips and midsection! It's perfect!"

Andy stopped pulling his hair, patted it down, and looked up from the crossword puzzle. He frowned while nodding his head positively. "Yup. Sounds like a winner."

Sparky had several demonstration twist boards made and applied for a patent. He had the girls at the club dance on the boards to help promote them and he imagined so much money flowing in that he would become very rich.

He actively promoted his Twist Board, before he introduced each dancer, every night for four months. But his hard worked resulted in exactly two sales. One was to Arturo Miller, a salesman who had stopped in the club on his usual round of selling discounted champagne. Miller said he would try to see if his boss would be interested in marketing it in Milwaukee. The other sale was to his sister, Eva. After four months, Sparky was so thoroughly frustrated that he put away the Twist Board.

Two months later Sparky received a call from a Sales Manager in Milwaukee. "I found your business card attached to the back of some board."

"Yeah, that's mine," he said hopefully. "Do you want to market the 'Twist Board'?"

"I don't know what you're talking about," the manager said. "I called to let you know that Arturo passed away in a car crash last Thursday."

"Oh," he said. "I'm sorry to hear that."

"Were you a steady customer of his?"

"Who, me? Yeah, we bought a few cases of champagne now and then. But it don't sell that much here. Yeah, Arturo. He stopped in my club for a drink now and then."

"So you do you need any more champagne?"

"Well, you know, I bought a case now and then from Arturo."

"Terrific, I'll have Miguel Sanchez stop by on his next trip through Texas."

Sparky thought, "Arturo" and now "Miguel." What kind of outfit was this? but he wanted to steer the conversation back to his Twist Board.

"Alright, take care," the manager said.

"Wait," static noise fuzzed over the long-distance call so he spoke louder. "Did he talk to you about my Twist Board?"

"No, sorry."

"It's my own special invention. It combines doing the twist with ex—"

"Look, I got a lot of long-distance calls to make to tell people about Arturo. I'm sorry." The guy hung up. No goodbye or nothin'. It was his only lead for sales and it was gone just that fast.

Another two months went by and Sparky had not sold any boards. People were just not as excited about exercising as he was, and doing the dance called the twist was quickly fading from popularity. He still couldn't understand what went wrong. But he finally decided he had to let it go and find another way to make more money. The Twist Board simply didn't catch on and he was out fifty bucks.

34)

Sheep dipping

Lee wore his best jacket, dress pants, a plain white collared shirt and tie, his shoes were highly polished, twice, and he still felt underdressed. He always felt uncomfortable in situations with very rich people because they seemed to have something that he didn't, like a crest on a jacket that signified acceptance to the finest club in the region. But it was something more that his mother had engrained in him and he was sick of it, constantly fighting against it, because he knew that it did not matter. What mattered was the information they had. He tried to relax and knew there was nothing visible to set them apart other than incredible jewelry, the accoutrements of fine purses and stickpins, of silken dresses, crested jackets, and monogrammed shirtsleeves.

"Focus on the job," he repeated to himself. But he kept thinking about the cost of the babysitter, how little money they had, and how little money he made. He tried to ignore all of those things, too, but every rich accoutrement that he saw reminded him of just how poor they were.

Agent Raikin in New York had arranged Lee's first meeting with George de Mohrenschildt and now de Mohrenschildt was at least twenty minutes late to this exclusive tea party. He wondered if he would be a no show then thought maybe he and Marina should leave. He didn't want to be noticed as someone who did not belong here and de Mohrenschildt was his only connection to the party.

He had never been to a tea party before. As he waited, he realized he had never even known anyone who had been to a tea party before. Marina must have noticed him fidgeting and said, in her broken English with a beautiful Russian accent, "Relax. Have coffee."

Then he was tapped on the shoulder and, turning around, saw de Mohrenschildt with a statuesque blonde woman.

"So nice to see you," de Mohrenschildt said. "May I introduce you to my lovely wife, Jeanne."

"My pleasure," he said.

George de Mohrenschildt was taller than he imagined, or taller than the p-file stated. He was about six feet two, thinner than the 180 pounds in the file, but just as elegant and sophisticated as described. He carried a cigarette holder, wore an ascot, and spoke with effortless grace. "I'm so glad you could make it. Have you met the Hunts?"

"We've just arrived," he said casually, eyeing Mr. H. L. Hunt, the host of the party, wearing a navy blue blazer and white ascot. Hunt was an older, large man with greasy silver hair and a yellow-toothed grin.

Lee turned toward de Mohrenschildt but extended his arm toward Marina. "Please allow me to introduce you to my wife, Marina. We met in Minsk."

"Ah, Minsk—an enchanted place," de Mohrenschildt said and bowed, then pulled Marina close and gave her a kiss on each cheek with a third kiss on the right cheek. His blue eyes twinkled with charm. "It's beautiful by the Karchina River and the opera house is wonderful." He patted her handshake with his left hand and laughed easily. "Although I imagine it is just now becoming warm!"

A moment later de Mohrenschildt gave a wink and a graceful excuse, touched Lee's arm, and they left their wives to talk with each other. From across the room, he observed Mr. Hunt ogling Marina with his yellowish grin but then de Mohrenschildt introduced Lee to yet another group of "very important people."

He noticed that de Mohrenschildt had charm and grace that allowed him to move effortlessly from one topic in a conversation to another without the least hint of prying or intrusion. Lee remained quiet, simply watching de Mohrenschildt, and saw how he steered the conversation to oil exploration in the Caspian, or coffee plantations in South America, or to the United Fruit Company in Guatemala. In each case it sounded like casual conversation but at the same time he was gleaning information from all these people. What were their connections? Were they simply foreign businessmen, or diplomats, or were they playing for the other side? In spite of the fact that de Mohrenschildt was now on "our side," Lee kept thinking of two items in his p-file: his photograph on an official Nazi document and an agent's report that de Mohrenschildt attended pro-German rallies in America during World War II.

After an hour of seemingly effortless conversation, they were back with Mr. Hunt and his wife, a glamorous looking trophy wife with a beehive hairdo with too much jewelry—she wore a ring on each finger and several gold bracelets on each arm—and a tall drink. Hunt was eating yellow cheese off a silver platter as a waiter in a tuxedo with white gloves stood as still as a statue. de Mohrenschildt gave a tight-lipped smile, excused himself, bowed slightly, and moved away as if headed for another casual conversation.

Lee followed de Mohrenschildt outside to a patio with a large peanut-shaped pool with a huge fountain with a Greek statue of a maiden pouring water from a pitcher at the far end of the pool. de Mohrenschildt lit his cigarette with a gold-plated lighter engraved with his initials and relaxed his smiling face as if he was an actor finally off stage. He exhaled the smoke through his nose.

Lee glanced over his shoulder to confirm that they were alone and then joked, "Seems like you're ready to invest in oil and bananas."

"Mmm. Perhaps Uncle Sam is," de Mohrenschildt chuckled good-naturedly.

He nodded and, having thought about this moment for days, decided to launch into his prepared speech. "I was stationed at Atsugi Air Base in Japan. Radar operator for the U-2 flights over the Soviet Union. I went on a couple of missions in Japan and, ahem, 'defected'." He cleared his throat again for effect, "Ahem. For almost two years. Minsk, as you know, doesn't have much in the way of military or strategic importance. But it was an interesting experience. By the end I was bored stiff. Thank God I met Marina along the way."

"Who kept you board stiff."

He laughed. "Yes, she's a good woman."

"What brings you here?" de Mohrenschildt stood above Lee and locked eyes with him. He stared back.

"You do." de Mohrenschildt seemed as if he were evaluating him, so he simply spoke what he knew to be true to try to impress him. "You were born in Russia to nobility but your father had to escape to save you and your family in the Bolshevik revolution because your father supported the White Russians. You grew up in Poland, learned equestrian riding, and probably a good deal more about the nobility and upper classes. You received a university degree in Belgium and when World War Two broke out, you fought with the *French* resistance despite your Russian background. You came to the United States, lived in D.C. with a British agent and a U.S. Naval intelligence officer, and offered your services to the O.S.S. We were very happy to have you, starting up as we were, but you also continued spying for the French as well. Some people say you were recruited by the Nazis in the United States, but I'd like to think you were just keeping tabs on them when you went to pro-German meetings."

He carefully observed de Mohrenschildt's reaction and waited for him to speak.

After a moment, de Mohrenschildt exhaled and blew a smoke ring. "Do I honestly cut such a dashing profile? You make it sound," he chuckled affably, "oh, very mysterious and dangerous!"

"Considering that you probably knew people fighting in the Warsaw ghetto two thousand miles away, I doubt that you considered going to a pro-German meeting in a posh American suburb as dangerous work."

"Well, let's think about that." de Mohrenschildt took another puff and again exhaled it through his nose. "If the French think you're double-crossing them, they'd kill you straight out. If the Americans think you're supporting the Nazis, they'd deport you and give the French the sordid details before your arrival in Europe. If the Nazis knew you were spying on them, they'd either torture you for information, or cut the brake lines in your car, but either way you'd be dead to them as well."

"I see your point. But it couldn't have been as bad as the Warsaw ghetto." He walked casually behind de Mohrenschildt so he could keep the patio glass door in view in case anyone from the party came outdoors and approached them. Beside the pool were several black metal chairs, and one table with an umbrella, but they remained standing. "So why'd you attend the Nazi rallies?"

"Do you know a better way to get inside their organization and find out about them?"

He nodded.

"But, sir," de Mohrenschildt said politely with a grin, "you make it sound so easy. Let me ask, How do you think I gathered information on pro-German activists?"

"I would expect you followed them."

"That's unreliable and slow. I had to go to every pro-German rally and get as much information on every person who attended, especially the leaders."

He rubbed his chin. "Yes, that would be very dangerous, especially if you were caught."

"They'd see me as a traitor. Meanwhile, most Americans saw me as a Nazi sympathizer going to pro-German rallies."

He nodded again. It *was* dangerous.

de Mohrenschildt said authoritatively, "It's called sheep dipping."

"And you're a wolf."

"You learn quickly," de Mohrenschildt gave a sheepish smile and yet he still seemed to be sizing him up. His next statement sounded more like a challenge than a question. "So why'd you tell me so much information about yourself?"

"Was there anything I said that you didn't know?"

"You're very smart," his thinly slit eyes revealed a glint of amusement as he examined his finished cigarette. "Tell me about yourself, not just information, something that is revealing of who *you* are."

He thought for a moment. He figured he had nothing to lose and wanted this badly. "I love my mother but I can't stand her. My father. . . Not a lot to say there as he died before I. . . I'm the son of an insurance agent born with a mean streak of neglect."

de Mohrenschildt nodded solemnly. "I had a background check done on you and Agent Moore also said you were okay."

"You didn't check with Mister Raikin?"

de Mohrenschildt squinted and raised an eyebrow. "I have my own sources."

He was impressed. This guy was the real deal. de Mohrenschildt didn't even trust agents in the Company. After another quiet moment he felt the need to explain why he had said so much before. "Okay, I wanted to let you know that we're on the same page. To save time in the long run."

de Mohrenschildt took the spent cigarette stub out of the holder and crushed it in a green glass ashtray on the table. "Just where is this 'long run'?"

"It's wherever you and Uncle Sam need me," he said.

de Mohrenschildt smirked, opened his gold cigarette case with his initials engraved on top, took out another cigarette and placed it in the holder, but did not light it. He raised one eyebrow precisely as Claude Raines had done in the movie *Casablanca.* "It looks like this is the beginning of a beautiful friendship."

He chuckled as George put his arm around him. He liked George's reference to *Casablanca* very much as it implied that they were two fighters in a secret resistance against the fascists. "Come, I'll introduce you to Robert Stovall. He's the President of Jaggars-Chiles-Stovall. An old *Navy* man, too."

They entered the house again and George weaved his way through the party, nodding and exchanging pleasantries with everyone, and suddenly stopped in front of a well-dressed businessman. "Bob, this is a *very good friend* of mine."

Lee was dazed by his words and looked at him closely, while Stovall and George spoke to each other with familiarity. He had introduced him with such acclaim and sounded very convincing.

He returned his attention to their conversation. George said, "Well, if you can name one other man in all of Texas, who already has a high-security clearance, has worked with U-2 cameras, loading and unloading them, and knows photography, well, go hire them."

"Alright, George! You've made your point!" Stovall beamed and wore a diamond-studded tiepin. He set down what was left of a whiskey sour in a cut-crystal tumbler on a table to focus on shaking hands with authority. "Bob Stovall. I'm very protective of my employees. I need to be. It's government work, you know."

"That's fine, sir. I'm a Navy man myself, Marines, so I totally understand."

Stovall looked hard at him and continued to shake his hand, still quite firmly, and turned his wrist to see his Marine Corps ring. "Very good. You have clearance?"

"Yes, sir. Absolutely."

"That's fine. Just fine." Stovall finally stopped shaking his hand, eyed him closely for another moment, then continued. "We need someone to unload and develop the film from their special cameras, and then coordinate that to government maps. They enlarge some photos, I think, transpose them, I'm not really sure. It's all done in a dark room in the back."

"Yes, sir, I can do that. I have been trained in various camera techniques and, as Mister de Mohrenschildt mentioned, I have high-security clearance and experience with the U-2 program."

"Okay, okay," Stovall laughed and picked up his drink again. "You're hired! I'll talk to John in personnel and he'll set 'er straight."

It was only four days after his arrival in Dallas but he had met his contact George de Mohrenschildt and got a job at a job with high-security clearance working with U-2 photographs. He recalled his life in Minsk and was thrilled. For a change, everything went very smoothly.

35)

You never forget your first cherry

Sparky stood in an old beer hall in Chicago, back in the union organizing days, and the union guys were making speeches and laughing. He could see that it was going well. But then someone shot the President, by mistake of course, and the guy died. So his boss took over as the Union President and the music "Happy Days Are Here Again!" played. But then the cops came and got the idea that something wasn't right. The cops screamed, "This isn't kosher! This isn't kosher!" louder and louder, trying to be heard over the music. "This isn't kosher! This isn't kosher!" and then they started asking him questions, yelling at him, and the music was gone, and the cops kept after him. First the cops, then the lawyers, and then one judge, a huge, giant judge with enormous eyes under his wire-framed glasses like his second foster father, and through it all there was a vile smell. It was hideous. He tried to explain it all again to the gigantic judge. "This asshole started mouthing off, slow at first, like they always do, little snide comments." Then suddenly the asshole was up on the witness stand talking to everyone like it was his personal podium. His boss, Paul Dorfman yelled from the crowd, "Do something for Christ's sake!" Then short little Leon Cooke charged up to the witness stand with his black jack and hammered the asshole pretty good, wailing on him with his thick black rod. He pushed his way through the crowd, wanting to get in his own good licks, smack this asshole a good one, when the jerk started fighting back! He grabbed his pistol, the heavy, used rod from Mr. Capone, and shots rang out! Loud blasts and men screamed! He wanted to shoot his gun. Maybe he could hit that asshole from here, way in the back of the room, and take him down. "Come on," he thought, squeezing the gun, "I want to pop that asshole!" The crowd of men drew back, showing an opening, and the guy was laying in a pool of blood, holding his side, curling up like a baby and going to sleep for good. But it was Leon! His good friend, Leon, who lay still on the cement floor, not the asshole. Leon stared fish-eyed at the ceiling. A colossal grunt and Leon was dead with his skin decomposing into a dark gray-blue. The gun felt hot in his hand. It was stiff and he tried firing a few shots to break up this crowd before the police arrived, and he pulled the trigger but nothing happened. He pulled it again and again and nothing happened. What was wrong with this gun? A bullet dropped out of the barrel. A tiny turd hit the floor. He had to get rid of this gun! Then the police came pouring in, clowns out of a Keystone cop car, laughing and hitting everyone over the head with rolled-up newspapers repeatedly. It was only a matter of time until they got to him. They were working their way around the room and getting closer. He felt hot, sweat was seeping from every pore, and he wanted to put the gun somewhere. He had to hide it! He looked around for a hiding place, maybe under a beer barrel, or toss it in the river, and he looked up to see a reddish-brown spot on the ceiling. Why was there a spot on the ceiling? What did that mean? The cops were getting closer. They would bust him next and he still had the hot gun in his hand. God, he had to do something and quick! What should he do? Leon was dead! He had to do *something! The police closed around him and grabbed him, they saw the gun!, and wrestled him to the ground. The cement floor was cold and hard and he struggled to get free but there were too many of them! He couldn't move but he held on tightly to the gun as if his life depended on it. They wouldn't get that from him. He squeezed the rod harder and thought, Hold on to it!*

Sparky awoke in a sweat, holding his dick. It was stiff and hot. Christ, not that dream again, he thought.

He rolled out of bed, went into the bathroom, washed off, and looked at his tattoo of "Leon" on his arm. He was glad those crazy days in Chicago were long gone. He had moved up so much since Leon's death, when Paul Dorfman ran Chicago for a while, and after that with Mr. Giancana. He had done well.

Still, he felt remorse that Leon had died, looking at nothing in particular except a god-damn stain on the ceiling. He wondered if Leon's family still missed him, even after all these years? Probably.

He splashed more cold water on his face. He had current problems to worry about, like making more money to pay off Carlos Marcello and Sam Giancana, keeping things running smoothly at the clubs, dodging the IRS assholes, and finding a woman for tonight. He hated going to these fancy parties without a real woman of his own, but he knew he could always get one of the dancers from the club to go with him. Yeah, he had his own problems.

Sorry, Leon, he thought. He looked at his tattoo again and fell into a daze, remembering how they went to so many meetings back in the union organizing days and shared beers and a lot of laughs over their good fortune. Then he remembered what Mr. Capone had said: "You never forget your first cherry." It had two meanings, but more importantly it was the first person you killed. Mr. Capone was right once again. He couldn't forget Leon, even if things did work out okay.

36)

George the Fourth

At another party, this one thrown by George H. W. Bush, oil magnate and political hopeful, George de Mohrenschildt questioned an oil geologist from Germany for several minutes. George had greeted Max Baer with a brief heil Hitler salute and a click of his heels but no one other than their immediate party and Baer saw the flash of a salute, except Baer's wife, who made a quick frown that she covered with a charming smile and handshake.

Baer chuckled slightly and extended his hand warmly, "Sehr gut to zee you again, Georges."

"The pleasure is all mine, all mine!" George replied. "I'd like to introduce you to my friend, Lee."

He shook Max Baer's cool, limp hand and was left with an aloof, unfriendly impression, which was par for this crowd. He continued to observe him and listened very closely as George carefully and deftly interrogated the geologist about the Caribbean, dashing through various oil fields and political regimes in Mexico, Haiti, Costa Rica, and Cuba—a country with a tumultuous government that seemed to be the hot-button topic of the conversation.

"Cuba has some potential," Baer said, "but this Castro is some character!"

There was a brief pause and he could tell that the issue of Castro was the key to the entire conversation. Where did Baer stand? How would George approach it?

"He's difficult to work with, that's true," George responded. Then he asked with an innocent tone, "Tell me, what do you think of General Walker's plan for him?"

"I'm not sure I know what plan you're referring to. Who, General Walker?"

"Yes, General Edwin Walker. The right-wing, hopeful senator from Texas."

"Oh yes, the one who's been making speeches," Baer said, obviously taking the moment to check the lay of the land and formulate his response. "He's got the right idea, if I follow you. But that's in regard to Cuba only. I don't know much about him other than that."

George half-chuckled under his breath and Lee understood, by the nature of that stifled laugh, that this was something to discuss later. The party continued for another two hours with lots of small talk about theater in Texas and art collections in various museums in the country and around the world. Mr. Bush tried to bring conservative politics into the discussion but George was not interested in him. Before the party, de Mohrenschildt had explained that he had known of Mr. Bush from the CIA, but didn't like him as he acted more important than he was and repeated bad jokes that were often off-color, which was an unforgivable personality flaw according to George. When the party ended, Lee and George and their wives were among the last people to leave.

Even though Lee was anxious to discuss a number of details and issues with George, he kept up polite conversation with their wives until George pulled his turquoise-blue '59 Ford Galaxie into the driveway of their rented bungalow. George parked the convertible and got out of the car to formally kiss Marina on both cheeks to bid her farewell. He then asked Marina to excuse Lee and himself for a moment, and she waved goodbye to Jeanne in the front seat and went into the house to greet their babysitter, who was holding June.

George put his arm on his shoulder and walked him halfway toward the house, away from the idling Ford and his wife, and quickly quizzed him. "What's your first point?"

"Baer agrees that Castro needs to be removed but he may not support it financially."

"Right. Two?"

"Also on one, you've got some oil investment potential in the other countries like Haiti," he said. "Two, I'm not positive but Baer appears supportive of any initiative against Castro but this needs further probing at a later date. But what's this about General Walker?"

"That's right. But you need to become an expert on Cuban politics and anyone remotely associated with Cuba. Practice a little speech about *every* side. If you knew about Walker's policies, then the way Baer dodged that shows he isn't ready for the extreme tactics Walker proposes."

"Yes, I'll do that." He was curious about many things, but stayed away from the heaviest concern weighing on his mind, and asked an item of curiosity instead. "Why the Hitler salute?"

"It was for their reaction. It's a quick gauge of someone's stance. Are they humored, infuriated, intrigued? You'll need to learn how to do something like this with great subtlety and deftness, as a quick background check on any source."

"Yes, I observed how you did it without anyone at the party noticing." He was still reluctant to ask his next question but instinctively knew that this brief conversation was headed toward this one, weighty issue. "Tell me, who is General Walker?"

"Are you kidding me?" George looked at him harshly, then seemed to let it go instantly. "I forgot for a moment that you've been out of the country for a while. You need to study politics. Walker is a fast-rising fascist, right here in America! He's a *dangerous* man and he's gaining in popularity almost daily."

"Hmm, okay. But why is—"

George cut him off bluntly. "Do you understand what one fascist, Lee, just *one* can do? Look at Hitler. If someone had stopped him at an early stage, the world would be a different place. I'm not saying World War Two would have been avoided, but consider the outcome if someone much less fascist than him would have been in power. We tried a few times, even later in the war."

"Yes, I agree with you."

"You need to be a hunter of fascists."

It was an order. Did George really mean it to the degree implied? Or did he simply mean to hunt down fascists with information? He had to ask because as an order it held grave consequence. He looked him level in the eyes. "Hunt them down through *information* and expose them?"

George squeezed his shoulder firmly as he returned his stare. "We are in the unique position to take action, son. And let me tell you this honestly. I have never met or worked with anyone that I consider myself closer to than you. Do you know this? You are like a son to me."

"Thank you, sir." He was truly touched. He smiled, "That'd make me George the Fourth!"

George chuckled at the joke but then glanced over his shoulder to ensure that Jeanne was still in the car and no one was approaching on the walkway. He added, "*This* fascist needs to be eliminated."

He swallowed hard. It was the ultimate assignment. *Again.* Except this time it was not a foreign leader like Premier Khrushchev. It was a rising fascist in the United States. He nodded slowly. He had heard through the grapevine of other important targets being eliminated in the United States and he was slightly surprised that *he* was tabbed to do it. Still, he had the training, had the experience, and knew he could do anything they asked of him. As he stared into George's eyes, his confidence was building with every passing moment. He was happy that this was his destiny. This was the best way to serve his country. It was his patriotic duty. "I'm ready. I'll do it."

"Good." George tore a five-dollar bill in half and gave him one half. "*Sergio* will have the other half. He'll know all the details. Go over the plan with him many, many times, and don't execute it until you're absolutely certain it will succeed."

He felt very proud. His country had given him another mission and was depending on him. He was also very happy that George had said he was "like a son" because he had grown close to him over the past few months. He viewed George as a mentor and a father-like figure, in place of his own missing father, and a growing emotion welled up inside of him of pride, respect, and love.

Yes, this was outstanding news! He would do everything in his capability to carefully execute his mission for George and for his country. He could do this. He was finally going to do something historic and he felt very proud.

37)

Denial in public

It was just after 5 p.m. Saturday afternoon and the Carousel Club was open and running smoothly. Andy and a second bartender, Budd, were already busy and the scheduled dancers were on time, which was a small miracle in itself, the drummer and trumpet player looked classy in their blue velvet suits, and the crowd was getting stirred up. Everything was going great.

Sparky was happy that the club had opened without problems because he wanted to go to his nephew's party at 7 p.m. Secretly he was hoping to get a few moments alone with the rabbi. In his daily life he denied being Jewish to cut off any conversation about it and he would tell people he was an atheist. It fit well with running a strip club, with his mob associates, and even among his family it was easier to say this and be done with it. But he was searching for more, for some meaning, and he wanted to ask the rabbi's opinion of denial in public and practice in private. Could that work? Was that possible?

He had brought his best suit to the club and stepped into his back office to change. He had just finished buttoning up the fancy white dress shirt when he heard a loud crash and the sound of breaking glass. Then he heard several men yelling and dashed for the main room. A man was onstage and clenched in combat with the trumpet player, who was trying to smash his right fist down on the man while holding his trumpet away at extended arm's length. The man was wearing a white cowboy shirt with brown piping and shiny buttons, and jeans. The straw hat on his head was cocked back and tilted to one side from wrestling with the trumpeter.

He leaped onstage, splitting the two fighters, and threw a right uppercut that caught the cowboy flush on the chin and sent his hat flying. The trumpeter looked at him wild-eyed, as if he was insane, or maybe he thought he had control of the situation, which he obviously did not. He pushed him aside but for some reason the trumpeter took a swing at him but he dipped down slightly to avoid the punch. The cowboy had recovered from his uppercut and threw a surprisingly crisp left jab that caught him on the cheek and he saw his own saliva go spraying across the stage. That made him more mad than hurt, he could always take a punch, and he rushed the man, pushing his face, then wrapping his hands around his body and lifted him off the ground. Then arching his back, he slammed him down while flopping on top of him. They crashed hard to the stage floor with a very loud thud.

"Shit!" the man yelled and began kicking wildly as he held on to his face with his hands. Then the man bit down on his right forefinger and son-of-a-bitch if he didn't bite off the last part of his finger. It felt wet and blood ran out like a garden hose.

His immediate reaction was to turn and lift up his hand to slow the bleeding and the jerk took that moment to ram an elbow into his gut. Now he was really pissed off.

He grabbed the man by his short hair and smashed his head down on the stage repeatedly until a tooth went flying. Blood splattered everywhere. The trumpeter and Andy were on him now, while the drummer and Pete, a regular and a good guy, pulled the cowboy away from under his grasp as they scrambled to their feet. The cowboy slipped as he stood up, his boots slid on blood, but he kept his balance.

He shook off Andy and the trumpeter, threw a quick right-uppercut, left-hook, right-cross combination and every punch found their target of chin-body-nose and left the man with buckling knees and fixed gray eyes. He was out cold on his feet and he wound up for one last big right hook to the mouth that snapped his head back and sent his front tooth flying. It was a damn fine punch. The guy collapsed to the floor.

"That's my cousin, Purdy," the trumpeter said.

"Yeah?" he said, breathing heavily. "So what?"

"He's my cousin!"

"Yeah, so?"

"I owe him forty bucks," the trumpeter shrugged and looked away. "He was trying to take my trumpet."

"Christ."

Andy and Pete picked up Purdy, still unconscious, and carried him through the club, down the stairs, and out into the parking lot. Sparky followed them, just in case, and outside the cowboy became conscious in the fresh air. He looked around while still in their hands, then felt his bloody mouth and mumbled something.

Andy and Pete dropped the guy to the dirt lot and he slowly got to his feet. He looked around as if lost, a few new customers were making their way to the entrance, and Purdy wiped his bloody mouth again.

"Get the fuck outa here!" Sparky yelled.

"You' be hearin' f'om my lawya!"

"Go fuck yourself!" he yelled.

The man wiped his bloody hand on his jeans as he stumbled two rows over to a specific car, apparently his, put his keys in, and started up the Ford. He rolled down the window and yelled something again but the revving engine and gravel kicking underneath the tires drowned out his words.

Sparky shoved his left middle finger up in the air, and then examined his bloody right forefinger again. The top portion was gone and the bright white knuckle was partly exposed with loose flesh around it. He took out his handkerchief and wrapped it.

When he went back inside Glen, another regular, was stepping down off the stage with a bloody towel in his hand as he had apparently cleaned up the stage. It was kind of quiet so Sparky hollered at the musicians to start playing again and just that easily Magical Melissa bounced on stage and everything was back to normal again. The second bartender, an ex-Navy guy named Budd who filled in occasionally on busy nights, had a shot of whiskey waiting on the bar. He picked it up and downed it in a single gulp.

"Yor hand's bleedin' like crazy and you got blood on yor shirt," Budd said, refilling the shot glass. He winked and placed a tall beer with a perfect head in front of him. "But I'd shore hate to see tha other guy!"

He smiled and chugged the beer. Andy pulled out the first aid kit that was behind the bar and took out some gauze and tape. He took off the bloody handkerchief, sprayed some seltzer on it, and then doused vodka over the nubbin. Andy glanced up with a steely, steady gaze, then quickly wrapped the gauze around the finger, twice, three times tightly, then taped the bottom, and it was done. Just that quick. He recalled that Andy had spent some time as a corner man for a boxer and he obviously had not forgotten his deft skills with a medical kit.

He nodded thanks and went to his back office to change out of his shirt and dress pants. He decided he'd call his sister to say that he couldn't make the party. He just didn't feel like going. He shook his head and raised his eyebrows. Maybe he'd talk to the rabbi another time. But then again, what was the point?

38)

Happy hunting

Lee met Sergio Arcacha Smith at the local laundrymat by matching their halves of the five-dollar bill that George de Mohrenschildt had given each of them. Arcacha Smith was a big man, about six feet tall and muscular, with a trim black mustache and dark complexion. He had rugged features and Lee recalled reading his p-file where a photograph showed him in Army gear as if he had recently been through training camp. In the file he had a New Orleans residence but he had been an official in General Batista's Cuban government and was very active organizing a military coup to overthrow Fidel Castro. He was also the head of the Cuban Revolutionary Council and, he suspected, Cuba was probably a hot-button topic for him. They went to a nearby park where they carefully planned the details of their mission.

Sergio was the spotter and driver as well the lookout and cleaner, and they planned the mission over several nights. Lee had taken reconnaissance photographs with his camera and they studied and discussed the details over a map and the photographs of the target's house. Sergio explained that as he was from New Orleans he would need to drive the planned route several times to become familiar with it, so he would need at least a few more days. They realized a church near the target's house would have people milling about on Friday night and so their presence in a secluded, rich neighborhood should not be noticed on a Friday. After their fourth meeting, Sergio felt the plan would not get any better.

He suggested the timing was right to execute their plan *this* Friday at dusk. Lee agreed.

He wrote a detailed note for Marina, in case anything went wrong, and left it on the desk in their bedroom. He wanted to look as inconspicuous as possible so he wore a pair of khaki pants and a white work shirt. He slipped his rifle into a long bag, tossed the cleaning gear in a separate drab-olive duffel bag, and waited for Sergio at the bus stop.

A little old man with a black walking cane and glasses hobbled up and sat down on the bench. The elderly man said, "Your bag reminds me of the one I carried in the Spanish–American War."

Lee said nothing and looked down the street for the bus. It was a little warm for April, puffy storm clouds were gathering overhead, and it felt humid like it might rain.

Finally, Sergio pulled up in a light green 1959 Ford Galaxie. Lee was stunned because this was exactly the same kind of car that George de Mohrenschildt had except this one was green and a hardtop. In all their planning, Sergio had not mentioned the specifics of the car.

He opened the door and tossed his bag and gear over the front seat and into the back. The old man on the bench said, "Happy hunting!" as he stepped into the car. It was a *very* odd remark and he figured the old man had been sent by de Mohrenschildt to check up on them, using the "hunter of fascists" words as code. He said nothing but stared at the old man, who adjusted his glasses on his nose to look closer at him, then leaned over to look at Sergio behind the steering wheel.

"Who's chore buddy?" Sergio said with his thick Cuban accent.

"No one," he said, and they took off.

Lee suddenly felt very nervous, as if he were being watched, because this was the same type of car that George drove coupled with the old man's comment. Also, he didn't like working with people he didn't know extremely well. He thought of his nervousness and wondered if he should mention it to Sergio, then quickly knew he should *not*. He recalled from his training it was better to remain focused and not be negative, so he remained quiet as Sergio drove their planned route, avoiding the freeway, by taking Griffin Street instead.

"Chew ever going to say somethee'n'?" Sergio asked.

"No."

"So chore all chummy with some old gringo on the beench, but chew doan say notheen' to me? Sheet."

"I just met the old man. No, I didn't really meet him. He said a few things. I didn't say anything to him. George may have sent him."

Sergio looked at him for a long moment, as long as he could before he had to look back at the road ahead of them. "Tha's loco, man."

"Alright," he said, not wanting to talk but preferring to focus on what they had to do. Then he thought, maybe talking relaxes Sergio? He said, "What do you want to talk about?"

"How 'bout Castro?" Sergio's accent was strong and he rolled his r's in "Castro."

"Sure," he said. He knew clearly what Arcacha Smith's position was but responded politely. "What do you think?"

"Fucker's crazy. He-e's got to go."

He did not move or say anything, and Sergio kept looking over at him. It was amazing what people would say about politics or religion without knowing the beliefs of whom they were speaking. But perhaps Sergio was blatantly testing him for a response? Should he go into politics? What did Castro have to do with *this* mission? Maybe Cuba and Castro were Sergio's personal litmus test.

"So—say sometheen'!"

"Okay, at first it seemed clear that he was trying to raise his people from under the yoke of General Batista, who I think we all agree, was quite a son of a bitch. But he was *our* son of a bitch, as they say. But Castro clearly stated, right in New York City, that he was open to many different approaches to government. He's a very smart man, he received a law degree from the University of Havana, you know, but he has swayed from his Marxist roots. His recent statements about the Soviet style of government was, I believe, more of a provocation on his part to seek a response from the United States but it's obviously backfired and now he needs protection, and he's being backed into a corner by his own words. I think it was a monumental mistake by the U.S. not to court him and embrace him when he first overthrew Batista, but that's all water over the dam. I'd advocate restoration of diplomatic relations and trade, but he's straying further and further from truly helping his people and clearly the U.S. should do something to step in and help, if not to overthrow Castro, then at least to help the Cuban people who are starving, many of whom are without electrical power, clean water, or sanitary facilities. It's a colossal tragedy that needs to be addressed politically, economically, and, if necessary, by force."

Sergio stared at him with furrowed brows. "Who da fuck are chew again?"

"Just another guy trying to help our country."

"Yeah." Sergio was quiet for the next few blocks but occasionally looked over at him. He had obviously passed Sergio's test but his little speech had also made Sergio uncomfortable as if it was *too good*, and he needed to be watched. Or maybe they were both being paranoid because this was their first mission together.

As they approached Turtle Creek Boulevard, Sergio spoke again, but in a quiet tone, a near whisper, as if someone may be listening. "Okay, I'm going to stop in de alley behind de target. Chew geet chore bearings, site de target, and I'll deeg a hole in de deetch on de back side of de car. When chore done, give me de rifle, I wipe eet down, put eet in de bag, an' we bury it together. I jump in from de passenger side and den we move slo-o-owly down de alley to Avondale and we're out of here."

He nodded with confidence. This guy was professional. "That's good."

It was nearing seven o'clock, dusk colored everything purplish-black, and it was very quiet as the tires crackled tiny pebbles under the car. Sergio peered over the dashboard and motioned toward a large house and spoke softly, "Is that eet? Did I miss somethee n'?"

He recognized the house from his reconnaissance mission the previous weekend even though it was becoming hazy dark. "No, that's it. When we're leaving, just act natural like we're pulling away from a gas station. Not fast, not slow."

"Okay." Sergio pulled off the road and into the alley, about fifteen feet wide, slowing down to find the precise spot to park.

No cars were in the target's driveway and Sergio threw it in park, across the alley from the distinctive lattice fence, but virtually blocking the alley. It was a secluded spot but it was almost time for the Mormon service to begin at the church at the end of the alley. Several people could be seen in the church parking lot about forty yards ahead. They milled about talking, with a few cars pulling into the lot from the street in front of the church. He and Sergio had timed their arrival in this exclusive, residential area so they would not be conspicuous as other people were around but some distance away. Still, they would need to be quick.

He reached into the back seat, grabbed the bag with the rifle, and slid out low to the car. Sergio left the engine running and came around with his head down as if he were looking at the tires. Nice move, he thought.

Lee knelt down by the front right tire, as if he were checking the pressure, and pulled the rifle out. He peered over the hood of the car and then moved casually to the lattice fence, keeping the gun next to his leg to conceal it. He examined the various windows until he saw the back of a man's head sitting in a den. A single lamp glowed under a green shade. General Walker was working at his desk and the rest of the house was very dark and quiet.

Sergio grabbed the duffel bag with the cleaning cloth from the back seat and took out a small green Army shovel with a swivel head from the back floor area. He dug powerfully by the side of the car into a drainage ditch that ran alongside the alley, with his biceps flexing under his rolled-up white sleeves. With only a few strong strokes Sergio had created a small trench four feet long and six inches deep. Sweat dripped off his forehead and he nodded to him.

He looked back at the target. He was unmoving at his desk. He swung the rifle up onto a notch in the latticework fence and steadied it. Peered into the sight. Drew the crosshair down to the base of his neck and the thickness between his shoulders, then raised it to his skull. Exhaled slowly. Squeezed the trigger.

BLAM! The bullet slammed into the window and the target was suddenly off the chair and on the floor. He couldn't tell if he hit him or not, but he was no longer in the window frame. There was no sound or movement in the house.

A cloud of smoke hung in the thick, damp air, and he could smell gunpowder. He turned around, hustled over and handed the rifle to Sergio, who had a cloth out and wiped down the gun swiftly. He slipped the gun back into the bag, dropped it in the hole, and they pushed and stomped dirt over the hole rapidly.

Sergio walked around the car to the driver's side and hunched in behind the steering wheel, as he opened the passenger door and slid into the front seat. The vinyl was warm and he could smell something in the car but couldn't identify it. He closed the door and they pulled away gently, gradually picking up speed. A little black boy came running out the back of a house into the alley and stared at them as they drove by.

"Jus' like clockwork," Sergio said, staring at road seriously. "See, no problem."

He looked at Sergio dubiously. He felt odd about leaving the gun there, but it was wiped clean and there was no way to trace it to him. No, it would be okay. He thought about other aspects, if anyone had seen them get out of the car, but he had not seen anyone. Perhaps neighbors heard the gunshot, but so what? Also, it wasn't his car, but it concerned him. "You're going to ditch the car in Dallas."

"No. Ee's my cousin's but as soon as we get back, I'm takeen' the battery out. He woan' be able to move it out of his garage for a long time."

There was an odd smell in the car. "Do you smell anything?"

Sergio shook his head no and sweat dripped off his temple. His white shirt was wet.

Okay, Lee thought. What else? Nothing. Everything had gone very well. Sergio did an excellent job. Is there anything at all to be worried about? No. There is nothing. It all went fine. Guess it'll be on the news. "Turn on the radio."

"I doan' like chore music," Sergio said.

"What music?" he asked.

"Western music. Country, I mean. Rock and roll ees okay, but I prefer salsa."

"Not music. Turn on a news station."

"Oh."

Sergio turned the dial and found a newsman reading stories haltingly. There was some white noise but the announcer could be heard above the static. He reported nothing for the entire drive back.

Sergio pulled over at the bus stop and Lee thought of the old man from earlier in the evening. No one was around, but he said, "Drive around for awhile."

"Sheet. Chew doan say notheen'. Ee's like torture." Sergio stared at him, then finally said, "I'll drive if chew talk."

"Just drive," he said.

They went downtown, followed the flow of traffic around the main avenues, and went by a few businesses that had neon lights glowing. It reminded him of his drive around Tokyo after his mission with Hiroshi and he smiled faintly. That seemed like such a long time ago.

They drove past a strip club that had a red neon sign that read "Exotic Dancers" and continued to listen to the news without talking. He wondered why there was no news on the radio but maybe it was still too early. Someone would need to find the body, call an ambulance, and so on. After a long time, he said, "Alright, take me back to the bus stop."

When they arrived back in his neighborhood, at the isolated bus stop, it was very dark and quiet. He got out of the Ford Galaxie and he almost said, "see you later," but that was one thing he did not want. He did not want to see Sergio ever again. This mission was over. "Bye."

He walked back to their bungalow and listened to the stillness of their neighborhood. Crickets called excitedly and bugs swarmed around a single streetlight. He quietly opened the front door of the house and glanced at the clock on the wall near the door. It was nearing eleven o'clock.

Marina stood up from the sofa, clutching a piece of paper that she raised at him angrily. "Where you have been? What is wrong? You are white like ghost!"

He said nothing, trying to avoid her, but she continued excitedly in her broken English. "And smell bad. Your shirt wet, sweaty. You are okay?"

Marina held his hand-written note and breathed deeply through her nose with her lips clenched. She furiously demanded, "What this note?"

39)

Close Call

Lee had left a note in Russian for Marina and, as he had not been caught, he knew she was worried over nothing. He arrived home around eleven p.m. and as soon as he walked in the door she confronted him with a barrage of questions that ended with a demand. "What this note?"

"I was out. I didn't want you to worry."

Marina trembled with anger and confusion. "Note says if captured or die? What? What you are doing?"

He knew leaving a note for her was a bad idea. Still, he had to take precautions. He would never do it again. He'd simply make any necessary arrangements with his CO and leave her some obvious items that would let her know he wasn't returning. Coming back home to this situation, because of the note, had backfired.

"You are to answer me?"

"I was worried about your feelings. It was a mistake."

Marina kept her distance from him. She lit a cigarette, paced, and clutched the crumpled note in her hand. After a few moments of pacing, she sat on the tan sofa with a crocheted blanket on the back but she immediately popped up, continued pacing, and stopped to confront him. "I don't understand. What you are doing?"

"I told you, I was out."

"What? What out? You must tell!"

He took her hand holding the note and sat down with her on the sofa. "It's not as easy to tell you as you would think. But I'll try. I'm involved in some things here and I can't give you all the details."

"What are 'some things'? Note says you may die!" she began crying. "I cannot live this life. What you are doing to me? To us? What of June? In Minsk you said 'No secrets!' "

He had thought about this scenario many times before and decided now was the time to let her hear it. "Maybe it's better if we separate."

Marina stopped crying and stared at him incredulously. His words hung in the still, heavy silence for a painful moment until she burst out crying again, but now even harder. After a few minutes, when she composed herself enough to stop crying, snot ran down her nose and her eyes were red. But she became angry again and returned to her earlier questions. "You're pale. What wrong?"

He did not respond and her voice gradually rose with her anger. "What you did? Why should we leave? Answer me!"

He felt very emotional and excited but tried to speak evenly. "I may have killed General Walker."

Marina's eyes darted back and forth wildly with fear. Confusion washed over her face. "No! You kill a man?"

"I don't know. I think so," he said. "I took a shot at him with my rifle."

"Who? Why? Oh God!" She cried hysterically and he went to her.

"I didn't want to tell you." He pointed his finger in her face. "What I do is very important."

"You kill a man? How is important?"

"How?" He was annoyed that he had to explain this but he spoke calmly. "Let's say someone killed Adolph Hitler before he gained power as Fuhrer of Germany. World War Two may have been prevented. Or maybe if Hitler was stopped, even during the early days of the war, say in 1939 after the

Polish invasion, think of how many millions of lives would have been saved."

"So this man next Hitler?" Marina said derisively and then added sarcastically, "with horrible army!"

His temper rose with frustration and he yelled. "He was the worst fascist in America!"

"Who?"

"General Walker!"

"Why I never heard of this man?"

He heard himself shouting and he took a few deep breaths to remain calm and not wake June. "Do you remember when I told you about the meeting I went to, where Walker was speaking. Remember? I got up and shouted that their organization was a bunch of right-wing neo-Nazis and anti-Semitic, and, and anti-Catholic?"

"Yes, I remember you tell me," she said, wiping her eyes. "*That* was brave. Shooting at man, no, no."

"Well, I shot him tonight. I think he's dead."

"Oh God! Is horrible!" She burst out crying again. "I do not believe this!"

"No, it's a good thing. No one will ever know it was me. History has been changed. America cannot be led into his fascist policies."

Marina stared at him with disbelief. "He is not *our* leader. He is not politician."

"He was going to run for senator and he was becoming very popular. And I've stopped him."

She shook her head again and charged off for the bedroom. A moment later she emerged and threw a blanket and pillow at the sofa, and he tried to hold her. "Stay away!"

"Shut up!" His anger rose instantly and his blood veins pounded in his temples as he maneuvered her against the wall. He watched her, intimidating her not to move with his eyes, a vicious animalistic stare that paralyzed her, and he slowly raised his hands around her thin neck. Tightened them until she clutched at his hands with great fear in her eyes. He spoke with as much conviction, power, and violence as his voice could throw. "If you say *anything*. . . to *anyone*. . . about this. . . I *will* kill you."

Marina's arms and body went limp, she fell to the floor, and then she jerked into a spasm of fear with her legs trembling. She cried violently and rocked back and forth.

She got the message. It had to be this way.

After several minutes she collected herself off the floor and scampered into the bathroom. He heard her vomiting and crying more, and he went to the door to help her, calling out her name softly, but she ignored his pleas to open the door. He checked on June, somehow she was sleeping soundly, and he settled on the sofa, sitting in the middle with the blanket and pillow on one end. A few hours later he heard her open the bathroom door and make her way to bed. He ignored her now and continued to think of what he should do with Marina and June.

It had been one hell of a day, but overall he regretted nothing. Nothing except the note he had left for her, which started the whole god-damned bitching confession. Once again his old worry about having a family and being an agent, the same worry that he had in the Soviet Union, resurfaced. He didn't think he could do it. And if he had to choose one or the other, he would choose his country and being an ONI agent. It was clearly more important to serve his country and he felt honored to do it. His daily ordinary life wasn't worth anything compared with these critical missions and international affairs, but there was no need to involve and destroy her life, and June's life, if that could be avoided. Yes, it would be much better if they separated.

He lay down on the sofa and pulled the crocheted blanket down over his feet and body, turning to plump the pillow, but he could not get comfortable. The old sofa sagged in the middle.

He thought again about the rifle buried in the ground outside of General Walker's house. What if someone noticed the overturned dirt, dug it up, and found the rifle? Also he would need to shut down his post office box so the authorities would not be able to trace the rifle back to him, even though he had used an alias when he ordered it from a catalog from a sporting goods store in Chicago. But he knew it would be better to go back and get the rifle tomorrow night, as soon as it was dark again, as long as no one saw him.

He thought of other details of the shooting, like Sergio Arcacha Smith's background, which seemed solid, and if he would talk, which seemed highly doubtful, and if he had taken care of the car as he said he would, and it was in Sergio's own best interest so of course he would. Then he thought of Marina crying. As many times as he went over the details of the day and any possible tracks that may have been left, he always finished by worrying about Marina. It wasn't right to involve her. He must keep his family at a greater distance.

Then Lee remembered George de Mohrenschildt and his wife Jeanne were coming over for lunch tomorrow. He began to think about how he would report back to George and thought again about the rifle in the ground, about the look of smugness on Sergio's face when he said he would hide the car, and a look of perplexity on his face when he gave his opinion on Castro and Cuba. He rolled over again. Could he trust this guy? Well, he had to, as George's man, as part of their unit.

Did he absolutely need to leave Marina and June? Maybe if he rented a room in a boarding house, so they would be kept apart from his activities. Would that work? Did she need to be completely out of his life? He wanted to be with her and June very much. How could he make this work? What would George recommend?

He plumped the pillow again and lay on his side facing the sofa. Birds chirped in the early morning light and he stretched. He sat up and looked at the small white clock on the end table. It read 5:35. Apparently he had fallen asleep.

He rose and made some coffee, and wondered why June hadn't awakened yet? But he knew better than to check on her, which would definitely wake her. He made some scrambled eggs, bacon, and toast, unhitched a tray from a t-v stand, and took it to Marina in the bedroom.

"Darling," he whispered, trying not to wake June in her crib across the room. Marina stirred. He whispered again, "I made you some breakfast."

She opened her bright blue eyes, reddened and swollen, and looked at him then blinked. She frowned, sat up, and looked at June in her crib. Her rustling had awakened June and she cried a soft murmur of calling.

He said, "I'll take her," handing Marina the tray. He went to June and picked her up, shushing and swaying her on his shoulder. He laid her gently on a small table covered with a baby's blanket and changed her diaper, which was wet.

Marina rose and went to the bathroom, and returned just as he finished changing June's diaper. June whimpered so he carried her into the kitchen to get a bottle and, looking back over his shoulder, watched Marina as she crept carefully back under the covers and pushed aside the tray of food.

In the kitchen he poured June a bottle of milk, holding her in one arm, and she eagerly took it. He bounced as he walked back into the bedroom. "Don't you want breakfast?"

"I am not believing you." She rolled over, away from him, and mumbled, "I no sleep all night."

June mumbled a soft whimpering as she saw her mother but he picked up the tray gingerly, while holding June in his right arm snuggly. "Remember, George and Jeanne are coming over for lunch."

She did not say anything. Her eyes were closed. He knew she must have heard him and it annoyed him that she did not respond. He took June into the living room, shut the bedroom door, and sat down with her on the sofa, holding her in his arms, and pulled the blanket around them both. He looked into her round blue eyes and he began crying. It wasn't supposed to be like this. If the police found out about his shooting General Walker, this may be one of the last times he would hold his daughter. She suckled on the bottle and stared at him. He realized he did not want her memory of him to be his crying, so he stopped.

"You're going to have a great life. I'm going to do whatever I need to do to help you live a wonderful life." He held her close and watched her as she drank more milk. "I'm going to look out for you. I love you."

June finished the last of the bottle, dropped it aside casually, and nestled into his chest and arms, and was soon asleep. He smiled and closed his eyes, feeling her gentle breathing on his chest.

It was mid-morning when Marina woke up. She was sullen and grouchy, and did not speak to Lee for a long time. He asked her, "Are you making something for lunch for George and Jeanne?" but she ignored him. He held June in his arms, rocking her as he walked around the kitchen, when a car horn honked twice.

Looking out the front window, he saw a white Chevrolet station wagon but he didn't recognize it. Then a man stood briefly from the driver's side and he saw Sergio Arcacha Smith, went swiftly back into the kitchen, and set June at Marina's feet on the gray-and-white checkerboard linoleum floor. "I've got to talk to somebody right quick."

"You are leaving?"

"No, no. I'll be out front. One minute." June gave a whiny cry and he tussled her hair. "Look out for Junie."

He hustled outside and jogged to the Chevrolet, looking up and down the block to see if anyone was out and watching. There was no sign of anyone fortunately. Sergio was behind the wheel with the motor running and Lee leaned on the open passenger's side window. "What's going on?"

"Package for chew!" Sergio was unshaven and thumbed toward the back seat, but it was empty.

"What?" he said.

"On de floor!" he angrily bit off his words. Something long and thin was wrapped in a blanket.

He opened the back door, saw dirt on the blanket, and lifted the drab olive bag, feeling its heft. It was his rifle. "Did anyone see you?"

"No. I went back before dawn."

"Are you sure?"

"Yes!" Sergio spoke firmly and stared with his deep, dark eyes now very bloodshot. He breathed heavily. "No one was around."

"Thanks. I've been thinking about it all night."

"Me, too." Sergio ordered him strongly, "Get *rid* of eet!"

"Yes, sir. Don't worry, I will."

"See de paper?" He handed him a newspaper, the Dallas *Morning News,* and it was folded open to reveal small headlines that read

Rifleman Takes shot at Walker

Close Call

General Walker Survives Shooting

Sergio's anger exploded and he cursed in Spanish, "¡Usted jodiendo perdió!"

The car lurched and then sped away just as Lee shut the back door. He had to twist awkwardly to reach out and push it shut with his right hand, clutching the newspaper, with his left hand while holding the wrapped gun. He looked up and down the street, on both sides, and looked again. The only person in sight was a tall gangly boy who pushed a lawn mower over the front lawn three houses down and across the street but he seemed preoccupied.

He carried the blanket-wrapped gun at his side, with the newspaper under his arm, and walked swiftly around the side of the house to the back. He realized he didn't have his keys and the garage was always kept locked. He tip-toed up the few wooden stairs and peered into the kitchen window. Marina and June were not there. He carefully opened the back door and heard Marina with June in the bedroom, and then saw potatoes in a pot of boiling water on the stove. He could hear Marina as she spoke softly to June while changing her diaper and then began to coo a Russian lullaby.

Lee set the newspaper on the kitchen counter, looked around quickly, and opened an upper corner cabinet. It was mostly empty except an old two-quart pot that he pulled out and set on top of the newspaper. He stashed the rifle in the cupboard and pulled the dirty blanket out. He realized he would need to wash the blanket as soon as possible, as soon as George and Jeanne left, when he heard Marina say, "There. All done!" and she returned carrying June in the crook of her arm. She glanced at the boiling potatoes with a blue flame underneath the pot and he closed the cabinet nonchalantly. He grabbed the empty two-quart pot and opened a lower cabinet to put it away but it was full of other pots and pans.

Marina said, "Good, take her. I finish lunch."

He set down the old aluminum pot on the back of the counter, took June, and leaned over to kiss Marina but she turned away.

"We talk. Later."

"It's alright," he nodded at the newspaper, bouncing June in his arms. "I missed. No one knows."

She said nothing, eyed the headline, and then went to work by opening the oven door to check on the rosemary chicken broiling in a pan. Next she took out a large frying pan and opened two cans of baked beans.

He could tell she was not going to talk to him, so he carried June and the blanket through the living room and into the bedroom. With his free hand, while holding June carefully, he placed the blanket in the laundry hamper and then went back into the living room. There was a pile of children's books that his mother had brought over and he tenderly set down June next to them. She pulled out one of the books and was immediately entranced by the pictures so he straightened up the entire living room and dusted it with a rag and some furniture polish. He then sat on the floor with June and looked more closely at the books. They were books that he had read as a child and it brought back memories of sitting alone, trying to read them, and staring at the pictures while trying to remember the whole story. His mother worked as he was growing up, and Robbie would rarely play with him, so he was often alone. One book was about a curious monkey that always got into trouble and, as a child, it had some big words that he didn't know but he liked the monkey. He thought the monkey was funny in spite of getting into trouble. At first he hated those lonely times but he came to enjoy reading more and more, and now preferred being alone. Reading was one of his favorite pastimes. He read the book to June but she was still too young to be interested in the story, but she looked at the monkey and giggled with him as he pointed and said, "Silly monkey!"

Marina had just finished preparing a nice lunch of chicken, potato salad, and baked beans when Jeanne and George de Mohrenschildt arrived. Marina scooped up June in her arms as Lee opened the door for them and welcomed them into their house. This was the first time they had come over and he felt self-conscious about its appearance. He also felt badly that he and Marina had fought and hoped that the hangover effect was not too noticeable.

He said, "It's so great to see you again, Jeanne, George."

Jeanne kissed Lee on the cheek and George bowed slightly and handed over a stuffed rabbit toy for June—Easter was coming. Lee smiled with playful, wide eyes and said to June, "Oh, lucky you! What do you say to Uncle George?"

"Fank you," June said, squeezing the rabbit to her chest and smiling broadly.

He shook his hand firmly, but George curled his lip in a snobbish snarl and looked away, obviously annoyed.

Lee wondered, Did Sergio say something to him? Did something else go wrong? Had the police called George?

"Well this looks like a nice, little place," Jeanne said to Marina, who stepped aside with June, "show me around."

"Okay," Lee said, but Jeanne cut him off and pressed his forearm. "Marina, honey, you show me around and let the men talk."

Marina started toward the bedroom so Lee set down the stuffed rabbit on the sofa and went in the other direction, toward the back of the house and the kitchen, and George followed him.

"Here's the kitchen and we've got a small backyard," he pointed out the window, "and there's the garage." George did not say anything but he was obviously irritated and very upset.

"What do you want me to say?" he asked.

Marina came into the kitchen, still holding June in her left arm, but opening the kitchen cabinets with her free hand. "Kitchen is nice. Plenty space."

She kept opening more cabinets. He watched her, knowing the stowed rifle was in the next one, the corner cabinet, so he tried to cut her off. "I'm sure they've seen dishes and pans before."

But she reached the corner cabinet and opened it, exposing the rifle. Everyone stared at the gun.

It was very quiet. No one spoke.

"That's my rifle," he finally said. "The garage was locked."

Now everyone stared at him. He felt the need to explain it so he said, "I like hunting."

"George was a hunter of fascists during the war," Jeanne joked and George picked up her cue with his charming laugh.

Lee tried to chuckle but a fake laugh came out awkwardly and he heard it, sounding strange, and stopped. Marina had a look of confusion mixed with anger and she shot him a fiery stare.

George covered for him, chuckling with grace, and continued on Jeanne's comment. "Oh, the war was so long ago!" Then he turned to stare at him and added, "General Walker is the only fascist I know!"

Now Jeanne laughed. He was shocked and embarrassed, again tried to laugh with her but his chuckling came out awkwardly. Marina's face flushed dark red.

George stood over him and his incriminating eyes fixed on his. He asked point blank, "How is it that you missed General Walker?"

No one spoke. It was very quiet. He was clearly flustered and didn't know what to say. Marina's lips were pursed together and her cool blue eyes squinted with a look of resentment and fear. Why was George asking this in front of everyone? What was going on? He could feel his upper lip twitching and he tried to laugh again but only a crude grunt came out. His eyes watered and he thought of the seriousness of blowing this assignment. And now, tragically, his family was involved. Why was George confronting him—here and now?

Then, as suavely as if he were at a posh party, George patted him on the back and with his charming laugh said, "Well, it's not like shooting rabbits! Maybe you need a new sport like bowling!"

He laughed again and looked at the women, but they were equally stunned and speechless. June gurgled and then reached out for Jeanne's dangling earrings. It was awkwardly quiet.

Finally Lee said, "I do like bowling. Do you have a favorite place?"

"Honey," Jeanne pressed Marina's forearm, "what is that delicious smell? Are you baking a pie?"

The conversation was moving again and the inquisition had passed. What in the hell was that all about? He would definitely follow-up with George on the purpose of that.

Their lunch went smoothly as George told stories of his travels in Costa Rica and Guatemala. He also mentioned he was going to Haiti soon on an extended business trip, he knew what that meant; although George explained it was in an effort to broker an oil deal. Later George said he had arranged an interview for him in New Orleans, with an ex-FBI agent who was running a lot of "business" deals out of his office, and that he should go there as soon as possible to "look for work."

Lee realized that this meant he had been reassigned to New Orleans after all, and this period of time with his mentor was over. He smiled politely and said yes, of course, and drifted off in his thinking as Jeanne excitedly described a new dress she had bought for a fancy party next weekend at the Hogg mansion in Houston. He smiled again as he thought of how good it would be to be back in New Orleans.

Around three o'clock the de Mohrenschildts said their final goodbyes. Marina waved with June from the front door and he walked out to the driveway with George, who stopped at the front of the car. He waited and watched as Jeanne walked around the Galaxie, got in, and then George turned to him and spoke crisply, "People who are more demanding than me, and more unwilling to accept your answers than me, will ask you much more vigorous questions than I did today. After any mission you should be prepared to respond to any question, even the most direct question, at *any* time. The best tactic is to remain calm, admit nothing, deny everything, and *counter* with a question on some other topic. Is that clear?"

"Yes, sir. Thank you."

"Good. Get it clear in your head. You failed. When you fail on a mission, *everyone* will deny all knowledge of you."

"I can do it. Give me another chance."

He looked at him with disgust and spat on the ground. "Forget it. You're too hot now. But on the plus side you showed once again that you weren't afraid to take risks. And you followed orders. Now, get your ass to New Orleans immediately."

"Yes, sir," he tried to smile again, felt his upper lip quivering strangely, and extended his hand for a grand, final handshake of thanks, good luck, and hope for the future. But George turned away coldly and got in the car.

"Thank you!" he called out and waved.

George started the turquoise-blue Galaxie impatiently, revving the engine so uncharacteristically uncouth, and backed out of the driveway with a sudden start. He didn't acknowledge him as he continued to wave goodbye. The car sped off down the street.

Lee thought, Shit. He had blown it, several people knew, and now he wouldn't have George to advise him. Also, he still had to face Marina—again. Well, he wasn't taking any shit from her. Maybe this would be good practice for him. He'd deny it, remain calm, and change the topic. If she questioned him too much, he'd yell at her, or beat the crap out of her. Or follow up on his threat to kill her and perhaps take her within a heartbeat of her life. Yeah, that should work.

Back inside the apartment the air was stuffy. Marina fixed June a bottle in the kitchen and he approached her just as she screwed on the top. But she handed June to him and said, "I'm in trouble. I'm losing my faith," and she walked out the back door and into the Texas heat.

He gave June the bottle, cradled her in his arms, and rocked from side to side. He peered out through the kitchen window, over the sink of dirty luncheon dishes, as Marina stopped in the middle of the back yard, covered her face with her hands, and cried in great sobbing heaves.

40)

Didn't quite catch your name

Sparky didn't mind helping out the girls at the club. He felt it was his duty. As his mother often said, his second foster mother, "women need help." His foster mother needed help—that was certain. She was weak and always needed something. Okay, he'd help any woman who asked. How hard could that be?

A woman from his club, Connie Trammell, had said she wanted to get a job in the business world, so he said he would help her. She said she had office skills, knew how to type or something, and he set up an appointment to introduce her to his best business connection, Mr. Lamar Hunt. He had other business to do there anyway, so what could it hurt to take Connie along?

Sparky and Connie walked into the Mercantile Bank Building and he acted like he owned the joint. His father had taught him that, his real father, the one who emigrated from Poland and made America his home, made Chicago *his* place, owned it. He taught him to never be intimidated by a place simply by its appearance or by who runs it. His father often said, "Walk in like you own the joint."

"Wow, Sparky," Connie said. "This is some swanky place."

It was a conventional office building, although rather tall, with a marbled floor lobby but it also had a bank of elevators trimmed in gold-plated oak leaf. Because he had been there before, and knew Mr. Hunt well enough to get an appointment, he knew which elevator to take and which floor his office was on. A dark-skinned Negro closed the gate, and then the doors behind them, and they rode up in silence as Connie, who had pretty green eyes, watched the flashing numbers of the floors light up. He smiled, thinking of the sweet treat he'd get for this simple favor.

Connie's eyes moved back and forth to the rhythm of the alternating lights and her mouth was open in amazement. He took his right forefinger, the one that had part of it bitten off in a bar fight, and touched her lips softly. She was startled from her reverie, shook her head, licked her lips, and giggled. "Gosh!"

The elevator stopped, the Negro boy opened the gold-painted gate and doors, and a shiny silver sign on the wall behind a receptionist's desk read,

Hunt Oil Company

"Gosh!" Connie said.

"It's okay, honey," he said. "It's just another office building. All office work, right?"

"Yes, sir," she giggled, then put on a straight face. She reminded him of Shirley Temple in one of her movies because Connie had a cute girly face with freckles and short red hair that was very curly, too. It made her look younger than her age of twenty-two.

"Welcome to Hunt Oil Company. May I help you?" a bright, dark-haired lady asked politely. She had a bouffant hairdo and wore a blue cotton dress. She smiled nicely, had a pencil in one hand, and ignored the ringing phone on her desk. She had class.

"I'm here, we've got an appointment to see Mr. Hunt," he said. "That is, I do. She's here for a job."

"Alright, honey, fill this out," she offered a clipboard with an application form on top and answered the telephone before its third ring, "Thank you for calling Hunt Oil Company. How may I help you?"

The receptionist had pretty blue eyes that sparkled and when she noticed he was looking at her, she winked good-naturedly. He imagined her stripping at one of his clubs and tried to see down the neckline of her dress. She had smallish breasts, but maybe they were perky.

"No, sir, Mister Hunt declines to comment for the press at this time. If you like I can send you our annual report that has—" The person on the other end had apparently hung up. She chuckled, "Annual report gets 'em every time! Now, honey, she's filling out the application and you had an appointment, is that right?"

"Yeah, that's right." She had everything on the ball. He found her very attractive in her smart, competent way. He had never been with a woman this bright and then recalled that some of the women he had bedded were brainy smart but didn't have as many tricks in the sack. But maybe this one was different? She seemed so quick and chirpy. How could she be a lousy screw?

"Ah, yes, I see it here. You're the two-fifteen. Go right in, sir."

Sparky wondered, how did she know? Did she remember him from his last visit? No, that was almost five months ago. He headed for the large office door but stopped to look back at her. "How'd you know?"

"Mister Hunt has been expecting you. Mister Braden is already inside, too."

He thought, Braden? Who's Braden? She must have meant Brading, who he was expecting, but nodded and went in. Behind a very large desk, Mr. Hunt had his hands behind his head. He did not have on his suit coat, it was hanging over his chair, and he had a big pot belly. His father, Haroldson L. Hunt, better known as H. L. Hunt, was an oil magnate and this was just one the many companies he owned. They were ultraconservative and he wondered how Brading was doing with Mr. Lamar Hunt. Also, should he act like he knew Brading? Then he had a slight panic as he suddenly forgot some of what Mr. Civello and other connected guys had told him about Brading. But his main concern was if Brading was classy enough to meet with Mr. Hunt and in his office, too?

"Howdy," Mr. Hunt said. He had greasy dark hair beginning to gray at the temples and yellowish teeth. "Come on in. Cop a squat."

He put his hand out but Mr. Hunt didn't shake it. He tried to remember if Mr. Hunt shook his hand last time. A tobacco spittoon was just off to the side and some tobacco juice stained the wooden floor around it. A huge pair of Texas Longhorn cattle horns, at least six feet from tip to tip, was mounted on the wall behind him.

"Jim Braden," Brading said to him, shaking his hand as if they hadn't met last year in Las Vegas. He was taller than he remembered, well over six feet three, and had a receding hairline but grew his dark hair long and it was slicked down with some kind of greasy hair product. Sparky recalled the long discussion the bosses had at the Thunderbird Hotel with Mr. Hoffa and his people, Mr. Marcello and his people, Mr. Pecora in particular, and a few others. He was sure this guy had said his name was Brading then, and was certain the mob guys had given him the inside scoop on "Brading." He remembered now: They had said *Brading* was a good shooter, got things done, but was sloppy, too. They said Brading was caught way too often but at least he kept his mouth shut.

"Didn't quite catch your name—Brading?" Sparky said, as if he didn't know him. He hated playing these charades, maybe because it reminded him of his own name changing. Just do it and be done with it and move on.

"Braden," he said clearly, rolling back his shoulders and looking around the office as if someone else may be listening. "Official two weeks ago."

That was smart, he thought. The cops wouldn't be able to get a read on him if they picked him up for any reason. "That's good. Okay."

Mr. Hunt unfolded his hands from behind his head and wagged a finger back and forth. "You two fellas know each other?"

"No," Sparky said quickly.

"No," Braden said. "Nope. Not at all."

"Oh. 'Cause Carlos said he had a pilot lined up, Gerry, Ferrie, something or other, guy *you* knew," he pointed firmly to him, "but *you* needed the ride," he pointed to Braden.

"That's right," Braden said. He shifted a lot in his chair and was clearly nervous, but maybe Mr. Hunt saw nervous guys all the time. Maybe Mr. Hunt made guys nervous on purpose, just to see if they'd be up front and honest.

"Yeah," he said. "I think we have some common friends."

"I'm sure we do!" Mr. Hunt said, laughing. "But let's not get into that! Ha! Ha! Ha!"

"Yeah, so the plane will be waiting for me at Bluebird Airport," Braden said. "And your guy, Ferrie will—"

"It's Redbird Airport," Mr. Hunt said, laughing again. "You ain't from around here, is ya, boy?"

He laughed just to amuse Mr. Hunt, as if he were a Texan, too, and a good old boy. It made Sparky uncomfortable. Not only was he *not* a local Texan, but if Mr. Hunt knew he was Jewish, being a John Bircher as Hunt was, he'd probably run him out of his office and sic his good ol' boys after him for a good ol' lynching. All these guys worked the same, Sparky thought. They all play as if it was their ball, their field, their game, and he was lucky just to be playing. Okay, think that, you redneck asshole.

"No, sir," Braden said. "I sure as hell ain't from around here."

He watched as Braden smiled, like he was sucking up to him, but he knew that violent smirking look from other tough guys. Even though he was smiling and laughing, he knew that if this were a back alley, Braden would have roughed him up by now and Hunt would be wearing a smiling bloody gash from ear to ear.

Braden continued, "But from what I see, you grow 'em big down here!"

Mr. Hunt grabbed his crotch and jostled it. "The bigger the better—that's what *she* said!" and then laughed loudly, spitting tobacco juice to the side of his desk and into a brass spittoon.

"Anyway, it's all set," he said quickly and stood up, wanting to get out of here before someone crossed the line and said something wrong, or said too much.

"That's a businessman, for ya!" Mr. Hunt said, and rose from his black leather high-back chair. They shook hands firmly.

Sparky motioned at the longhorns behind Mr. Hunt. "Hook 'em Horns!"

Mr. Hunt released his handshake and made the University of Texas longhorn sign with his first finger and pinkie extended. "You bet!"

He thought, This is all a fun game to him.

Braden, who had stood up after Sparky did, looked over at him, chuckled, and slapped him hard across the shoulder. "Let's get the fuck outa here. Gimme a ride to the motel."

They walked out of Mr. Hunt's office and the reception area was quiet. The secretary politely got rid of another telephone caller as he and Braden looked over to Connie, who was flipping through a magazine. Sparky asked, "You done?"

"Yeah," Connie said.

He gave her a confused look and then stared with intimidation at the secretary, in an attempt to help Connie, but the perky secretary simply raised her eyebrows and gave a tight-lipped smile.

Connie said, "They don't got no openings 'cause I only type thirty-five."

"That's it?" he said, looking back at Connie. "Crap, I type that. Bunch a mistakes sure, but I do that. I thought you said you could secretary."

"No, I never said that." Her voice squeaked. He knew that her ex-husband used to smack her around and now, when she sensed a beating coming, she got nervous and her voice squeaked, "You did."

"What?" He felt himself getting angry but he tried to hold his temper in this office. It wouldn't be good to get out of line in front of real business people because the word could get around and that would hurt business for his club.

"I said I wanted to do somethin' different," she squeaked with wide eyes, "and *you* said I could do business, and I said, sure why not?"

"You know this broad?" Braden asked, tapping his arm repeatedly but staring at her tits.

"Yeah." He wanted to leave quickly. This whole situation was spinning out of control and he wanted to hit someone, but not here and not now. He glanced at the secretary—she was minding her own business fortunately—she was professional. Then he gave another vicious stare at Connie before looking Braden level in his bloodshot eyes. Braden better not try anything now. "Come on, I'll drive you over to the motel."

"You," he pointed two fingers at Connie, doing all he could to keep from yelling, "you owe me. You got some explaining to do."

"Sure, Sparky," she said, throwing in a sweet smile and a wink. Her freckles were disarming and she wrapped her curly red hair around her ears. She stole a look at Braden's crotch as she stood up and that just about did it for him, but he grabbed her by the arm and led them all out of the office toward the bank of elevators.

"You owe me," he said again, feeling he was just about to explode and pulling her along. Braden said something from behind them, but he was thinking too many things to hear him or pay him any mind. He wondered, Why was he always doing things for other people when no one cared about *him,* no one gave *him* any respect, and no one could do anything without *him?* He was sick of it. Sick of kissing up to these assholes! This had to change. It had to.

He looked at Braden, waiting for the elevator and bouncing on his toes, and thought, if Braden says one word he's gonna get smacked in the mouth. He breathed heavily, squeezing Connie's arm as she mumbled complaints of pain. It was very quiet until the elevator bell dinged and the doors opened.

He said, "I'm disgusted with you," as they all got on the elevator.

"I know," Connie squeaked. "But it ain't my fault!"

"Yeah, but just so you know. Disgusted."

Connie swallowed hard and looked up at him with her pretty eyes. He liked seeing her big eyes, staring up at him, and his heart raced faster in anticipation of getting back to the office and having her suck him. That would be something, he thought, for having her embarrass him in front of Mr. Hunt. The thought of Connie licking her lips around his shaft made him grow thicker in his pants and he gave a slight smile to Braden, who didn't notice as he was still staring at Connie's tits. The elevator doors opened and they all left the building.

41)

544 Camp Street

Lee climbed the steps to the second floor offices at 544 Camp Street and wiped his brow. It was very hot. He had moved his family, Marina and June, into a small bungalow apartment in New Orleans and had easily established his connection with his CO, Guy Banister, but he still wasn't accustomed to the humidity here.

He opened the front door and could see past Delphine, Guy Banister's secretary, to a dark-haired man sitting in Mr. Banister's office. The visitor had the look of a Company man: clean-cut, black tie, white shirt. He wondered why a Company man would be here, even though he knew Banister had ties to CIA, but it seemed odd. Something was happening and he wondered if it had anything to do with his current mission. He had carefully built a cover reputation as a supporter of the communists and, as instructed, started a local chapter of the Free Play for Cuba Committee. He handed out leaflets for them and even recruited an old Marine buddy to help him, of course he had to pay Mike Torrey the minimum wage of $1.15 per hour, like most Americans after the Bay of Pigs disaster he wouldn't be caught dead with a pro-Castro pamphlet in his hand, but Torrey did it for the money. But now the sight of a Company man from Langley in Mr. Banister's office had the look of something *much larger.*

"Hot enough for ya?" Delphine asked, chewing her gum.

Lee smiled at her poor joke—New Orleans was *always* hot and humid—and he motioned to the CIA man with an inquisitive look. "I reckon it's hotter 'n two rats goin' at it in a wool sock."

Delphine picked up his silent cue but shrugged that she didn't know who the Company man was, then put one finger to her lips in a "hush" motion. "You sure are a card. Did you finish all them pamphlets?"

"Yes, ma'am." He clutched his black tie and fluttered his short-sleeved shirt back and forth to get some air on his sweaty chest. More sweat trickled down his temples and his armpits were wet. He lingered near Delphine, not wanting to go into his back office yet, and recalled a few days ago he had made a mistake by passing out some Fair Play for Cuba Committee leaflets with "544 Camp Street" stamped on them and somehow word got back to Mr. Banister. He suspected Delphine had snitched on him—even though she was the one who had relayed the story back to him of Mr. Banister's reaction, which was to laugh, and he thought that was an odd reaction for a hothead like Banister. Delphine told him that Mr. Banister had said, "Don't worry about him. He's a nervous fellow. He's just confused. He's with us," and then when she told Banister that some of the leaflets had his 544 Camp Street address stamped on them, Banister blew a gasket, waited in the office for him to return, and hollered at him to destroy *all* of the leaflets with their address on them. Still, he watched Delphine closely and wondered what her intent was in asking if he had "finished all them pamphlets?"

Then from out of a back office Sergio Arcacha Smith led six men. Most had an olive complexion and a few spoke Spanish, and one mentioned something about Castro as they sauntered past him. They had a rugged, angry look about them. Two of them wore baggy green Army pants and Sergio gave a quick nod to him as he led the men outside the office and down the stairs, quickly moving around the building, toward a back alley. He watched them from the front door. He figured they were part of Sergio's band of men called the "Cuban Revolutionary Council" and he looked back over his shoulder at Delphine with a raised eyebrow and, again, she shrugged.

Suddenly the Company-looking visitor called out, "Come on in!"

Lee marched to Mr. Banister's office and poked in his head casually as if he had not been giving them any attention. "Yes, sir?"

The visitor eyed him up and down while Mr. Banister had one shoe pressed against his desktop.

"Lee, this is Frank Bender. Frank, Lee."

He stood over Mr. Bender, who looked to be in very good shape in spite of a small paunch and a few gray hairs mixed in his dark hair. He shook his hand with a slight bow as Mr. Banister continued, "I think you may know of him."

"Yes, sir," he said. "Pleasure to meet you." Then he turned to Mr. Banister and reported, "I've finished handing out the pamphlets but there wasn't any action today."

"Okay, keep trolling." Mr. Banister folded his knotty hands behind his head and crossed one leg on top of the other on top of his desk. "Get some rest. You've got that radio interview coming up. Study for that."

"Nice breeze in here." He turned to the oscillating circular fan and grinned. "Outside it's hotter 'n—"

"Got it," Mr. Banister said, immediately silencing him.

"Ya know," Mr. Bender said, raising his glass of iced tea, "I bet you'd appreciate hearing this, being a Marine and all."

It did not surprise him that Mr. Bender knew that he had been in the

Marines. He had probably read his p-file. But was Mr. Bender really here for *him?* Either way, he knew that he had to play along. "What's that, sir?"

Bender chugged a long drink of the tea, raised it high to finish it, and sucked on an ice cube as condensation ran off the glass and splattered onto his white shirt, before he spit the ice back into the glass. "I was telling Guy here about the Bay of Pigs. I was sitting in the White House, in the oval office with about ten other officers when we landed on the beach."

"Yes, sir, I'd like to hear about that," he said. "I was overseas at the time."

Mr. Bender set the empty glass down on Banister's desk and a ring of water instantly formed around the base. "We listened to our boys dying on the beach. We were at this big long table and everyone was staring at the radio, just like the old days before T-V. We had a direct link radio communication to our boys on the beach. You could hear the shells coming in, exploding, and our men screaming. They were slaughtering *our* soldiers!"

Mr. Banister took his feet off the desk and leaned in as Mr. Bender continued, "You could hear the gunshots, the Commies firing on our boys, churning up the beach, and that piece of shit Kennedy let them die. *He* let them *die!*"

Mr. Banister punched his desktop with his bony right fist and spoke slowly with disgust. "He heard our boys gettin' the livin' shit kicked out of 'em, *dyin'*," Banister slammed the desk again, "and he didn't send in air cover or the Marines or *nothin'?*"

"Our boys got squat."

"Why didn't anyone *do* anything?" he asked.

Bender was irate. "I damn near smashed his teeth down his God-damn throat. They had to hold me back."

"What?" he said.

"Yeah, I was yelling and screaming at him."

"At Kennedy?" Banister asked.

"Damn right. Jumped out of my chair and grabbed him by his jacket."

"Then what happened?" he said.

"I don't know for sure," Mr. Bender shook his head and thought. "There was a sense of confusion. A spirit of desperation. General LeMay was there. He wasn't too happy neither. His boys were ready to fly. They were minutes away! I think his brother Bobby and McNamara, or somebody, grabbed me from behind. And Howard Hunt took me by the back of my collar and my arm, and twisted, and took me down. They tossed me out of the room."

"Jesus," he said. "How awful."

"Awful don't touch it boy. It was torture." Mr. Bender sucked his teeth, pursed his lips tightly, and then continued in his harsh tone of voice. "We figured as more reports came in the administration, the President would feel more and more obligated to unleash some American power to equalize the situation. Anyone who heard that radio call for help could not stand by and *not act*, unless he was a God-damn commie sympathizer."

"Shit," Banister said.

"That's right. It was a failure of nerves. This administration set this whole thing in motion and they abandoned it at the point when our fine men were being destroyed on the beachhead! Part of our national will to prevail *failed* right then and there." Mr. Bender reached over and nudged the door shut, and stared at him hard with a look that conveyed everything: a life in the balance. He lowered his voice but it was an undeniable order, "And now you know why we've just got to *do* something about it."

He returned a confirmed look of knowledge being passed. "Yes, sir."

"Good."

"There comes a time," Mr. Banister's steely eyes locked onto him, "when the world's problems can be better solved with the bullet than the ballot."

"That's right," Bender continued, "George and Guy have told me a lot about you, what you've been involved in, what you've been doing. We've got something special planned for you, Lee. Don't be discouraged by all this pamphlet shit."

He quickly wondered what George de Mohrenschildt and Guy Banister would have reported about him, but responded coolly. "Oh, I know it's sheep dipping."

Mr. Bender chuckled. "That's right. You're getting names and addresses of anyone who wants to join, see what activities they have participated in, or maybe planning, and so on. That's good useful information. But we've got something *very important* coming. Be ready."

A brief smile crossed his lips until he felt it and he immediately bit his tongue to become serious. He knew this was his chance. It reminded him of his other *big* missions, to hit Khrushchev, then Walker, and he was excited for another chance at redemption. He knew this would probably be his *last* chance. Opportunities from someone as high up as Mr. Frank Bender do not come along every day. "Yes, sir! I'll be ready."

42)

When were you arrested?

Lee figured that his boss and CO, Mr. Guy Banister, had obviously recommended him for another assignment to Agent David Phillips, who was CIA Chief of Covert Operatives, which was why Agent Frank Bender had come down from Langley to confirm that he was the right man for this job. He knew that he must have passed Bender's examination because his new mission raised the stakes to an international scale, which pleased him, but also the assignment was twofold. First, he was to create some newsworthy event that would clearly show the new Cuban government, under the highly undesirable Fidel Castro, that he seriously supported their revolutionary movement and, second, that he was a deserving ally who should be allowed to defect to Cuba.

He wrote a letter to the Cuban Embassy in Havana, explaining that he should be given a visa because he believed in their cause and, as a matter of fact, he had been arrested for fighting anti-Castro activists in the streets of New Orleans. It was just after lunch when he showed the letter to Mr. Banister, who sat in his office with a toothpick in his mouth. "That's fine. When were you arrested?"

"Day after tomorrow. The Company Chief, Mister Phillips, arranged it with Mister Carlos Bringuier."

"How's that? You called the Bureau?" Mr. Banister meant his old employer, the FBI.

"No, Mister Phillips arranged it. He gave me Agent Bateman's name as a contact at the Bureau. But Mister Arcacha Smith's man, Carlos Bringuier, will start an altercation on Camp Street."

"Bull crap! Don't do it around here!" Mr. Banister shouted and threw the toothpick into a black wastebasket half-filled with crumpled paper. "Go downtown. Hell, make it easy on yourself and do it in front of the police station."

He smiled, "Now that's a little too obvious, don't you think?"

Mr. Banister chuckled, stood up and walked around his desk, and slapped him on the back. "No notes for Marina this time, okay?"

Lee's smile slammed into seriousness. How in the hell did Mr. Banister know about that? George must have told him. But wait, no, he never told George about the note to Marina. Maybe Marina mentioned it to someone? But who? To Jeanne, who told George, who told Mr. Banister?

He was so mad he couldn't speak. He grabbed the newly printed leaflets off the table and stormed out of Banister's office. He heard Delphine call out as he flew down the steps, "Don't forget your money!"

Mr. Banister always paid cash in an envelope, but he didn't want to go back up. To hell with him for now. Banister had revealed that he had used his FBI or Naval Intelligence skills to gather information about him and it was much more information than he cared to have known.

Lee thought, Shit. Shit, shit, shit. And they needed the money, too.

~ ~

The day was typically steamy, and he wavered in his performance of a happy politician. He wore his best white shirt and a crisp new gold tie that gave him a professional appearance. He handed out leaflets for about thirty-five minutes and Sergio's man, Carlos Bringuier, was late. A television cameraman came by and shot some footage of him distributing the leaflets, which was okay. Hell, that might even be helpful if the right people saw it. But the object was to physically fight for "the cause" and he was starting to wonder if this guy Bringuier was coming at all. He hated operatives who were late.

As planned, someone from Chief Phillips office anonymously called the police at 12:45 to report a disturbance on the 700 block of Canal Street. Police officer Mickle arrived a few minutes later. Policeman Mickle was stout with a pudgy face and he looked around with some confusion. "What's going on here?"

"Hello officer," he said. "I'm handing out some literature about Cuba."

"Oh, okay. Do you have a permit?"

He saw the name Mickle on his badge and its shininess made him wonder if he was a rookie. "No sir. I don't believe a permit is needed to distribute literature on public property, so long as the people willing accept the fliers."

"Yes, that's right. But we had a call—"

"Yes, sir, officer, and I'm sure that if you *stay in the area,* you'll be needed."

"The hell you say." Officer Mickle stared at him with some attitude as he obviously did not like being told what to do. "I'm on my way to lunch and I'm overdue to meet a friend."

"Yes, sir. If you must." He wiped some of the sweat from his brow with two fingers and flicked it on the sidewalk as Mickle walked away. The heat was making him sweat and ruining his best shirt. "Don't go too far."

Policeman Mickle turned to give him a strange look and wandered across the street to Beauchamp's Grille. He looked over his shoulder again and he waved to him with the leaflets before Mickle went inside the restaurant.

Finally he saw two men approaching and one was Carlos Bringuier, his skin darker than when he last saw him, and his black hair neatly trimmed. He also noticed dark mascara highlighted his eyelashes. Bringuier walked with eagerness in his stride and he seemed ready.

Bringuier said, "Hey, it's Lee!" to the other man, who was shorter but rough-looking. The other guy looked Cuban, with muscles rippling under his short-sleeve cotton shirt and he immediately wondered, Who in the hell is *this* guy? Then he recognized the second man as someone he had seen with Sergio Arcacha Smith in Mr. Banister's office. Bringuier was late, the policeman was probably suspicious, and Bringuier was supposed to come *alone!* Well, this would make it more real, as long as it didn't turn into his fighting *both* of them.

"What are you doing?" Bringuier asked.

"Nothing." He handed out a few more leaflets, checked that his gold tie was clasped to his shirt, and said, "Fair Play for Cuba!"

"What de fuck!" the shorter guy said. "He was at our meeting!"

Bringuier said, "Yeah, what are you doing?"

"Nothing. Mind your own business." He reached out for a businessman in a gray suit. "Free Play for Cuba!"

"God damn you!" the muscular guy shouted.

"Yeah, so what?" He turned to Carlos, who didn't look upset, but his friend was seething mad. He wanted to avoid that guy, so he stepped right into Carlos's face, which smelled faintly of rum. "What are you going to do about it?"

Carlos grabbed the leaflets from him and threw them in the air. He wanted to get this over with, to avoid the short tough guy, so he skipped much of their rehearsed script and smiled, "Okay, Carlos. If you want to hit me, hit me."

"Why are you doing this? I thought you were my friend!" Carlos was still speaking his opening lines, but his friend was ready to explode. He knew there wasn't time to slowly build up the confrontation.

"Hit me," he said. "Go ahead."

"Um, I can't believe you *betrayed* us!" Bringuier was fumbling with his scripted lines. "You were *in my house!*"

"Would you hit me already?" He couldn't stand how badly Carlos Bringuier was doing this. He was a handsome Cuban and at this moment it reminded him of a bad television actor selected for his looks instead of his talent. It was ridiculous and annoying, but for some reason he chuckled.

"He's laughing at us," the short guy yelled. "I'm going to kick his ass!"

He saw him rushing at him from the corner of his eye and felt the rough crush like a hard football tackle in the area of his left ribcage. He grabbed Carlos by the shirt collar to hold himself up and took a swing that deliberately missed his jaw but grazed his chest. At last Carlos punched him on top of his head, but it was more of a slap. It hardly felt like anything at all. He was getting more upset at how badly this was playing out and wanted to punch the shit out of Carlos, but resisted, and threw a couple of body punches into his soft belly for effect. Meanwhile Bringuier's tough buddy snapped a sharp right hook into his kidney that stung and he doubled over. Son-of-a-bitch! And now the bastard was grabbing his right leg and trying to lift him up, so he spun away from this madman's grip and popped a quick left jab between Carlos' dark eyes that landed flush on his long, straight nose and seemed to get his attention. Bringuier's eyes watered and widened, and he wound up for a here-it-comes haymaker but in spite of all the wind-up he stood his ground and took it square on the jaw. It had some jolt to it. Not bad.

Lee heard someone yell, "Hey! Hey!" probably officer Mickle from across the street but he was closing fast. He looked over at the shorter guy who was leaning back for his own haymaker. He thought, one of those was enough, so he pushed his head into Carlos' belly and turned away. They danced a few wrestling steps as he jerked Carlos' shirt up into his throat and then he felt the policeman's hands pulling them apart.

"Alright, break it up! Break it up!"

He had never heard a cop actually say that before, except on television, and he almost laughed again. He thought, Thank God the cameraman had left otherwise this would go down as a traveling comedy act.

Officer Mickle separated them, got out his handcuffs, and Lee offered his wrists swiftly. The short, tough guy took off running and Mickle yelled, "Hey stop! Police! Stop!"

This guy is unreal, he thought. Officer Mickle called out again, "Get that guy!" but the pedestrians turned to look at Mickle and then watched the Cuban zigzag through them down the street.

"Take me, too," Carlos said.

"Gee, do you think so?" Mickle said.

At the police station, it took over an hour to be booked for disturbing the peace, and another hour before Lee received his allotted telephone call. He called Agent Bateman, his FBI contact from Regional CIA Chief David Phillips, and for some reason he sounded completely ignorant of what was happening. In some odd way this made sense because why should the CIA Chief contact a Bureau man, but this made him even madder because the entire event had been so poorly executed by Phillips's contacts. He wondered if Chief Phillips had delegated this aspect and someone didn't follow through. He vowed he would never trust them again. It was one thing to work with ONI people but if they screwed up something as simple as this, what would they do when it was a more serious assignment? Exasperated, he simply told Bateman, "Get your ass down to the city jail and bail me out!"

The Precinct Sergeant, a big Cajun–Irishman named Mulally, had watched him make the call and grumbled, "Serves ya right! Who da heck da ya t'ink ya are, callin' the holy FBI fir a disturbin' the peace arrest?"

He grew furious as another two hours passed. The asshole Bateman wasn't coming! He demanded that Sergeant Mulally call the FBI to send someone over, but apparently no one was on duty at this hour on Friday night. Finally, someone called back Sergeant Mulally and said they would arrange for an FBI field agent to meet with him first thing Saturday morning.

After another hour, Lee asked for, and was fortunately given permission for another telephone call. But it took the police almost one hour and thirty minutes to escort him to the telephone area again and this time he called his Uncle Charlie, but he wasn't home. He asked Aunt Lillian to tell their neighbor Sam Termine, Carlos Marcello's chauffer, of his situation. Apparently Sammy called Emile Bruneau, who was also a friend of Uncle Charlie's, and coincidentally, a close friend of Nofio Pecora, who was Carlos Marcello's right-hand man.

Within fifteen minutes of that phone call, Emile Bruneau stood in front of him in the jail's holding pen. Unfortunately, it took another one hour and forty minutes to process the paperwork for his release.

The on-duty field officer for the FBI, Agent Quigley, arrived just as he was being processed out, so he spent a few minutes answering his inane questions. Mr. Bruneau discretely stood off to the side in the hallway as if uninvolved, but he could tell Bruneau was listening carefully.

Agent Quigley obviously had *no* information on who he was or what he was doing in his effort to create a "Fair Play for Cuba" background. At this late hour, he was not about to explain it to a stooge who was only standing in front of him because he had less experience and had to cover the weekend shift. He gave Agent Quigley a telephone number where he could be reached and demanded, "Tell Agent Bateman and Guy Banister to call *me* immediately."

"Well, answer me this," Quigley snapped back. "What were you doing distributing these leaflets?"

"I was doing what I was told," he said. "Following orders."

"Is Five Forty-Four Camp Street your office?"

Damn, he thought. How in the hell did that leaflet get in there? He thought he had destroyed all the fliers with the 544 Camp address as ordered by Mr. Banister. Maybe someone had planted it? But he quickly answered, "I was distributing them out of patriotic duty, as a patriotic American citizen. Aren't you patriotic?"

Agent Quigley was appropriately dumbfounded by his question. The tactic of denial followed by a tangential counter-question had worked.

It was nearing 6 a.m. when he walked out of the police station with Emile Bruneau and into the emerging New Orleans heat. He again thanked Mr. Bruneau, shook his hand vigorously, and immediately thought of how he would explain his arrest to Marina. This was getting old. He would definitely need to separate himself from his family, so she would never know of any of his activities. Somehow, he would have to move, or arrange for Marina and June to move into another house. Perhaps he would need to arrange for them to live in another city? That would be one way he could continue his work for the ONI without any interference from her and without having to constantly explain himself. He knew he had to do this. He would visit Marina and June as much as possible and whenever possible. He decided right then, in the breaking New Orleans dawn, that he would make moving out of their home a priority.

43)

Wants to see you

J.D. was young and handsome with dark hair, a solid jaw, and clear blue eyes. He ran his fingers over the bumpy knobs of the steering wheel of the patrol car and fantasized about his girlfriend while his partner, Billy Ray, rambled on about deer hunting in Big Bend country. J.D. liked having a girl on the side and she was a damn good lay, too. He often fantasized about their hot fucks and imagined new places to meet her. He didn't care that she was married, or that he was married too, for that matter. But even though she was married, she was often separated from her husband and that made it a lot easier. He just needed to manage his own nosy wife and that was simple: He wouldn't tell her spit.

J.D. figured he was obliged to have another woman and so what if her husband complained? That was *her* problem.

"Being in the Dallas police department has its privileges," J.D. told his rookie partner, Billy Ray. This was one of them. He could do anything he wanted, as long as he wasn't seriously breaking the law, and he wasn't. He was getting a little action on the side, that's all, and being handsome and wearing a police uniform got him plenty.

Plus J.D. got to carry a gun, which was another hell of a perk. It scared most people shitless and that was kind of cool. All you had to do was unsnap your holster, along with a few choice words, and they'd get the message loud and clear.

J.D. thought about his gal's tight thighs and the way they looked from behind when she bent over. A perfect pair of poles holding up that sweet meat, all juicy, right plum in the middle. It made him hard just to think about it. Suddenly a call came over the radio and Billy Ray asked, "Should I pick it up?"

"Hell, no," J.D. said. "We're getting' off in twenty minutes and I gotta be some place."

"Hittin' that 'tang again, J.D.?"

"Damn right."

Billy Ray grinned. "Why don't you tell me her name?"

"Why don't you kiss my ass? I clean-up enough of your shit without havin' to listen to more about her."

After the shift ended, J.D. quickly changed into his civvies. He enjoyed walking by the bank of telephone operators on his way out of the building. Maxine, a pretty blond with a very nice voice but a rail-thin body, called out, "Officer Tippit!"

Maxine handed him a pink note. It was a regular telephone message but he stared at it perplexed. It read, "Mr. Whitherspoon" for the name, which immediately alerted him. That was *her* husband. How in the hell did Witherspoon find out? Did she rat on them?

Then the second startling point, a box was checked: "Wants to see you."

J.D. looked at the time, next to today's date, and Maxine had written: 3:17 p.m. He looked over the counter at Maxine. "He say what he wanted?"

"No, sir."

"He say when he wanted to meet?"

"No, sir," Maxine adjusted her telephone headset and looked up at him with her small dark eyes. "Strange guy. Acted all secret. It was like pullin' teeth just to get his name."

"Thanks." J.D. tucked the note in his cowboy shirt pocket, turned, and walked out to the parking lot. When he got to his red '62 Chevy Impala SS, he pulled out the note again and looked for a telephone number. Nothing.

J.D. thought, To hell with this. I'll meet him on *my terms:* When I'm working, with my police uniform on, and you can bet your ass *with* my gun. Okay, big guy, now whatdya got to say? That's what I thought. You ain't sayin' spit.

J.D. wadded up the pink note and threw it on the ground. He decided he'd lay low and ignore Witherspoon. First, he'd catch up with his own wife and that ought to keep her mouth shut for a while. Hell, he might even be nice to her if she did something nice for him. As he drove home, he thought of the pink note and "Wants to see you." It tumbled through his mind over and over again: "Wants to see you."

44)

The best place for all this to happen is in Dallas

Lee had made the decision long ago that what he was doing was the best for his whole family, but that didn't make the actual event any easier. He felt incredibly guilty about doing this with Marina pregnant with his second child, so close to coming into this world, but he knew that this was how it must be. He prepared a number of special things to say but all of them had a sappy jukebox sound to them and avoided the main issue of his being an ONI agent, which he could never tell her. He knew she was often unhappy and many young couples go through that unhappiness of imperfection and the harsh reality of day-to-day life. Many husbands devote themselves to their work and struggle to make time for their family, but he had to keep his work completely separate from his family—for the good of his country and for the good of his family.

He knew that by doing this that other people would gossip, but every couple endures that, too, and ultimately that would not matter if their bond was strong, and he knew it was. But what would Marina say? How could she hear any words he would say and *not know*, to the very core of her essence, that he was lying?

He also loved his daughter June deeply and would do anything for her. But the worst of part of it was knowing that he would not be there for their next child, who was due in October. Marina would need so much help and he would not be there, and that hurt. But he would try to resolve any problems they had when he had the chance. With all this weighing on his mind, how could he say anything of separation that would ring true for *their* best interest?

He had packed his Marine duffel bag earlier in the week and placed it in the front closet. It was almost two p.m. on Saturday when Marina put June to sleep in her crib for her afternoon nap.

He took Marina by the hand and led her to sit down on the sofa. He took a deep breath to steady himself to explain everything as clearly as he could, just as he had prepared it.

"It is my firm belief that every child should have two loving parents," he began slowly and with assurance. "I know first-hand how difficult it is growing up without a father and I want to do more for my children than was given to me."

He paused for a moment, feeling choked up with emotion already but knowing that the international importance of his work trumped everything he had just said and yet he couldn't tell her about his work at all. He thought of discussing himself but that was so complex with many layers of deception and untruthfulness that he decided to focus on her in spite of what he had prepared.

"You need to improve yourself, both for our family by working, and in the sense of weaving your life into the fabric of your new homeland. I grew up in poverty, needing good shoes, and I often wished for more. So, I want better for you and for our family. It would be to your own betterment to find a good job." He had been staring into her clear blue eyes but was becoming overwhelmed with emotion and looked away.

He continued, "And the physical space away from me will enable you to spend more time with your friends, Ruth, and activities. It will improve your situation. And the best place for all this to happen is in Dallas."

"I am not believing words you say," she said in her broken English. She held his hands tightly in hers. "My life? You, us. Family *is* my life."

He felt trapped by her hands pinning his, so he broke free then tenderly stroked her extended abdomen. It was an instinctual reaction, one that he had done many times before but he felt it was misleading her so he stopped with his hand resting on her abdomen. "I'm sorry I'm poor. But with Ruth's help, you'll have a nice place to stay for now. You and Junie and the baby. And you can take some classes, maybe typing, work on your English with Ruth, or get a job. It will be a lot better."

"How better?" she demanded, pushing his hand off her. She leaned back on the sofa and crossed and re-crossed her arms angrily over her mid-section, trying to get comfortable. "Man and wife. One life. How Lee? How you do this?"

He rose from the sofa, opened the closet, picked up the duffel bag, and walked past her. He knew that if he stopped to hug her, to kiss her, to express any physical involvement again, that he may weaken and not make it. He paused near the doorway, looking down at his scuffed shoes, and said his well-rehearsed lines. "I left an address on the coffee table where I'll be. I'll visit on the weekends. Every weekend. I need to do this... for *us*. It's for the best."

He opened the screen door and heard Marina crying, softly at first and then bursting out in a heavy sob, but he did not stop. He did not look back.

PART V

45)

Mexico City

Three days after Lee walked out he helped Marina, six months pregnant, and June board a bus bound for Dallas. Two days after that, he bought a ticket for Mexico City. The bus left in the high heat of mid-afternoon, did not have air conditioning so all the windows were open and CIA agent William Gaudet sat next to him for the long ride from New Orleans. He quickly became bored with Agent Gaudet, he was a devoted Company man, but he did not find him intellectually stimulating. He left his seat to talk with some of the other passengers bound for Mexico.

He eased down next to a young girl who looked to be about fifteen, sitting alone near the back of the bus. She had a hardened, faraway stare as she gazed out at the flat, dry landscape. He asked, "Got a cig?"

"No, I don't smoke." She looked around nervously. She had pretty blonde hair but tired eyes of faded blue. A few freckles dotted her face and she wore a simple gray cotton dress. "I… Shit, I smoked 'em all."

"Oh." He noticed her tobacco-stained teeth and reluctant smile. "Your daddy know where you're headed?"

"My *step*-daddy can go to hell."

He suspected she was running away from home. "Oh. I'm headed for Cuba. This is the bus to Cuba, right?"

She giggled. "You can't get to Cuba on a bus! It's overseas."

He noticed a small welt near her left temple, perhaps as fresh as this morning, and figured that may have been the last blow her stepfather threw. He watched her staring at the desolate countryside of cacti and tumbleweeds. "Rough country out there, hey?"

"You got that right."

He observed her, letting her absorb the cleansing sparseness of the landscape. But he also wanted to begin practicing his pro-Cuban role, and she was an easy mark, so he pressed a little more. "Okay, why are you off to Mexico of all the god-forsaken places on earth?"

"I could afford the ticket."

He waited. After a moment she turned to him but remained quiet. She seemed to want to say more. He waited. Finally she spoke again. "I heard it's nicer. The men are nicer, more gentlemanly."

He nodded, although he wanted to say, Aren't you a bit young to be interested in gentlemen?, but knew she must have already had her share of rough experiences.

She continued, "My friend Doris said Latin men are the best!"

He chuckled. "If you really want to experience Latin men, you should skip Mexico and go straight to Cuba. Shoot, Cuba's the best country in the world! The men there are suave, sophisticated, and they'll treat you like a queen."

She seemed shocked, although a hint of a smile crossed her face. "You better go back to your seat."

"Alright. But it's true. The men there are true gentlemen. They wear white pants and dance the salsa." He did a little salsa step in the aisle and watched her giggle as he danced away.

Next, Lee stopped in the aisle next to a young couple who were snuggling together. He sized them up and made a quick guess. "You two on your honeymoon?"

"Why, yes," the young lady responded. She had dark hair and wore a very pretty green dress with tiny yellow roses. Her husband had a blonde crew-cut and wore a simple white tee-shirt and jeans. "Well, the best hotel in Mexico City, by far the best hotel in all of Mexico is the Hotel Cuba. That's where Fidel Castro stays when he's in town."

The couple was smiling until he said "Fidel Castro" and their smiles dropped. He winked and returned to his seat, feeling better that these conversations had warmed him up for the role he would play in Mexico City. It put him in a "performance" frame of mind that Castro, Cuba, and its people were great. It was the role he would be acting for the next three days and hopefully longer.

Lee's mission in Mexico City was to impress upon the Cuban Embassy that he admired their new system of communism under Fidel Castro, he had formed his own local group in New Orleans at some risk to his own life, and he had information, as a former radar operator with top-secret clearance, that the Cubans would love to have if they would allow him to defect. Once in Cuba, as part of the bigger project with many, many other agents, he would gather information on their military capability, seek out Cuban agents and find out who their contacts were in the United States, and, if the opportunity arose, to kill Castro. It was Minsk all over again except now he would try to defect through Mexico City with the aim of living in Havana. He felt clearly focused on his mission with his family well out of the way and he was confident he could do this.

The Company man who sat next to him, CIA Agent Gaudet, had a different mission, which was to be yet another tourist attempting to travel to Cuba, to visit a sick relative, in the hope that by some miracle the Cubans would allow Gaudet to enter their country. But Gaudet's main goal was to observe Lee's attempt to defect to see how the Cuban officials reacted at each step of the process.

Together he and Agent Gaudet also had another, less pressing mission, which was to turn a Cuban Embassy employee, a local named Silvia Duran, into an asset. They had information that Duran had a weakness for blue-eyed, blonde

Americans, their source had called her a "puta," and they planned, with Lee's sweet-talking attention, to use Duran as a source of information inside the Cuban Embassy.

In Mexico City he and Agent Gaudet checked in with their CO, CIA Regional Chief David Phillips, who was tall with a slim build and had thinning blonde hair. Lee was a bit surprised that Chief Phillips looked so young, perhaps in his late thirties, as he was now the CIA Director in charge of the Western Hemisphere. Chief Phillips wore a nondescript gray suit and there was absolutely no paperwork or files of any kind in his office. It was barren except for a telephone on his desk. During their brief meeting, Agent Gaudet spoke to Chief Phillips, who nodded or shook his head but he did not say one word. At the end of the meeting Lee extended his arm to shake his hand but Chief Phillips stared at him with his hollow, very light blue eyes.

The next morning he and Agent Gaudet entered the Cuban Embassy shortly after it opened. Lee waited in the ornate lobby of dark brown marble with gold-leaf framed paintings on the walls as Agent Gaudet observed him from across the room, pretending to fill-out the paperwork for a visa request. An officious oaf named Eusebio Azcue accepted Lee's completed forms and stated reflexively, "Cuba is not accepting any Americans without a two-week background check!"

He put on an air of importance and urgency. "I *need* to get to Cuba! Listen, I have information *you would be interested in* and I know you can pay my way."

Suddenly his stomach hurt—a sharp pain in the side. He ignored it, stared at the official, and then smiled slightly.

Consul Azcue replied curtly, "I doubt you seriously, senor, but I will call Havana directly." Azcue turned and went back into his office.

He took a deep breath and pressed his side, which had mellowed to a dull throbbing ache. While waiting for Consul Azcue, he took notice of an administrative secretary in a group of four secretaries typing at an island of four desks facing each other. He noticed her because she was eying him. He presumed she was Silvia Duran, so he went to the waist-high banister separating them and spoke with glowing admiration. "You sure are a good typist."

"Thank you." Her English was almost perfect. She wore a white dress with a large floral print of red rose buds and green leaves, had pretty brown eyes, caramel-colored skin, and a brilliant smile. She seemed very receptive to his attention but Consul Azcue returned quickly, summarily handed back his form, and said, "Your application is denied."

The whole process had taken less than five minutes. It was so fast he wondered if Azcue's "telephone call" to Havana was simply to retrieve information about him from a file on hand, perhaps from the Soviets. Regardless, Consul Azcue looked him over, up and down with obvious disgust, and spoke firmly. "You are denied a visa. Please leave the Embassy."

He bowed graciously, watched Consul Azcue walk away, and then turned directly to the secretary, who was staring at him. He smiled, cocked his head to her, and shrugged.

She immediately offered, "I know many students who, on some occasion, are allowed to travel to Cuba to study. If you like, perhaps I could introduce you to some of them? They are having a party at the university tonight."

"Yes, I'd love to go," he smiled warmly and winked.

She blushed, but only for an instant, and walked to the railing, wrote down "Silvia" and the address of the party on an official Embassy notepad, and handed it to him. "I will meet you there."

As he took the note, he looked over his shoulder and saw Consul Azcue shaking his head as he sat down at his desk.

He stared deeply into Silvia's eyes. "I can taste you on my lips and it's sweet like sangria."

Silvia blinked. Her mouth surrendered and opened. She was captivated, but she walked away casually then turned very fast like a flamenco dancer to look back at him longingly. He walked slowly backward, staring at her, and then left.

The CIA Regional Chief, Agent David Phillips, who controlled the entire Mexico City office with phone calls and paperless messages, had arranged through another source for Lee to meet a newspaper editor named Oscar Contreras. That afternoon, as part of his role to gain attention and notoriety for his support of the Cuban cause, he went to newspaper's offices and spoke with Mr. Contreras for almost an hour about the struggling Cuban nation, their efforts to instill a new form of communist government, and of how this was an exciting time in Cuba's history much like Mexico's own revolutionary struggles. Mr. Contreras was rather dumbfounded throughout the interview and, in closing, stated that he would try to place an article somewhere in their newspaper but he could not promise it. Lee politely nodded with a short bow, shook his hand, and thanked Mr. Contreras for his time.

After the newspaper interview, he checked in with Chief Phillips at the central office. Chief Phillips introduced him to another Company man, E. Howard Hunt, who was slightly taller than him, with dark hair and hardened features. But the striking thing about Hunt was his black pork pie hat. Lee recalled from his meeting with Agent Frank Bender, in Guy Banister's office, and from his conversations with George de Mohrenschildt, that Hunt had a lot of experience in the Caribbean dating back to Guatemala. He knew Hunt was an important person but he was feeling a bit tired so he said slowly, "Excuse me, I need to get some dinner and a nap back at the Hotel Del Comercio. I've got to prepare for this evening's mission."

Agent Hunt chuckled, his square chin jutting out under his pork pie hat, and forcefully put his arm around his neck. "It's another fucking party. Fucking. Party. Fucking. Come on."

Agent Hunt pulled him, still in a headlock, and guided him out of the office and onto the streets of Mexico City. Outside, Hunt finally released his headlock but kept his hand in a tight grip on the back of his neck. It was the same thing Uncle Charlie did to people when he was upset with them. The whole prospect of what was coming next worried him. They walked much further than he expected, for quite a while, and then into a park with many trees and finally into an isolated area of the park, and Hunt suddenly let him have it. "Of all the pansy-assed, two-bit shitheads I've seen for a lousy excuse of an agent, you're the motherfucking worst fucking asshole I've ever seen! You had a simple assignment at the Cuban Embassy, shit, you'd even done it in the fucking Soviet Union that is ten times the operation of the Cubans in Mexico, and one, shit-eating, piss-ignorant official stopped you from gaining access to the Cuban higher-ups, never mind defecting, and he had you fucking turning tail like a bitch with water thrown on her? Of all the dumbshit, asinine, piss-for-brains retards I've had come through here, you take the cake! You're a fucking disgrace to the Navy boy, and I'm sorry I have to even talk to your lousy, miserable, good-for-nothing, excuse of a turd face!"

"I tried to make—"

"You shut the fuck up when I'm talking to you!" Hunt boxed his right ear with a swift open-hand karate punch that stung. He grabbed the side of his face and Agent Hunt followed up with a thwacking finger pop to his upper lip that burned with pain.

"Jesus fu—"

Hunt grabbed him by the back of his neck and forced him down while thrusting a vicious knee-kick into his forehead. He crumpled to the cracked sidewalk.

"I thought I told you to shut the fuck up when I'm talking. Don't you know who I am, dickhead?"

"Yes, sir!"

"You bet your ass, you know. Now show me some respect, you two-bit, shit-faced cunt!"

He stood up quickly, brushed himself off, and stood at attention. Agent Hunt didn't speak but eyed him suspiciously. He resumed his grip on the back of his neck and they continued walking.

Lee checked his nose to see if it was bleeding. It wasn't, but it was running with snot and he wiped it again and again. His stomach started burning with that familiar hot pain in his side.

Agent Hunt spoke with very strong, opinionated words about Cuba and the President's policies, while occasionally flexing his strong grip on his neck. He then he spoke tangentially and Lee knew that this meant something important was about to be said, or *not said.*

Hunt said gruffly, "Either result of your next mission will be fine. Succeed—great! But if you fail, we can blame the assassination attempt on Castro and arouse enough indignation among the American people to create a movement to support another invasion of Cuba, but this time with *full* American military support. Hell, we might even lead the charge."

Further in the park Agent Hunt pointed to a bench. He directed Lee, "Wait here for a colored guy. He's got a package for you, *then* you can get some rest."

Agent Hunt still seemed very upset, made a clucking sound, and shook his head. He shoved him by the neck toward the bench. "Fuck."

He watched as Hunt walked away casually, pushing up his pork pie hat and wiping his brow, as if he were enjoying the shade of the park in the blazing Mexican heat. The air was thin and dirty. He felt his nose again, massaging it tenderly, then it occurred to him that Agent Hunt had the same last name as the wealthy Hunt family, who had the party where he met George de Mohrenschildt. He recalled H.L. Hunt's silvery hair and yellow-toothed grin as he eyed Marina lasciviously. H.L. Hunt's entire appearance and personality oozed wealth and attitude. There was no way Agent E. Howard Hunt could be related to him.

Nearby children played on a swing set and sang a bouncy song in Spanish. He thought of Junie and wondered what she was doing at this very moment. Probably eating dinner with Marina.

He felt very badly after Agent Hunt's tirade and wondered what he could do to improve himself on his next mission. He remembered his training: be confident, be smart, be quick. You can do this, so remain calm and confident.

A few minutes later a tall Cuban and a younger black man came and sat down next to him with the black man closer to him and the Cuban at the end of the bench. As they sat down, the Cuban handed the black guy a small paper bag. He knew that this was his "package" as Hunt described it. He wondered what this was all about, but knew it had to be a mission related to Cuba.

"I was there on the beach," the Cuban said, meaning the Bay of Pigs invasion. He spoke with a very slight accent, although his English was flawless. "I would love to do this myself because I lost friends there. Loved ones, do you understand?"

"I understand you, sir," he said.

The Cuban had a wizened, creased face. He looked as if he had been through jungle training, or lived it, but his dark eyes were tearing up. He looked away and the black guy, thin with a short Afro, picked up the conversation.

"We'd stand out—we'd be spotted. That's why we can't do it," the black man said. He wore a white tee shirt and baggy, olive-green pants. Then a Mexican in a business suit walked by very slowly, fooling with some kind of electronic device in his hand, but the black guy didn't seem to notice and spoke too loudly, "I want to kill the man."

He stared at the passing businessman, who acted as if he wasn't concerned about their conversation, which he obviously was, as he stopped to fiddle with the palm-sized instrument that looked similar to a transistor radio. Lee spat in the man's general direction, which got a disgusted response, but the guy moved on.

He waited for another moment before speaking, waiting until the businessman was well out of listening distance. He wasn't quite sure exactly what he was agreeing to do, but he was pretty sure it had to do with killing Castro, or another top official such as Che Guevara. He wanted to succeed very badly. These guys were acting with bravado, hard-earned machismo, and he knew that he had to act stronger than them, so he played the part. Plus in his heart he knew he could do it. He said, "You're not man enough. I can do it."

"I can't go with you. I have a lot to do," the black man said. He shrugged his shoulders and handed him the package. "This isn't much compared to our desire for justice."

The black guy stood, tapped the Cuban, who was openly weeping and wiping his eyes, and they left.

He waited for several minutes, checked to make sure the "businessman" wasn't around, he wasn't, and then peered into the bag. There were a lot of twenty and fifty dollar bills. He closed the bag nonchalantly and casually walked out of the park, pausing to watch the children play. He again thought of Junie, watching as they jumped rope, drew with chalk, and tossed a ball. He looked around again and continued on his way back to the Hotel del Comercio, thinking of Junie and Marina until he got back to his room, where he opened the paper bag on his bed and counted the money: $6,500.

This must be *very big*, Lee thought. He had never dreamed of this much money. He stuffed the cash in the bag and tucked it under the mattress, then collapsed into a deep sleep. He dreamed of Marina's soft skin, kissing her neck gently, and tasted a sweet spray of perfume. He hugged her tenderly from behind and softly stroked her full abdomen as they watched Junie play in the back yard.

~ ~

Later that night Lee met Silvia Duran at the party, which was held at an off-campus apartment of a professor in the philosophy department. Several students were there and a record player blasted a rock 'n' roll song. He approached Silvia as she danced a twist. She wore a black dress with a red floral print of blooming roses and she immediately brightened and danced with him. They did the twist for twenty minutes, including several moments when he was clearly not dancing as much as he was simply keeping his face inches from her while moving his hips. There was a break in the music and Silvia introduced him to her brother and then to the professor hosting the party. A few minutes later they left the party for his hotel room, where they were twisting the night away.

In the morning Silvia acted rather cool toward him as she dressed. "I would love to see you again, but my husband, he's been away on business, and he will be back today."

He acted appropriately surprised and upset that she had not mentioned a husband before, but he already knew about him from her p-file. After a moment he pretended to calm down and took hold of her hand. "Can you meet me during your lunch break? You could bring me the paperwork for a student visa and. . . " he winked and smiled, "we'll fill it out here."

That afternoon Silvia returned with the student visa paperwork and they danced for nearly two hours during the afternoon siesta. Afterward he quickly filled out the paperwork and escorted her back to the Cuban Embassy to submit it. As they approached the building, he stopped to allow her to enter first, avoiding any surveillance cameras that would show them together, and he entered a few minutes after her. He acted very business-like as he handed her a completed student visa application to travel to Cuba. She personally handed it to Consul Azcue, who looked at him harshly.

"Come back tomorrow!" Azcue said with disgust.

The next day, Lee's student application was denied. A few days later, he again tried to "defect," letting them know clearly and without mincing words that he had *privileged* information. But Consul Azcue was now completely annoyed at the very sight of Lee and not the least bit interested in helping an American. Azcue said directly and strongly, "Get out!"

He tried to raise the issue into a physical confrontation, screaming and creating a scene, but Azcue remained professionally calm and called for security to take him from the building. Two large guards promptly lifted him off his feet and dumped him on the sidewalk outside.

He had failed on his mission to enter Cuba. He did make a significant contact with a source, Silvia Duran, inside the Cuban Embassy, but it would be up to ONI and CIA on how to use that source as an asset at a future date. There was nothing left for him to do except to return to America.

He stood in the sparse office of his CO, Regional Chief Phillips, who sat behind his empty desk and stared out the window at the Mexico City skyline shrouded in a thick yellow haze of smog. Chief Phillips wore a gray fedora very low over his eyes but Lee recalled his vacant look and extremely light blue eyes. Chief Phillips acted as if he wasn't in the room.

He explained that his wife and family were now in Dallas, not New Orleans. Chief Phillips may have nodded slightly as if he already knew this information. "Mm."

He waited for another moment but Chief Phillips sat sphinx-like, staring out the window. The drone of a generator hummed at a nearby construction site. He decided he would wait to see how long the silence would last, or how long Chief Phillips would remain motionless. After several minutes it occurred to him that Phillips's slow, deep breathing may be a sign that he was asleep. He waited a few more minutes then softly stepped away. At the office doorway he heard, "I'll contact you."

He took a bus back to Dallas and checked into a rooming house. He tried to reach George de Mohrenschildt but the phone rang and rang and rang. He suspected George had already left for Haiti.

The following Monday he walked to the local bus stop to ride downtown, a blond boy with black glasses on a bicycle handed him a newspaper then rode away quickly with playing cards strumming the spokes of his wheels faster and faster. It was about 6:30 a.m. and Lee gazed about quickly. There was no one else on the suburban streets of Dallas. The row houses all had neatly trimmed hedges and lawns but no one was in sight. Then he noticed that the boy wasn't delivering newspapers to any of the houses as he turned a corner and rode out of sight.

He looked more closely at the newspaper and saw the number 9 was circled in the date. He quickly flipped to page nine and found the words "supervisor to give briefing tomorrow at the DalTex building" underlined in an article about sewage treatment. He interpreted that to mean Chief David Phillips was now in Dallas to coordinate his next mission and to give him instructions. He suspected that the next mission probably had something to do with Cuba because other than the Soviet Union that was where all the action was.

Lee was mentally exhausted by his failures, on so many missions, and decided that if he was going to fulfill his burning ambition to do something historic, he needed to perform at a much higher level. He rededicated himself and was determined his next mission would be a success. He desperately wanted to prove his worth. He wanted to prove it to his missing father, to his mother and brother, to his immediate family of Marina and June and their next child, but most of all he wanted to do his patriotic duty for his country.

46)

You ever been in prison?

Sparky pulled over at the intersection of two dirt roads, DeWitt and Jefferson, in an isolated piece of flatland and swamp with absolutely nothing around it for miles, outside New Orleans. Cicadas hummed wildly in the desolate swampy heat.

Sparky watched as Lee's wife, eight months pregnant with pretty blue eyes and holding a spray of pink flowers, waddled up, said something to Lee in broken English, and got in the front seat of his new white Oldsmobile. Hmm, Sparky thought. She just jumped in the front seat! This guy can't control his woman. He must be a wimp to marry this twat.

He opened the trunk and showed Lee a few rifles and pistols he had.

"That's nice," Lee said.

"What?" Sparky asked.

"The B-A-R. Military issue."

"It's all military," Sparky said.

Lee picked up a Colt .45 and checked the action. It was smooth. He placed it back in the trunk by a jug of radiator fluid and picked up another pistol. "This isn't. This is a standard thirty-eight."

"Yeah," Sparky said. "Colt."

Lee looked around the open trunk to make sure Marina wasn't listening or paying attention to them. She had stayed for one week with Uncle Charlie and Aunt Lillian in New Orleans, while June stayed in Dallas with a friend, as Lee attended a training camp near Lacombe. Then Lee brought Marina out here by bus to catch a ride back to Dallas with Sparky, who had worked with his uncle's boss, Nofio Pecora, and also knew Sam Termine.

Sparky's white car had a shiny brown vinyl interior and was parked on the shoulder of a dirt road, not far from the camp where Captain Dave Ferrie had arranged for Lee to take target practice with his rifle alongside a group of anti-Castro rebels. The rebels called themselves Alpha 66 and they were a patchwork of Cuban exiles pulled together and organized by the CIA and led by Sergio Arcacha Smith. They used the camp to train in guerilla warfare techniques and hardly noticed Lee taking extensive target practice with his rifle. He had recently bought a new scope and needed to calibrate it to this gun as well as become accustom to its peculiarities under various weather conditions of wind, humidity, and glaring sunlight.

Lee was still miffed over Captain Dave's comment that he "couldn't hit the broad side of a barn with that piece of shit Italian rifle with a Japanese scope," and everyone laughed. It was an unusual combination but it handled similarly to the rifle he had in the Marines. But then Captain Dave said, "Plus it spits fire like the devil's asshole!" and everyone laughed louder. So examining these guns made Lee consider getting something new. The derisive remarks had also reinforced Lee's motivation to *not fail.*

Lee extended his arm and looked down the barrel of the Colt .45 at a telephone pole up the road. He liked the way if felt, squeezed the trigger, and BLAM!

A shot rang out and smacked the telephone pole near the edge, sending a wood chip flying.

Marina jerked around from the front seat and screamed. "Lee!"

"Christ, you keep it loaded?" Lee said.

"Yeah," Sparky smirked. "You never know."

"It's alright!" Lee called out. He gave Sparky a harsh look. "Jesus."

"It's a sweet piece. Treat 'er nice and she'll love you forever." Sparky pulled his keys out, slammed the trunk, and walked for the driver's door.

Lee was left holding the gun. He slid on the safety and carefully put it in his jacket pocket. Damn. He walked around the passenger's side and opened the front door, telling Marina, "Get in back."

"But I'm comfortable and—"

Lee screamed, "Get in back!"

Marina wheeled out of the brown vinyl seat, placing one hand on her abdomen and holding the stems of the pink-petaled obedient plants in her other hand, and glared at him.

Lee shook his head disapprovingly. What in the hell was she thinking?

As Marina opened the back door she glanced at him again so Lee raised his hand as if he would slap her a good one. Damn. One more reason to keep her the hell out of everything. How in the hell did she persuade him into visiting New Orleans? Just because she wanted to see his family again? That was a big mistake. He should have realized there was a chance she'd run into these people and now he had to get her back to Dallas. He should have never allowed it. In spite of all the money from the Mexican mission he didn't want to stick her on a bus, alone, and in her condition, so when Nofio Pecora, a connected friend of his Uncle Charlie, offered that this guy Sparky could drive them back it seemed easy enough. Shit, it was a big mistake. But there was nothing to do now except contain it.

Marina started to say something as Lee closed the door so he hollered, "Sit there and shut the fuck up!"

As Lee got in the front seat Sparky gave him a slight smile of approval and put it in gear. His heartburn flared up his throat and he felt that odd pain in his side again, but he turned to look at Sparky, who accelerated until they were doing eighty-five. The wind howled through the rolled-down windows but it was still stifling hot in the steamy, late-morning heat. The sun baked through the front windshield and the pistol barrel felt hot on his side through his gray jacket.

"You in the Army?" Sparky said.

"Marines," Lee said.

"Semper fi."

"You too?" Lee asked.

"Air Force. I grew up in Chicago."

"Oh. I was in the Civil Air Patrol plus I was stationed at an air base."

The car hummed over the blacktop. Lee looked into the backseat at Marina and she had a tissue to her nose. She was upset, tears were in her eyes, and she moved her left hand over her abdomen. He thought of the forming baby, hopefully growing strong in spite of everything.

Lee turned back around. "She barely speaks English."

Sparky said, "Yeah. I saw."

"So you don't have to worry about what you say." Then Lee quickly added, "But I don't want to talk about anything."

"You got something against talkin'?" Sparky said.

"No. I meant the details of what we're doing. Anything about it at all."

"I ain't a fuckin' moron." He tightened his fists around the white steering wheel and breathed heavily.

"I didn't say you were," Lee countered.

"Well, I'd have to be to talk about it," Sparky snapped. He thought, This guy's an idiot and already treating me without respect. Where did they get this asshole?

"Alright, take it easy," Lee said. He thought, Geez, this guy has a short fuse. Where'd they find this asshole? But he was at the meeting site on time and Nofio Pecora said he was reliable. And he had delivered guns for Guy Banister's Cuban operation, under Carlos Marcello's financing, so that was another good sign. He probably knows Captain Dave, too. Just watch his temper.

Sparky rolled his neck, loosened his grip on the steering wheel, and exhaled heavily. He thought, I'll try to be nice to this jerk and make some polite conversation. "So'd you serve overseas?"

"Yes, I was stationed in Japan for a tour, then my mother got sick so I got an honorable discharge. Shortly after that I served in Minsk for about two years."

"Minsk? Where the fuck is that?"

"Minsk is located in the Soviet Union. It's a small city that was obliterated in World War Two but was rebuilt by the Soviets."

Sparky stared at him out of the corners of his eyes with scorn. "The Soviets? You a commie?"

"No sir. I'm a Marxist–Leninist and there is a distinct difference. It's a philosoph—"

"She a commie?" Sparky snapped.

"No, she has no political affiliation. Leave her out of it. She's my wife and that's it."

"Okay." Sparky breathed heavily again and twisted his fists around the steering wheel tightly. Sweat rolled down his temples to his white shirt collar. He wasn't wearing a tie or jacket, and his t-shirt and shirt were sticking together from all the sweat. "But with so many women, why'd you marry her?"

"It's none of your business. She's my wife. That's it."

Sparky thought, who does this guy think he is? He wanted to ask another question, just to bust his balls. "Did you have to?"

"Leave it alone," Lee said. His side ached again but he resisted rubbing it. If this kept up, he may need to see a doctor.

"Yeah, okay."

Sparky took one hand off the wheel, dug into his pants pocket and retrieved a medicine bottle, shook out a preludin into his mouth, and then picked up a pack of Lucky Strikes that had been on the floor. He punched in the lighter and stole another long look at him. The lighter popped out almost immediately with a red-hot glow. He lit the cigarette to little crackling noises and took a deep drag, exhaling thickly threw his nostrils. "I know a lot of women, take care of you real nice, if you know what I mean. If you want me to fix it up, I can."

Lee spoke firmly, "That won't be necessary."

"Yeah, okay. I know how a guy can be married for a time and start to have urges, you know, and I'm just saying I can make it easy for you, if that's what you need."

Lee was furious and spoke as evenly as he could. "I love my wife. Please refrain from talking about her *ever* again. Do I make myself clear?"

Sparky took another drag on the cigarette and stared at him. He blew smoke directly into his face and thought, How do you like that? Yeah. You and your Russian bitch want to get out and walk you're welcome to. You ungrateful shit. I gave you a gun. Why do I always do stuff for people and get no respect? Mr. Marcello better reward me plenty for this. I didn't ask for hauling around assholes and their high-minded cunts like some goddamned bus service.

Lee could tell Sparky was fuming, so he tried to make light conversation. "What do you think of the Texas football team's chances this fall?"

Sparky grunted and said, "Hook 'em horns!" It was a simple reflex from years of living among the local Texans. The truth was he didn't give a shit about any college team. "Yeah, they'll do alright, but I'm more of a Bears fan. Pro teams."

"Okay. They've got Ronnie Bull out of Baylor and with Wade at quarterback their passing game isn't too shabby, either. Plus Coach Halas is one of the finest in the game. It all starts at the top."

"Yeah. But Wade doesn't run the bootleg too good and he gets sacked too much. But, yeah, I bet on them almost every Sunday. Except when I *know* they're going to lose," Sparky laughed loudly. "If you know what I mean!"

Lee wondered, What's so funny? He must know guys that fix games. That wouldn't be a surprise. He runs with the mob.

He felt the gun, still warm, and carefully slid it out of his pocket. He bootlegged it, keeping it away from Sparky, and lowered it to the floor but held onto it.

Sparky said, "Makes for a nice little side income, you know?"

"Yes, I bet it does."

"You bet on sports?"

"No, sir, that's not an interest of mine," he said. "I like to watch the games when they're on television but I can't really afford the luxury of betting on teams. I have a limited income and a family to care for."

"Yeah?"

"Yes, I have a wonderful little girl named June." He let the gun slip slowly from his hand to the carpeted floorboard, still cradling it tenderly in his hand. "We call her Junie. She's almost two. Twenty months."

"Where's she now?" Sparky asked.

"We have a friend, Ruth, who's watching her for the week. Marina wanted one last trip to get away and see my family. She's big on family but I'm not." He pointed the gun away from him to the front and side, and let it rest on the floor. He inched his fingers away from it. Touched it again, still warm. Let it lie. He pulled his hand up and sat up straight. He'd let Sparky find it later.

"Yeah," Sparky said. He took another drag on the cigarette before mashing it out in the ashtray. He thought about family and how important it was to him. But "family" also extended to a few select people, very special people who you had to put your life in their hands and vice versa. Family is *very* important, he thought. It was the ultimate "unit." Mr. Capone had talked about it often. Santo Trafficante had recognized it when he visited him in prison. But this guy said he *wasn't* big on family. Hmm. This guy was more than a bit off. How can anyone put down family? Maybe this guy had a bad family experience. Then he thought of how prison can change people and he had a hunch. He asked, "You ever been in prison?"

"Yeah," Lee thought of his recent jailing for disturbing the peace, then of the brig in Japan for a fistfight with an officer, detention centers growing up, the various interrogation techniques he'd experienced, especially the time when he was being held by the KGB and that goon thought it was his masochistic duty to beat him, and decided it would be best not to talk about any of it. "I'd rather not discuss it."

"Yeah, me too," Sparky said, but he thought, This guy is a real prick. He had been arrested plenty of times and the guys who had something to hide were the ones you had to watch out for. They'd try to pin something on you, or use you to their advantage. It was better to shut up around those pricks. But he decided to be nice with him, being as this was a guy that Carlos Marcello and Nofio Pecora picked, but to hell with dealing with him. "I know what you mean."

They did not speak for the remainder of the ride. Occasionally Lee looked over at Sparky. Occasionally Sparky eyed Lee. A few moments would pass and they would eye each other again, suspiciously, as if the other was crazy and dangerous. The Oldsmobile screamed down the highway, a white-hot rocket riding on the crest of a wave of heated ideas and secret planning about to crash on the streets of downtown Dallas.

47)

You will *do dis t'ing*

Sparky sat in his bar reading the Dallas *Morning News,* checking his ad to make sure they got the girls' stage names right, when he was very surprised: Jimmy Hoffa walked through the swinging doors of the Carousel Club in the middle of the afternoon. He had seen him on the television but he was shorter than he expected, maybe five feet nine, wore a neat suit and tie, and he had a brown valise in his left hand. Plus he was with Joe Civello for Christ's sakes!

Sparky jumped off the barstool and eyed the valise again as he shook their hands. Hoffa smelled of sickly-sweet cheap perfume. Mr. Civello also wore a suit and his dark hair was neatly trimmed. He pulled out a chair at the first table and motioned for them to sit down. "Can I offer you a drink? Rum and coke? Sambucca?"

"That'd be nice," Mr. Hoffa said. He had thick jowls and round piercing eyes, and he looked around the room with a trace of dissatisfaction. He sniffed as if he smelled something unpleasant while setting the valise on the table.

"Andy! Three Sambuccas! And keep them coming." He wished he had the carpets cleaned last week. But it seemed that no matter how much he had the place cleaned, it still smelled of spilled beer and puke. "You want anything else? A sandwich? I got all kinds in the back."

"No, t'anks for your concern," Mr. Civello said politely and smiled. His smile was very unnerving. He always smiled but the fact Mr. Civello was here, in his bar, meant serious business. And sometimes when he smiled, well, you better watch your back.

"Listen, I'll keep it brief," Mr. Hoffa said bluntly with his round, serious eyes staring at him. "We need you to clean up a situation."

"Yeah, of course. You, Mister Hoffa, I'd do anything to help you out. I believe in the Union. I'm a Union man from way back. You know that."

"Dis ain't about unions," Mr. Hoffa turned to Mr. Civello as if he resented something, probably someone should have talked to him first, but Mr. Civello shrugged. Mr. Hoffa raised his eyebrows and pushed on. "It's another t'ing."

"Oh." He was silent and immediately feared they were here to take his club. He was late on his payment, as usual, but things had not been going well lately. The club wasn't a good earner and the IRS was breathing down his neck for back taxes. He owed the IRS an impossible amount of money, $40,000, and any time the club had a good week, he tried to give something to the IRS to keep them from pressuring the local cops to shut him down or worse, to bust him for tax evasion like Mr. Capone. Now, here's Mr. Hoffa, a Union man, but connected, and Mr. Civello sitting right there, too, and he was afraid they'd make him a "deal" that would cost him his club.

Andy, the jug-eared bartender, set three shots of Sambucca on the table and wheeled away quickly without asking if they wanted anything else.

Christ, offer them a sandwich! Sparky thought. There's plenty in the back room. "You sure you don't want a sandwich, nothin' to eat?"

"Salute!" Mr. Civello said, and they all clinked glasses and downed the clear sweet liquor.

Sparky noticed Mr. Hoffa eying Andy, maybe to make sure he was out of hearing range or maybe just sizing him up, so he said, "Don't mind him. Andy's close. He did some time, a raw deal, but he can be trusted."

Mr. Hoffa gave him an evil look that showed this was no ordinary business. Holy shit. This was it. He nervously glanced at Andy, who was checking stock and making a list of liquor to be ordered, but stopped when he saw him and grabbed the Sambucca bottle and filled three more shot glasses.

Mr. Hoffa opened the valise and pulled out stacks of twenty dollar bills, wrapped with red rubber bands, and set them on the table. "Here's seven large."

"Whoa!" Sparky said. "Now I—"

"Shut up," Civello said. Oh Jesus Christ, this was it! They'd make an offer and then take his club in about one month.

Hoffa continued, "When you get the word, you do what you're told. Is that clear?"

"Yes, sir."

"It may be," Hoffa said casually, "that nothing has to happen on your end. That's fine. Consider this a gift. But if we need you, you do this t'ing."

"Yeah, of course," he said.

Andy placed three more shots on a tray but Hoffa stood at the table, closed his valise, and walked over to the bar. He picked up a shot, knocked it back, and then looked over his shoulder. Civello stood up at the table, frowned "no," and Hoffa picked up a second shot and threw it back, leaving one glass on the tray.

"We done a lot for you, Jackie," Civello said, smiling broadly. "Got dis business going, kept it going. . . "

Civello's face changed instantly and he stared down at him with vicious intimidation. "You *will* do dis t'ing."

"Yeah."

Civello nodded solemnly to seal the deal, and then looked at Hoffa at the bar, and walked away.

"Atta boy!" Hoffa said, following Civello for the swinging doors. Two very large men were standing by the doorway and he recognized Robert "Barney" Baker, who was over 300 pounds and was known as Hoffa's main enforcer. They had been there the whole time but he now realized he had been staring at Hoffa and Civello with fixed fear. He was very nervous about this "thing" and noticed he was sweating profusely and breathing heavily.

As Hoffa followed the group of men down the stairwell, he slapped Barney Baker's huge back, said something and laughed, then disappeared down the stairs.

Andy watched them leave and spoke from behind the bar. "What was that all about?"

Sparky left the stacks of money on the table and went to the bar. "Give me the bottle." He took out his preludins, popped two in his mouth, and slammed back the last remaining shot. "Don't you say a fuckin' thing."

Andy looked at him evenly and handed over the bottle. He nodded okay and said, "You the boss."

"I have no idea what that was about," Sparky mumbled, but he knew that it meant something very, very serious. Hoffa and Civello had been sent and he must do this thing or . . . but there was no "or." He would do it or he would be dead. He took a long hit off the bottle, stared into space, and said, "It ain't good. It sure as fuck ain't good."

48)

Who's my contact at the theater?

"Don't worry. We have a back-up plan to take care of you."

Lee didn't see who said that and looked around Chief Phillips's sterile office. It was empty and cool with a weird odor of formaldehyde.

Chief Phillips acted like everything was under control, but he felt uneasy and, following George de Mohrenschildt's advice to not give *trust but to make every person* earn *it— he did not trust Chief Phillips. It was Phillips who engineered the miscues in New Orleans: First Carlos Bringuier was sloppy and then Phillips's FBI contact, Agent Bateman, never came to the police station. In this new mission something smelled out of line but he didn't want to question the entire mission—just anything relating to Chief David Phillips. He asked, "What's the back-up plan?"*

"I can't talk," Chief Phillips said stone-faced. Then he looked closely and saw his lips did not move. Perhaps this was some type of magician's trick? After a long pause, a low, ghost-like groan bellowed, "Fixed."

"Well, who's in charge of the back-up?"

"Ja-a-ack."

"He's a—" He caught himself from saying too much. He thought they were alone in Phillip's office but cautiously looked around the sparse room to see if anyone would hear him say "mob guy" and there was Nofio Pecora, Uncle Dutz's associate, leaning against the bare wall. Pecora seemed to understand him anyway but shrugged as if no offense were taken. Then Pecora began laughing hysterically, throwing his arms up and down with convulsive laughter.

He continued, "How will Sparky handle it?"

"Don't worry!" Pecora said in an exaggerated Italian accent.

"I know him," he said. "He gave me a ride from New Orleans."

"Good," Chief Phillips smiled. His light blue eyes were haunting and his mouth did not move as the word seemed to come from nowhere. Maybe Phillips practiced ventriloquism? "Good."

"Seemed like an asshole to me. He has no respect for women and—"

"He's got conneggions wit da police!" Pecora said, smiling at Chief Phillips, who smirked and then stifled another laugh. "He been done working dem for over ten year! Dey look at him and see a friend. So if anyone can back you, it Jack."

"Okay, true dat." He heard his words come out in a N'awlins drawl, looked down briefly, clenched his lips, and shook his head. He knew from speaking with Uncle Charlie that Sparky was associated to Carlos Marcello. If he was okay by all of them, then he should accept him as his back-up. "Okay."

But when it came to the key points of the escape route for the mission, he did not want any slip-ups. He wanted confirmation of each important detail. "But the main plan is the same. I change, go to the theater, your contact meets me there, drives me to the airport, and Captain Ferrie flies me out of the country."

Chief Phillips nodded positively, put his hands out, and smiled broadly. "Like clockwork."

Did he actually say that? Lee thought, and then decided he should not question his CO. "Alright. I'm counting on your man to get me to Captain Dave. I have no worries about Captain Dave, except that one time, that one time was horrible. But your man better not screw up."

"Don't worry!" Pecora shouted. "He a good driver. There be no problem. Sammy a good driver and so is dis guy. He meet you in de dark theater, you slip out the back door into the alley where he have a car waiting, and zoom off you go to de airport."

"Okay." It seemed rock solid. "Who's my contact at the theater?"

Nofio Pecora clutched his small, muscular fist to his mouth to keep from laughing and for some reason this was very funny to Chief Phillips, too, and he also laughed and then caught himself. Phillips started to speak, to actually move his lips, but he laughed hard, caught himself, and then said through a giggling little-boy's voice, "Car-los Br-ha-ha, Brin-guier."

Shit, he thought. Bringuier was late in New Orleans. He knew this smelled bad.

Chief Phillips noticed the concern on Lee's face and was suddenly very serious. He stared at him with his fixed, cool blue eyes and said solemnly, "Do you have a problem with Bringuier?"

He thought more about the details of the street fight, recalled that eventually when Bringuier did arrive, it went okay and the objective was met. Bringuier was also fine in the staged radio interview, the following week, and he could keep his mouth shut. "Yeah, I guess he's okay."

Chief Phillips nodded to Nofio Pecora and both men shared a knowing look and immediately burst into hysterical laughter. They both began pointing at his feet but he ignored them. Their laughter continued until they were both doubling over and pointing at him. He looked around to see if it could be anyone else, or some other thing in the room, but no, they were definitely pointing at his *feet.*

He looked down and was horrified: his shoes were dirty, torn in tatters with holes in the toes, and one sole flopped loosely.

Lee awoke from his dream, which seemed very real except for the maniacal laughter. It was the same damn recurring dream of being embarrassed of his shoes. He lay still, with his heart racing, and sweat in his single bed. His stomach burned and he tried to figure out what was so disturbing about the rest of the dream. It was times like these that he missed Marina with her comforting touch and gentle reassurances. He had taken this single room in a boarding house run by Mrs. Earlene Roberts in Fort Worth, not too far from Marina and June, and yet far enough, and he was able to visit them every weekend. In many ways it was good that Marina wasn't here to see him upset over another mission.

The dream had given him an unsettled feeling especially because his CO and the other key players had not held a group planning meeting yet. But the disturbing issue wasn't anything he could identify, yet something felt odd like the smell of formaldehyde. Something wasn't quite right. He knew it to his core. There was something wholly wrong. He simply knew it. But what could it be?

Then suddenly, there it was, dazzling right in front of him: the combination of Uncle Charlie's connections and his ONI contacts working together on a mission. It was so completely unlikely that it felt either contrived or serendipitous. He thought either he was being set-up for another failed mission, or he was born for this historic moment. It disturbed him. But as he lay still, thinking about it all, he preferred to think it would be his historic moment, focused on that, planned on that, and smiled slightly. Yeah, it's okay. It must be. This is my historic moment.

49)

You ain't sayin' much

Lee looked around the decrepit, smelly strip club and then observed Sparky, who had given him a ride from the Lacombe training camp. He was a half-loony want-to-be-hoodlum and chatted up a lot of cops who didn't know how small their own lives were. Sparky tried to be both host and intimidating bouncer. It was a stupid combination that any right-minded manager would easily avoid, but he wasn't that bright. He was also not a menacing intimidator. He had witnessed Marines, ONI agents like E. Howard Hunt, or Uncle Charlie, or Sammy Termine and plenty of their associates be intimidating when they had to be, and Sparky was not in their league. Not even close.

The cops appeared to be mid-level policemen who had stopped trying to get ahead through good work and started taking the extra money that was floating around. It was only appropriate that these cops had found company in these hoodlums. The cops were trying to be important, but the most important thing they could do was arrest someone under false pretenses, write parking tickets, and act like they had everything under control. Not only did they not have *anything* under control, they didn't even know who they were sitting with. Or did they? Perhaps they were sheep dipping, the same way he had pretended to defect to the Soviet Union, and pretended to be pro-Castro, all in order to gain information and set-up the enemy for a big blow that would come later. He watched them very closely: they were mesmerized by the dancers. Then it struck him that maybe they *did* know who they were sitting with and they just didn't care, which was even worse. The whole situation made him sick.

A stripper named Jada swung around a brass pole in a spotlight on the stage. The band, which would never pass for a band in New Orleans, was a drummer and a trumpet player. That was it. They played some amorphous grinding tune that wasn't really a song. The odorous funk of spilled beer, sweaty body odor, stale sausage, and a hint of vomit hung in the air.

"You ain't sayin' much, mister," Sergeant Dean said. "You got a secret?"

He watched Sergeant Dean roll his bottle by its long neck in a circle to see what was left of his beer. Sergeant Dean had said earlier in the night he had been coming to the Carousel Club for ten years and Sparky always stopped by his table to take care of him. He also said that during the holidays, Sparky doled out bottles of whisky, or "favors" from some of the girls, to Sergeant Dean and to any policeman who would take it. Lee shook his head with disgust.

"Ain't you got nothin' to say?" Sergeant Dean asked him.

"Leave him alone," Sparky said. "He ain't hurtin' nothin'."

"Give me something worth talking about," Lee said.

"Yeah, okay!" Sparky said. "You like sports, right? Football?"

"Looks like the only sport he's interested in is Jada's titties!" Officer Julius Kimball said as he elbowed his partner, Blackie Harrison, who was wearing a beige business suit and a white Stetson. They all laughed.

He chuckled, too, because it *was* funny. He had been staring off into space, then up at the stage despite trying to *not* watch Jada. The trumpet player was very bad and her grinding was slow, crude, and slightly awkward, but he couldn't take his eyes off her pasties. She had very nice full breasts and the pasties were dark and very round over her perfectly placed areolas, which reminded him of Midorii back in Tokyo. He wondered if Midorii was still working at the Queen Bee? Probably. If she hadn't retired when she turned 25, as she said she would. When was that? Oh, right, she was the same age as him, 24, so she would not "retire" until next year.

"He can't speak. He's hyp-no-*tized*," officer Kimball joked. They all laughed again.

"Come on," Sparky said, a bit more forcefully. "Leave him alone."

Sparky was becoming embarrassed. He didn't like his clientele mixing it up like this, especially with off-duty policemen. It only led to trouble, with someone getting arrested, and it was bad for business.

The joking cop, Julius Kimball, put one heel of his black cowboy boots up on their table and leaned back in his chair. Kimball took a drink of his beer and smiled, revealing a dimple on his cheek. His blue eyes were quick and yet there was something alarming about him. He locked eyes with Lee and pushed back his straw cowboy hat with two fingers. "You a Sooner fan? Y'all don't talk like y'all f'om around heah. Where y'all f'om?"

"No, sir," he said. "I was born in Slidell, Louisiana."

" 'S'at so?"

"Yes, sir. And no, I am not a Sooner fan." He stared back at him. "I think Auburn should do very well again this year, but it's a long year. But Coach Bear Bryant is one of the best coaches in the game and Alabama will also field a very competitive team."

Officer Kimball slapped the back of his hand against Sergeant Dean's arm. "I liked him better when he was staring at her tits."

They all laughed again.

Lee stood up and walked for the black swinging doors. He could see Sparky eying him the whole way, but he didn't care. He didn't need these idiots. He had a mission to complete and he was going to do it. He would do this job and that would finally show George that he was a hunter of fascists, it would show his CO that he could finish a mission successfully, demonstrate to his brother that he was as smart as he was, show his mother that he was not a burden to anyone but was a fine, worthy person, and prove to the memory of his missing father that he had done something historic. He would be an all-American hero. Yes, he desperately wanted to prove himself. He would do it.

50)

From the op book

Lee knew the best way to assassinate a protected figure, such as a political leader, is to use triangular crossfire. That's from the op book. That was a given. But on the whole parade route, there was no place three teams could set up.

Mr. Guy Banister explained the logistics to the group and CIA Regional Chief David Phillips and Nofio Pecora were looking at a map of Dallas with the parade route marked in red. He stood quietly off to the side, between Sergio Arcacha Smith, the spotter and driver from the General Walker mission, and Carlos Bringuier, the handsome but terrible actor and street "fighter" in New

Orleans. Then he recognized that most of the people in the room were based in New Orleans and not familiar with Dallas and its peculiarities. But it was *their* mission and he remained quiet, absorbing as much as he could.

"What about over here? Dealey Plaza." Chief Phillips pointed to the odd-shaped park where hundreds of spectators would be lined up on Main Street before the caravan merged onto the highway for the Trade Center.

"Yeah, dat could work," Nofio Pecora said, tweaking the short, dark whiskers on his chin with his small fingers. He bounced on his toes and twisted his chin hair into a point. "Elm Street."

"It's not on the parade route," Mr. Banister said, turning away from the group and using his craggy index finger to follow Main Street as it led in a direct line to the freeway entrance. "The parade route is a straight shot to the Stemmons Freeway and from there to the Trade Center."

"So change the route," Chief Phillips said in a matter-of-fact tone, as if it was already done. "Have 'em turn here Houston, to, ah, Elm. It happens on Elm."

Lee chewed on a medicated tablet for his stomach and thought, Who in the world could change the route of a presidential motorcade? Only someone involved from the inside. But why would those people agree to do it? Wouldn't this raise questions in the Secret Service to the area of the new route and draw specific attention to them? Who in the Service would agree to a hard right turn onto Houston, followed by a tight left turn onto Elm, when the entrance to the freeway was less than one hundred yards away and in a straight line of the current parade route?

There was no way, he thought. Then he realized if they could change the route, then powerful people were involved. He looked at Chief Phillips, who was in charge of the CIA Western Hemisphere as well as Chief of Covert Operations, and realized there weren't too many people above him. Okay, he nodded to Chief Phillips and then to Nofio Pecora. It must be a go.

"We'll put a team here," Chief Phillips said, now firmly showing that he was the force behind the mission. He tapped the map on the southwest portion of the overpass. "Here," he glanced at Sergio Arcacha Smith and pointed north of the plaza but near the overpass, and then turned a level-eyed stare at him, "And your team will be here."

"Roger," he said but thought again of the route change and couldn't stop from speaking his mind. "How will you change the route without drawing suspicion?"

"It's *fi-i-i-ixed!*" Chief Phillips groaned with irritation. A few people from the other teams mumbled, including Braden, a tough-looking tall man with greasy dark hair that was receding far up his high forehead. He decided he had to let go of the route change. If they could fix it, so be it.

Braden said, "There might be people on the overpass, being it's a parade. Cops, too."

He observed Braden closely and was reminded of the hucksters and con men who hung around the pool hall beneath their apartment in New Orleans. He had the same steely-eyed gaze of the sharks who moved constantly with a shifty nervousness.

"We gonna have a pick-up truck stalled right der," Pecora pointed to the base of the overpass. He tapped Braden on the shoulder, trying to relax him. "You can get a shot from de overpass."

"I'm not that good a shot," Braden continued, flexing his hands open and shut quickly. "How 'bout if I go up here? One of these places. How 'bout this? What's this DalTex building?"

Chief Phillips looked at Pecora, who nodded imperceptibly, smiled, and squeezed Braden's shoulder. "Sure, Jimmy. Sure."

Chief Phillips reaffirmed it with authority. "We can get you in. That'd work."

Sergio Arcacha Smith and some of the others were beginning to mill about, perhaps thinking the meeting was finished. A few guys were making smart-aleck comments. But Lee was still worried about several issues.

"My best shot is when they're slowing down for the second turn," he tried not to sound too worried about his marksmanship, but he was, in fact, extremely worried. "They'll be right under me and practically stopped."

"Forget it," Phillips snapped. "If you shoot then, the whole motorcade will look up and see you. Be patient. Wait until they pass because from that point on they're in the triangle, the kill zone, with two other teams focused on them."

"Zhat's a tough shot," a bony thin man said with a French accent. He waved a cigarette with two fingers in the European fashion, over the map by his perch and over the DalTex building. "Moveeng away *and* down zee hill, pfft!"

"No, it's not easy," Chief Phillips said calmly. His professional demeanor was steeped in confidence. "But you're here. Any of the three marksman can hit the target."

"Okay," Lee said. "But if I'm supposed to wait, how do I know when to start?"

"Any time after this turn," Chief Phillips touched the map carelessly, actually pointing to Commerce Street, but he spoke firmly. "After the limo clears the second turn, it's open season. Your shots will be increasingly difficult but theirs will be increasingly easier. It'll work."

"Okay." He turned to Mr. Banister, who looked very satisfied but rubbed his arthritic hands. "Let's go over the escape routes again."

"We've been over that ten times!" Banister snapped, wheeling around in aggravation. Mr. Banister must have noticed that the others were not paying attention as Sparky and Pecora joked with the Mafioso and Company shooters, Sergio Arcacha Smith and the French guy, and Braden with his team. Lee had more confidence in Sergio and wished they were on the same team, but realized

Sergio must be a shooter because Bringuier was his spotter. And yet he, Sergio, and Bringuier were meeting in the same rendezvous spot? Normally each team split up and had their own rendezvous spot with a separate guide to take them away.

Sergio and Bringuier chuckled with the others, so he tapped Sergio's muscular arm and snapped his fingers at Bringuier. He said, "Let's make it eleven."

"Okay." Banister's steely gray eyes looked at him coolly but he spoke slowly and clearly above the rising din as if it were the first time. "Lee leaves the window. Carlos takes the gun, wipes it down, disassembles it, collects the cartridges, goes down the elevator, and out the back of the building. Lee goes down the far stairwell, down to the second floor, into the lunchroom. Someone will give you the news the target's been shot, and you'll proceed with the crowd out of the building."

"I'm a little worried about that 'someone,' " he said.

"Don't worry," Banister said flatly. His wrinkled face showed no concern as if his experience had tempered away any worry long ago. "That "someone" is your alibi that you were in the break room the whole time. People will be in a panic and they'll spread the news fast, you can bet your ass on that."

"Well, I am."

"Don't worry so much!" Chief Phillips said sternly. He was running the whole operation and seemed miffed that he expressed doubt over any aspect of the mission. "We've done this before. It's all by the book. It works like clockwork."

"Okay, then what?" he said.

Banister continued slowly, "You go home, change clothes, and two cops will take you to meet Arcacha Smith and Bringuier in the Texas movie theatre."

He recalled the street fight and Bringuier's tardiness. He turned to Bringuier, jabbed his shoulder, and said firmly, "Don't be late."

Bringuier raised his eyebrows and glared at him as if he were beyond reproach. After a beat he cursed under his breath in Spanish, calling his mother a satisfier of fascist pigs. His voice cracked near the end, so it came out comical, but no one laughed.

Banister continued, "Sergio will drive Lee and Carlos to Redbird Airport. It's a small little field so no one will notice you. Ferrie will be waiting to fly you all out of the country."

"Where?" he said.

"To a safe haven in Guatemala."

"Okay," he thought, that will work, and nodded in confirmation. He was excited about this historic mission and he would do his best not to screw it up. He knew he needed more target practice with his rifle, the scope wasn't working well and he would need to adjust it at the firing range, but he was dedicated to the success of this mission. He would make the time to do whatever was necessary.

But he did feel bad the target was someone he respected, someone he once admired a great deal, but the s-o-b had shown he was soft on communism and let our boys die on the beach without lifting a finger to help them. Also, it was not his place to question orders. He had learned in the Marines, and through his ONI service, not to question orders. He had a mission and he was going to place himself in the best possible position to succeed. His country depended on him and he was ready to make any sacrifice for his country.

51)

The Egyptian Lounge

Sparky knew the best way to whack a guy was to make him think he was with friends. He'd never suspect a thing and BLAM! That was an unwritten part of the code, but all of the guys knew it, which made almost everyone edgy and paranoid.

He met one of his oldest and closest friends, Joseph Campisi, the restaurateur of the Egyptian Lounge, for dinner. It was a first-class place with beautiful chandeliers, dark blue walls, and a motif of ancient Egyptian wall paintings, statues, and reproduced artifacts. He ordered a steak and it was a real thick cut of prime rib, top quality and tender, and another friend, Ralph Paul, got the Alaskan king crab and steak combination. He didn't want to drink, but Mr. Campisi got out his finest champagne, maybe he was showing off how well he was doing, and they all had a glass and toasted, "To good friends and good times!" For dessert they all had lady fingers, or it looked like lady fingers in rum, but they called it some fancy name.

After dessert, Mr. Campisi leaned over him and whispered in his ear. "We need to send our dancers to the Cellar Club after hours."

He didn't like having his girls go to another club but he nodded. "Yeah, okay."

"Some Secret Service guys will be there," Campisi leaned away from his ear and stared at him, "and they want them entertained until dawn."

"Yeah, okay. I'll make sure a few girls get there."

This was an odd request but Sparky knew something big was happening. Then he became even more concerned. Jimmy Hoffa's top man, Barney Baker strolled into the Egyptian Club. Baker made a definite impression. He was six-feet-four and 370 pounds and shook Mr. Campisi's hand, but then turned and nodded to Sparky, not a normal nod, but a show of respect, *at last.* He wore an overwhelming amount of the same cheap perfume that Hoffa had worn. Baker extended his open hand toward him and announced to everyone at the table, "This is the guy who's going to make it happen."

He was on the front line now. He felt like he was in a daze as he shook hands with Baker and then, almost like a dream, Sam Giancana, his old boss and one of his mentors in Chicago, came into the restaurant with a phalanx of well-dressed Mafioso. Mr. Giancana wore his signature fedora, trench coat, and dark glasses with tinted lenses. His face was sagging with more wrinkles but he still had that strong, square jaw with a cleaved chin. Mr. G paid his respects to everyone in the room, shook a lot of hands, hugged people, and then walked directly up to their table, filled with Mafioso top brass and musclemen, wolfing down steak and dressed like they were ready for a Saturday night party. Mr. G spoke as if had been standing there and had heard Barney Baker's comment, "Yeah, Jackie here's gonna handle da whole t'ing."

One of Mr. G's henchmen, a tough-looking thug with dark hair and a round scar on his cheek, spoke up. "A guy should take a knife and stab and kill the fucker, where he is now. Somebody should kill the fucker. I mean it. But I tell you somet'ing, I'll kill. Right in the fucking White House. Somebody's got to get rid of this fucker."

Mr. Giancana and a few of the men nodded and said words of agreement. Sparky pulled on his collar to loosen his tie and rubbed his fingers over and over again. It was happening. Maybe not this guy talking, but Braden and others for sure, and that would lead to his clean-up job. A few of the other toughs nodded or laughed, offering up their favorite methods of killing someone.

The rest of the evening at the Egyptian Lounge was ordinary except some of the big shots like Mr. G and Barney Baker stayed for more than an hour, just being regular Joes. Sparky had a few drinks with the guys, and then went back to the Carousel Club to check up on things. He used some of the seven large from Mr. Hoffa to handle a small money problem for Little Lynn, one of the dancers, cautioned the new drummer about groping the girls, roughed up some wimpy drunk who was mouthing off, paid off some of his losses to his bookie, and made arrangements, as requested by Mr. Campisi from higher up, for a few of the girls to go over to the Cellar Club and party with the Secret Service men until dawn. Some of the girls were tired and complained, so he paid them all up front. He gave the girls extra money for beer, wine, or hard liquor, and told them to "party 'til dawn." He then went back to the Egyptian Lounge for a nightcap but most of the guys had left by then—it was almost midnight—and they must have gone on to other parties, or maybe even the Cellar Club.

Then he saw Braden having a drink in a corner booth that was covered in dark blue vinyl with hanging white drapes and short palm trees nearby. Braden had on a dark suit coat and tapped the table repeatedly with his knuckles. Next to Braden was another shifty guy and two bleached blondes, but he simply waved and smiled to them. He didn't want to talk with Braden or get to know him too well.

The whole thing gave him a sense of impending doom. One of these guys was going to be whacked. Who would it be that he had to "handle"? Anyone who didn't get away cleanly. Of course he'd do it, but it was the pressure—all the way to the top bosses—Mr. Hoffa and Mr. Giancana stopped by for Christ's sake! It was so overwhelming that it made him very, very nervous.

He popped another preludin and swallowed it dry. He nodded goodbye to the guys, then went over and shook hands firmly with Mr. Campisi. He was a good, stand-up guy. He was glad he paid his respects to him and then he left the lounge.

Outside it was very dark with a stormy and dusty cool breeze blowing in from the southeast. It was heavy with moisture and clumps of raindrops spattered his Oldsmobile as he got in. He sat for a long time, clutching the white steering wheel, and stared through the windshield at the wavering neon lights in the heavy black sky.

He was going to do whatever he had to do. If it was Braden or any of the others. He had to do this thing. He had to do it right and finally gain their full respect. He had to do it. The car rocked from a strong gust of wind.

He would do it. He had to. He had to.

52)

My lips are sealed

J. Edgar Hoover looked at his partner, Clyde Tolson, as the chauffer parked the Cadillac. Hoover tapped the light cream on his hair, all were in place, and licked his lips. He had been disgusted by the President's inability to stop his philandering—in spite of his visit to the White House with a complete dossier of information and photographs of what his agents had learned, and especially with the potential security risks—so he felt comfortable with this meeting. Clyde could be trusted. He had shared other tawdry events with him and he never told anyone, but Hoover was excited to have Clyde attend this meeting at the home of Clint Murchison, a Texas oil baron with political connections.

Hoover wanted to let Clyde in on a secret because he knew Clyde would enjoy that and would reward him later, and not just tonight but perhaps for months to come. He was already thinking of various scenarios of feathered garments and lace, and tried to resist any improper thoughts now. He needed to remain focused on the job at hand, which would make celebrating later all that much sweeter.

"You've got to make me a promise," Hoover said, clearing his gravelly voice and adjusting his tie.

"Oh no, not again, Jay," Clyde said. He gave him a quick, flirty laugh and said, "You know my lips are sealed."

"I know," Hoover said, tightening the knot and shooting a scowl at him. "This is critical. Not only for you, but for me, for our country."

"You start this way every time."

"Shut up!" The chauffer stared straight ahead as still as a statue. It was quiet in the car, the engine crackled as it cooled in the Texas night air, and Clyde's dazzling blue eyes watered. Hoover readjusted himself on the soft leather back seat. "You need to appreciate what we're doing here tonight and then promise me that you'll never say *one word* about this to anyone *ever*. Is that clear?"

"Of course, Jay," Clyde swallowed and composed himself. He gave him a slight smile with a raised eyebrow—a look that was both knowing and sexy. "You know I'm as tight-lipped as a rooster in the dark."

Hoover grunted. "The rooster knows there's a killing in the barn at dawn but he still crows. *You* can't ever say anything."

"Alright already!"

Hoover snapped open the car door and exhaled heavily with frustration. He strutted impatiently for the entrance and the huge wooden door opened as they approached. A butler in a tuxedo with white gloves bowed and kept his eyes downcast. Clyde hurried to catch up as Hoover stepped inside the mansion and shook Clint Murchison's hand vigorously. Murchison was a tall man with thick jowls and horned-rimmed glasses.

"You know Clyde Tolson," Hoover said out of the corner of his mouth as he continued inside, making his way to the middle of the great room where several socialites were chatting in formal wear and holding cocktails. Hoover didn't see anyone he was looking for so he glanced back at Murchison. "Anyone else here?"

Murchison broke from shaking Clyde's hand, Clyde had a tendency to shake everyone's hand for too long, and jumped to answer Hoover. Murchison spoke with a thick Texas drawl, "H. L.'s here. A few more of the eight eff club. Some Company boys."

Hoover looked around the large room at the partiers, saw a few underworld figures, Joe Campisi, a restaurateur, and his wife; Jack Rubenstein and a cheap-looking call girl; Carlos Marcello and Joe Civello having cigars; Sheriff Bill Decker and Mayor Earl Cabell, an ex-CIA executive in charge of the Bay of Pigs operation, and his wife; an agent he recognized from his p-file as Robert Morrow; and then he spotted the ex-Vice President Richard Nixon, who smiled when he saw him.

Hoover crossed the room to shake Nixon's hand, which was wet with perspiration, and tiny beads of sweat dotted his upper lip and forehead. Nixon looked uncomfortable in his gray suit but Hoover always tried to compliment the few people he liked. "Good to see you again, Dick."

"Likewise," Nixon said, swirling his clear-colored drink in his glass. "Another damn hot Texas night. Did you see that Alabama football game? Those boys played their hearts out."

Murchison had followed Hoover into their conversation and nodded at a woman sitting alone in a corner of the room on a blue loveseat. She was very pretty with long dark hair, a shapely figure in a bright yellow cotton dress, and Hoover remembered her from the photographs with Vice President Johnson. She was Madeleine Brown, a stunning beauty with big, wide-set eyes and her dark hair puffed up like a doll. She was out of place here, in her nice but simple dress, among all these extremely wealthy people.

Just then Lyndon B. Johnson entered the front door, tall and imposing, wearing his Stetson hat and a beige suit. The room was momentarily quiet until a few ladies chatted and Murchison said, "Come on, boys!"

Murchison led a select group of Johnson, Nixon, Hoover, and Hunt into a study room off to the side. It was lined with tall bookcases and a billiards table was in the middle of the room. Two burgundy leather wing chairs were at each end of the pool table and Nixon and John McCloy, a former president of the World Bank, immediately went toward the chairs to the right but Murchison cut-off McCloy. "You can't come in John. This is a private meeting."

McCloy, mostly bald and wearing a neat gray suit, looked annoyed but nodded and backed out as Murchison closed the door behind him.

H.L. Hunt shuffled over to a fireplace mantel, set his drink on it, and began speaking but Vice President Johnson quickly interrupted, "Is this sum-bitch gonna happen or not?"

"We're ready," Hunt replied. Hunt was becoming old with thinning gray hair but still wielded great power and had a lot of connections, including oil deals with Murchison as well as other business dealings with Murchison's financial partner, Carlos Marcello.

"I don't want, we can't have. . ." Johnson said, following Hunt and standing in his face. Hunt looked up at him, slightly surprised, and Johnson stepped closer, belly to belly, using his tall frame to dominate over the frail man. "We can't have another Chicago or Tampa Bay slip-up!"

Hoover adjusted his coat sleeves then stood with his hands folded in front of him and looked around the room. Apparently no one else in the room knew of the earlier failed attempts in Chicago and Tampa Bay. Murchison had settled in a wing chair on the other side of the room, in the corner with a tall brass reading lamp next to it, and comfortably crossed his legs.

"Well, it looks good," Hunt said.

"God dammit! Is it happening or not!" Johnson's face was red with anger.

"Yes." Hunt's yellowish grin faded into a hardened, cold stare and his faint blue eyes still had some fire.

Hoover was surprised to hear Hunt sound unsure and he didn't blame Johnson for yelling at the elder Hunt, in fact, it pleased him to see Johnson's take-charge authority.

Hunt backed away from him, like a boxer slipping off the ropes and out of the corner, and walked over to the billiard table. Hunt grazed his hand over its smooth green felt. There were no balls on the table and a fully loaded cue rack was in the corner.

"This has been planned as our back-up for some time," Hunt spoke strongly, regaining his confidence and authority. He picked up a tiny nap of felt and flicked it away. "There is no sure-fire, cinched deal. But we're ready for the big event."

Johnson put one hand in his pocket and leaned on the mantel with the other. Nixon took the momentary pause to speak up. "This will help with our position in Cuba. We'll have—"

"Be quiet!" Johnson said.

Nixon stood up from the wing chair and walked over to Hunt, squeezing his shoulder, but facing down Johnson. "If Howard says it's a go, it's a god-damn done deal."

Hunt smiled mischievously and looked at Johnson. "Do you want to go into the details?"

"Hell no!" Johnson snapped. "And don't you ever use a condescending tone with me again!"

"We need to discuss the investigation. Our boys will handle it," Hoover said, wanting to diffuse the tension. "And of course, the succession."

Hoover waited for a response but when there was none he continued, licking his lips quickly. He had done this with six other presidents and he made it clear he was not about to relinquish his power in spite of another transition. He also included a mention of Nixon and his people, knowing that Nixon may one day hold the reins. It was a brief meeting and everyone seemed satisfied that "the big event," as Hunt called it, would happen. The transition would be smooth.

The men filtered out of the room and Johnson, red-faced and anxious, went over to Madeleine Brown, who jumped up with a big smile on her face. Hoover followed Johnson closely, wanting to hear whatever he would say to Brown. Maybe she was his closest confidant?

Johnson grabbed Madeleine forcefully by the hand and led her toward the front door. She winced from the pressure, his large hand crushing hers, but she said nothing—not even hello. Hoover thought she was a smart woman, waiting for her man. A few giant steps later Johnson finally let it out, speaking directly into her ear in a grating whisper, "After tomorrow those goddamn Kennedys will never embarrass me again. That's no threat. That's a promise."

Hoover stopped by the door and looked back around the room, saw Clyde with his usual white Russian drink in his hand, and raised one eyebrow and smiled. Clyde smiled back and downed the creamy white drink while staring at him, then licked the cream off his upper lip with his tongue.

53)

Buy June some shoes

It was late Thursday afternoon when Lee had slipped into Ruth's house while they were all away. He wrote out a note carefully, being slightly vague in case he escaped and to avoid the repetition of the General Walker fiasco, but with enough peculiarities for Marina to know this was serious and probably the end for him. He wrote,

Marina—

I love you very much!!! I'm so happy that we are coming together again. I'm sorry that this had to happen but it was part of my mission in life.

Love,

Lee

He suddenly thought the word "mission" was too obvious, but folded the note and laid it on the dresser bureau. He then took out his wallet, removed all the money he had, $186, saved sixteen dollars for himself, and put the wad of $170 in the bottom drawer under some of her neatly folded blouses.

He sat on the edge of the bed and thought back to meeting Marina at the crowded dance in Minsk. They had been through a lot together and he realized being with her was the happiest time of his life. His work with ONI was challenging and important, but for him personally, knowing Marina and creating their life together, with June and now Rachel, was the best part of his life. Rachel was a healing blessing to their marriage and Junie was becoming an angel on two feet, running around and speaking more and more each time he saw her, and displaying more and more of her vibrant and joyful personality. She seemed to be the best of both of them. He was saddened to think that he would not be there to help his children more, but he knew this mission was beyond his small life.

He thought about the note again and knew it said too much. He stuffed it in his pants pocket and decided to write something very simple that, combined with the $170, would be powerful in retrospect. Just then he heard the front door open. He wrote swiftly,

Buy June some shoes.

Love,

Lee

He slipped the note under the jewelry cup and made his way out of the bedroom and saw Ruth, the owner of the house. He casually said, "Hello."

"Oh, hey, Lee." Ruth had pale skin, dark hair, and, following her Quaker religion, was very meek. "I didn't know you were here."

"Yeah. Just looking for Marina."

"She's at work. And Junie and Rachel's at day care."

Ruth had several paper bags full of groceries in her arms and he took one to help carry them into the kitchen. "Yeah, I realized that on my way over but thought I'd come on anyway."

She smiled and nodded. "Well, you're always welcome. Thursday or not."

"That's good." He set the groceries on the kitchen counter and Ruth began putting away the perishables in their new yellow refrigerator. He wanted to say something to her, about how grateful he was that she had been such a good friend to Marina, to look out for her and June, and now Rachel, too, while they patched things up, but he knew that anything so emotional, or out of the ordinary, may cause suspicion. Instead he asked, "How are you?"

"Well, pretty good, you know. Work's the same. Marina should be home in—" she looked at the brown leather watch on her thin arm, "—forty-five minutes or so. How 'bout a piece of pie while you wait?"

He glanced at the covered pie-plate and smelled fresh apples and cinnamon. "No, thank you, ma'am. That's very nice of you all the same. I'll just do a little reading until they get back. I've got an important meeting tomorrow."

Ruth was nodding until he came to the part about a meeting and she looked confused. She had helped him get the job filling orders at the book warehouse and he realized he had made a mistake as soon as he said it.

"Actually it's somebody outside of work," he said. "I'm doing a job for them and hoping, well, it will make things better for all of us."

She smiled again and crossed her fingers. "That's nice. Good luck with it."

"Thanks," he nodded and walked past her and out the back door.

Outside it was warm for November and he sat on the back lawn, took out *Life* magazine from his back pocket, and read. He thought about how he wanted this last meeting to go, decided it should be as normal and average as possible, for Marina and June's sake, and would try to be upbeat and happy in spite of the fact it was, perhaps, the last time he'd see his family.

When Marina and the children arrived, he cherished every moment. Time seemed to slow down and almost stop: as he and Junie ran on the front lawn to catch whirligigs of oak seeds spinning in the autumn air; throughout dinner as he watched Junie play with her food and then eat it quickly; as Marina softly pampered newborn Rachel, so innocent and pure with her delicate breaths.

Marina was happy to see him, which he was very grateful for, although she was always a bit wary now. The tender moments—her smile, a touch, the way she curled her dark hair around one ear—all filled him with infatuated rapture. It was a glorious, full evening.

~ ~

The next morning Lee awoke early. He quietly had a cup of coffee and left most of it in the cup in the kitchen sink. He went back into Marina's room with the girls and slid off his wedding band, his Marine Corps ring, and placed them in the jewelry cup on the bureau. He gazed at Rachel in the bassinette, then Junie in the single bed, and Marina asleep in the double bed. They were all peaceful, all content, all just fine. He gazed at this perfect setting and, within his mind, took a final snapshot to remember this moment of quiet bliss.

He silently made his way out of the house in the early dawning light. He walked for Buell Wesley Frazier's house, a nearby neighbor and co-worker who gave him a ride from work on Mondays when he visited Marina and the girls. He stood near Wesley's back door and garage, leaning on his green Chevrolet so as not to miss him. He thought of Marina and wondered when she would find the note. Maybe tonight. If she tried to call him at work he wouldn't take a break to answer the telephone, or call her back. No, this was it. Everything's set and in motion. After this historic mission, then he would make it up to her. He would show her how much he loved her by trying to find a house together. One that would be large enough for all of them, including June and Rachel having a room of their own. Of course, it may take time, and they would need to work out this "problem" in their marriage, but after this mission life should be a lot easier for all of them.

A large elm tree shaded the back door area and the sun's low rays shot past the tree trunk and through the bushes surrounding Frazier's property line. The elm's leaves had changed color to brown and rust, they rattled in the light breeze, and a few leaves and seeds fell. He readjusted himself against the car, felt the lack of rings on his hand, and played with his ring finger. It felt odd and weird. He needed to remember not to play with it at work to avoid suspicion from co-workers. Something like that would be the last thing he'd need—for someone at work to ask him why he wasn't wearing his ring, and then someone would ask how Marina was. No, that would be too distracting, so he had to concentrate to not fidget with his hands.

Finally, Wesley came out the back door. He was tall with dark hair and a mustache, and there was a surprised look on his face. "Oh hey, Lee. Didn't expect to see you today."

He explained, "You remember I said I had to pick up some curtain rods." He noticed Wesley glance at the long paper-wrapped package as he opened the car back door and placed it onto the floor area. He smiled politely and slid into the front seat, knowing he was on his way to the most important mission in his life. He felt a bit nervous but he had prepared his entire life for this. He was ready.

He deftly took out the crumpled first note to Marina from his pocket and held it loosely in his hand, out the window, as Wesley drove down the street. He loved Marina very much, more than she would ever know, and he was very happy June was doing so well, and Rachel was healthy. He became very sad again that he would not be there for them but knew, deep down in his core, that this was so much more important. It required sacrifice and he wanted to give it. This was his most important mission and Marina would take good care of their family.

He squeezed and wadded up the note, let his arm hang out the open window, feeling the wind take the note and tumble it in his hand, up and down and around and up and over, and he opened his hand to release it.

He was ready. This was his historic moment.

54)

The sixth floor

Lee crept up the stairs to the sixth floor and immediately saw Carlos Bringuier standing among the stacks and stacks of cartons of books. Bringuier had obviously had no problem in stealing in the back entrance to the warehouse. He took the rifle out of the brown wrapping and handed the paper to Bringuier, who nodded without a word and began neatly folding it into a tiny wad and set it next to the rifle cleaning gear. He held the Mannlicher-Carcano in his right hand, walked around a wall of stacked books that he had made yesterday, and knelt down by the window at the far corner of the building. He looked down to the street at the crowd of people around the steps to the colonnade and noticed a peculiar man with an umbrella in his hand. It was a sunny.

Because of the wall of boxes around the first open window, Bringuier went to the second window, which was closed, and looked down at the street. Bringuier pointed across the plaza to a red truck parked off the road by the overpass. "There eez the pick-up."

He noticed the excitement of the crowd of people, but everyone was focused on looking up the street in the direction of the motorcade that was to come. He then scanned over to his left and saw a few prisoners standing by the windows of the Dallas County Jail. One man in particular seemed to observe him and he jerked back further into the room. He wondered, did he see me?

He then looked across the street to his left, down to the fire escape of the DalTex building. Down below, he saw Braden, tall with dark hair, just inside a third floor window, setting up a tripod, and his partner, the spotter, a heavyset guy who stood with his back to him and was probably watching the entrance to the room, just as Bringuier should be doing. They were also in place and ready.

Seeing the prisoner notice him had spooked him and, remaining deep in the building, he slowly checked to see if the prisoner was still watching. He saw a man in a prisoner's uniform looking vaguely in his direction, but he knew he probably couldn't see inside the darkened building. It was sunny, which helped.

"Go check the stairwell," he said to Bringuier, who walked casually across the floor, opened the door a crack, and listened.

It was quiet. Bringuier frowned and nodded, "Ee's clear," then closed the door behind him, picked up the rifle-cleaning cloth and pull-through cord, and walked back around the stacked boxes behind him before returning to his post at the second window, albeit facing the wrong way.

Lee was cautious to not lean out the window but looked down at the crowded street again. The umbrella man stood calmly. He tapped the point of the umbrella on the pavement, looking around casually in comparison to the excitement of the crowd. After a moment he turned with all the others and watched as the motorcade made a hard right turn, off the main street that led directly to the highway, and onto the side street that took them north of the plaza. The crowd began to applaud. The man opened the umbrella—the motorcade was coming! It was a go.

He adjusted the scope and looked down to his right again, following in his mind's eye the course of the motorcade. Envisioning it. Again he had that eerie feeling that someone was watching him. He quickly looked left and saw the prisoner. He stared at him and he reflexively pulled away from the window. "Got damn!"

He tightened his grip on the rifle and crouched over the windowsill. Bringuier stood at the next window, holding the weapon-cleaning equipment and gazing down at the plaza. "Wha's zee matter? I doan' see notheen'."

He clenched his teeth and pulled back the bolt action, loading a live round into the chamber. Always God damn somethin'. He exhaled with control as he had been taught. It was a simple mechanical release to let the air flow shallowly, slowly, smoothly out the nostrils. He could hear the cheering of the crowd growing louder. Then suddenly there they were, the motorcade of policemen on motorcycles, and then the main limousine, open, in sight, approaching directly below him on Houston, followed by another limousine, and a truck full of cameramen and reporters.

"They're comeen'," Bringuier said excitedly. "Ee's happeneen'!"

He inhaled deeply, snuggling the butt of the rifle to his shoulder. Lowered the barrel out the window. It stuck out about six inches. Not too bad. He rolled his eyes down and to the left, picked up the lead limo out of the corner of his eyes. Yep, there they are.

Time slowed down. The limousine braked, larger than life, to make the hard left turn onto Elm. God they're huge. They're right there. The target and his wife. . . and the Governor and his wife. He exhaled shallowly. Rested his arm on the ledge. Balanced the rifle in his left palm. He was distracted momentarily by the second limousine but quickly returned to the lead limo, picking up speed ever so slightly as it came out of the turn.

"Shoot!" Bringuier said. Panic laced his voice. "Shoot! Shoot!"

He looked above the oak tree in front of him, anticipating the limousine's path, and waited for the target to clear the tree and then—

Snap! Someone else fired! Probably Braden from the DalTex building, before he was ready, before the limousine had cleared the tree, before it was in the field of play, and BLAM! He fired as a reaction, not ready, not even aiming. He felt the gun pull right as he fired—maybe he hit the target in the back?

Nothing happened in the limo. No brake lights. No reaction by anyone.

"Jesus, chou meessed!"

Yeah, he thought. And Braden must have missed, too.

He jerked back the bolt and ejected the spent casing, ramming home another round. Slowly drew the crosshairs down onto the target. Mid-back, raising to the center. Exhaled with control, thinking, "quick is smooth," squeezed, and—

BLAM! The bullet flew high and right again. Did he hit the Governor?

No reaction! Again! Maggie's drawers! Got damn, a lousy shot. But wait, the target clutched at his throat. Whoa. Someone got him. He didn't hear anything so that shot must have come from the front, maybe from the pick-up near the overpass. The wife looked at the target, taking hold of him by the shoulders lovingly with concern.

Son-of-a-bitch. Two missed shots! He pulled back the bolt, spinning out another cartridge that tingled onto the wooden floor. Glanced at Bringuier sweating. Wasn't he supposed to be gathering the cartridges?

He could smell the gunpowder. Felt his palm on the warm gunstock. Slowly drew down the scope, to the back, then slightly up to the head, but the target's leaning down, the gun's pulling right, and—

BLAM! The bullet flew high, too far left, and ricocheted with a spark off the windshield molding. Missed! Son of a —

Snap! Another shot fired and that bullet exploded on contact with the target's head—burst open in a halo of blood spray and flying clumps of gray matter. The wife, in her pink dress, climbed onto the back of the limo, grabbing something.

He stood up to look more closely. Yes, the target was hit. He's finished. Probably a shot from Sergio or the French guy as they used bullets that exploded on contact. A Secret Service agent jumped up on the back of the limo, motioned at the wife, and she slid down into the back seat.

He glanced across the street and saw the prisoner staring at him. He then looked over at Bringuier, who stood wide-eyed in disbelief and shock. He hurried around the wall of books and handed the rifle to Bringuier, who grabbed it with the oily cloth. He said, "Pick up the shells!" and quickly zigzagged his way through the stacks of books, across the floor, and to the far stairwell.

He glanced over his shoulder to check on Bringuier, who was wiping down the rifle with speedy hands, and went out the door, scampered down the steps as quickly as he could, trying not to breathe too hard but taking deep breaths. Turning, and again, and again, hearing more clearly the screaming on the street and someone yelling. Another flight of stairs, turning, and another turn, and quickly now. A siren. Another turn and the last flight and finally reaching the second floor cafeteria. A quick deep breath and exhaling calmly. Opening the door quietly.

There's Carolyn Arnold. She was eight months pregnant and she sipped water from a cup at one of the break tables.

He nodded politely to Carolyn from across the room and suddenly felt hot. He turned away from her, wiped his brow, and dried his hands on his pants. A couple of coins in the soda machine. Bingo. Cold cola. Opening the cap in the machine. A refreshing drink. It hit his stomach and it immediately flared with a burning sensation in his gut all the way back up to his throat.

He thought, Okay where is that "someone" with the news? Let's go, let's go! He couldn't wait any longer. He decided to walk out the cafeteria when he heard someone running up behind him. He turned to see a policeman with his gun drawn—pointed right at his chest!

"Hey!" the cop yelled. "You there!"

He froze and stared at the cop with his heart racing, trying to remain calm. Then Roy Truly, one of the managers, hurried into the break room behind the policeman.

"Come here," the cop said, looking very official with his badge on the crown of his pointed policeman's hat. He turned to Mr. Truly and asked, "Do you know this man? Does he work here?"

"Yes, he does," Mr. Truly said.

The cop turned away quickly, ran for the elevator, and Mr. Truly followed him. He looked at Carolyn Arnold as if to say, "What was that about?", but he knew very well why the officer was running around and waving his gun. He drank some more of the cola, felt its bubbly sensation fire the acids in his stomach, set down the bottle, and walked down the stairs and out onto the street.

Pandemonium reigned with shouts and cries, tires squealing, sirens wailing, and some people were dazed and looking about, holding their faces like the person in the painting "The Scream"—silent and horrified. Others sat motionless on the grass, while policemen and brave men ran for the grassy knoll over to the right. Policemen seemed to be everywhere in the street and around the plaza, running in various directions, and now forming in groups of two, three and four, to block off the entrance to the book warehouse and other buildings in the area.

He shuffled down the sidewalk with his head slightly down and saw an idling white bus with brown stripes stuck in traffic on Elm. He quickly approached it and tapped on the glass door. The driver, a thin white man, opened the door, he climbed on, paid the twenty-three cent fare, and felt some comfort among all the others. He walked to the back and slid into a seat and faced the road, away from the sidewalk, and stared into nothingness away from the other passengers. At least in here he could sit on the bus and not be examined by every cop who ran by. The bus inched forward.

A few more policemen ran by and one officer looked into the bus to scrutinize the driver and then went methodically to every window, jumping up and down to get a good look at the passengers, bouncing on the sidewalk, until he arrived at the back of the bus. The cop stared hard at him. He stopped jumping and a long moment passed. But then another cop ran up and grabbed the staring policeman by the arm, and they turned and sprinted for the rail yard. After the bus crawled a few more feet, another cop ran up to the bus door but he dashed away at the last instant—a distant yell could be heard.

He couldn't stand inching along any more. Up ahead he saw the Greyhound bus station and a line of waiting blue taxicabs with their white trunks and white hoods. He rose, headed to the front, and asked the driver as politely as he could, "Would you please let me off?"

The driver looked at him oddly—didn't he just get on the bus?—but he opened the glass doors and he bounded out, making his way quickly for the taxi stand.

He wanted to get in one as quickly as possible, to get away from here, but when he got to the stand an older woman approached at about the same time. He politely motioned for her to take the first cab and he closed the door behind her. He stood motionless as the next blue and white cab pulled up and Lee got in. "Five hundred North Beckley."

The cabbie, a middle-aged white man with dark hair, put it in drive and they pulled into the congested traffic that inched forward slowly. He tried to look around casually, with slow movements, and saw the driver's license on the dashboard: William Whaley. He was heavyset with a large lower lip and sagging jaw line, and looked at him in the rear view mirror, so he looked away. The traffic gradually picked up speed, they finally seemed to get out of the jam, and pulled away at a normal speed. He smiled briefly and exhaled, long and slow, and gazed at the leafless trees whizzing by.

When the cab got to the corner of Tenth and Beckley, the driver pulled over and threw it into park. He paid the eighty-five cent fare and jumped out, walking briskly for the rooming house. He was behind schedule. It was almost one p.m. and he was due at the movie theater *now* but he still had to change his clothes and get there. At least Sergio Arcacha Smith and Carlos Bringuier would be there. Sergio had better wait for him, he thought. God, how did he blow it again? Three shots and he missed every time! Maybe he hit the target in the back? And maybe one shot hit the Governor? Well, it was over now and there was nothing to do but get the hell out of town.

Okay, he thought, he was running late, but Sergio had better be waiting for him at the theater. Yes, of course Sergio would wait for him, because he was a professional. He knew that from experience. Sergio would not leave a man behind.

He tried to clear any doubts and all thoughts of failure out of his mind. Still, he had a nagging feeling that Sergio would not be there and yet his life depended on it. Sergio had god-damned better be waiting for him at the theater.

55)

Dealey Plaza

Sparky paced at the back of his white Oldsmobile. He didn't want to watch. Shit, he liked the guy. No, he loved him, in spite of his arrogant Boston accent. Yes, the President had been an amazing inspiration for him, personally, as well as for lots of his friends and lots of Americans. He took a drag on a cigarette, got in his car, and drove toward the offices of the Dallas *Morning News,* not far from Dealey Plaza. He couldn't help imagining what it was happening:

SNAP! Was that it? The crowd was cheering, just over the knoll, along the street and then someone screamed, then another scream. He took another drag on his cigarette and slowed down behind a bus, knowing the newspaper office building was just ahead, but thinking of the chaos happening behind the grassy knoll:

The two-man team, with a third man, Taggart, serving as the lookout, rushed away from the wooden picket fence. The shooter, a thin French guy dressed in a Dallas police uniform, handed the rifle to the spotter, Sergio Arcacha Smith, who dismantled it and dumped the parts into a bag, and split off toward the railroad overpass. The shooter, a mafia connection from Marseille, walked briskly toward the railroad employee's parking lot and was soon part of a sea of swarming policemen, empty handed, and like any other of the many curious men rushing in various directions. After a brief moment the French guy was so much a part of the crowd of policemen that no one could tell who he was. The spotter, Arcacha Smith, had dumped the rifle somewhere, Sparky thought, maybe in a sewer drain, and was joined near the railroad overpass by two more men, Hunt and Sturgis, and Hunt led them toward the rail yard where they would hop a freight car to anywhere.

Sparky parked his Oldsmobile in the newspaper parking lot, got out, and mashed the cigarette stub into the blacktop. He knew, at this very moment, all hell was breaking loose:

Men yelled from the grassy knoll below and one man came through the railroad employees' parking lot, between two parked cars, and over the parking guardrail, but Taggart stopped him with his hand to the guy's chest. Taggart flipped open his wallet, showing his pseudo Secret Service badge, and the guy turned back in the direction Taggart pointed, back across the employee lot, and away from them. Two, three, and now a fourth policeman popped their heads over the wooden stockade fence. From about twenty feet away, Taggart pointed them in the direction of the first guy and they all dashed in that direction.

Sparky entered the newspaper offices and walked down the hallway to the advertising department, as he had done so many times before. He met Tony Zoppi, who was tall and thin and wore horned-rimmed glasses, at the reception counter. He told Tony that he wanted to check his ads, but he was still thinking of the melee in Dealey Plaza:

A railroad employee stood on the bridge of the dispatch tower, near the booth, watching all the activity. That guy would need to be whacked, depending on whether he saw anything and if he reported it to the police. About fifteen men were running toward the parking lot and the back of the stockade fence but Taggart pointed the lead guy in the direction of the others, then shrugged his shoulders to a second and third guy, and walked casually away. Down by the freight cars, a group of policemen closed in on Hunt, Sturgis, and Arcacha Smith.

Sparky pretended to examine the ad for his club, smiled and nodded politely to Tony, who stood behind the counter in a short-sleeved white business shirt with a dark tie. The usual hectic atmosphere of the newspaper was in full swing. Tony checked the details of another ad with a red pencil while he waited for him. At the end of the counter a radio console played a song by The Chiffons when a news flash came on. Tony looked at the radio's beige cloth speaker.

"This KLIF bulletin. . . from Dallas, three shots reportedly were fired at the motorcade of President Kennedy today near the downtown section. KLIF News is checking out the report. We will have further reports. Stay tuned."

Tony turned to him with a look of deep concern and his eyes were filled with tears. He also got choked-up and thought, Damn, he loves the President, too.

Tears burst out and flowed freely, and he let them go, crying into his fists holding the crumpled newspaper ad. Tony patted him on the shoulder and, after a few moments, he composed himself, shook his head to Tony to mean he couldn't speak, and left the room quickly.

He needed to be sure the job was done. The bosses would expect nothing less. He walked quickly to his Oldsmobile, looking around the empty newspaper parking lot and thought, all the newsmen must be with the motorcade or at the Trade Mart. He fired up the engine, floored the accelerator, laid a patch of rubber on the blacktop, and flew onto the street, weaving around some stopped cars, and was quickly on the highway and headed for Parkland Hospital. It was just a few minutes away, honking down the freeway, and he started crying again.

He pulled into the hospital parking lot. Cops, photographers, and reporters swarmed around the emergency entrance. He noticed the "AMBULANCES ONLY" sign and pulled off to the side, behind two other cars double-parked. He recognized officer Steve Sharp among six policemen and other agents hovering around the black limousine. Patrolman Sharp waved him away, but he got out, wiped his eyes, offered to shake hands, and said, "It's me!"

"Oh, hey," officer Sharp said, pushing down on his nightstick and waving off another car. "I didn't recognize you Sparky."

"I won't be more than a minute," he said.

Officer Sharp was so preoccupied with so many vehicles pulling in that he simply nodded and continued to wave off other cars.

He walked briskly through the open doors into the hospital. The entryway was spilling over with reporters, policemen, doctors and nurses, all going in different directions. He saw Seth Kantor, a veteran reporter he knew from the Dallas *Morning News*, and Sparky stood off to the side near Kantor in the hallway. He thought to ask dumbly, "What happened?"

"Someone shot the President," Kantor replied.

"Yeah, I heard on the radio. It said there was a shooting, but it didn't say who." There was a lot of noise in the lobby and he looked around as a nurse pushed through the sea of reporters. "This is insane."

"Yeah," Kantor looked a little frazzled but was working just the same, reviewing his notes and scribbling down questions on the top page of his note pad.

"What's going on?" he asked in rapid-fire succession, "Is the President okay? Is he going to make it?"

Kantor raised his eyebrows, shook his head negatively, and then exhaled. "It doesn't look good."

"Where was he hit?"

"In the head, throat, back, maybe more," he flipped back through the pages of his notepad to confirm what he had said. "They got the Governor, too."

"Yeah? The Governor was hit?" He felt a need to explain himself. "I heard on the radio, that's why I came over."

Many people scurried about but the gravity of the moment was intense. Another reporter in a suit and tie with dark hair graying at the temples leaned against the wall. He openly wept. Every seat of the waiting chairs were taken and a woman in a brown dress, clutching her purse, rocked back and forth convulsively sobbing. Another man in a suit, maybe a Secret Service man, had blood on his hands and stood in a daze with one foot propped against the wall. The man turned around suddenly and punched the wall. Another guy in a suit yelled a long string of obscenities and began arguing with a doctor, who wore scrubs for surgery with blood stains on it but his hands were very white. A cop, holding a motorcycle helmet, had dried blood splattered on his face. His eyes were dazed as he stared into nothingness.

One of the hospital administrators, in a dark suit with a thin tie, pushed his way out of the corridor and into the receiving area. He was escorted by three doctors, who peeled off and made their way down another corridor. The administrator motioned for a few reporters to move their things and he made his way into a lecture room, behind a new steel table with a brown faux-wood Formica top and in front of a green-colored blackboard with the single word "Parkland" written on it in white chalk. Reporters crammed in behind him and scurried for position, not bothering to sit in the chairs but instead standing on the wooden desks. Television cameras began rolling and photographers flashed pictures.

The spokesman began without introduction. "President John F. Kennedy died at approximately one o'clock Central Standard time today here in Dallas. He died of a gunshot wound in the brain."

The newsmen were still clambering for position, climbing on the desks in the back to get a clear photograph, and yet the room was momentarily quiet until a reporter, Tom Jackson, did his job: "Were there any complications or other wounds that may have caused his death?"

The spokesman was visibly shaken and his voice choked with emotion. "Doctor Berkeley told me that it, it was a simple matter, Tom," he pointed to his right front temple area, "of, ah, a bullet right through the head."

Sparky felt sick to his stomach. His throat was thick and he couldn't swallow. Tears dripped from his eyes and he looked around to see others crying, too. He walked out of the emergency room into the sunny, crowded parking lot. The open limo was parked there with a few policemen nearby. Crumpled remnants of a bouquet of red roses, mangled petals, lay on the back seat, with blood on the back rest, blood on the seat, blood on the floor, smeared blood on the back trunk, blood seemingly everywhere.

He wiped his eyes and looked around. Policeman Sharp was gone.

He went to his car, getting in slowly. He felt very, very bad and lay his forehead down on the steering wheel and wept. After a moment, he composed himself a bit, punched the top of the dashboard, and started the car. He let it run for another moment and, when another car honked at him, he eased out slowly.

He drove slowly to police headquarters, knowing that anyone the cops picked up would be brought downtown for questioning. He parked in an alley behind the building, entering through a side door, went down the steps quickly, opened a metal door, and walked through the basement parking garage, through the glass doors, and into the lobby.

He wasn't sure if he could just wait here, knowing the President was dead. He thought, How could he just stand around and wait to see who they brought in? He paced among several reporters for a few minutes. The glass doors at the front of the lobby swung open and they brought in Hunt, Sturgis, and the spotter, Arcacha Smith.

He thought, Shit. How am I supposed to whack *three* guys? He turned to face the wall and kicked the base with his shoe. "God damn it!"

Another reporter looked at him and exhaled heavily. "Yeah, what a tragic day."

Then two more cops brought in Braden, tall and taking long, lanky steps, and he looked directly at him with a smirk. The fucking smiling bastard!, he thought. That was one guy who it would be a pleasure to whack. The bastard. But now it's up to four? Damn.

He felt he couldn't take it any more. He mumbled, "I'll have to leave Dallas," noticed that a reporter heard him, and became even more nervous. He took out his cigarettes, lit one up, and walked out the front doors, then down the side alley for his car. A knot in his stomach rumbled and became tense. He thought of the four guys in there and recalled Hoffa saying, "Jack's gonna handle the whole thing." A lot of killing was coming or *he* would be killed. He had to do it. But four guys? He almost made it to his car but the churning in his stomach suddenly surged up his throat and he puked all over the alley, leaning on the rear trunk of his car. He thought of the bloody back seat of the limousine and heaved again, splattering coffee and mushy, dark cereal onto his shoes. "Oh, crap."

He dropped his cigarette in the puddle of puke and thought more about the four guys inside the police department. What should he do? He finally decided that he should go back to his apartment, see if anyone was charged or released, and wait for a call. They would let him know who was left and who got away. Right now it looked like no one got away. Damn, Sparky thought. Maybe his friends inside the police force would persuade the top cops to not press charges? Who knows? Maybe they didn't have any evidence. He'd just have to wait and see.

He popped another preludin, wiped the top of his shoes on the back of his pants, and fired up the white Oldsmobile. He'd wait for orders from one of the bosses, or for more information from someone inside the police department. Either way, it gave him an awful sense of anxiety. His stomach tossed and turned, and he chewed on his already stubby fingernails as he drove slowly back to his office. He would wait in his office for the phone to ring.

56)

Texas Theater

Lee changed his shirt in a flash and heard a car horn honk twice. He pushed aside the white vinyl window shade and saw a police car by the curb with officer Julius Kimball looking out of the passenger side up at the house, smiling with his mad-dog grin and dimple showing. He grabbed his Smith & Wesson .38 off the closet top shelf, his light jacket, hustling out to catch his ride. He said nothing in response to Mrs. Earlene Roberts, his landlady, who said something low and quiet with sheer horror in her voice.

Outside he was startled: the patrol car was gone. What the hell was going on? What was he going to do now?

He put on his jacket and thought of the quickest way to get to the theater. It would take too long to call a cab, have them come all the way out, then take him back downtown, and he was already late, so he walked quickly for the bus stop. It was only a few blocks away and it ran regularly.

Another police car pulled around the corner, slowed down up ahead and, at first, he thought it was his ride doubling back but quickly knew that it wasn't. This cruiser had a single cop behind the wheel. Shit, Lee thought. What should he do?

He crossed the street and the cop car pulled over in front of him, about twenty feet away. He continued walking, straight ahead, as casually as he could.

Suddenly a man came out of seemingly nowhere, somewhere off to his left, running hard, and charged straight for the police car. The man looked madder than hell.

He stopped and watched the policeman get out of his vehicle, a handsome man with dark hair and a solid jaw. He walked around to the front of the car, and then he saw that the angry man held a pistol by his side!—raised it to the officer's chest as he approached and, without saying a word, he fired—BLAM!

Jesus Christ! he thought, and crossed the street again, away from the car, only about fifteen feet away from the shooter, and hoped the shooter didn't turn around. Should he run?

BLAM! BLAM! Two quick shots rang out. God damn, this guy was pissed! He moved quickly away, onto the grassy boulevard, and looked back at the shooter as he pointed the pistol straight down over the officer's head and—BLAM!—shot again. Then the killer looked straight at him! He jogged on the sidewalk and down the street, looking over his shoulder as the killer turned around, back toward a parked car that he got in and sped off.

"Stupid. . . That's a cop!" He said. What in the world was that guy thinking?

Then he saw another man who was crouched behind a pick-up truck and stared at him oddly with a severe look of disgust. He wondered, Did this guy think I shot the cop?

Then he saw a woman staring at him from the corner across the street. She put her hands up over her face like a child hiding. What the hell?, he thought.

Another man stared at him, standing on his porch across the street. He now realized they were all watching *him* because they had not seen the shooter, only heard the shots and came out to see him walking nearby. He definitely needed to get away. He ran a few steps across Patton Street, cutting the corner across someone's lawn, and found an alley that ran parallel to the main road. He had to figure out something and fast. He stopped jogging, but continued walking very quickly, and looked back again. No one was following.

Up ahead yet another man stood watching, holding a wrench and a greasy rag, as he came out from a Texaco automobile garage. Its back entrance was open with cars needing repair lined up. The mechanic gazed at him so he put his head down and moved faster.

"Hey, man, what the hell is going on?" the mechanic yelled.

Holy shit! he thought, and ran down the alley and cut through a backyard.

The man screamed again, "Go after him!"

He came out onto Jefferson Street and moved rapidly. He looked back down the avenue but did not see the bus coming so he kept moving on foot. He sure as hell couldn't stand around this neighborhood waiting for a goddamn bus.

It would be crawling with cops soon and the woman had seen him near the police car, and then the guy on the porch, and the mechanic. At least one of them would think he was involved in the shooting of the policeman or at least an accomplice to the shooting. He was that close. Why in the hell would anyone shoot a cop? And the killer fired so many times—maybe he knew the cop? Yeah. Maybe that's why the killer was so pissed. The shooter knew the cop.

He moved swiftly down the street, noticed that most of the people were walking away from town, of course, and put his head down again. Looking up briefly, he saw the Texas Theater and hoped that Banister's men—Sergio as the driver and Bringuier—were still there. He slowed down to catch his breath and looked back again. No one.

He walked casually up to the ticket booth but it was empty. No one was around so he went inside the building without buying a ticket. He was running late and he wasn't there to see the movie anyway. He'd meet his contacts and they'd leave out the back as planned.

Inside the lobby there was no ticket taker. Across the lobby a young kid was counting ticket stubs on the candy counter. Maybe he was supposed to be selling and taking tickets, but he wasn't about to ask and find out, especially as the guys should be waiting inside. He opened the theater door, stepped in, and waited a moment for his eyes to adjust to the darkness.

Inside a film was showing and on the bright screen Van Heflin was making a tough-sounding speech to some Filipinos. His eyes adjusted and he saw an older gentlemen gawking at him from near the back. As he looked around, he saw there were only a few people, maybe seven in all, in the audience. He thought, Jesus Christ! They aren't here!

The old man turned around completely and stared at him so he took a seat in the middle back where he could see anyone come into the theater in case they hadn't arrived yet. Maybe Bringuier was late again? Maybe all the chaos and congestion had delayed the others, too? No way. Not this late. Maybe Sergio had already come and gone? No, he wouldn't do that. Sergio would follow through with his assignment if at all possible. Then he thought, maybe they were waiting for him in the back alley? Should he walk to the front and go through the exit door by the movie screen and into the alley? Of course, they must be waiting for him there.

The main theater door opened again and he turned around to see who it was. It was the young kid from the candy counter and two policemen. Jesus Christ! he thought., and he turned forward quickly. What are the cops doing here? Okay, okay. Play it cool.

The door to the right of the movie screen opened. He could see the back alley. He stood up, wondering if that was Sergio and Bringuier coming into the theater from the back alley.

No, it was more cops! Christ! The police came flooding in one, two at a time, four, five, and then the other door to the left of the screen opened and more cops rushed in from that side, eight, nine, and more. He turned to look back at the two cops with the theater clerk and there were now six cops with him. Two officers with flashlights shined their beams on the faces of the people in the audience. Now a flood of cops came in the back from the other side.

He moved down the aisle toward the candy clerk when a cop grabbed his left forearm from the row behind and yelled, "Where are you going?"

"This is it." He tried to twist his arm free, looking toward the front where more and more policemen poured in from the doors on each side of the movie screen. What was going on?

The cop who had grabbed his arm whacked his head, so he took a swinging punch at his exposed ribs, and another haymaker came down on his head, then a billy club, from out of no where, down across his left eye that sent him back onto the seats. There were so many policemen he thought he should surrender and he reached for his pistol—to take it out and show them so they wouldn't get the wrong idea—and another cop put both his hands on his wrist and slammed it down on a seat armrest. His hand squeezed tightly on the gun, the trigger released, and the hammer came down, but one of the cop's fleshy fingers jammed in-between, stopping it from firing. The first cop punched him again and again, slamming his head against the seat back while someone grabbed his other arm and twisted it behind his back, lashing his shoulder socket into severe pain. He screwed down to the floor with the twisting to try to make it stop. Another fist came down on the back of his head and handcuffs went around his right wrist. He dropped the pistol. They jerked that hand around and handcuffed it to the other wrist, pulled his arms up before he was ready to stand, sliding his legs up under his chest, and a fist came down on his back. The lights came on but the film was still running: one of America's greatest heroes was still talking and talking. They pulled his arms up again, ripping the shoulder sockets backwards, and he stood up reflexively, catching his balance underneath him.

"He's the one!" the clerk shouted. "He didn't buy a ticket!"

Lee thought, This is a lot attention for someone who didn't pay for a movie ticket! Now what? He looked around the theater. He had never seen so many policemen. There must be thirty of them. They pulled him by his handcuffed arms and led him to the back of the theater, where, finally, the projectionist stopped the film and the sound came to a groggy halt. He was pushed and shoved by several policemen out of the theater, through the lobby, and outside.

In front of the Texas Theater were more cops and a huge crowd of 100 to 150 people. He tried to look past them, up and down the street, as they pushed him toward one patrol car in particular. He briefly saw a car that looked like Bringuier's blue Chevrolet but no one was inside or near it. They must have left. Where was his back-up? Where was Sparky? Who were all these people and how in the world did so many cops and so many people find out so fast? Now what? He mumbled, "It's all over now."

They shoved him into the back of the patrol car and he tightened his lips. He had to think. What should he do? They would take him downtown to the police station but what should he do? If he were in New Orleans he would call Chief Phillips or Guy Banister. Uncle Charlie could fix this—if this was New Orleans—but it isn't.

What should he do? Call Banister? Chief Phillips? Call Nofio Pecora? Carlos Marcello? Where was Sparky? Should he call him? Call Captain Dave? Yeah. Captain Dave, come fly me the hell out of here!

God damn, he thought. Now what should he do? He'd been in worse situations. The police would try to sweat him like the KGB in Moscow, but he wouldn't talk. Admit nothing, deny everything, and ask questions with counter-accusations. But, no, he had nothing to say. It was their turn to talk now.

He thought again, Who should he call? But of course any person that he called would tip them off to his connections. Maybe he should call Ruth to instruct Marina not to worry. Tell Marina that he'd been in worse situations and this would all work out.

Damn, he thought. Why did so many cops come to the theater so fast? Someone must have tipped them off and the police broadcast it over the radio. Thirty cops don't show up for someone sneaking into a movie house.

The arresting officers said they were taking him downtown to ask him "a few questions" for a "few minutes." It was a quick ride and when the policeman driving pulled into the basement parking lot, under the Dallas Police Department main building, the officer pointed in the direction of a glass wall. "Look at that."

Dozens of reporters were swarming in the hallway. The cop next to him said, "Hunh. Listen, we can take you down to another corridor, to a more secluded entrance. Or you can use one of our jackets to cover your face."

"Why should I hide my face?" he replied calmly. "I haven't done anything to be ashamed of."

The policemen led him out of the patrol car, one officer opened the swinging steel doors that led to the police department, and the throng of waiting reporters turned and rushed for them. The first policeman pulled him by his cuffed wrists and another cop shielded away the reporters on the other side, holding his elbow, guiding them through the barking reporters.

He was escorted through the huge crowd of media and he kept his head up, focusing on where they were going, making their way through the crammed hallway and now the media room, and they stopped by Chief of Police Curry, who was a big man with a good ol' boy potbelly, a very high hairline, and polished-metal glasses. Chief Curry wore a suit and tie, and he spoke near a group of microphones on stands to the many, many press members to inform them of the basics of what the police knew. As soon as they stopped by the microphones near Chief Curry, a storm of questions surged loudly:

"Why did you do it?"

"Over here!"

What a lot of racket, Lee thought. What was the purpose of this? Remain quiet.

"Hey! Why did they arrest you?"

"Did you kill the President?"

They think I killed the President, he thought. That confirms it. Someone eliminated the target. He wanted to argue that he had missed, maybe hit his back, but he remained silent.

"Were you in that building? The book depository?"

Lee realized that the reporters seemed to know as much as the police: how is that? The information had traveled incredibly fast, much too fast, and, instantly, he knew he had to begin protecting himself. He leaned back toward the microphones as they continued to pull him along. "I work in that building."

"Were you in that building when the President was shot?"

"Naturally if I work in that building, yes sir." He was led by his handcuffed wrists and the reporters followed in his wake.

Sergeant Bobby Ray "Bull" Anderson, a burly Swede, hollered, "Hey, back up!"

"Did you shoot the President?"

"I didn't shoot anybody, sir," he said. "I haven't been told what I'm here for."

"Do you have a lawyer?

"No, sir, I don't."

"Did you shoot the President?"

"No, they're taking me in because of the fact that I lived in the Soviet Union."

The policeman leading him pulled harder, taking him into an elevator, where they rode up one floor, then exited and weaved their way through desks in the middle of the floor, around typewriters on stands, past a bench against the wall under a large map of the city of Dallas, by a stand of flags, including the Texas and U.S. flags, and entered Room 317, which was an office with a sign that read "Robbery and Homicide" over the door.

Lee braced himself and thought he sure as hell wasn't talking to the police. How did they have so much information so fast? Yes, he must be completely silent and let them talk. When he got the chance, he'd call Ruth and ask her to sit down with Marina to explain to her, and make her understand, that everything would be okay. It was going to be okay.

57)

Close de book on loose talk

Sparky sat in the office of his Carousel Club. He knew the telephone was going to ring, but he didn't want to answer it. There was no good news to be had in any of it. The police had picked up so many guys and now *he* had to clean it up. Shit. Maybe he could take off and get out of here. Go somewhere where no one would know him, or his past. No, that was no good. They had guys everywhere. They'd get to him. He *had* to do this thing. But how many guys would he need to kill and how could he handle so many?

Andy, the bartender, stuck his head in the office while holding on to the open door. "You want some coffee, boss?"

"No. Just, um. . . Are the other clubs open? I think I should close. What do you think?"

Andy nodded his head solemnly. His sad, drooping eyelids and dark skin made him look particularly mournful. "Yeah, I think some the others closed. I can check. But, yeah, I can tell you think you should close, so yeah, you should close."

"Yeah, I'd like to close. I'll put an ad in the paper saying we're closed. That way our regular—"

The phone rang and Sparky flinched in his chair.

"Shit," Andy said. He knew enough to leave and close the door behind him.

He picked up the receiver nervously.

"Listen." It was Nofio Pecora's gravelly voice on the other end, but he had the authority of Carlos Marcello. "We can forgive dis debt, you know, all dat you owe us. But somet'ings gotta be done. It makes de whole country look bad—all dis talk on a level of conspiracy."

"Yes, sir," he said, wanting to offer something. "We can't have that. There's—"

Pecora spoke over him brusquely, "If de feds go in der, man, and shake Oswald, shit he liable to tell dem everything, man. He got dis. He got dat. You don't know what de motherfucker do."

"Yeah, I mean, no, we can't have that."

Pecora's voice was firm and to the point. "I'll tell you what de people want. Dey want dis Oswald to vanish. Dat's how you close de book on loose talk."

Sparky remembered the sign on the Marcello's conference table of Churchill Farms: Three Can Keep A Secret If Two Are Dead. A chill raced over his spine as Mr. Pecora spoke slowly with a violent, threatening voice. "People want him off de map, Jack. He's a nuisance to behold."

"Yeah. Okay, yeah," he said, although the sound on the other end was the constant humming of disconnection. Marcello had given his order, through Pecora, who did not wait for a response before hanging up. He didn't need a response. No one refused Marcello's order.

So there it is, he thought. Oswald. Maybe the others had been taken care of, or maybe the police let them go. Oswald. That's it. In a way, it was a relief that it was just the one guy and he immediately began to focus on how he would do this.

He used a white kerchief to wipe the sweat dripping from his temples and knotted it around his right fist like boxing tape. He stood up and began pacing around his desk, swinging his fists at an imaginary boxing opponent and thinking. Shit. How would he do this? He had to do this. He had to do this *now!*

58)

Room 317

Lee sat in Captain Will Fritz's office, staring blankly ahead at the laminated brown desk covered with reports and folders. A lanky policeman sat next to him in the corner, watching his every move in spite of the fact that his hands were still handcuffed together in front of him. Officer William "Blackie" Harrison, wearing a white Stetson hat, stood quietly in the opposite corner of the office, near the door, guarding anyone from entering. Detective L.D. Miller put his boot up on the desk, his crotch a few inches away from his face, and pushed back his Stetson. He overheard someone outside the door say, "We didn't find any cleaning cloths. Only three cartridges and one in the rifle," and another man responded, "okay, keep looking."

The door suddenly opened as Captain Fritz used his keys to unlock the door and officer Harrison stepped aside. Captain Fritz had short dark hair neatly combed straight back, quick brown eyes, and he seemed to notice everything all at once as he carried a paper cup of coffee in one hand and a fat manila folder in the other while juggling his keys back into his brown suit pants pocket.

Lee stood up out of respect, with cuffed hands in front of him, making Detective Miller take his boot off the desk and back away. The older, taller man, Detective Miller, flicked his cowboy hat and looked up at the ceiling, obviously annoyed at his show of respect, and said with a slow Texas drawl, "Shee-e-t."

Captain Will Fritz set down his coffee cup on the desk and looked around the crowded room. They often used his office as an interrogation room and today there were just too many people, the media and gawking public, downstairs. The two detectives continued to stare at him viciously and with loathing.

He returned a harsh look at Miller, then sat back down and folded his hands in his lap. Captain Fritz settled in behind his desk, forcing Harrison, the shorter, thin detective, to move in front of the door but he continued standing. Then Harrison said to no one in particular, "I'll go get another chair," and left the room.

Lee thought of the interrogation by the KGB when he first arrived in Moscow and wondered if the Dallas police would hit him during their interrogation? They had already roughed him up pretty good in the movie theater and the swelling over his eye ached.

"I understand we're not getting too far with you," Captain Fritz began warmly, as if he were his friend and smiled.

He remained quiet as trained. Let them play their cards, he thought. Name, rank, and serial number? Ha! Bullshit. Let them figure out *all* of it.

"You don't have a driver's license?" Fritz was smooth.

He looked down at the gray, linoleum-tiled floor. Should he mention no one drives in New York City because they all ride the subway? Or that no one drives in Minsk because they all ride the bus or walk? Hell, most people in Minsk don't even own cars. No, he didn't drive, so why would he need a license?

"Your identification says O. H. Lee. That you?" Fritz stood briefly to take off his brown suit coat, revealing his white short-sleeved shirt. He noticed Fritz's dark tie with a polished brass tie clip as he sat down again and smiled. He remained silent and glanced over at the filing cabinet in the corner overflowing with paperwork.

"You've also got this library card that says David Ferrie," Fritz said. "But that's in New Orleans, so I reckon that's somebody else's and not yours."

Someone knocked twice on the door and Detective Miller opened the door. Detective Harrison entered with another office chair, maneuvered to close the door behind him, and handed a note to Captain Fritz while leaning over to whisper something that sounded like "cleaning gear" that made Fritz's face sour slightly. Harrison then stared at him, sat down, smoothed his hand over a pad of paper, and wet the pencil lead in his mouth.

"Hmm?" Captain Fritz continued. "What'd you say to that?"

"You're the cop. You figure it out."

"Oh, we *will* figure it out. How you shot Officer Tippit and so on, but we'd save a lot of time if you told us who you are."

Officer Tippit?, he thought. That must have been the cop that was shot. That's why they brought me in. Those witnesses thought I shot that policeman! Stay calm and deny everything.

Captain Fritz opened the folder and started to go through the papers, which looked like an FBI file as several of the documents had the FBI's stamped logo at the top of the page. One of the documents had his Marine enlistment photo clipped to it. "We already know a lot about you."

He was well aware that what they "knew of him" was one of three sometimes fictionalized background stories and none of the three were complete without the other two. Then he realized only a select few people would be able to pull it all together and thus he would be labeled a killer by the entire world, and for the wrong reasons. That thought, along with the fact he had worked his whole life to become a special agent and would forever be misjudged, made him very sad. "Everybody will know who I am now."

"That sounds like a confession," the tall Detective Miller said, putting his boot up on the desk. "Is that why you did it?'

He scoffed. What did Miller know about patriotic duty? What had he done in the way of self-sacrifice? Loyalty? Did he ever serve his country in the armed forces? Did he ever serve overseas on the front lines? Or better yet, to serve behind enemy lines where *no one* is to be trusted?

Sparky saw a sign that read "Robbery and Homicide" and found what he was looking for: Room 317. He felt the loaded, snub-nosed revolver in his pants pocket. Reached in with his right hand, grabbed the gun and pulled it out, but kept it near his leg. He felt nervous because the door had a glass window but he could see the group inside, including Oswald, who sat off to the side. He looked around quickly—no one was watching. Now was his chance. He tried the doorknob: locked.

It was almost seven p.m. They had held him in custody for about six hours now and Oswald could have said anything. He could have spilled it all.

Sparky tried the doorknob again: locked. Should he bust in? Slam through the door and shoot him quickly? But what if one of the cops questioning Oswald interferes, stops him? No, he must wait for a clear shot. "You must make sure this is done," Carlos had said.

"Hey!" A police officer in uniform walked up the hall quickly. He held a paper cup of coffee in one hand and his other hand pushed down on his nightstick. "You can't go in there, Jack!"

He nodded, turned his head down and turned his body away from him, slid the pistol back in his pocket, and walked for the far stairwell at the end of the hallway even though the elevator was directly behind the policeman. He'd find another opportunity. He would make sure.

"We've got your Smith and Wesson thirty-eight caliber revolver," Captain Fritz said.

Lee thought, That's not a crime. Anyone can own a gun. It's in the first amendment to the constitution. You can look it up.

Another rapping sounded at the door and the shorter Detective Harrison looked up from his notebook. Captain Fritz nodded to Miller, who opened the office door, and another policeman came in, handed another folder to

Fritz and crammed his way into the far corner, where he stood at attention, sipped his coffee, and then folded his arms in front of his chest.

Captain Fritz flipped through several typed pages in the latest folder, reading them carefully. "Seems you were employed at the book warehouse. . . "

He remained quiet. Okay. So? That was my job. Filling book orders.

"We sealed off the building after the shooting and did a head count. You were the only employee who was not there. Why'd you leave?"

"I didn't think there would be any more work that day."

Captain Fritz continued, "Did your boss say it was okay to leave?"

His "boss" had told him to go home, change clothes, two cops would take him to rendezvous at the theater, where he would meet two men who would take him out the back alley and drive him to Redbird Airport, where Captain Ferrie would fly him out of the country. But the cops fled, then Sergio and those assholes weren't at the theater. They all abandoned him. Hmm. I wonder why thirty officers would respond to someone not buying a movie ticket?

"Did you dislike the President? Were you upset with him?"

"No, sir, I am not a malcontent."

"What did you think of his policies?" Captain Fritz was obviously fishing for any background information.

"As you apparently are considering me a suspect, I think any answer I give you may be misconstrued," he spoke calmly. "But I will say this. Since the president was killed, someone would take his place, perhaps Vice President Johnson, and his views would probably be largely the same as those of President Kennedy."

"Uh-hmm." Captain Fritz seemed a bit unsure of where to go next. He had three fat folders of paperwork in a matter of hours. He pulled out a picture of Lee in the backyard, holding a rifle and some Soviet magazines. "What do you have to say about this picture?"

"That's not me." His mind was racing. How in the world did they get that photograph so quickly? It was a photo he made Marina take with his Imperial reflex camera, and he had used the darkroom at Jaggars-Chiles-Stovall to reduce and manipulate the image. "Since I've been here, you've taken my photo and superimposed it onto someone else's body. No, that's not me. It looks like me, but that's not me. That's just my face."

The captain flipped it over and on the back was the note he had written in Russian Cyrillic to George de Mohrenschildt:

To my friend George

from Lee Oswald

Hunter of fascists Ha-ha-ha!!!

Damn. That was *fast!* He tried not to move, flinch, or breathe irregularly. Don't sweat. Damn, another betrayal! George! He did his best to look around the room casually.

Captain Fritz flipped through a few more documents. He pursed his lips into a frown as he studied one, and then looked up. "You want to know what really gets me? I see a lot of stuff in here about you. . . but a lot of it, and I mean a *lot* of it, just plain *don't. . . make. . . sense.* In the Marines, defecting to the Soviet Union, coming back here without so much as a thorough tongue-lashing let alone being arrested for the possibility of giving away government secrets, but I'll come back to that, and since that time you basically worked piss ant jobs. You owed Uncle Sam about four hundred dollars for a loan of repatriation money and here's a note saying your brother had to purchase your airplane ticket, so you owed him, what, another two hundred?"

He knew where this was going. There was no way they could follow the money. It was all cash and from various sources. The sources flashed in his mind. George paid cash. Banister paid cash. Phillips, Marcello, Hunt all paid cash. No, they had nothing.

"Your IRS statement from last year shows you made four hundred and ninety dollars." Captain Fritz looked at some of the officers standing in the room. "For the whole year!"

He was annoyed by Fritz's drawn-out presentation, exhaled a long sigh, and was immediately smacked on the back of his head by Detective Miller. Captain Fritz gave Miller a scowl but did not say anything to Miller. He continued, "We have a statement from Mrs. Earlene Roberts, your landlady, which says your rent was sixty-eight dollars a month. Plus you've got a wife and two kids to support, and pay your bills. And yet last year you paid off the entire government loan of three hundred ninety-six dollars, bought a rifle and a revolver for another fifty dollars, and bought this fancy spy camera. Did it all on wages of four hundred and ninety dollars. So what I wanna know is, who's giving you money?"

You'll never find out, he thought. Too many separate sources. All cash. All covert. They'll never talk.

"Who's in this with you?"

He shook his head and shrugged. "I don't even know what you're talking about. You haven't told me anything. Am I being charged with a crime?"

Captain Fritz again looked at the other detectives and policemen. The exasperation on his face showed this was not getting the results he wanted. "Alright, let's start gathering evidence. Test him with paraffin to see if he's fired a gun. Jim—" he paused to look over his shoulder at the latest policeman to enter, in the corner behind him, "let's get a warrant to search his house."

Captain Fritz stood, his wiry forearms flexing on his desk, closed the folder, held it, swatted it in his hand, and dropped it on his desk. "You've obviously been trained in resisting interrogation techniques."

The shorter Detective Harrison spoke with a sarcastic smile, "Your self-control is wound tighter than a Swiss watch. Like you been rehearsed."

"Or programmed like one of them Commie *Manchurian Candidates,*" the tall Texan scuffed his boot on the floor as if bullshit were on it. "You know what I think. I say we should show him how we do it down here in Texas."

"Sir, I am entitled to legal representation," Lee said.

"Oh, you'd like a lawyer?" Fritz smiled. "What for?"

"You're stating that somehow I'm implicated in a crime."

Captain Fritz nodded solemnly, "Yes, you will be charged with the murder of Officer J.D. Tippit. You want a lawyer?"

"If you can find a lawyer who believes in anything I believe in, and believes as I believe, and believes in my innocence as much as he can, I might let him represent me."

"There ain't no such person on the face of God's green earth," Miller walked for the door, made a lasso-type loop with his hat as if waving to a crowd, and stepped out of the office. "Let's go, Will."

"There is a Mister John Abt, a New Yorker I believe, who may do this."

A few of the men scoffed, Miller reached back and grabbed him by the handcuffs, jerking him out of the chair, and they led him out of the office, down the hallway, down a staircase and three flights of stairs, and out into the first floor hallway where dozens of reporters anxiously awaited him and began peppering questions at him as soon as they saw him.

"How are they treating you?" a reporter yelled.

"I'm being denied my basic hygienic rights like a shower. . . and a book. These people have given me a hearing without legal representation or anything."

"Did you shoot the President?"

"No, I didn't shoot anybody. No, sir."

The officers hustled him away and Lee thought he was probably headed for more questioning. His mind raced over how many people had already betrayed him, then recalled George's instructions and other training from his very first CO: if captured, we will deny knowing you and you're on your own.

He had to start fighting for himself! He suddenly realized that he may not have the chance to speak to the media again, so he turned back to them and yelled, "I'm just a patsy!"

59)

Who are you with?

It was almost midnight and Sparky proudly wore a red badge that read

President Kennedy Visit to Dallas
Press

Sparky felt slightly out of place, but knew that no one in the media would know or care about his presence here. The newsman had gathered in the media room of the Dallas Police department but there were so many of them, and arriving hourly by the planeload, that there was standing room only. They smoked cigarettes and rehearsed their opening lines, performed camera and sound checks, and went over their notepads full of questions. One talkative reporter asked, "Who are you with?"

He said, "I'm a translator for the Israeli Press."

The whole room had a somber tone, but was very businesslike. The press had to get their story and to them, he was just another guy on the beat. The police were his friends, of course, and most were happy to see him or were too busy to say anything. He would stand in the back, where no one would notice or care, and if the opportunity arose, he would be *ready*. He recalled the telephone calls and his meetings with the bosses from Sam Giancana, Barney Baker, Jimmy Hoffa, Nofio Pecora, Carlos Marcello, Pecora again, and felt the Colt .38 in his pants pocket. He *would* do this thing.

Chief of Police Curry came into the room from a back door. He tugged his belt over his large belly, adjusted his metal-framed glasses, and nodded as he came to a stop by the microphones. The frenzy of questions began:

"Where is the suspect?"

"Has he been charged?"

"Is he a communist?"

"One at a time! One at a time!" Chief Curry called out but most continued yelling until Sergeant Bull Anderson hollered, "Order!"

It was briefly quiet and in that lull Sergeant Anderson, the big, muscular Swede, pointed to a thin reporter near the front of the crowd and said, "You!"

The thin reporter, with dark hair and beads of perspiration rolling down his temples, held a tape recorder and pushed out the microphone toward the Chief. "What's his name?"

Chief Curry spoke clearly, "Lee. . . Harvey. . . Oswald."

"Is there any doubt in your mind Chief that Oswald is the man who killed the President?"

"I think this is the man that killed the President."

A television reporter, standing next to a cameraman, called out, "Can you describe the evidence you have against Oswald and the President's wounds?"

"The President was shot twice. Once in the throat and the fatal head wound. The bullet struck his head," he pointed to his right front temple area, "about here."

"From the right front?" a national magazine reporter with a crew cut asked, but before Chief Curry answered, the first reporter followed up his question. "How was it the President was shot in the throat if the motorcade had already passed the book depository?"

"The President turned around to wave to people." Chief Curry was firm, undeniable in his fact-giving. "Next."

"Will there be an autopsy?"

Chief Curry pursed his lips tightly. He had read a police report of a fight at Parkland Hospital between the Secret Service agents and hospital's doctors. It was wildly rumored among the press people that some officers from the Navy, or the Secret Service, had pulled their guns on the attending physicians to remove the body. Now Chief Curry was being placed in the spotlight of commenting on where an autopsy would take place and who would conduct it. He had received calls from J. Edgar Hoover, the State Department, the CIA, and a special radio transmission from the newly sworn-in President Johnson, and all stated the same information: He had to follow orders. He said, "That's a federal matter."

"Is it true Oswald is a member of the communist party?"

Chief Curry, showing the effects of the long day, rubbed his forehead and replied from memory. "We really don't know whether. . . if he is or isn't. We have uncovered some information which indicates he was connected with a group while living in New Orleans, the ah, Free Cuba Committee."

Sparky knew that was wrong and, not wanting this error to go out to the whole country, that Oswald was *for* the liberation of Cuba from Castro, he said, "Sir, it's Fair Play for Cuba Committee."

"Yes, that may be, this Fair Play group."

Suddenly there *he* was—Oswald—being led through the horde of media by two policemen. Sparky felt the pistol in his pants pocket, but there were too many people around. All these reporters. How could he be sure to hit him? He was in the back row, behind all these people. Maybe he could push through the crowd to get a clear shot. No, Oswald was too far away and the reporters flooded around him. Damn. Maybe he could lunge through the crowd?

Lee was tired of the way he was being treated, led around like an animal on a leash, and upset he had been denied all of his requests. When they reached the first floor again and stepped off the elevator, he raised his fist to show the reporters, photographers, and television cameramen that he was still in handcuffs.

A reporter with a blonde crew cut called out quickly, "What is your response to the charges?"

He answered as he was pulled along. "It's not just the facts as you people have been given. But I emphatically deny these charges. I'm really not sure what the charges are."

"Why'd you do it?"

"Are you a communist?"

"Are you aware of the evidence mounting against you?"

He pulled back strongly to stop the officer from tugging him in order to respond. "I know nothing of the so-called evidence. All I know is I was arrested at the movie theater and brought here."

Sparky needed to maneuver his way through all the reporters, get close to him, and then shoot. There were just too many people and the cops would notice him coming. It wouldn't work. Next time, he'd be in the front, or very near the front. Next time, he'd have a clear shot. He was going to do this thing, but next time, when the conditions were right. When he could be sure. He had to be sure.

"Do you know you're being charged with killing the President?"

"I don't know about that," Lee said. "You all seem to know more about that than I do."

"What's happened to you since you've been arrested?"

"Well, I was brought before Judge Johnson and I protested at that time that I was not allowed legal representation during that very short and sweet hearing. Ah, I really don't know what the situation is about. Nobody has told me anything except that I'm accused of ah, of ah, of murdering a policeman. I know nothing more than that and I do request that someone come forward to give me legal assistance."

"Did you kill the president?"

"No, I have not been charged with that. In fact nobody has said that to me yet. The first thing I heard about it was when the newspaper reporters in the hall asked me that question."

"Nobody said what?" The reporter yelled from the rear. "Nobody said what? We can't hear you back here."

He was pulled away from the microphones and he exhaled with frustration.

"How'd you get a black eye?" a reporter yelled, extending his arm with a microphone. "How?"

He stopped, leaned toward the microphone, and said clearly, "A policeman hit me."

"Do you have a statement?"

He felt inclined to say something in the form of a statement, but didn't know where to begin. He had to say something in his defense, but it was all so complicated, so he was silent and they pulled him further down the hall.

"Come on, Oswald! Statement!"

"Make a statement!"

"I did not do it." He looked at the crowd of reporters and they all had a look of disbelief. They did not care. "I did not do it. I did not shoot anyone."

The police officers took him in the elevator to an upper floor that had a group of jail cells with single beds. An officer opened the steel-barred gate at the entry to the corridor, he heard it clang shut behind them, lock, and they led him into a cell on the left, uncuffed him roughly, closed the door, and locked it. One guard remained standing in front of the door, one stood at the end of the hallway where they entered, and another unlocked the gate, exited, and locked it behind him. Across the aisle, a black man sat on an upper bunk bed and leaned against the cinder block wall, staring at him.

His cell had a single bed and he sat down on a stained mattress without sheets. It smelled of piss. Some of the metal bars were rusted brown and there was a smooth cement floor. He had a lot of thinking to do and, finally, he had a quiet moment. He wondered who he should call *if* he was given the opportunity. The police weren't too keen on letting him making contact to outsiders. Perhaps he should call a lawyer—Mr. Abt? Or maybe he should call someone who had some power to help him. His mission CO—CIA Chief David Phillips? Or someone from the New Orleans connection—Guy Banister? Carlos Marcello? Nofio Pecora? Uncle Charlie? The man who bailed him out in New Orleans—Emile Bruneau? Or FBI Agent Quigley? Or maybe his back-up, Jack Ruby? Perhaps his mentor, George de Mohrenschildt, even though he had betrayed him by supplying the damning photograph? Maybe in private George would help him? No. No, no, no, no. No, no. No. No. He was alone.

After an hour of circular thinking, he realized that there were many people who had betrayed him. No, they had *all* betrayed him and the wall of denial had been formed. They were probably burning his files now, if they had not already burned them.

Then he realized, after this initial session of questioning, they had nothing. They had no evidence. They were trying to make him admit something but they had no physical evidence. In spite of that, he knew he still needed help. And what was he going to do about this Officer Tippit? Deny everything and redirect them with questions.

Okay. He had done well so far, but they were only beginning their investigation. The cops had so much information on him and, meanwhile, he was stuck alone in this squalid, small cell without a lawyer or anyone helping him.

He knew he had to be more assertive for his rights. He had the right to make a phone call. He had a right to legal representation. He had to speak out about all these injustices and about his treatment at any opportunity he had. Still, in spite of it all, so far he was doing well.

He lay back and closed his eyes, knowing he would need his rest to remain calm and composed. He needed to sleep. He also needed legal help and he couldn't help but think about all the people who had abandoned him. How could he sleep now?

He recalled the first arresting policeman who had said they had "a few questions" that would take "a few minutes." It had lasted eleven hours. He was mentally tired and exhaled heavily. He smelled the funky mattress, covered the crook of his arm over his nose and mouth, and tried to sleep. He had to sleep.

60)

The visitor's room

Lee was led into the visitor's room, which was divided by a heavy green metal wall with three thick-glass windows in it. Marina stood on the other side of the wall, behind the glass window in the middle, clutching the black receiver of a telephone by her neck. He went to the booth across from her and looked over his shoulder at a heavyset policeman, who stood at the door but was still very close. Another officer was standing at the end of the wall and watched him meticulously.

"What're you staring at?" he said, but the man did not blink. His reddened face was leathered with deep-cut wrinkles, apparently from too much time in the Texas sun. He wore a Texas Ranger badge on his crisp uniform.

He turned to Marina and she smiled through quivering lips. She motioned at a bag of clothes that she had brought for him, in a paper grocery sack behind her, but said nothing. A tear dropped out of her eyes and then another, but she gazed deeply into his eyes.

He picked up the telephone and said, "Come on, now. We've only got a few minutes. Let's not be sad."

Marina brought up the phone to her mouth. "Your eye! They beat you?"

"Oh, no, they're not beating me. They're treating me fine. You're not to worry about that. How's Junie? Rachel?"

"I'm worried," she said and looked around nervously. "Can we speak?"

"Of course, we can talk about anything."

"Fine. Fine." She took a deep breath and seemed to compose herself. "They are with your mother. Did you—"

"My mother? Why are they with her? Where's Ruth?"

"No, I meant right now. Your mother came over to Ruth's. She. . . She—"

"She what?"

"Nothing." Marina started crying again. Tears flowed from her pretty blue eyes and she put one hand over her trembling mouth.

"It's a mistake," he said. "I'm not guilty. There are people who will help me. There is a lawyer in New York." He knew something else was wrong because of her tears. Was it something his mother had said or done that made her so upset? He didn't want to discuss his mother so he let it go. Their time was short and he didn't know when he would be able to speak with her again. "Don't cry. There is nothing to cry about. Try not to think about it. Everything is going to be all right."

That seemed to help, even though he knew it was a lie. He knew it most definitely was *not* going to be all right. The government stonewall of denial was firmly in place, the media was misinforming public opinion, and no one had any idea of who he was or what his past had been. It would certainly not be revealed in a trial. No. No one would ever find out. He would need an outstanding lawyer and even then he'd need a lot of luck. But the prosecution couldn't have much evidence, as long as Bringuier did his job. But what of the other shooters? Sergio or the French guy or Braden? Why hadn't he heard about them? They must have escaped as planned. "Did the newspaper or radio say anything about what's going on?"

She looked at him with bewilderment. "Is *only* thing on radio and television! Are you serious?"

"No, no. Anything about *me* or any others?"

She spoke reluctantly, "They said you are 'a lone nut.' "

He wanted to laugh because in that simple phrase he saw how they were manipulating public perception and setting him up to be *the* fall guy. Of course. *He* was all they had, so they had to make him out to be *everything*. But he would never talk about anything he had done with ONI, the Company, any source, the Mafioso, any of their connections, or Uncle Charlie, or anyone at all. He was rock solid on that. They would never be able to figure it all out. To hell with them. But he definitely needed help in proving that he was not the one who killed the President. That could still be proven. "Get in touch with Attorney Abt for me."

"Who?"

"There is a lawyer in New York named Abt. He represented some people in the Smith Act case. See if you can convince him to represent me. I think if he were to understand me and my philosophies, then he might be able to represent me."

Marina wiped her eyes with a tissue and looked at him again. He didn't know what more to tell her. Of course she's afraid. She had a pre-existing paranoia of government agencies from the Soviet Union and KGB, but now she would be scrutinized and perhaps threatened by the ONI, CIA, or the mafia, all trying to cover their own trail, anyone who thought he may have confided in her, like the FBI or the Dallas police, and he didn't know who *he* could go to for help much less be able to help her on the outside. But he wanted to make her somehow feel more comfortable. He also knew she would be worried about deportation by the State Department. "You have rights. You're married to a U.S. citizen and that gives you and your family rights. Rachel was born here, for God's sake. If they ask you anything, you have a right not to answer. You have a right to refuse. Do you understand?"

She nodded yes. It appeared she was so emotionally overwhelmed that she was unable to speak so he continued, "You are not to worry. You have friends. They'll help you."

She blurted out, "What if they don't!"

"If it comes to that, you can ask the Red Cross for help. You mustn't worry about me."

She smiled through her tears, wiped her face with a tissue, and blew her nose delicately. She took another tissue out of her purse and the Texas Ranger at the end of the partition stepped closer to them and wrapped his baton on the desk. She looked at him with squinted eyes and took out another tissue and waved it in the air at him, mocking "surrender." He retreated and she seemed less nervous.

"Take care of the kids," he said.

"Yes, of course. They stay with Ruth."

"No, I mean, always. The kids have a better chance here. It's a better life for them than the Soviet Union."

"Yes, yes." She shrugged her shoulders, "Of course, yes."

It was quiet and he wondered if she would have the strength for all of this? It was only beginning and she appeared so distraught and fragile. But she was here. She was by his side in spite of everything. He gazed at her soft beauty and felt very proud of her. She would be fine. His family would be fine no matter what happened.

"Your mother thinks you are government agent."

Ah, so that was what had bothered her, he thought. He didn't react outwardly but inside he rejoiced for a millisecond, the tension around his eyes relaxed, and in that brief moment he saw Marina recognize a glint of admission. He then changed and spoke forcefully, "She's stupid."

Now her eyes registered a look of confusion, but she carried on with her probing, apparently wanting to get at some truth. "She said you were great man. Perhaps greatest hero this country ever had."

"She's stupid," he continued, "and now even you can see that she's stupid."

Marina shook her head and cried more. "I'm sorry. I can't help it."

"You mustn't worry about me."

Again she tried to compose herself. Then something, a thought, seemed to dawn on her and she looked at him with bewilderment. "You're calm."

He raised his eyebrows but then felt a knot in his stomach pinch him. Fluids floated up his esophagus and burned his throat. "My stomach hurts."

The heavyset guard watched the big circular clock on the wall and, when the red second hand reached its zenith, at precisely 1:30 pm, he called out with disgust, "Time!"

Lee put his hand flat against the glass separating them and Marina reflexively put her delicate hand up. She was crying again. The guard grabbed him by the upper arm and pulled him away.

He felt he had only a slim chance to avoid prosecution, to remain alive and continue to see his family, to see them grow up during their visits in his life behind bars, so he spoke clearly, "Call a lawyer named Abt. He's in New York."

The big guard pulled him harder by his elbow. "Kiss Junie and Rachel for me. I love you!"

She was quiet.

The guard jerked the telephone receiver from his hand, so he raised his voice before the man replaced it in the cradle. "Be sure to buy shoes for June!"

Marina nodded and looked down, quietly hanging up the phone.

It was around 3 p.m. when Sparky received a telephone call in his office. A dark voice whispered, "Oswald is being transferred to County."

He immediately left the Carousel Club and rushed over to the County jail. He stood among the reporters near the entrance and tried to remain calm with the loaded pistol in his pocket. As more newsmen arrived he jostled his way to the front, to remain near the door.

The time passed slowly with no news. He chatted briefly in a friendly manner with the other newsmen in spite of the fact that he could feel himself sweating in the Texas heat. He tugged at his shirt collar, loosened his tie, and checked once more to make sure the gun was readily available. A reporter, a pudgy man with a blotchy complexion, turned to him and asked, "What's the matter? You're as nervous as a long-tailed cat in a room full of rocking chairs."

"Nothin'." He smiled and shrugged his shoulders.

Sparky and the newsmen waited several more minutes. He gazed at his watch: almost four o'clock. A policemen from the County Jail came out in full uniform and called out in a loud, officious voice, "They postponed the transfer until tomorrow morning! Sorry, guys!"

He walked away brusquely, slamming open the metal door. Another chance lost. When he was out on the street, he took a swing at the air, throwing a sweeping left hook and yelled, "Son-of-a-bitch!"

61)

The phone call

Sparky's roommate Dick lounged on the sofa with his hairy, bare feet up as he read the Dallas *Morning News*. He occasionally made a remark that sounded like a wild, stupid rumor but he couldn't tell if it was Dick's uninformed opinion or the newspaper article.

"Stay the hell off the phone," he warned. "I'm expecting a god-damn important phone call and I can't have it tied up." He took a preludin and tapped his fingers on the Formica countertop of the kitchen, hovering over the olive-green phone that was supposed to compliment the brown-green refrigerator. His own nervousness made him upset so he stood up and paced the kitchen floor, looking at the odd color of the refrigerator. What made this odd green, with a tint of shit-brown mixed-in, attractive? Who in the fuck ever bought this piece of shit and who designed this crap? He hated that he lived in a rental apartment, at his age, and the first thing he would do when this was all settled would be to buy a proper house. That would be soon, he thought. As soon as he did this thing Mr. G and Mr. Marcello would forgive his debt. He would be free and clear to make some real money, then he could get out of this piss ant place.

He opened the fridge and took out a can of dog food, using the spoon still sticking inside it, and scooped out some food into a bowl. Sheba, his favorite dachshund, came over quickly when she heard the sound of the spoon on the can. He bent over to pet her as she wolfed down the reddish-brown, nasty-looking food. "You love that shit, don't cha? Only the best horsemeat for you!"

The phone rang and he dropped the can on the floor, picking up the phone before it rang a second time. "What?"

The voice was faint, high-pitched, and pleading. It was one of his strippers, Little Lynn, wanting cash, wanting it now, wanting it because the club was closed and she had no money for food. Get off the god damn phone, bitch, he thought, but tried to be nice. "How much do you need, honey?"

"Twenty-five. But I don't have any way to come in to Dallas to pick it up. Can you wire it to me?"

"Wire it? Hunh?"

"At the Western Union telegraph office. You give them the money and they send it to another office and I can pick it up there. Okay?"

"Fine. I'll send it this morning."

"But it's already ten. It's after ten."

"Yes, this morning."

"I need it bad, honey."

"I said I'd send it. Now get off the fuckin' phone!"

Sparky slammed down the receiver. Cunts. You tell them you'll do what they ask and they still bother you with nagging.

Dick mumbled something about a "lone nut assassin" from across the room but stared at the newspaper. The phone instantly rang again.

"Yeah."

It was Detective Blackie Harrison. "I called before—the line was busy. They're doing it now."

"Now? Like right now?" He could hear in the background the sounds of clanking of dishes and silverware as if Blackie were in a diner.

"Yep, fifteen, twenty minutes. Get down here. Take the alley door, down the stairs—"

He didn't let him finish. He knew where to go. He patted his pants pocket to make sure he had the .38, his other pocket to feel the wad of cash—two grand—picked up Sheba, who was licking the bowl for the last morsels of food, and hurried out the door. Dick said something as he left but he wasn't listening to him. He had to hustle, had to get to Western Union, and then to the police station. It would be tight, but he knew he could make it. He floored the accelerator, kicking out gravel under the car and smoking the tires on the blacktop. Sheba pranced around on the front seat to keep her balance, and then put her paws up on the front window that was partially rolled down.

He was going to do this thing, take care of it for them, and then he'd be a hero. He'd be free of all debt and finally, finally, he would be respected by the big guys. He was definitely going to do this thing.

62)

The transfer

After a lot of delays, the detectives and a few other policemen finally came to his cell to transfer him to the Dallas County Jail. Lee knew that the media would be there, with all their television cameras and newspaper reporters and photographers, and he didn't want to look shabby so he asked for some different clothes that Marina had brought. He picked out a black sweater to slip over his shirt. That would make him look a little better and keep him warm in the cool, late-November air. He felt a little better.

Officer James R. Leavell handcuffed his own wrist to his, grabbed his belt, and escorted him out. Two other officers stood watching and two more were at the elevator, with another one holding the doors for them. Chief Curry was in the elevator waiting for them, two officers got on first, then he and Leavell, and finally officer L.C. Graves, followed in behind them.

The six of them were quiet riding down the elevator until officer Leavell said, "Lee, if anybody shoots at you, I hope they are as good a shot as you are."

Leavell intended it to be gallows humor, meaning that they should hit their target and not himself, but the implication was that he *did* do it and he wasn't about to say anything related to that. He was tired of arguing with everyone. "You're being melodramatic. I don't think anybody's gonna shoot at me."

"Well in the event that they do shoot at you, you know what to do." He was quiet so Leavell continued, "You will be on the floor immediately."

They reached the basement and the elevator doors opened, where another policeman was waiting. Down the hallway, a lot of reporters were gathered around the parking area and officer Leavell led him steadily with Graves on the other side. Four more policemen followed behind. Very bright lights flooded the area for the television cameras. Through the glare he saw Lieutenant George Butler, who was normally calm but looked visibly nervous with his lips trembling. Why should *he* be nervous?

A reporter called out, "Do you have anything to say in your defense?" A police car backed up toward the crowd, honked its horn, and then it happened quickly, a dark figure striding out of the pack, people seemed to be moving in slow motion. Leavell saw it coming first, from beyond the blinding television lights, and jerked him by his belt to twist him away from this man lunging out of the crowd.

Lee thought, Who is this? What's happening? Then he saw it was Sparky, his back up. A day late and a dollar short. He looked determined, no, mad beneath his gray fedora. Black suit and angry—a charging bull coming fast—with his hand rising, bootlegging something black, but what is it? What's in his hand?

BLAM! A shot hit his left side and he felt immediate, intense pain. "Unh."

He fell, the hall hurtling sideways, and the cement floor smashed his body and face. He saw policemen wrestle in a tangle of bodies onto Sparky, like football tacklers sacking the quarterback in a huge pile-up.

BLAM! BLAM! the room flashed brightly, briefly, with each exploding round. He heard the chaos of yelling, struggling grunts, fists smacking a face, and clothes tearing. Sparky's voice was clear above the din, "I'm a hero."

This is it? Lee thought. A poetic and meaningful moment, the ending of an opera when it all comes together, but. . . How will they know? To know with certainty.

From deep within the tangled wrestlers, Sparky's voice called out again, "Hey, you all know me! I'm Jack Ruby!"

He thought of Marina. Junie and Rachel. All my love. "Unh."

A reporter stood over him, then knelt down on his knees and spoke loudly into his ear, "Did you do it?"

Admit nothing, deny everything, and ask counter questions on a different topic. *They,* of course, will deny everything, too.

Sparky was the back-up. Shit. Some back up. It's all becoming dazzlingly clear now.

Mother. You always knew me best.

Robbie. What can I say or do that would ever satisfy you? Nothing. So screw you, you asshole. I never liked you anyway. I don't care what you think. Why didn't you. . . I was your brother.

Someone pulled off his handcuff and he couldn't hold his arm up. It hit the cold cement floor with a dull flap. A stretcher was rolled out and emergency workers lifted him. The reporter leaning over him shouted, "Did you shoot the President?"

He felt his body rising and his eyes rolled back. The light was dim. Now the light was blinding but it faded. The hard stretcher beneath him rolled into the white station wagon. A siren sounded. Every muscle went limp. Exhaling without effort, collapsing, "Unh."

Where is the light? The poetry of the moment? All gone, he thought. Who will know? Yes, of course. No one will know. No one. My historic moment. I did it. God bless America, I did it.

63)

My life is in danger here!

President Kennedy delivered his inaugural speech on a cold January day and his warm breath misted the air with tangible possibilities. He said, "Ask not what your country can do for you. Ask what you can do for your country." That patriotic challenge inspired the best people in America into enthusiastic action. His rousing words captured the imagination of even the mediocre to make of themselves, and of this country, something better.

Sparky knew in President Kennedy's death people had lost so much that they did not know where to turn for leadership, or for answers to their many questions surrounding his murder. It was in this atmosphere that new President Lyndon B. Johnson brought together a panel of seven people headed by the Chief Justice of the Supreme Court, Earl Warren. President Johnson assigned the Warren Commission to investigate the killing of their beloved President and, subsequently, to interrogate him to provide some answers for what happened. He knew the people wanted action, they deserved answers, and President Lyndon Johnson empowered the Warren Commission to give it to them.

Sparky sat in his Dallas County jail cell and read in the newspaper that along with Chief Justice Earl Warren, the Commission included the former Director of the CIA, Allen W. Dulles; a wide-eyed U.S. Representative from Michigan named Gerald R. Ford, who was rumored to be a member of an exclusive secret society; Representative Hale Boggs from Louisiana; U.S. Senators Richard B. Russell and John Sherman Cooper; and John J. McCloy, who was former president of the World Bank. To Sparky it seemed an odd assortment of people including the powerful ex-heads of the World Bank and the CIA.

President Johnson had asked them to conscientiously dig for the truth to expose the full truth of what happened. Sparky thought about that, to let *everything* be known.

Later that month he read in magazines like *Life* and *Time* the Warren Commission was eager to find out the truth and they immediately began their task. He knew investigators start with the shooter but Oswald's dead, so he would be next. He was ready for any questions of who he was, what he knew, any connections he had, and why he shot Lee Harvey Oswald. But instead the Commission did not interview him first.

As month after month went by, he read more newspaper and magazine reports that gave details of the botched Dallas police investigation, their method of bullying witnesses, the Secret Service's manhandling of people including drawing guns on doctors in Parkland Hospital to get their way, the FBI's bungling of various tips including more than one person who predicted that President Kennedy would be assassinated in Dallas during the few hours he would be there, the CIA's tight-lipped refusal to give any information even though they had many files on Oswald, and the Armed Forces blunt, disgraceful discharge of Oswald after several years of service. Instead of answering questions, more and more were raised.

Sparky began to wonder what was going on. One day his brother Sam came to visit and he watched Sam closely on the other side of the glass wall in the visitor's room. He told Sam he doubted the Warren Commission was really after the truth. He said, "They're avoiding the main witnesses and when an answer doesn't fit into their report? Forget about it."

Sam agreed, pursed his lips, and shook his head sideways as if the fix was in for him. "So, you gonna talk?"

He rubbed his face and looked away. An overweight guard with a Texas Ranger badge eyed him. When he looked back at Sam, he seemed to pick-up his thoughts and Sam said, "One nagging feeling I have is, can the best lawmen in America *all* be this bad? Of course not. So what are they hiding? What do the Dallas police know?"

He nodded firmly and Sam continued, "What do the FBI and CIA have in their files? And what of the powerful Office of Navy Intelligence? Some say Oswald worked for them. And why does the fuckin' Navy run the autopsy? That's where they'd start to gather evidence of the wounds and direction of the shooters, and so. . . What does ONI know? What's in their files?"

Sparky nodded again and thought. Yeah, they all fuckin' know. What are they hiding?

The media also wanted to know more about him. Why did he shoot Oswald? Did he act alone or was he working for an organization? They wanted to interview him, but somebody decided he couldn't talk to the media until the Warren Commission had questioned him.

In the meantime, his lawyers, Joe H. Tonahill and Tom Howard in particular, questioned and advised him. They sat at a table in a holding cell, with briefcases overflowing with papers, photographs, and other evidence, and Attorney Tom Howard, clean-cut and wearing an expensive-looking suit, waved his hands over all the paperwork and then smacked the table with his hands like he was giving up already. He asked, "Why'd you shoot Oswald?"

He said, "I'm a hero. People will see me and say, he shot the guy who killed the president."

Attorney Howard looked at him in astonishment. Millions of people had watched the live television broadcast. "No, when someone, anyone asks why you shot Oswald, you say, 'I wanted to save Mrs. Kennedy from coming down here for a trial.' "

"Hunh?" he said. He wondered, Who are these guys Civello sent? Sure, they were part of the team that had helped others, they knew Paul Jones and other guys, but what was this cock-and-bull story? Well, if that wouldn't work, he'd try another answer that some connected people gave him. "'Honestly, I thought it would bring more money to my club. You know, people would want to go to the Carousel Club because I'd be famous.' How's that?"

"No, that's no good either." Howard loosened the knot of his fancy tie and smirked at Joe Tonahill, who chuckled, before looking back at him. "That sounds self-serving and profiteering. No, you did it because you felt bad for Mrs. Kennedy. You wanted to save her the terrible trauma of testifying in a trial."

"Yeah, okay. I can say that." He felt a little down. Even now he was playing a game of concealing the truth for *them* and not a single one of his "friends" had come to visit him in jail. He knew he wouldn't be receiving Mr. Trafficante, as he had visited him in Havana, and Mr. Trafficante even seemed to appreciate it, but what of the other guys? Sam Giancana had shown so much interest in him from the very beginning in Chicago but now nothing! Not a word from Mr. Hoffa or his man, Barney Baker, or from Carlos Marcello, or Nofio Pecora, or any of the New Orleans guys. Besides his family the only one who came was his friend Joe Campisi, the owner of the Egyptian Club, and he brought his wife, like he was going somewhere else and happened to be in the neighborhood! The whole thing made him feel like he was jinxed with bad luck.

"You know what else you have to say," Attorney Howard continued, after taking a drag on a cigarette, "is that a feeling suddenly came over you. That an emotional impulse of patriotic duty just took you and you did it on the spur of the moment. Otherwise, it sounds like you planned it, which would have been pre-meditated murder."

"Oh." He scratched his chin, feeling the stubble of a beard. He thought of how long he had stalked Oswald, trying the door while he was interrogated, in the pressroom during one of Chief Curry's talks with the media, hoping he would have a clear shot, and he knew that this was another lie. He felt obligated to do this thing, coerced, because if he didn't do it, they'd take away his club, and probably whack him. "Yeah, well, I guess I could say that but, you know, I had to do it. I was framed into killing Oswald."

"Framed? What do you mean framed?" Howard had a confused look on his face. "The whole country saw you do it on national TV!"

"Well, not framed, you know. I had to do it. I was co—" he caught himself before he said coerced, not wanting to give this schmuck too much because you never know what words would make it back to the big bosses. "Um—obligated."

"Obligated. Okay, we'll work on that." Howard flicked the cigarette ash on the cement floor and crossed his legs, looking off to the side at the concrete wall painted white as he formulated the proper words. "You had to do it because this emotional patriotic feeling came over you. . . that you were obligated because you felt you owed this debt to our beloved President. . . to save Mrs. Kennedy this ordeal of coming back. It was a sudden impulse and when you shot him you said, 'You killed my President, you rat.' "

Attorney Howard looked at him with a condescending smirk. It made him mad and he tensed his eyebrows. Howard was making him sound like James Cagney in a gangster movie. But wait, he thought, Jimmy Cagney is a good guy. Yeah. "Yeah, I can say that. You killed my President, you rat!"

Attorneys Tonahill and Howard briefed him many more times and gathered evidence in his defense but through it all he knew his lawyers were *theirs*, looking out for *their* interests. He didn't trust them. If he said the wrong thing, said things about who was involved, about Hoffa and the seven large, about the money they had forgiven him to do this thing, they'd whack him. He had no doubt about that. He decided he needed to shut up with his attorneys and only speak in court when he had the chance.

~ ~

The Warren Commission interviewed hundreds of witnesses in various parts of the country including Washington D.C. It was during a brief delay in questioning witnesses, when Chief Justice Warren, a large man with gray hair, adjusted his wire-rimmed glasses and asked a high-ranking CIA agent, Richard Helms, if Oswald was one of their agents. Trained to deny everything, Agent Helms seemed intent on shining some knowledge onto the investigation. Helms responded as trained with very carefully chosen words. "I would have thought he was the Navy's responsibility. As a Marine, he was a Navy man first."

Chief Justice Warren squinted his eyes in understanding, but then asked, "How would a CIA officer deal with an inquiry into an agent he had recruited?"

CIA Director Dulles, wanting to cut off this questioning as quickly as possible, answered even before Helms could respond. "He wouldn't tell."

"Would he tell it under oath?" Warren continued.

Dulles responded curtly, "I wouldn't think he would tell it under oath."

"Why?"

"He ought not to. . . tell it under oath." Dulles appeared compelled to explain more, took off his glasses, wiped them with his pristine white handkerchief, blinked twice, and replaced them. "Maybe not tell it to his own government, but wouldn't tell it any other way."

Chief Justice Warren was still curious about their procedure and asked, "Wouldn't he tell it to his own chief?"

Dulles smiled. Justice Warren was beginning to understand the vagaries of a secret agent. "He might or he might not."

There was a long pause. Agent Helms looked around the room, made sure no one else could hear him, and repeated his first statement. "As a Marine, he was a Navy man first."

Justice Warren cleared his throat and scratched the back of his neck. He shuffled some papers for effect, glanced at the witness list, and proceeded in calling the next witness, a young woman who had been on the far side of Dealey Plaza. The woman testified she hadn't seen the actual shooting but that a lot of policemen and other men ran in the direction of the shooting on the grassy knoll. Her official statement was re-worded to say that she was "unsure of the direction" of the shots fired, and her statement about the pursuing men and officers was dropped altogether, as was done with many other witnesses.

Finally, after six months of delays, with everyone from the average citizen to the media hypothesizing various scenarios with myriad theories of accomplices ranging from right-wing groups, to a rogue element of the military intelligence—specifically, the Office of Naval Intelligence—to the CIA, the FBI, discouraged anti-Castro groups, the Mafioso, Castro himself, and more scenarios, the Warren Commission interviewed Jack Ruby in the interrogation room of the Dallas County Jail.

Throughout the process of questioning, Sparky spoke carefully. He was cautious to say the wrong thing and there was a timidity and reluctance to his answers, or to speak forthright on the events and his involvement. Representative Gerald Ford noticed this and said, "Are there any questions that ought to be asked to help clarify the situation that you described?"

"There is only one thing. If you don't take me back to Washington tonight to give me a chance to prove to the President that I am not guilty, then you will see the most tragic thing that will ever happen." Sparky paused to give his words emphasis. "Maybe something can be saved. Something can be done! What have you got to answer to that, Chief Justice Warren?"

Warren shifted in his seat and brushed his hand over his white hair. "Well, I don't know what can be done, Mister Ruby, because I don't know what you anticipate we will encounter."

He noticed one of his lawyers, Joe Tonahill, shifting around in his chair and holding a "statement" that Tonahill had prepared that was supposed to be his written version of what happened but he knew it was riddled with lies and incompleteness. He looked around the room. There were many people he did not know and a few of them looked like the type of person who would know Carlos Marcello or Nofio Pecora, or Sam Giancana or Jimmy Hoffa, or Santo Trafficante, or Guy Banister or David Phillips, or any one of many brutal people involved in this thing. "If I am eliminated, there won't be any way of knowing. . . but he has been told, I am certain, that I was part of a plot to assassinate the President."

Warren deftly avoided his statement of "part of a plot" and redirected him. "The President will know everything that you have said. Everything that you have said."

"But I won't be around, Chief Justice! I won't be around to verify these things."

Attorney Tonahill spoke up with an incredulous tone. "Who do you think is going to eliminate you, Jack?"

He knew immediately that statement was meant to remind him of who was keeping a close eye on him and who Tonahill was working for, but he ignored him. Then another man in a stiff suit came into the room with a briefcase in one hand and several folders thick with papers in the other hand. Chief Justice Warren said, "This is another man on my staff, Mister Specter," and proceeded to introduce him around the room.

He didn't like the way this was going. He had spoken for only a little while, had been interrupted often, sworn in later, and asked irrelevant, stupid questions. Now more people were coming into the room, it was getting out of control, and he didn't feel safe. "Is there any way to get me to Washington?"

Chief Justice Warren replied, "I beg your pardon?"

"Is there any way of you getting me to Washington?"

Warren said, "I don't know of any."

"I don't think I will get a fair representation with my counsel, Joe Tonahill. I don't think so. I would like to request that I go to Washington." He rubbed his fingers over and over, but tried to be calm. "I am at a disadvantage, gentlemen, telling my story."

Chief Justice Warren ignored him, readjusted his glasses to review the transcript, and said, "You were right at the point of where you had it culminating—"

"That is untrue! That is what I wanted to read." He slammed Tonahill's notepad of his "statement" on the table. "Gentlemen, unless you get me to Washington you can't get a fair shake out of me. If you understand my way of talking, you have got to bring me to Washington to get the tests. Do I sound dramatic? Off the beam?"

"No," Warren replied, "you are speaking very rationally, and I am really surprised that you can remember as much as you have remembered up to the present time."

What? He thought. This guy thinks I'd forget who is breathing down my neck and all the circumstances because six months have passed? He wasn't getting it. "Unless you get me to Washington, and I am not a crackpot, I have all my senses, I don't want to evade any crime I am guilty of, unless you get me to

Washington immediately, I am afraid after what Mister Tonahill has written here, which is unfair—"

"Why don't you read it?" Warren asked.

Sparky glanced at the notepad. "This is the girl—"

"*Thing*', isn't it," Tonahill interrupted.

"This is the '*thing*' that started Jack in the shooting!"

Tonahill clarified, "Kathy Kay was talking about Oswald."

"You are lying, Joe Tonahill!" he said. "You are lying!"

"No I am not."

"You are lying! Because you *know* what motivated me."

"No."

"Yes you do." He breathed rapidly. How could he continue with all these people, with all the knowledge that certain individuals know, and who have people here watching for them, and are listening now? "It is too bad, Chief Warren, that you didn't get me to your headquarters six months ago."

Justice Warren brushed off some pencil erasures from the desk in front of him. "Well, Mister Ruby, I didn't want to do anything that would prejudice you in your trial. I wish we had gotten here a little sooner after your trial was over, but I know you had other things on your mind, and we had other work, and it got to this late date. And as I told you at the beginning, if you want a polygraph test of some kind made, I will undertake to see that it is done. Now if you will proceed with the rest of your statement."

He thought, This guy isn't getting it. Either that or he was one smooth son of a bitch. "I don't know how to answer you."

"Well, you have told us most of what happened up to the time of the incident, and you are just within a few hours of it now."

He turned to Sheriff J.E. "Bill" Decker, who stood nearby in his full brown uniform, and asked softly. "Will you do that for me, that you asked a minute ago?"

"You want us all outside, Jack?" Sheriff Decker asked.

"Yeah, alright," he said.

Sheriff Decker spoke loudly and clearly, "Will everyone clear the room!" and then in a normal voice to him, "I will leave Tonahill and Moore," who Sparky knew was a U.S. Secret Service agent.

"Bill, I am not accomplishing anything if they are here," he waved in the direction of Moore and his attorneys, "and Joe Tonahill is here. You said *anybody* I wanted out."

"Jack," Sheriff Decker spoke loudly, "this is your lawyer."

"He is not *my* lawyer!"

They waited a few moments while Sheriff Decker, the law enforcement officers, his lawyers, and the other counsel lawyers left the room. Chief Justice Warren exhaled as if this were all a dramatic show and when the room was clear, except for him, Sheriff Decker, the stenographer, and a few other Commissioners, Justice Warren continued, "Yes, go ahead."

"I want to tell the truth and I can't tell it here. I can't tell it here. Does that make sense to you?"

"Well, let's not talk about sense," Chief Justice Warren gave a hint of a smile. "But I really can't see why you can't tell this Commission."

He looked over at the stenographer, a thin young man in a suit, oddly without a tie, who was still typing quietly. "But this isn't the place for me to tell what I want to tell."

"The Commission is looking into the entire matter, and you are part of it, should be."

He knew that this guy needed to be set straight. Warren had no idea who he was dealing with so he decided to be more direct. "Chief Warren, your life is in danger in this city, do you know that?"

"No, I don't know that. If that is the thing that you don't want to talk about, you can tell me, if you wish, when this is all over." Warren smiled again. "Just between you and me."

He took his condescending smile like a punch to the gut and gazed at the remaining Commission members, examining them one by one, to see if they had condescending smiles to hit him with and some did. Some were idly tapping their pencils or pens. They were all a bunch of "yes" men and he returned his gaze to the Chief Justice. "No, I would like to talk to you in private."

"You may tell me that when you finish your story."

He was deeply frustrated. So this is all a "story" to him? Who did he think he was? "I bet you haven't had a witness like me in your whole investigation, isn't that correct?"

"There are many witnesses whose memory has not been as good as yours. I tell you that, honestly."

"My reluctance to talk. . . You haven't had any witness in telling the *story,* in finding so many *problems*. . . " He waited for this guy to catch his drift.

Warren nodded, "You have a greater problem than any witness we have had."

He nodded. At last. Maybe he *was* getting it. "I have a lot of *reasons* for having those problems."

"I know that," Warren said quickly. "I came here because I thought you wanted to tell us the story, and I think the story should be told for the public, and it will eventually be made public. But at all events we must first have the story that we are going to check it against."

He felt confused. Maybe Warren did get it and he was stonewalling him? He had to be sure so he thought for a moment, then spoke slowly and clearly. "If you request me to go back to Washington with you, right now, that couldn't be done, could it?"

"No, it could *not* be done," Chief Justice Warren said flatly, wanting to end this. "It could *not* be done. There are a good many things involved in that, Mister Ruby."

"What are they?"

"Well, the public attention that it would attract—"

He laughed out loud. What, in the entire nation, had more public attention than him testifying? Nothing. It was absurd that he had said such a thing and he laughed loudly again.

Chief Warren continued, "The people would be around. We have no place for you to be safe when we take you out and we are not law enforcement officers, and it isn't our responsibility to go into anything of that kind. And certainly it couldn't be done on a moment's notice this way."

He shook his head. This guy was something else. His words echoed in his mind: "There would be people around." Hmm. Was that a threat? Were there worse people than those around here? The people who wanted to get at him, *here. . . now?* And then he thought, wait, this is the biggest guy in the whole justice system and he can't make a safe place for him?

He cleared his throat and tried another angle, trying to make it more personal for the judge. "Well, from what I read in the paper, they made certain precautions for *you* coming here, but you got here."

"There are no precautions taken at all."

He lost his temper and snapped back, "Gentlemen! My life is in danger here!"

There was a momentary silence after his outburst and Sparky thought he had finally got their attention. "Not with my guilty plea of execution. Do I sound sober enough to you as I say this?"

"You do. You sound entirely sober."

"From the moment I started my testimony, have I sounded as though, with the exception of becoming emotional, have I sounded as though I made sense?"

"You have indeed."

"Then *I* follow this up." He waited a long time before he spoke. They all stared at him but he waited even longer. They were finally ready. "I may not live tomorrow to give any further testimony. . . Chief Warren, if you felt that *your* life was in danger at the moment, how would you feel? Wouldn't you be reluctant to go on speaking, even though you request me to do so?"

Justice Warren looked at him hard. "I think I might have some reluctance if I was in your position, yes. I think I would figure it out. . . *very carefully*. . . as to whether it would endanger me or not. If you think that anything that I am doing, or anything that I am asking you, is endangering you in any way, shape, or form, I want you to feel absolutely free to say that the interview was over."

"What happens then? I didn't accomplish anything!"

"No, nothing has been accomplished."

"Then *you* won't follow up with anything further?"

"There wouldn't be anything to follow up if you hadn't completed your statement."

He knew that was it. Warren *was* stonewalling him and would be happy to *not* follow up on anything he would have to say. Warren didn't give a shit if he lived or died, told the truth, or let it be. All right, he thought. I'm going to hang this son of a bitch for who he is, because the court stenographer is still right there, taking notes. "You said you have the power to do what you want to do, is that correct?"

"Exactly."

"Without any limitations."

"With the purview of the Executive order which established the Commission. We have the right to take testimony of anyone we want in this whole situation, and we have the right, if we so choose to do it, to verify that statement in any way that we wish to do it."

"But you don't have the right to take a prisoner back with you when you want to?"

"No. We have the power to subpoena witnesses to Washington if we want to do it, but we have taken the testimony of two hundred or three hundred people, I would imagine, here in Dallas, without going to Washington."

"But those people aren't Jack Ruby."

"No, they weren't."

"The thing is this, that with your power that you have, Chief Justice Warren, and all these gentlemen, too much time has gone by for me to give you any benefit of what I may say now."

"No, that isn't a fact. It isn't too late."

He shook his head negatively. "I tell you, gentlemen, my whole family is in jeopardy. My sisters, as to their lives."

"Yes?"

"Naturally, I am a foregone conclusion. My sisters, Eva, Eileen, and Mary. My brothers Sam, Earl, Hyman, and myself naturally. . . My in-laws, Harold Kaminsky, Marge Ruby, the wife of Earl, and Phyllis, the wife of Sam Ruby. They are in jeopardy of loss of their lives. Does that sound serious enough to you, Chief Justice Warren?"

"Nothing could be more serious. . . *if* that is a fact."

"Sir, it is. Will you take me to Washington?"

The Chief Justice of the Supreme Court evaded him deftly. Chief Justice Warren was the highest-ranking official of the entire judicial system in the United States. He wasn't the first to lie and he has not been the last. He lied, "No, we *can't* take you to Washington."

During his time in prison, Sparky had visits from his family and doctors, who came more frequently. The doctors said he had cancer and then the Warren Commission published its report stating there was no "significant link between Ruby and organized crime."

The doctors came again and gave him shots. He never heard of shots to cure cancer and he told anyone who would listen the shots *were* the cancer, the doctors had put it into his system, because *they* didn't want him to talk. Within months he was dead.

The End

www.ingramcontent.com/pod-product-compliance
Lightning Source LLC
Chambersburg PA
CBHW020613310726
48979CB00008B/1467/J

* 9 7 8 0 9 8 8 4 5 9 7 3 1 *